More praise for

EARTHQUAKE GAMES . . .

"Compelling . . . Ramthun has done the improbable . . . She has produced a second novel that manages to equal if not surpass the promise of *Ground Zero*." —*The Denver Post*

"Ramthun, a former war gamer for the Department of Defense, handles the mechanics with straightforward, credible authority." —*The Washington Post*

"Highly atmospheric . . . [Ramthun] weaves in a couple of personal subplots—a love interest for Reed and the surprising emergence of someone out of her past—that give her story warmth." —*Publishers Weekly*

. . . and for Bonnie Ramthun's previous thriller, GROUND ZERO . . .

"Like getting to wear a top-security badge and being admitted into fascinating places you'd never otherwise get to go." —*Nancy Pickard, author of The Blue Corn Murders*

"Gripping, fast-paced, high-tech . . . superb." —*Robert Louis Stevenson III, author of Bright Star*

"A well-conceived tale of murder, espionage, and terrorism." —*Publishers Weekly*

"Puts a new spin on the old locked-room mystery." —*Richmond Times-Dispatch*

"Quite clever . . . Ramthun obviously knows her stuff." —*The Gazette*

"A topical, high-tech locked-room mystery for the millennium. It has all the ingredients for success." —*Dorothy Simpson, author of Once Too Often*

EARTHQUAKE GAMES

Bonnie Ramthun

J

JOVE BOOKS, NEW YORK

1769 0031

This is a work of fiction. Names, characters, places, and incidents either are the product of the author's imagination or are used fictitiously, and any resemblance to actual persons, living or dead, business establishments, events, or locales is entirely coincidental.

EARTHQUAKE GAMES

A Jove Book / published by arrangement with
G. P. Putnam's Sons

PRINTING HISTORY
G. P. Putnam's Sons hardcover edition / September 2000
Jove edition / November 2001

Visit our website at
www.penguinputnam.com

ISBN: 0-515-13177-6

A JOVE BOOK®
Jove Books are published by The Berkley Publishing Group,
a division of Penguin Putnam Inc.,
375 Hudson Street, New York, New York 10014.
JOVE and the "J" design
are trademarks belonging to Penguin Putnam Inc.

PRINTED IN THE UNITED STATES OF AMERICA

10 9 8 7 6 5 4 3 2 1

For my father, Lee John Droege

Acknowledgments

Writing a book while raising three children and with one on the way was a bit of an effort. Sometimes I felt like I was trying to launch the space shuttle with a '67 Chevy and a set of jumper cables. This book happened because of my friends and family, and I'd like to acknowledge them here.

Marcy Zipke picked my first book, *Ground Zero,* out of the slush pile at Putnam. She edited *Ground Zero* and now *Earthquake Games* with superb skill. In the past year, I have come to know her as an editor and as a friend. Stacy Creamer, senior editor at Putnam, generous and brilliant, patiently explained every step of the publishing process to me and guided *Ground Zero* and now *Earthquake Games* to a successful launch. She and Marcy are wise, witty, and honorable. I'm lucky to know them.

When my deadline for *Earthquake Games* loomed and I was falling behind, my sister Roxanne offered to look after my boys and me at her house while I wrote. This was heaven for everyone, since her house is a ranch in Wyoming. My boys swam, trampolined, fished, hiked, walked 4-H sheep (did you know they have to be walked like dogs?), and generally had an incredible time. I wrote every minute I could, and this helped put me over the top. Heartfelt thanks to my handsome and athletic nephews Aaron, Eric, Brandon, and Jim Tomich for babysitting my little ones with good cheer. Also thanks to Andy Tomich, who did the daddy bottle duty for my husband, who couldn't be there, and of course, thanks to the incomparable Roxanne.

I'd also like to acknowledge the friends I made simply by

having siblings. My brothers married smart, strong, gorgeous women. Okay, I guess my brothers are kind of cute and bright and all, but still, how did they manage this? My sisters-in-law Lara Long, Sharon Droege, Jan Droege, Dawn Butler, and Jodi Butler have been an inspiration and a help. My brothers-in-law Michael Larson and Andy Tomich, on the flip side, are kind, funny, superintelligent guys. Thanks also to Kim Goggin, my terrific sister-in-law, and my in-laws Gary and Cindy Ramthun. They are generous, kind, and wise.

Thanks to Megan Silva, friend and physician, who researched the medical information in this book. Any mistakes are mine, not hers.

I am frequently asked how I manage to find time to write. I have a high school girl come over twice a week after school. She babysits for two hours and I write like a maniac. My first babysitter was Duabhav Vue—smart, kind, and lovely as a song. When college classes started to interfere with her baby-sitting, she found a friend, Kia Lee, to help. Kia is as terrific and lovely as Duabhav and now my boys eagerly ask me if it is a "Kia" day. The babysitters' help allows me to leave the real world for a few hours every week, knowing that my children are safe and happy.

If you've slogged through the acknowledgments this far, you must be either a member of my family or a very dedicated reader. This book is not autobiographical, but in a sense it is a tribute to my father, Lee John Droege. It is a tribute to my foster parents, Dick and Judith Butler. It is a tribute to every human being that has ended up with more than one set of parents, no matter how it happened. I love my parents with all my heart, and I am lucky to be their daughter.

Finally, thanks again to Bill, my husband. He's the reason why.

1

Colorado Springs, Colorado

"I think about it a lot," Eileen said. "That's only natural, I guess."

"What's *it?*" Gerri Matthews asked, leaning back in her armchair. "Shooting Teddy Shaw, or seeing what he did to Jeannie Bernowski?" Gerri's clipboard rested comfortably on one knee but her pen dangled, point up, in her relaxed hand. Her relaxation was a ploy, Eileen thought, just like the exquisitely shabby little room, like her kindly face, like the delicious smell of the hot tea she served in thick pottery mugs. Gerri was the court-appointed psychologist for shooters. Cops who killed. Six years on the force, and Eileen Reed had finally joined the ranks.

"What?" she asked Gerri.

"Shooting Teddy, or seeing Jeannie?" Gerri repeated patiently.

"Shooting him, of course," Eileen said.

"Okay," Gerri replied. She was forty and looked a weathered twenty-five. Perhaps it was all the bike riding, she'd said during their introductions. Or perhaps because she and her husband didn't have children, and thus she always got a good night's sleep. This was said with a twinkle and a chuckle as irresistible as a little girl's. Gerri had sandy blonde hair and dark blue eyes, and she dressed in clothes that looked so comfortable they could be pajamas. On a plump woman they would have looked awful, but on Gerri's spare little frame, her baggy pants and shapeless pullovers looked terrific. Eileen wanted to like her immediately, and felt her ears pull back like a horse about to bite. Everything felt different since four days ago, when she'd shot Teddy Shaw.

"Do you have dreams about Jeannie Bernowski?" Gerri asked calmly.

Eileen closed her eyes momentarily, and the death scene unrolled in front of her. The backs of her eyelids had developed a sort of VCR-like capability, it seemed, and whenever she closed her eyes she was treated to what was now the number-one movie in her head.

"No, I remember Teddy," she said.

It was a fine summer night in Colorado Springs, Colorado. The mild night air blew through Eileen's open car window, carrying with it the scents of summer roses, recently mowed lawns, and sun-heated pines. The breeze felt good in her hair and against her face. One thirty in the morning on a Tuesday. There was no one else on the roads.

Eileen was on her way home after filing a report on a homicide, an easy one. She'd stayed late so she could take off Friday and Monday, thus giving her a four-day vacation. She'd planned to spend it in the mountains with Joe Tanner, her boyfriend. There was a persistent rumor that the Pike National Forest held the remains of an F-16 crash. The plane crashed twenty years ago and was seen only by the occasional hiker, or so the story went. No hiker had come forward admitting they'd seen the wreck, but the story persisted. The ghost of the pilot was said to haunt the plane, since he had never been buried and was, it was said, still strapped into his seat. Since the plane was never found, it was supposedly still full of equipment, including missiles and ammo for the dead pilot's pistol. It was the *Flying Dutchmen* of mountain wrecks and a juicy target. The fact that the plane probably didn't exist only fueled Eileen's desire to find the thing. She was excited about the adventure and happy to get away from the city.

Eileen was so wound up, in fact, she gave in to an impulse. The city seemed to be completely asleep and the night air was intoxicatingly warm. She turned off the main road and into the Briargate Subdivision, a housing community with long, curving streets. She clicked off her headlights. After a second or two of terrifying darkness, the night world sprang up around her. The houses were dark, and her car made little sound at thirty miles per hour. When she was seventeen this was one of the favorite sports of the high-school ranch-kid crowd. Driving at fifty miles per hour down moonlit Wyoming highways, they would turn off the headlights and laugh and yell their favorite lines from *Star Wars*. Driving without lights was unearthly and scary and fun, and Eileen hadn't done it for years.

"*So that's why* Teddy didn't hide from you," Gerri said.

"Yeah," Eileen said. "I didn't exactly put that in my report, you know."

"Of course, and as you can see, I'm taking no notes," Gerri said. "I'm a psychologist. You can tell me anything, and it will go no further than this room."

"You said that already."

"I'll say it until you believe me, chum," Gerri said comfortably. "Now tell me what happened next. You've set the scene. I can see it in my mind."

"I saw Teddy—a man—walking from a house carrying a large gym bag. He was walking very quickly and his van was running. But the van was at the curb and the driveway was empty, and there were no lights on in the house. That all added up to a robbery. I had just turned the corner in a long swooping curve. I knew the street was a long, straight one, so that was going to be my run at the *Death Star* ventilation tube."

Eileen looked sharply to see if Gerri was laughing, and she

was. But there was nothing mocking in Gerri's face. She was just laughing.

"Use the force, Luke!" she said.

"That's right," Eileen replied and couldn't help but smile. "Keep on target! All the great lines. I swooped around the corner in full Rebel Alliance mode and there's Teddy Shaw with little Alice Gherkin in his bag—although I didn't know that then, of course."

"But you knew there was something going on."

"Oh, yes," Eileen said grimly.

The man didn't see Eileen at first, because he was very nearly at his van. He had almost made his snatch, and his whole focus was getting to his vehicle. Besides, she didn't have her lights on. Teddy Shaw would die with a petulant look on his face, the look of a little boy who was beaten at a game where the other side hadn't played fair.

Eileen flipped her lights on and aimed her car at the burglar, her mood changing in an eyeblink from vacationing lover to police officer. She expected him to run for his van, and perhaps even to have to chase him down, but her perceptions were all wrong. This was not a burglary. The man dropped the bag—which fell to the ground and bulged in a funny shape, a shape that was familiar and unidentifiable at the same time, a shape that was somehow horrible—and drew an enormous contraption from his long coat. The contraption looked like a homemade bazooka, a monster black muzzle with a tiny handle on the end.

Eileen stamped on the brakes and threw her car into a skid and ducked, and the windshield blew out of her beloved Jeep Cherokee with a coughing sound. There was no boom of a gunshot. At thirty miles per hour, Eileen was stopped in four seconds of skid, four very long seconds. She had time to consider her choice of weapons. She had a Sig Sauer 239 in a shoulder holster, 40 caliber with seven rounds in the magazine, cocked and locked for quick firing. She also carried a .38 Ladysmith in an ankle holster, a revolver with five shots. She decided on the Ladysmith since she was bent double underneath the dashboard anyway. The Sig Sauer was too hard to reach.

As her car stopped, she rolled out the door, keeping her Jeep between the shooter and herself, dropped to the asphalt, and aimed at the feet on the lawn from underneath her car. A low slung car wouldn't have given her line-of-sight, but her Jeep was fairly tall.

"Police!" she shouted, and the Jeep's side window blew out. There was no time to do anything else. Instinctively, she made sure the black bag was not going to be hit by gunfire and pulled the trigger three times.

The feet disappeared in a black burst of blood, black like an old movie because there wasn't enough light for her eyes to register color. The man fell down as Eileen rolled to the back of her Jeep. She leaped to her feet and stepped out from behind her car, gun held steady, hoping the man was clutching his ruined feet and not his gun. The man still had his weapon. The bazooka Eileen had seen was an ordinary .357 revolver with a homemade silencer on the end, made of a perforated cardboard tube stuffed with cotton. The cotton was now on fire but the man didn't seem to care. He was trying to bring the gun up and aim it at her, and in a microsecond more, he was going to get there.

Eileen fired the gun twice more—Tap! Tap!—and she was out of bullets. A tiny black mark appeared in the man's forehead and another one pinned itself on his chest. Eileen dropped her Ladysmith to the grass and pulled her Sig Sauer from her shoulder holster. One click of the safety and she was armed again.

The man leaned backward slowly, like a child's punching bag with a hole in it. The bazooka-like silencer continued to burn. Teddy settled to the grass, no longer looking much like a human being, no longer alive. Eileen stood blinking, suddenly aware of her racing heart, her lack of breathing, the stink of gunfire, and the richer stink of blood. She gasped and her arms started to tremble. Looking around, she saw nothing, no one else. The van still idled at the curb. The back door was open.

"This is the police!" she shouted. "Come out with your hands up!"

There was a response from the van. A tiny, squealing sound, like a rabbit when it is struck by a hawk or a fox. Eileen sidled along the side of her Jeep until she could get to the passenger-side door, keeping the back door of the van and the very dead man in her sight. She fumbled out her cell phone and called for backup.

"Then you decided to look in the van," Gerri said.

"I did," Eileen said. "I should have waited, but there was that tiny little sound. Maybe a bullet had ricocheted and I was listening to someone dying. I had to see."

"Nobody came out of the house? None of the neighbors?"

"A .38 makes a popping sound, not a big boom. The .357 makes a good-sized noise, but Teddy built that stupid half-ass silencer. The windshield made the most noise. Lights started to come on in a few houses, but my backup arrived before anyone came out of their houses. Besides, the whole thing had taken maybe thirty seconds."

"So you looked in the van," Gerri said, and took a measured sip of her tea.

Eileen took a sip of her own tea and sighed. The tea was herbal, light and sweet and dainty. A little girl's drink.

"Yeah, I looked in the van. And there was Jeannie Bernowski, whose face had been on every telephone pole and in every supermarket in town for a week. I knew her instantly and I was just flat out amazed. Do you know how often we get a kid back alive?"

"Not very often," Gerri said.

"Statistically speaking, never. I remember the whole Heather Dawn Church search. That little girl was snatched from her bedroom during the early evening, and they had helicopters from Fort Carson combing the Black Forest that very night. Finally, a year later, they came across her bones. That's what everyone expected for poor little Jeannie. If a child isn't snatched by a parent, their chances are slim and none. And

Slim left town," Eileen added. She grinned a hard and un-mirthful little grin.

"And yet there she was," Gerri said.

Eileen made a diving roll past the back doors of the van, getting a nightmare glimpse of the horror within. The van was running and the interior light was on, which gave color to the blood. There was a little figure huddled against one wall, and some sacking and other materials were puddled on the floor. Nothing large enough to hide a man or woman. Eileen wasn't going to have to shoot anyone else. She climbed to her feet. The little figure looked vaguely human, but her one flashing glimpse didn't give many details.

She walked to the doors and looked inside, gun still held at the ready, and there was little Jeannie Bernowski. There was no one else in the van. In the distance, sirens warbled briefly as her backup negotiated some red lights. Jeannie raised her head slowly, sensing someone, but her eyes had no more sense than a gutted doe. She was covered with bruises and worse. There was quite a bit of blood. She was handcuffed to a steel bar welded to the side of the van. On the other side of the van, another steel bar waited.

Eileen looked back toward the black bag. She took two long steps away from the van and bent over the bag. She had time to marvel at the warmth of the breeze, the stars, the beauty of the Colorado night. Then the zipper came open with a long buzzing sound and a choking smell of ether and there, duct tape firmly over mouth and eyes, was six-year-old Alice Gherkin, unconscious.

"So what made you go back to the van?"

"I don't know," Eileen said. "But that wasn't very popular with Captain Harben. I crawled up in that van like my brains had run right out my ass—that's what Captain Harben told me, anyway—and wrapped the little girl up in my arms."

"Captain Harben didn't approve," Gerri said, and laughed.

"Captain Harben did not approve," Eileen said. "He

chewed me out good, he did. Disturbing a crime scene. Destroying evidence. Et cetera."

"But she was talking when the ambulance got there, that's what the report said."

"She's a tough girl," Eileen said. "He'd done a lot to her, but he hadn't killed her. Inside, or outside."

"Now you're a hero. But you got that way by killing someone."

"Teddy Shaw," Eileen grimaced. "I know. So fix me, Gerri."

"I have no magic wand, Eileen." Gerri smiled, glancing at her watch. "And our session is over for today."

"I have to come back?" Eileen asked in dismay. "I thought this was just—you know."

"What, for show?" Gerri asked. "No way, lady. You're mine for at least two months. Maybe more. Once a week, my tea, your choice of flavors."

The sun was setting over Pikes Peak when Eileen walked outside. Gerri's office was in an old Victorian house, surrounded by gorgeous elm trees and lilac bushes and stuffed full of psychologists and social workers. Eileen paused and took a deep breath, smelling the warm earth and the flowers that grew in lovely hundred-year-old beds. A woman hurried up the walk past her, her head down and dark sunglasses failing to cover the fading remains of a spectacular beating. Eileen stood for a few moments more, her hands in her pockets, listening to the door open and close and the distant sound of voices. Next week, same place, same tea. And eventually, if Eileen wasn't careful, Gerri was going to figure out the places where she had lied.

2

The Great Sand Dunes, San Luis Valley, Colorado

Five days later, at dawn, Marcia Fowler found the body of the dead girl. At first she didn't know what she was looking at. She walked across the sand dunes, squinting in the near darkness of early morning, her mind flipping through a series of mental images and discarding each one as they did not fit. What was that dark object? A rock? No, it was too familiar-looking to be a rock. Someone's discarded coat, blown across the sand during the night? No, it was too large. A cougar crouched down and waiting for her?

Marcia stopped walking, the last of her breath wisping away in a vapor from her open mouth. She was in the Great Sand Dunes in southwestern Colorado. There were cougars in this part of the state.

This could be a cougar. It didn't move. Marcia didn't move. She'd dropped into a steady hiking pace a half-hour ago, wanting to reach the top of the first range of sand dunes before the glorious early fall sunrise. Now she stood, panting a little, wondering what to do. There was a campground full of people less than two miles away, most of them still asleep. It was cold in late August in this part of Colorado.

There was no steam of breath from the object. Shouldn't a cougar breathe? The light was becoming clearer by the second as the sun rushed to its rise above the range of mountains to the east. The mountains to the west suddenly flared with light from the rising sun. The snow at the peaks turned an impossible rose color, delicate and lovely. This was called the alpenglow and should have thrilled Marcia to the bone. She could see the dawnlight from the corner of her eye as the racing light swept down the mountainside across the valley. The prairie to the west lit up with amber grasses. The line of light swept out to the sand and took the grayish sand to gold.

Marcia's knees were trembling with fear and tension, in a face-off with the unknown thing. It was hard to stand still. She was traveling to the Great Sand Dunes to hear the famous Taos Hum, because she'd read that the hum could be heard best of all in the huge expanse of Colorado's version of the Sahara. The dunes were made of fine ground quartz with a great deal of iron, a material that some said was a source of spiritual power.

Marcia believed in spiritual power. She was a retired teacher of high school biology. She'd been married once, but the marriage didn't last. She had no children. She was only fifty-five, having taken early retirement, and she spent her free time exploring the paranormal.

This was the third trip she'd taken in the glorious freedom of retirement. There weren't enough years left for her to visit all the places she wanted to visit. This place was one she'd read about for years. She stood frozen in a waiting game with whatever-it-was, trying not to think that this trip might be her last. The light was almost bright enough to see now.

Then the morning sun reached her discovery and illuminated it brilliantly. The light was not kind to the body, for a body it was.

Marcia's terror changed instantly to horror. A young woman lay before her, sprawled on her side. Her nude body was ivory and pale like a statue, as though every ounce of blood had been drained from her. Her eyes were open and filled with sand. There were no footprints around her. She was laid on a sloping curve with tiny ripples of sand spread all around her. The ripples, formed by wind and dry days into a crunchy plaster, were undisturbed around her body.

She was laid out like an offering to the gods, but not to the God that Marcia worshipped. Her shoulder and arm looked odd. Marcia realized she was seeing places where the girl's skin had been cut away. She turned away, the image burning in her eyes, and started to run toward the entrance to the dunes. Suddenly a hum filled the air, a low moaning tone that invaded every inch of her body. It was the Taos Hum, at last, and it wasn't exciting at all. It was more horrible than she could have imagined.

She staggered, flailed, lurched in the sand. The ground seemed to be heaving under her feet. The ground *was* heaving under her feet. Marcia fell to her knees as the dunes quivered and rolled in enormous waves. She curled up on her side, her arms around her head. Tons of sand around her shifted and writhed, threatening to bury her like an ocean wave of sand. The moaning tone made her dental fillings ache fiercely and vibrated in her head until she thought she would go mad. The rolling started to slow, then abruptly stopped. Marcia heard a high, piercing shriek that went on and on. A while later she realized the sound was coming from her, and she stopped it.

"Earthquake," she said to herself. Her voice came out in a husky whisper, cracked and broken.

She struggled to her feet. The sand hadn't buried her. Her ankle didn't want to work properly and her daypack hung sloppily from one shoulder. She straightened her hair, brushed off her shorts, and adjusted her backpack. She looked back at the body of the girl and it was still there. She took a brief drink from her water bottle. She tried out her voice.

"Colorado has earthquakes," she said. "They're very rare, though." That was better. The shaking was a normal event, though rare, just a perfectly explainable natural phenomenon. Just an earthquake. What the hum meant, she wasn't sure. No time for that now.

She didn't have to look at the dead girl again. It was no trick of the light. There was a dead body on the Great Sand

Dunes, and Marcia had to get the word to the park rangers before anyone else came along. Earthquake or not, the poor girl needed to be taken care of. Marcia let her years of teaching stiffen her like a good brace. She straightened her shoulders and started limping toward the campgrounds as fast as she could.

Westside, Colorado Springs, Colorado

Eileen Reed directed traffic.

There was nothing else to be done. The ambulance had to get through and the traffic lights were out. Eileen stood in the intersection and waved her arms. She was in a pair of sweatpants and a white T-shirt. Her shoulder holster was clearly visible, which was perhaps why she was commanding respect from the alarmed Colorado Springs drivers.

The traffic streamed through the intersection. The ambulance went through slowly with lights flashing. The ambulance drivers gave Eileen a wave. Their faces were still pale, but there were clear signs of recovery. They grinned at Detective Reed in her workout clothes, directing traffic like a rookie cop.

Eileen grinned back. A few more minutes and the traffic would sort itself into a four-way stop, orderly streams of cars first going one way and then the other. Colorado Springs lost power quite often when the famous summer thunderstorms came barreling down Pikes Peak. The cars wouldn't be in a snarl if people weren't so completely poleaxed by this weird earthquake. Eileen could hear the car radios, most tuned to the KALT radio station. An enterprising disc jockey at KALT had called a disc jockey in California, who was now dispensing earthquake advice over the Colorado airwaves with a casual and calming nonchalance.

With a final wave, Eileen left the intersection and ran for her apartment, two blocks from the stoplight. During the earthquake, Eileen had ended up on the lawn with the other residents, wearing bra and panties and a towel that shrank to washcloth size as soon as the earthquake was over. She would have faced a lot worse than the very real threat of a gas explosion to find some clothes. She'd heard the wailing of the siren from her bedroom as she started to get dressed. She abandoned her attempt to put on work clothes and pulled on the first things that came to hand. The ambulance had to get through, and the intersection by her house was a snarl of confused drivers—she had to help.

By the time she returned to her apartment, the building manager had turned off the main valve, educated by the cheery California disc jockey about the dangers of broken gas lines. Just to be sure, the manager had turned off the electric power as well. Eileen finished dressing quickly in her eerily quiet apartment. With no running refrigerator, fans, or clocks, her apartment seemed to be holding its breath.

Betty, her cat, was stiff and outraged and silent underneath the bed. The earthquake was completely Eileen Reed's fault, and Betty wasn't going to forgive her any time soon. She was an adopted alley cat, ferociously independent, a bright and improbable orange, and would not be coaxed out from under the bed when she was in a huff. Eileen didn't even try. She left her an open can of cat food and a small handful of cat treats, a sort of cat bouquet, as an apology.

Her cell phone began ringing as she reached her car.

"What took you so long?" she said into the receiver.

"Uh, er, Detective Reed?" a voice said. "This is Cathy at dispatch."

"I'm on my way in, Cathy," Eileen said, starting the car.

"Thank you, ma'am," Cathy said, and broke the connection. She sounded frayed. It was going to be a busy day at the police department. Eileen figured she wouldn't be doing much detective work that day. Today would be a day spent in the trenches, keeping citizens happy and looters unhappy.

She started to speed dial Joe's number, just to check on him. Joe was a solid type. If he wasn't beyond help, he wasn't going to do anything stupid.

Eileen saw the first broken storefront window and the small crowd in front and turned off her phone in mid-ring. She pulled over to the curb with a warning yelp of the tires and slammed the car door, hard. The crowd dissolved as she strode up to the storefront, trying to look about seven feet tall. It was going to be a long day, she sighed to herself. A long day.

Scenic Viewing Site, San Luis Valley, Colorado

The sight of Blanca Peak nearly took Alan Baxter's breath away. He'd never been to the San Luis Valley before. The peak sat at the end of the Sangre de Cristo Mountain range like an enormous post at the end of a fence. The top was a pure and blinding white in the early morning sun. He couldn't believe any amount of summer could reach the top of that peak and melt the snow. Across the valley he could see the San Juan Mountains, another tall range of mountains with snow-capped peaks. The San Luis Valley lay in between, a peaceful patchwork of farmland and grazing cattle. In the distance, up the valley, he could see the tan pelt of the Great Sand Dunes. What a beautiful place.

Alan had pulled off at the viewing site and gotten out to stretch his legs. He stopped every two hours, because if he didn't, he had a tendency to stiffen up. He'd been driving since early morning and the cold air was delicious. There was no one else at the viewing site, which was perched on the edge of an enormous drop-off and gave a gorgeous view of Blanca Peak and the San Luis Valley. The bathroom had an out-of-order sign, so Alan leisurely watered some wildflowers off the side of the guardrail and zipped up. He stretched and sighed and grinned. With luck, he'd be on the Rio Grande in the afternoon, seeing what kind of bugs the fish were taking today. He'd never fished the Rio Grande. He'd meant to get down here for years, but there always seemed to be somewhere else to go. The summer fishing in Yellowstone and Montana were too good to pass up. Then there was the Frying Pan, or the Gunnison. Alan just never made it down to southern Colorado.

Then Sam Williams ended up at his table at the bar in West Yellowstone, Montana, earlier that winter. They'd been warming up after a day of bone-chilling fishing, and Sam had joined their table because he knew Alan's friend Dietrich. Dee introduced Sam to Alan, and the conversation turned, as it always did, back to fishing.

Sam owned a small cattle ranch down in the San Luis Valley, it turned out, and he talked up his Rio Grande like it was the best fishing since the legendary Millionaire's Hole on the Henry's Fork. The wild trout intrigued Alan. Sam Williams, from a ranching family that went four generations back, loved company. Like many ranchers, both he and his wife liked visitors. His wife Beth, particularly. They'd love to have Alan down for a month or so. Hell, all summer if he'd like.

"I hear you're a computer type, too," Sam commented. "Beth has a PC. I think she'd have fun talking computers to you." Dietrich rolled his eyes. Alan's particular eccentricity was well known among the fisherman. His was fairly mild compared to some. One fisherman carried around a bag of ashes collected in small handfuls from every fire he'd ever sat around. The bag was getting kind of big; the man was nearly seventy. He never explained his habit and wasn't required to. He was, of course, required to take a ribbing, just as Alan had to take jokes about his little portable computer and *his* Internet.

"Alan likes them cybersex bulletin boards," Dietrich grinned.

"You know I read about them in *Time*," Jack mentioned from the next booth over. "Them girls are all fat and pimply and can't get dates, which is why they's at home pretending to be sex queens on the Net."

"I thought you liked 'em like that, Jack," Alan said mildly, and there was general laughter.

Alan, in fact, did have a special friend on the Net, but he wasn't about to let the boys know that. Her name was Krista Lewis and she was twenty-six.

Krista was supposed to be in the San Luis Valley this month, another unspoken reason why Alan Baxter suddenly decided he had to fish the Rio Grande. She suggested they get together for dinner. He couldn't pass up the chance to meet her face to face, even though there was a whole generation between them. It was just dinner, after all.

Alan headed back to his Bronco. First he had to find the Williams's Ranch and catch about six hours of sleep. That would put him on the Rio Grande in the early evening, a good time for dry-fly fishing.

He put a hand on his car door handle and thought for a second that his car engine was still running, though he was holding the keys in his other hand. The Bronco suddenly lurched away from him like something alive. The ground twisted and heaved under Alan's feet. He shouted something foolish, something that might have been "Hey!"

The guardrail where he'd stood moments before sagged outward and down. A moment later there was a high, sharp sound, like a guitar string breaking. A section of guardrail twisted abruptly into the air. Alan left his Bronco and staggered toward the road, away from the edge of the scenic drop-off. He had time to regret his favorite fly rod, an old eight-footer he'd had for years. He'd lose everything if the Bronco went over the cliff. But the only thing he could think of was the faithful eight-footer, catcher of a thousand fish. As he reached the asphalt of the highway, he was thrown to his knees. The shaking abruptly stopped. There was a roaring sound. Alan looked up in dumb wonder as an avalanche of rocks and dirt swept from the mountainside over the far end of the diminished scenic viewing area. A small scattering of rocks bounced against the tires of his Bronco. The avalanche swept serenely over the restroom, lifting the wooden structure and smashing it down the mountainside after the vanished guardrail.

The roaring stopped. Alan got slowly to his feet in a profound silence. The squirrels and the birds were silent. The road was buckled in a few places, but it looked like the Bronco could make it. The Bronco itself was completely untouched. One half of the parking lot was somewhere down below with pieces of the mountain on top of it. If Alan had parked six slots to the left, he'd be walking to Alamosa right now. Or he'd be dead. Alan's knees felt watery for a moment.

It was too unreal to be believed. Who'd ever heard of earthquakes in Colorado?

The dust started to clear as he made a slow and careful way down into the San Luis Valley. After a while, he heard the birds begin to sing again.

Briargate Subdivision, Colorado Springs, Colorado

When an earthquake happens in California, people know what to do. They react instantly. They drop what they're doing and run for bracing doorways and away from deadly windows. They do not, as the Coloradans did, stand with wondering gaze and try to figure out what the hell is going on.

Joe Tanner didn't know what was going on. He was standing in his living room eating a bagel and watching Fox news when the first tremor hit. The sun was up and the air was fresh and clear, with a coolness that would dissolve into early summer heat by mid-morning. Rush hour hadn't quite started in Colorado Springs since it was only six A.M., but half the city was up and getting ready to go. Joe was in his version of a business suit, a pair of jeans and a cotton T-shirt. As a computer programmer, he could dress as he liked. Like many programmers, he liked comfortable clothes. A rattle shook Joe's living room panes and made his screen door quiver just a bit. There was a faint booming sound, as though a jet from the Air Force Academy had broken the sound barrier too close to town. He saw movement from the corner of his eye and looked away from the television to see an amazing sight outside his living room window.

There was a man in the street wearing nothing but a pair of white Jockey shorts. His face was covered with shaving cream, and he held a cheap disposable razor in his left hand. It was Ralph Morrison, Joe's neighbor. He had moved from California that year and seemed like a nice man. Joe had thought when he met him that he looked just like the actor Danny Glover. He was wearing blue socks too, Joe noted with amazement. Danny Glover in blue socks, elderly Jockey shorts, and shaving cream, standing in the middle of the street.

"Quake," he bellowed in a huge voice. "Quake!"

The earth quivered under Joe's feet. Joe, who had never been in an earthquake before in his life, felt the floor underneath him start shaking like it was turned to gelatin.

The word Ralph Morrison was bellowing finally reached the proper slot inside his brain. Joe tried to run to the door but the ground was heaving under his feet. He staggered with bruising force into a bookshelf and was flung into the doorway and through the screen. He rolled with the fall and crouched on the pads of his feet, vaguely proud that the training his girlfriend Eileen had made him go through seemed to be working. So far the gun training had been useless, though fun. But the martial arts seemed to be coming in handy. His house, behind him, gave an awful and human-sounding groan. Joe scrambled on hands and knees away from his house, towards Ralph the California man. The earth itself seemed to be screaming. The asphalt of the street writhed under him, a feeling so loathsome that he cried out in disgust and tried to crawl away, back towards his house. Ralph kept his feet, bellowing, his shaver clutched in his hand.

Just as suddenly as it had begun, it was over. Joe crouched on hands and knees on the sidewalk, jeans stained with mud and grass. He saw other figures up and down the block, most in bathrobes, some clutching wailing children. Ralph looked up and down the block and held up his shaver. He waved it back and forth.

"Don't go in your houses!" he bellowed. "Gas pipes may be busted!"

"What can I do?" Joe said, getting to his feet and stepping into the street. He balled his hands into fists to stop the shaking that wanted to take hold of his body. Ralph looked at him, startled, then nodded sharply.

"Right," he said in his normal Ralph Morrison voice. "You take this side of the street. I'll take my side. Tell people to stay out. I'll start turning the pipes off. If you find anybody who's in shape to help, send them to me."

"Okay," Joe said firmly. Ralph peered at him closely then gave him a startling, unexpected wink.

"We'll be fine, boy," he said. "This was just a baby quake. Sure don't feel so great though, does it?"

"No shit," Joe said, and bit back a jagged laugh.

Ralph Morrison turned around without another word and marched to his side of the street. Joe started off in the other direction, on his side.

"One other thing," Ralph shouted back at him. Joe turned, to see Ralph's grin as white as the shaving cream on his face. He waved. "If someone has a spare bathrobe, send it along."

Peterson Air Force Base, Colorado Springs, Colorado

Jim Leetsdale knew he was going to die. He'd known it since he made the decision to unmask the project. They were going to kill him and it was going to be today, and he hadn't finished yet. There was still so much to package together, so many calls to make, and there was Krista Lewis. Krista was his conduit, the way he planned to break the news to the mainstream. With the array of data that Krista was gathering in the Great Sand Dunes, he could present proof that could not be denied.

Yet there they were, at the end of the hall, walking without any particular hurry. The earthquake hadn't slowed them down; the earthquake had helped them by clearing the building and distracting the guards. The Air Force guards were just past being children anyway. They couldn't face these men and win. Who could?

There were two of them, lit intermittently by the hallway emergency lights, heading toward Jim and his office and all the proof he had to unmask the project that had killed his wife. They looked ordinary but tough. One was gray-haired and wide, with a belly just starting to go soft. The other was younger and smaller, with merry black eyes and a slight curve of smile. They were Death come to collect him.

Jim turned and closed the door to his office. It had only two locks but was made of metal. It would take a while. He realized he was shaking, and his breath was a pant in his own ears.

"Lori, babe, be waiting for me," he whispered, just in case it took a while for the angels to collect her from wherever she was and get her to the other end of the tunnel. Lori was never late. Even pregnant and weary with morning sickness, she was on time and waiting to pick him up when a Los Angeles earthquake dropped a cinderblock wall on her and another person at the Burbank Airport. Lori and their unborn baby and a young, unemployed actor named Stephen Brill were killed, the only three fatalities in the latest shake from the San Andreas. Their deaths didn't even make the national news.

He started copying files to disk as fast as he could, scattering paperwork throughout his filing cabinets while each disk finished loading up information. Unless they burned his entire office, they might miss something, and Krista might find it later. He ignored the tiny sounds coming from the office door, the little chittering sounds that might be mice but were not. He had shoved a sturdy Air Force office chair against the door handle, but he knew that wouldn't be enough.

He wrote Krista's name on a yellow Post-it note, and put the note in his palm. What to do with it? He needed to leave her name in his office but he didn't want the soldiers to find that, certainly. They would kill her, too. Jim gave a hiccupy laugh, thinking how brave he was trying to be while his whole body was shaking. His body didn't want to die. His ancient brain, his lizard brain, was dumping adrenaline into his system in preparation for a fight to the death. Well, he was going to do that, he promised the lizard. He was going to try and take those bastards with him. But he'd seen what they could do, that one time in the dunes when they'd finished with Max O'Dell. O'Dell had tried to quit, too, which branded him a traitor. A traitor just like him.

The door shuddered in its frame. Jim spun toward the door, his breath accelerating into a pant, his heart thundering in his chest. Just a few seconds now. He looked at Krista Lewis's name on the Post-it and breathed a prayer. Then he reversed the note and stuck it quickly on the underside of his desk.

"Go gettum, Krista," he said quietly, and pulled out a file

cabinet drawer. Armed with this frail weapon, he waited as the door shuddered again and then fell open. Jim Leetsdale was no longer afraid. He felt a remote kind of calmness and thought again of Lori, waiting on the other side.

"Coming, sweetheart," he whispered.

3

Great Falls, Virginia

"My life," wailed Lucy Giometti, "is over."

"No, it's not," Carolyn Giometti said. Her voice was a
deep maple-syrup tone that reminded Lucy of a nature film
narrator. In person, Lucy's sister-in-law was short, round, and
merry, with snapping black eyes and hair so deeply curled it
looked like black yarn. Right now her voice on the phone was
all Lucy had, and she needed it.

"Hank didn't sleep much at all last night," Lucy said, trying to keep the wail out of her voice. Right now her darling
son, Henry Theodore Giometti, one year old, ready to be
weaned and showing no signs of wanting to let go of Lucy's
milk supply, lay sleeping against her exposed breast. His little
mouth, so much like her husband's, so beautiful, was smeared
with milk. His lashes lay against his rosy cheek, like a cherub
in a child's book.

"Think of this as World War Baby," Carolyn said.

"World War Baby?" Lucy asked. She wasn't sure she'd
heard right. Her eyes were grainy and her back ached.

"World War Baby," Carolyn said matter-of-factly. "You

get pregnant, you bear a child, for the next three years you're fighting the equivalent of a war. You're never relaxed, you're always dirty and frazzled with exhaustion, you never get enough sleep."

"Oh, exactly," Lucy sighed.

"Right, and the war is first to keep this little creature alive, and then to turn it into a nice human being. Housebroken, with a full set of teeth, willing to share a toy and not bash another kid in the head with it. It's a war. You may be at home, but you're not, really. You're in a foxhole in France somewhere with people shooting mortar rounds past your head."

"I'd rather be in a foxhole in France," Lucy said, shifting a little in her armchair. Hank stirred but didn't wake. He'd had an awful night last night with teething pain. The new tooth had caused his nose to run, and he couldn't breathe well. Lucy had given him acetaminophen and rocked him half the night, nursing him until her breasts were sore, and at dawn he'd finally fallen into a deep sleep. She was in her armchair in her office, her computer in front of her, and she never felt less like working in her life.

"At least you have a stay-at-home job," Carolyn said. "Although you don't have to work if you don't want to. My brother can take care of you."

"I know, but—"

"Exactly," Carolyn interrupted. "Without an outside interest, your brain would melt. Look at me, for example. Now that my house is done, I'm trying to figure out what to do."

Carolyn and her husband had bought an ancient Victorian house in Chicago when her children were toddlers. Now her youngest was twelve and her gorgeous house was refinished from attic to basement, work that Carolyn had done herself, by hand.

"Buy another house," Lucy suggested.

"I might," Carolyn said. "I might not. But I have the luxury of contemplation. You, on the other hand, are surviving on basically no sleep. How's the government research work going in the middle of all that?"

"Pretty good," Lucy admitted. "I'm surprised that I can still accomplish anything, but research is fun." What Lucy had never told Carolyn was that she worked for the Central Intelligence Agency. She was an analyst, specializing in computers, a tiny worker bee in a huge organization, and was as far away from fieldwork as a person could be.

Well, sort of. Lucy had ended up in the midst of an undeclared war when she was six months pregnant with Hank, a nuclear conflict between the United States and a terrorist group. They'd launched a nuclear missile from a captured missile silo in Uzbekistan and if Lucy hadn't been in Colorado, the bomb might have taken out most of the Midwest. Instead, she and a group of newfound friends had used the top-secret missile defense program to shoot the bomb down. This was all pretty much an accident, but her analysis of the terrorist group and her warning had arguably saved the world.

This led her and Ted to a very private dinner at the White House and a medal that she could show to no one. Her one regret was that she had to wear a pregnancy dress to the White House dinner. The most exciting dinner of her life and she looked like a humpback whale wrapped in black velvet.

All that happened before Hank's arrival. When he was born, everything changed for her. She'd pushed for two hours before her doctor delivered Hank's head, and then the rest of his little body slipped out painlessly. She'd lain back in the birthing bed, exhausted with the pain and the effort, and the nurse had swept her gown aside and laid Hank on her bare chest. He was still attached to her by his umbilical cord, and he was covered in blood and fluids—he was the most beautiful thing she'd ever seen. She held him and Ted held her and they'd both cried, and Hank who was supposed to cry didn't wail at all. He just lay in her arms and looked at the two of them with his bright eyes.

When she gave her notice at the CIA, panic ensued. The CIA hadn't had many successes lately. She was their golden girl of the moment, pretty and young and brilliant, proving to the other bureaucracies, and most of all to the White House, that the CIA had a purpose.

"They set up your office at home and everything," Carolyn interrupted. Lucy had to smile. Steven Mills, her horrid boss, had talked her into working at home. Imagine that. To a man like Steven Mills, working at home must be the worst idea ever. He was a fifties-style boss, a micromanager, and hated Lucy. Her medal and her status didn't change his loathing of her, but he was a *smart* horrible boss. He was determined to keep her.

He arranged a secure encrypted T1 phone link into her house and used some newfound pull to get her basement office shielded electronically. She stepped through a strange doorway lined with brass plates to get to her computer and her walls had an odd sort of cardboard look, but Hank's playpen and diaper-changing table stood in the corner, and her dog, Fancy, lay on Lucy's feet and snored while she worked. Her work wasn't at the highest levels, but it was still analysis. If she really needed some sensitive materials, she was still allowed to go to the CIA building and look at them there. It was better than no work at all.

Not that she was working right now. She was talking to her sister-in-law and wondering if she could even focus on her computer screen.

"I feel better just talking to you," she said. Carolyn laughed. "Hey, you know, you could write a book about child-raising. You could call it *World War Baby*. Or you could get a job reading books-on-tape. You have a great voice."

"That's my Lucy," Carolyn said warmly. "Always trying to solve everyone else's problems. Set down that nephew of mine in his playpen and get just an hour or so of work in, then get some sleep. Teething doesn't last forever, it just feels that way."

Lucy sat for a few minutes, smiling at Hank, after Carolyn hung up. She was so great to talk to. Carolyn had been through it all. She'd survived the war.

Hank muttered somewhat when Lucy laid him in his playpen, but when she tucked his blanket around him, he sighed and fell asleep again. As soon as she sat down, her springer spaniel nudged her.

"Yes, darling," Lucy said, stroking her little dog's ears and head. "Time for a little bit of Fancy. Then work, and more Hank. When Ted gets home, I'll pay attention to him, and when he falls asleep Hank will wake up." Lucy bent her head over her dog's silky ears and cried a few silly tears, tears of self-pity and tiredness. She despised herself for crying them, but she couldn't help herself.

Finally, she sat up and blew her nose briskly and put her hands on her computer keyboard. Time to work.

Special Investigations Bureau, Colorado Springs, Colorado

"I'm glad you're okay," Eileen said with a sigh. She'd been trying to get through to Joe all afternoon, and only just a few minutes ago realized he was probably at work.

Joe Tanner worked at Schriever Air Force Base on a top-secret system that Eileen shouldn't know about but did because of a murder there a year ago. He was a programmer in the missile defense system and Eileen had learned all about the system that wasn't supposed to exist. She'd learned how the system worked firsthand, actually. She still had dreams about the nuclear missile arcing through the sky and heading toward the United States, the missile that she and Joe and a few friends had shot down.

Joe and Eileen had been together ever since. Joe was smart and funny, and his looks made her weak in the knees. Best of all, he seemed to feel no urge to turn her into a little home-maker who'd cook his meals and darn his socks, if that's what homemakers did nowadays. If a case kept her out late, he simply woke up enough to make room for her in his bed when she crawled in, with never a murmur of complaint. He was just about perfect, and she was entertaining serious thoughts about permanence. Not that she'd tell Joe *that*. Some things a girl had to be old-fashioned about.

"I'm fine. I'm glad you're okay too," he said cheerfully. "The systems out here came through with no problems. I called once to make sure you were in, but they told me you were busy so I didn't leave a message. I guess I should have."

"I should have figured you'd be out there," she said. "I was stuck doing street-cop stuff all day long." She was now at her desk trying to wade through the paperwork she had to file on each incident. The office was boiling with noisy activity. All the off-duty police had been called in after the earthquake, and they were all trying to catch up on paperwork and go home. Captain Harben ran an efficient department, even when his homicide detectives were working street detail.

"Looters and lost children?" Joe said, and the half-teasing, half-sympathetic tone of his voice sent a brief run of pleasurable goosebumps down Eileen's spine. "But no lost boyfriends, now," he added. "What about dinner tonight?"

"Everyone in Colorado Springs will be going to dinner tonight."

"I'll pack some snack crackers for the wait in line."

"It's a deal," she said, laughing. "Call me if something comes up."

Eileen held the button down on her phone, staring out the window at her mountain, Cheyenne Mountain. It didn't look any different than it had before, but Eileen felt different, looking at it. The ground wasn't supposed to heave like that, to quiver and shake like loose mud. Even the huge Cheyenne Mountain had shaken with the quake, if reports were true. NORAD, the underground base in the mountain, had shut down its outside power lines just like it was supposed to if a nuclear weapon had gone off. The drill, apparently, had worked perfectly and with the exception of a small shower of rocks near the entrance, nothing was changed. That was the report from CNN, at least. CNN had exhausted the mystery of the Colorado quake a while ago and was now doing "human interest" stories like Cheyenne Mountain.

"Hey, there's one good thing about this fucked-up day," Peter O'Brien called out to her. He was just sitting down at his desk. His shirt was damp and his forehead was beaded with drops of sweat.

"What is it, Pete?" Eileen asked, smiling.

"You're old news now, hero," he smiled. Eileen froze in her chair. Had she really forgotten Teddy Shaw? Had she spent an entire day without thinking about killing a man?

"I forgot," she said, her voice small in her ears. O'Brien grinned even wider.

"So has everybody else," he said. "Now Teddy can fertilize some trees and never kill any more kids and you can go back to being Eileen Reed, that quiet, intelligent, pretty detective that always solves her cases—"

"Stop it, Pete," Eileen said, blinking hard. Damn Pete O'Brien. If he found a weakness, what he called a hot button, in another detective, he hammered it relentlessly until the detective exploded like a stepped-on ketchup packet or got over it. Until now Eileen had escaped ribbing. O'Brien figured out very early that Eileen didn't care about her looks, one way or the other. If some people thought she was pretty, that was okay. If they thought she was ugly, that didn't matter either. But now O'Brien had scented her concern about shooting Teddy Shaw, and he was out for blood.

"That red-headed gal, the one who used to be a hot-shot Air Force pilot, the expert interviewer who gets every suspect to spill their guts—oops."

There was a brief silence. O'Brien eyed Eileen and she glared back at him.

"One way or another," O'Brien added with a charming small smile, and Eileen couldn't help it. She started laughing. O'Brien stood up at his desk and waved his fists around like a winner in the boxing ring, revealing rings of sweat under his armpits like a slice of an ancient tree and sending an enormous scent wave of Dial soap in Eileen's direction.

"The champeeeon," O'Brien crowed.

Eileen, still laughing, waved at O'Brien like she was shooing a fly. O'Brien was better than a thousand sessions with Gerri Matthews. Besides, O'Brien would never try to find out what really happened in the back of Teddy Shaw's van. With luck, Eileen could keep Gerri from finding out too.

The Great Sand Dunes, Colorado

The park ranger was much younger than Marcia Fowler and frightened half to death by the earthquake. Consequently, he was horribly rude, which awoke a faint sense of amusement in Marcia and helped her regain her calm. This was no strong and capable Authority, but a tiny puffed-chest youngster barely on the edge of control.

After assigning another, even younger park ranger to keep anyone from entering the dunes, he walked with Marcia out into the sand. His stride was heroic and his Smokey-Bear hat brim was suitably lowered, as though glowering at the old lady tourist and her ridiculous vapors. Marcia made no attempt to keep up with him, although without the sprained ankle, she could have easily matched his pace. Marcia was a regular at her local fitness center and ran 10k races occasionally just for fun. She sometimes got whistles from her rear view. She had nothing to prove to Mr. Puffy Chest. Twice he stopped and waited for her to catch up, then marched on ahead after a nice rest for him, no rest for her. Marcia plodded on a steady, ankle-saving pace and ignored him. Finally, he reluctantly dropped his pace back to hers.

"How far, ma'am?" he asked brusquely, after ten minutes of silent hiking together.

"About a half mile," Marcia said. The dunes stretched behind them for nearly a mile in almost pancake flatness. The ripples of Medano Creek rushed across the center of the flat stretch of sand. Medano started in the far Sangre de Cristo Mountains and ran under the dunes. The creek surfaced in bare sand and ran for a mile before vegetation took over at the edge of the dunes. The creek was bathwater temperature in the summer and was no more than seven inches deep. During a warm day, like yesterday, Marcia had seen hundreds of children playing in the warm sandy water, splashing and shrieking with delight. Marcia's rubber sandals were already dry after splashing through the creek. The ranger's boots were wet and likely to stay that way, another source of amusement to her. Why would you be a ranger at the Great Sand Dunes and not have a pair of sandals to wear on the sand? Because sandals didn't convey the proper profile of authority, she answered herself.

After nearly a mile of flat sand, the dunes really began. The first few slopes, miniature foothills, took no more than fifteen minutes or so to climb. After the first hills of sand came mountains, then mountains even larger still, until the tan of the sand met the sizzling blue of the Colorado sky. The sheer amount of sand was astonishing. Marcia had gotten through the first set of foothills and was beginning her first major climb when she'd found the body. At dawn the sand had been full of color, various shades of tan and blue and black. Now the sand was uniformly pale brown and featureless and radiated heat in waves. It smelled, too, a vague and faintly spicy scent that Marcia couldn't define.

They crested the last of the foothills and Marcia saw the forlorn shape of the girl. Ranger Keith strode on, hat lowered. She put a hand on his arm and when he stopped she pointed mutely. His face blanched, and for a moment he looked very much like a bewildered, small boy. Marcia knew he'd convinced himself she was a fruitcake, probably one of those UFO nuts, and he was in for a long walk in the sun for nothing.

"Oh," he said in a little voice.

"We'll have to cover her, and post a ranger to keep people away. Then you can send someone to town to fetch the sheriff," Marcia said gently. Ranger Keith nodded. His face wore a floundering look, and she almost felt sorry for him.

"I have to make sure she's dead," he said gruffly.

"Well, make sure of it," Marcia snapped. "But she isn't wearing any clothes and she needs to be decently covered. I don't want people gaping at her."

Ranger Keith flushed bright red all the way to the brim of his Smokey-Bear hat. Marcia felt a brief flash of bitter hatred for the creatures that had left this poor woman to be gawked at. She felt fairly certain the ones who'd done this were Grays. In her long walk back to the ranger station, she'd had time to think about the lack of footprints in the sand and the mutilations. The dead girl was tumbled in the lee part of a dune and her body lay in a body-shaped outline. There were no other footprints around her. Some of her skin had been removed in strips. Marcia Fowler was not part of the UFO crowd that subscribed to the belief that aliens were benign, kindly watchers of humankind. She was firmly in the camp of the believers in the malignancy of alien visitations. She'd read the stories of abductions, mutilations, missing time, and men in black.

Never was a human body found. There were continuing rumors about the Air Force major found in the Nevada desert, skin sliced off, anus cored away, genitals removed, just like the many documented cow mutilations. But other than the rumors—and this was no more than a rumor—there were no cases of actual deaths.

This girl might be the first. Marcia felt a brief excited trickle in the pit of her stomach, thinking of the reaction in the UFO community. Then her eyes focused on the blushing ranger. Beyond him lay the sprawled and mutilated form of the girl, and she felt ashamed.

"Let's go look at her," Marcia said firmly. "Then we'll cover her and go back."

"Yes, ma'am," the ranger mumbled. He took off his hat, revealing a surprisingly pink and bald dome. He wiped sweat off the top of his head and put the hat back on. With the hat off, he was a mild and tender looking young man. With the hat on, he immediately became Ranger Keith, strong of jaw and with flashing manly eye.

They walked down the slope of the dune together, and there was the girl, whoever she was, eyes blinded with sand, dead. Marcia was a biology teacher and dead things were nothing new to her. As a young girl, she'd hunted deer in South Dakota with her father. The flies, the pale skin, the beginning of bloat, didn't make an impression. Marcia was looking at sharp laser cuts; skin sheared away at her shoulder and down her arm, bruises about the nose and back of the neck. There were bruises about the throat as well, faint marks. One arm was at an odd angle, without any swelling. She'd been killed shortly after her arm had been broken.

Ranger Keith was suddenly halfway up the dune, head down, hands on his knees. Marcia moved away reluctantly from the girl and walked back up the slope. The ranger hadn't thrown up, but it was a near thing. Beads of clear perspiration stood out on his cheeks and neck.

"I need to call this in, before we go back," he said hoarsely. His hand was fumbling again and again at the catch to his radio, failing to negotiate the small buckle. Perhaps he'd seen dead bodies before, but Marcia knew he'd never seen anything like this before. Fair enough. Neither had she.

"Right," Marcia said. She took one last look back, trying to memorize every detail, trying to get a picture in her mind that she could later look at and examine.

Once the sheriff took her statement, Marcia was planning to make some phone calls. She would contact some people who would suddenly take an intense interest in the San Luis Valley. Maybe, just maybe, this would be the case that would bring the UFO community into the mainstream. If that would happen, Marcia was sure that humans could defeat the Grays. Humans were stronger and smarter and were losing only because they didn't know they were in a war. The girl, the dead girl, might just unmask the war.

Special Investigations Bureau, Colorado Springs, Colorado

"Dead body," Harben yelled. "Peterson Air Force Base."

Eileen and Dave Rosen reached for their jackets. The late August weather had decided to pretend it was fall, with high gray clouds scudding overhead and a chilly wind tearing at the leaves of the trees, as though the weather was surprised at the earthquake, too. Tomorrow it could be eighty degrees without a cloud in the sky. There could even be surprise snowstorms in the glorious fall days of September and October, and when those happened, hikers always died, wearing nothing but sandals and light summer clothes and a surprised look. Colorado could be deadly to the unprepared.

"Great, another Air Force liaison job," Eileen grumbled to Rosen as they walked to Harben's desk.

"You'll be working with Major Bandimere on this one," Harben said, hanging up the phone. " I know you hate the liaison job, Eileen, but you two are just too damn good at it. As you well know."

"Where do we go?"

"Government Building 12-E, but that's okay, Major

Bandimere will be waiting to guide you. You don't have to find it on your own."

"Major Bandimere, oh boy," Eileen said dryly. Rosen and Harben exchanged deadpan looks. Major Deanna Bandimere was very pretty and wore a great deal of makeup. She was just about five foot three, and affected a little-girl, breathless Marilyn Monroe pout that put Eileen's teeth on edge. Eileen, who wore little makeup and didn't have the slightest idea how to pout, had little affection for the diminutive major.

"At least you don't have to have her hanging all over your every word," Rosen said under his breath. Bandimere flirted with every male over the age of twelve and Dave Rosen was an available target. "You have any ideas on how to approach this one, boss?"

"Be careful," Harben said absently, his eyes already returning to his computer screen. "Keep your eyes open. The major implied that it was a suicide, but I want you to make sure."

"No problem," Eileen said. At least this was a thankful change from all the damn earthquake reports. She and Rosen stood from their chairs, and Harben turned back to his computer terminal.

"Tallyho," Rosen murmured.

4

The irritating Major Bandimere was waiting at the gate, pert and curly and tiny behind the wheel of the large government truck. She rolled down the window with brisk little cranks as they pulled up.

"Hello," she said to Eileen. "How are you, Ellie? Nice to see you, Dave."

"Rosen," Rosen said frostily.

"We've got a suicide case out at 12-E," the little Major continued. "Just follow me, we'll be there in just a sec."

"I hate people who say 'sec'," Rosen said as Bandimere wheeled her Jeep around in a tight circle and headed back through the gate of Peterson Air Force Base. Eileen laughed out loud.

"Don't fret it," she said.

"I won't, Ellie," he said. Eileen shuddered.

"Aren't we lucky," Rosen murmured.

"I'd almost rather be filing more earthquake reports," Eileen said, then glanced over at Rosen.

"Almost," they said in unison.

There was a comfortable silence between them as they followed Major Bandimere, the comfort of nearly a year of police work as partners. Eileen liked Dave Rosen quite a bit. She'd been worried Rosen would try to take over the team, as many men naturally tried to do when their senior partner was a female. Eileen wasn't going to budge, not after working as junior partner to Jim Erickson for three years. But men didn't go into police work if they were the passive type. She smelled trouble, but it didn't happen.

Rosen was so quiet she found herself thinking that the racist stereotype of the silent Native American was true in his case. Eileen was almost positive that Rosen was Native American, but knew for sure that he wasn't Sioux. Eileen grew up in northeastern Wyoming; she knew the distinctive characteristics of the Lakota Sioux. Eileen thought for a while he had to be Navaho, but she knew he'd transferred from New York. Whatever he was and wherever he came from, he was the most perfectly balanced man she'd ever met. He never tried to take the lead in their investigations, yet worked as hard as she did. He was a man of few words, but the words he spoke were always sharp as knives. Eileen would talk and Rosen would listen and interject a comment or two, and they would solve their case.

Best of all, there didn't seem to be an ounce of romantic chemistry between them. Dave Rosen was six feet tall with ink-black hair and soulful black eyes and a handsome, chiseled face, and he didn't turn Eileen's crank one bit and never had, even when Rosen was a rookie and she was still working with Jim Erickson. Rosen didn't seem to find her attractive, either. Eileen read an article on pheromones once, and the theory of the researcher was that if two people were not genetically compatible—that is, if their offspring would be defective—then the two people would not be attracted to each other at all, no matter what they looked like.

Eileen expressed this thought to Rosen one night on a very boring stakeout, when they were sharing a messy twelve-inch meatball sub. If Eileen had been sharing a meatball sub with Joe Tanner, she would have attacked him the first time he put his fingers in his mouth and sucked off the thick chunks of spaghetti sauce, like Rosen was doing. Joe, not too physically different from Dave Rosen, drove her to distraction. Everything he did was intensely arousing. Joe was a fascinating man, she explained to Rosen, licking her own fingers one by one. It wasn't that he was some sexual passion, some meathead that she liked to sleep with. She loved him. He was just also incredibly sexually attractive.

"You two'll make pretty babies," Rosen said, typically brief. "You and I would make three-headed monsters with big noses and hair all over their bodies."

Eileen laughed so hard at this that she choked on a piece of sandwich, then whacked her forehead on the dash while coughing it up. Rosen offered her a sip of her Coke with eyes glittering with laughter.

Major Bandimere swung the Jeep to a stop and hopped out. She managed to make her standard Air Force uniform look like an expensive department store suit, something worn by a little mannequin with pertly curled blonde hair. Her triangle of blue skirt was tight and short and her pale blue shirt was tailored to her pointed, high breasts. A wave of perfume enveloped Eileen as the major stepped out of her Jeep.

"We're pretty sure this is a suicide," she repeated, pulling out two visitor passes from a leather folder. The passes had clips to attach to their shirts. "Major Jim Leetsdale, found in the park by 12-E where he worked. Gunshot wound, but nobody heard it. It was either during the earthquake, or maybe right after. We don't know." She handed a pass to Eileen and stepped over to Rosen. Ignoring his hand held out for the badge, she stepped close to him and attached it to his shirt pocket.

"There," she said, patting her little hands on Rosen's broad chest. Eileen smothered a grin as she attached her own visitor's pass. Peterson Air Force Base was a pleasant place, with trees and broad avenues. The buildings were twentieth-century cinder block affairs, but an attempt had been made to make them pretty with bushy green landscaping and groupings of trees. The parking lot where Major Bandimere led them was in front of 12-E. The building's designation was clearly painted in black letters nearly five feet tall. Only a few cars dotted the lot. Beyond the parking lot was a pretty little green space, a park, with a cannon on the rise of a hill. A soldier stood sentry near the cannon.

No, wait. Eileen saw the edge of a blue tarp. The soldier was standing sentry next to the body. Their body. She felt the taste in the back of her throat, the pleasant little taste like biting into something tart and sweet at the same time. She'd long ago gotten over the guilt about feeling so good. This is what she loved to do.

"Who found the body?" she asked.

"Private Amy Szneski," Major Bandimere said. "She's trying to get into Special Forces school so she's out running every morning at dawn carrying a big pack filled with rocks. At least that's what she says. We've got her in 12-E, in the break room."

"Okay," Eileen said, and sighed. Deanna Bandimere was competent, at least, if not any fun. "Let's look at the body."

The major gestured, and they walked toward the cannon and the sentry.

"Anybody touch the body?" Eileen asked.

"Just Szneski, feeling for a pulse. And me, same thing. I have a call into Doctor Durland's office. He'll have the crime scene team out here in an hour or so."

The sentry was bored and cold. The day was still threatening rain. The wind was chilly and the soldier was dressed in summer camouflage. He drew up and saluted Major Bandimere.

"Go get some food and pick up your jacket," she said. "Be back in an hour." The soldier dropped his salute and set off at a run.

Eileen drew on a pair of latex gloves. She kept a whole box of them in her Jeep. Rosen, too, silently put gloves on. Bandimere had her own set. Eileen stepped forward and pulled the tarp back carefully.

There he was. Major Jim Leetsdale, if Bandimere was correct. The man was very dead. He was lying on the slope of the little hill that held the cannon. His eyes were partially open and glazed. Some blood had trickled from his nose, mouth, and ears. His hands were at his sides, his palms open and up, his feet together. There were a few flies, made sluggish by the cold, crawling around his mouth. The gun was lying in his right hand, his finger still through the trigger guard. A single black hole marked his face, in his left eyesocket. The force of the bullet had knocked the eye out of true but hadn't destroyed it. The eye gazed forlornly off to the side while the other one stared indifferently at the sky.

Eileen felt her belly tighten. She gave a careful sidelong glance at Rosen and saw his tiny nod. She turned back to the body.

There was an empty wine cooler in the grass. A small puddle of a purplish substance was still in the bottom of the bottle.

"We'll want that tested," Eileen murmured. "When the crime scene crew gets here."

"If that's his," Rosen said.

"It's his," Eileen said, as Bandimere nodded. Eileen explained to Rosen. She had been in the Air Force. At every base, grounds cleanup was meticulously thorough. There were no cigarette butts, potato chip wrappers, or paper cups on any military base. As a recruit in basic training, Eileen had worked on countless cleanup crews. In a double line, they would sweep across a parking lot or a field and pick up every tiny piece of trash they would see. If the sergeant found the tiniest gum wrapper, there would be no weekend leave. This tactic was still used today and helped keep every base meticulously, even spookily, clean.

"So," Eileen concluded, "an object as big as a wine cooler bottle couldn't be left more than overnight."

"Seems like overkill," Rosen commented.

"I've got one word for you," Eileen grinned. "Mines."

"Oh," Rosen said, blinking.

"These guys occasionally get deployed to lovely spots like Bosnia," Eileen said. "Being meticulous is a good way to stay alive."

Rosen, economical with words as always, nodded. Eileen could almost see the busy librarian in Rosen's brain filing the information away, categorizing it, and extrapolating it to fit any future situation. Rosen was smart. It was fun to teach him something new.

"Was there a suicide note?" she asked Bandimere.

"Not that we found here," Bandimere replied. "But there might be one in his office. We sealed it off. Didn't even go in yet."

Eileen squatted down next to the body. She put one finger on his chest, a chest that was silent and still and flattened to the ground. Then she really looked at him, looked past the beginnings of bloat and the flies and the queerly aimed gaze. This was Jim Leetsdale, a man, perhaps a husband and father. What was he like? She saw the new lines of sadness and care in his forehead and bracketing his mouth, lines of sorrow so new they looked almost like cuts. Behind that were smile lines and fine crow tracks. The crow tracks looked like they were made squinting into wind or sun, tracks that spoke of boating or hikes or biking or some kind of good fun. His teeth, seen through the slackness of his mouth, were clean and straight, his arms were well muscled, his belly slightly soft. He had thinning blond hair that was cut short, with no pretense of comb-over or other nonsense.

"Was he married?"

"Married, lost his wife last year," Bandimere read from her folder. "Lori Leetsdale, killed in the Burbank earthquake. A wall fell on her and a couple other people. She was pregnant."

There was a small silence. Eileen, squatting by Leetsdale, looked up at Rosen. He met her eyes and didn't need to shake his head for her to understand the look. She nodded and turned back to the body.

No comb-over of the hair, good looking, soft in the belly from desk work but otherwise fit. A well-loved man, before a disaster took his family from him.

"Why a wine cooler?" Rosen asked abruptly.

Eileen stood up and shook out her legs. She had that thought too, although she was unhappy to think about it.

"A fruity sweetish drink. More like a girl's drink," she said, and grimaced. "Not that I really want to say that."

"Maybe the wine cooler has a drug in it," Bandimere said.

"Wine coolers are sweet and might mask a bitter taste. So he could work himself up to pull the trigger."

Eileen looked at Deanna Bandimere with new interest. This was more than she expected from the major.

"Hey!" shouted someone from behind Eileen, making her flinch. She spun around, instantly angry at being surprised like that. The man coming up the slope of the hill behind her was in a business suit. He looked furious. Bright pink burned across his cheekbones. He had thick brown hair and eyebrows and hazel eyes that were rimmed in red, as though he'd spent a sleepless night or had recently been crying. His skin was pitted with old acne scars, which gave him a rough, handsome look. He was tall and broad, a man who looked like he knew he was handsome, or at least thought he did. His hands were clenched into white-knuckled fists.

"Hello," Rosen said mildly.

"Mr. Mitchell," Bandimere squeaked.

"What is the meaning of this—travesty?" Mr. Mitchell's voice was deep and powerful and very angry. Bandimere nearly quailed, her little form shrinking under Mitchell's angry gaze. This made Eileen furious, not just with Mitchell's tone of voice but with contempt at Bandimere.

Women, of which she was one, should never, ever quail before men. She backed her belief with self-defense training and two guns. Eileen tried to arm women at every opportunity, and she found it odd and puzzling that most women, who got the best use out of guns and who rarely put them to bad use, were so adamantly for gun control. What, so if there were no more guns men would stop using their fists, too? Or they would abandon cotton pads soaked with ether and burglar's tools, like Teddy Shaw?

All this flashed through Eileen's thoughts in an instant.

"So who the hell are you?" she asked pleasantly, and was rewarded with Mitchell's angry gaze.

"Jacob Mitchell, director of Ops, 12-E," the man said. "Why aren't you taking care of this poor man?"

"We are, sir," Bandimere said in a voice so breathless and tiny she sounded like a cartoon mouse. Eileen could have kicked her.

"You call this taking care of Jim? He's dead, he's killed himself, and you're standing around him like a bunch of goddamned buzzards letting the flies crawl over him!" Mitchell turned his furious face to Rosen, ignoring Eileen.

"You, who are you? Are you in charge here?" he asked.

"I'm in charge here," Eileen said tightly. "Detective Reed. This is Detective Rosen. Colorado Springs homicide. Let's step away from the crime scene, shall we? I don't want you to accidentally contaminate evidence."

"You're calling suicides crime scenes, now? Don't you have anything better to do, like some real crimes?" Mitchell yelled. A chilly, gusty wind snapped the edge of the blue tarp and sent some stray leaves over the top, making a sound like cornflakes rattling into a bowl.

"Let's just step away, sir," Eileen repeated.

"I want you to take care of my friend," Mitchell said. His voice broke on the word *friend* and his cheeks burned pinker in the gray afternoon.

"We're sorry about your friend," Eileen said gently. "But we have to follow certain procedures. Let us take care of this, all right? Let's just step away, now." Eileen made the mistake of putting her hand on Mitchell's upper arm. The muscles of his arm were humming and writhing like a nest of cottonmouth snakes. He threw her hand off with a cry of disgust and stepped backward. The slope of the little hill made him lose his footing, and he nearly fell down.

"Major Bandimere, I want you to take care of this situation immediately!" he shouted, regaining his balance and shaking out his sleeves as though he'd been burned by Eileen's touch. "And you," he said, looking at Eileen, "I'll be placing a call to your superior and I'll have your job." Mitchell turned and walked toward his car, a brand new torpedo of a sedan that snarled like a jungle cat as he revved the motor. He puffed some black smoke out of the tires as he pulled into the street.

On the hill by the cannon, there was only the sound of the rattling leaves on the tarp and Deanna Bandimere's anxious breathing.

"Well," Eileen said. "That was unpleasant."

"He'd be terrible at your job," Rosen said, deadpan.

Eileen started laughing and then abruptly stopped as she saw Bandimere. The little woman was pale-faced and wild-eyed and looked entirely spooked, like a teacup poodle thrown into a pool.

"So who was that clown, Deanna?" she asked. "What's up with him?"

"Oh, no," Bandimere moaned, wringing her narrow hands. "We really, really can't make Mr. Mitchell upset. He's really important. He's got *power*."

"Not over us," Rosen said calmly.

"Fill us in, Deanna," Eileen said. "Don't forget, you can blame everything on us. We're protected all the way to Congress. Remember, they passed that law about military bases and capital crimes?" Bandimere nodded miserably. "No matter what Mitchell is at Peterson, he's got no power over us. He looks familiar but I can't place him. So who is he?"

"He's a former state congressman. Didn't you recognize him? He made a run for President a few years ago, but dropped out before the primaries were over. Now he's the project chief at 12-E," Bandimere said. "You guys must not follow politics very much." She sighed and blew a strand of blonde hair off her forehead, but her expression lightened as she looked from Rosen to Eileen. She spread her hands wide. "And before you ask me what that is, I'll have to tell you I don't have the foggiest idea. Something compartmentalized."

"What's compartmentalized mean?" asked Rosen.

"Above top secret," Eileen said absently. "Access only by special password. So if you are working on a compartmentalized project, you have a top-secret clearance and a special access code, like 'doom,' for example."

Eileen gulped and stopped abruptly. She had "doom" access clearance, clearance that she shouldn't have on a particularly dangerous piece of American history. Somehow the word just slipped out. Her and her big mouth. Luckily, Rosen and Bandimere were nodding without comprehension, as though she'd made up the word instead of spilling a special-access password. Damn secrets. Eileen didn't like them and didn't like keeping them.

"So Mitchell's on a special project," she said quickly. "So what?"

"It's something very big and powerful and he pulls a lot of money to the base, that's all I know," Bandimere said. "He's a politician. He really does have power. Can't we hurry and wrap this up, just to make him happy? You guys would really be doing me a favor."

Eileen glanced over at Rosen, whose shoulders raised a tiny millimeter. A whole conversation went between them in the arch of her eyebrow and the shrug of his shoulders. The gusty cold winds were getting fiercer and the light was fading. The day was tending toward real rain. Eileen looked toward the Front Range. The enormous bulk of Pikes Peak should have been clearly visible, but it was shrouded in clouds.

"Deanna," she said. "I would like to wrap this up, but we're going to have to do some further investigation."

"On a suicide?" Deanna wailed. "Are you trying to kill my career, here?"

"On a homicide," Eileen said. "This man didn't kill himself. He was killed, and he was set here to make it look like a suicide."

"Tarp," Rosen called. Eileen leaped to grasp the other edge of the tarp before a particularly heavy gust of wind tore it from the body. She and Rosen struggled for a moment before they secured the tarp with some of the loose rocks at the base of the cannon.

"When is Dr. Durland going to get here?" Eileen said as the first pellets of cold rain rattled against the tarp. She ducked her head as a spray of icy droplets swept against her cheek.

"Crime scene crew should be here within the hour," Bandimere said in a stunned, lost voice. "You say he was killed? You think he was killed?"

"He was killed," Eileen said, and Rosen nodded.

"They only missed a few things," he said. "They almost fooled us."

"Oh my God," Bandimere said softly. The rain plastered her blonde hair against her cheeks, making her look even younger and smaller. "Murder."

5

The Williams's Ranch, San Luis Valley, Colorado

Alan Baxter almost fell full across the bed, dirty and tired as he was, and let sleep take him. But he was sandy and dirty and this bed was sweetly clean and white. Beth Williams's guest room was a haven and he couldn't bring himself to foul the sheets on his first night.

He wearily stripped his travelling clothes and kicked them into a pile. The guest bathroom was freshly scrubbed and spotlessly white. The scent of cleaner still hung faintly in the air. Pale oak cabinets held everything from untouched toothbrushes to an electric razor. Thick white towels, ridiculously fluffy, hung from long oak bars. Beth Williams was happy to have guests, Alan decided, turning on the water in the shower. The water was hot in moments and stayed that way, all the way through his shower. He stood under the water and let the pounding spray take some of the ache out of his elderly muscles.

When he'd driven up to the gates of the Williams's Ranch, still elated he'd survived the earthquake that had taken half the rest stop, he'd found himself recruited immediately to help round up panicked and stampeded cattle. The ranch entrance was gated and locked, with a doorbell button on a pole for easy access from a truck. A small sign on the gate modestly said "Williams." Alan pressed the button and waited for ten minutes before he saw a truck raising a plume of dust down the ranch road. The truck held Beth Williams, Sam's wife, who was directing the salvage operation at the main house. They had never met, but Beth knew he was coming for a visit. Sam Williams had already been gone for hours, collecting his priceless scattered quarterhorses. Beth unlocked the gate and waved Alan through with wide arcs of her arm. She desperately needed someone to drive out to pasture four with water, coffee, and sandwiches. Alan immediately offered his Bronco and his services and fifteen minutes later found himself driving over bumpy pastureland with an enormous cooler and a huge Thermos of coffee strapped into the back. He hadn't even gotten out of his Bronco.

He found pasture four easily; there were no signs but the area was a milling, frantic mess of cattle and dogs and men in four-wheel-drive trucks. Four men were working with the cattle, although it seemed like a hundred with the noise and the dust. The men were using the dogs and their trucks to cut injured cattle out of the herd. Most were being patched up in a makeshift corral, although there were two forlorn corpses stacked neatly thirty yards away from the corral. As Alan drove by, he saw that each had been shot between the eyes. He parked next to the makeshift corral and wondered what to do next.

A man who seemed most obviously in charge came striding over with his hat plastered to his eyebrows and an outlaw bandanna tied around nose and chin. Alan just had time to notice that the man's shirt seemed to fit him rather oddly when the cowboy reached his Bronco and raised his head.

"Tell me my mom sent you here with food," a woman's voice said from the bandanna.

"In the back," Alan said, trying not to laugh out loud. Now that he could see her eyes and hear her voice, he wondered how he'd mistaken her curves for a man. Perhaps he should look into getting glasses.

"Well, get out and help me," the woman said, pulling her bandanna down and glaring at him. "We're dying out here. It's been hours."

Alan jumped out quickly and opened up the back. Within a few moments, three out of the four cowboys were gathered around his Bronco, drinking water from the plastic cups Beth Williams had thrown into the back. Water dribbled down their chins and out the sides of their mouths and cut clean streams through the dirt and grime that coated them. Two of the four dogs came trotting up and were given cups of their own. They were no neater than the cowboys, slobbering water out their muzzles as they lapped frantically. Alan found himself holding the cup for one of the cow dogs, and was taken aback when the dog gave him a measured, adult look before drinking from the cup he held. He'd never seen such intelligence in a dog's eyes.

The two dogs went back to the corral, and the other two cowboys came trotting to the Bronco. In the meantime, the remaining cowboys—cow people? Alan wondered, since the Williams's girl and one other were both female—dug into the cooler with little yelps of joy. The Williams's girl dropped a thick sandwich into Alan's hands.

"Ate today?" she said, her voice muffled by an enormous mouthful of food.

"No," Alan said, unwrapping his sandwich. His stomach woke up at the sight of the thick meatloaf. Homegrown lettuce was piled on top of the meatloaf and the bread looked homemade. He bit in. It was, and so was the meatloaf. He didn't think he'd ever had a better sandwich.

"Angler?" the girl asked, tilting her head towards Alan's Bronco.

"Yeth," Alan said through a mouthful of meatloaf.

"Friend of Dad's?"

This time he only nodded.

"Ever doctor cattle?"

"Not until today," Alan said after swallowing. He gave the girl a sunny grin and she grinned back. She was perhaps thirty, nearly six feet tall and with Sam Williams's round face and cheerful black eyes. Crow's-feet radiated from her eyes and her hair was damp with sweat. She looked magnificent.

"We'd appreciate the help," Sam's daughter said, and dusted her palms free of crumbs. She held out a callused and filthy hand. "Susan Williams."

"Alan Baxter," Alan said. "Lead me to it."

That had been twelve long hours ago. It was midnight, and they'd finished gutting and hanging the four cattle that were casualties of the earthquake only an hour ago. Beth Williams laid on a feast at the big country kitchen, steaks and eggs and country gravy over biscuits and an enormous spinach and lettuce salad with fresh cherry tomatoes and tiny carrots and peas, all from her own garden and tasting like heaven.

"We'll salvage two for the ranch," Sam told the family at dinner. "The others will go to Operation Relief. I'm sure they'll appreciate the donation."

"Operation Relief gives groceries to lower income families," Susan explained to Alan in a murmur. "Private, no governmental strings, just the way we like it."

"Thanks again, Alan," Sam said. "I'm sure glad you happened by today."

"Me, too," Alan said, and meant it, even though he was filthy and more tired than he had ever been since a summer working construction long years ago.

"So where were you during the earthquake?" asked Frank. Frank, short and dark, was from New Jersey, was emphatically Italian-American, and had bought a one-way bus ticket to Wyoming the day he graduated from high school. He ended up as a cowhand on a ranch in Jackson Hole and eventually found his way to the Williams's place. He explained to Alan that he always wanted to be a cowboy. He was just born with the itch and had it all his life. Frank told Alan this while expertly stitching a long gash in a heifer's haunch. Alan was sitting on the cow's head and holding her front feet, a position he found awkward and potentially dangerous. But Frank knew what he was doing.

He later explained to Alan about waking up in mid-

Wyoming and looking out the bus window at the bright and silent world of Sinclair, an oil-refinery town. He thought it was an amusement park, he told Alan, because he couldn't imagine that around the town of Sinclair there were hundreds of miles of nothing at all. The bright lights, the towers, and his exhaustion peopled the empty refinery structure with Ferris wheels and roller coasters and miniature golf towers. When he woke again he was seeing the dawn rise over the Wind River Mountains, and he knew he was in the land of his heart, his dreams, the West.

"I was at the rest stop coming down from La Veta Pass when the earthquake hit," Alan explained at the supper table. "But I wouldn't try to take a break there anytime soon. Most of it's at the bottom of the canyon." He was happy to have a story to tell and gratified at the stunned amazement of his hosts.

"We didn't think there was any damage," Beth said. "I hope no one was killed."

"We should catch the news," Sam said.

"I'll catch up in the morning," Alan said. "I need a shower and sleep more than I need to see the news right now."

His shower over, Alan pulled on an ancient and most-beloved pair of trout boxer shorts and a white T-shirt. He pulled back the covers and gingerly settled his body into the cool sheets and turned off the lights. He had a habit of thinking over his day while he settled into sleep, but tonight he was asleep before he began.

Joni's Restaurant, Colorado Springs, Colorado

"Tonight, I'll take every perk you can get us," Joe Tanner sighed. Joni's Restaurant was roaring with people. A crowd of waiting guests stood in animated clumps in Joni's gardens. Joni didn't allow smoking so only the smells of her cooking wafted out the front of the old Victorian house.

"I was right," Eileen said. "Everyone in Colorado Springs has gone out to dinner tonight."

"Eileen!" Joni called out. "And your handsome Joe! I was hoping you would arrive tonight. I have saved you a spot."

Joe put his nose in the air and pinned a smug smile on his face as they were escorted past the crowd of waiting people. Joni was tiny and wizened and adorable in her checked apron. Her thick white hair had been cut recently and upswept in the latest style, held back by the flowered headband she always wore.

"We can wait, Joni," Eileen protested. "I don't want to impose."

"Nonsense!" Joni said sharply. "Look at my gardens. These people are having a wonderful wait."

"True!" Joe said cheerfully. Joni's gardens were exquisite. Park benches and rattan chairs dotted the gardens and attentive waiters took orders for drinks. The late August evening was chilly but the afternoon rain had blown away and it promised to be beautiful tomorrow.

"Besides, if I know my Eileen, she has not stopped working today, am I right?" Joni said. "Making sure everyone is okay after the earthquake and taking care of people."

"More or less," Eileen mumbled, thinking of Jim Leetsdale in his silent box at the morgue.

"Here is your table," Joni said, settling them in what was once the dining room of the old house. Their table was in the bay window and it was arguably the best place in the house.

"Thank you, Joni," Joe said happily. He waggled his eyebrows at Joni and leaned forward for a kiss, puckering his lips extravagantly. Joni squealed in delight and stepped briskly away, making a slapping gesture at him.

"Stop that, you're Eileen's," she said. Eileen rolled her eyes.

"Only because you won't run away with me," Joe said mournfully.

"We'd better feed him before he gets any worse," Eileen remarked to Joni. Joni laughed and waggled her fingers at Eileen.

"We'll get you set right up," she said, and bustled away.

"So," Joe said, settling in his chair and taking one of Eileen's hands in his own. "Tell me about your day."

"A murder at Peterson Air Force Base." Eileen spoke in normal tones. The restaurant was positively roaring with conversation and cutlery clashing against plates as people brought every bit of Joni's fabulous food to their lips. The earthquake was the only topic of conversation as people spoke in bright, animated tones to one another. There were no reported fatalities, so the atmosphere had a tone of celebration. The noise level was outrageous.

"Yikes, a drug case?"

"No," Eileen said reluctantly. Homicides at the military bases in Colorado Springs were usually drug-related. The last big nondrug homicide Eileen had worked was at Schriever Air Force Base, which had led her to Joe and "doom" clearance and a friendship with a CIA agent named Lucy. "This one is odd. He was laid out to look like he killed himself, but he was definitely murdered."

"How do you know?"

"Rolls! Your supper will be out shortly. Here's some iced tea for you, my dear, and some iced coffee for my Joe." Joni breezed away as quickly as she had appeared, leaving behind steaming fresh rolls and a small tub of butter along with their drinks. The iced drinks were beaded with moisture.

Eileen took her glass and drank gratefully. She smiled at Joe as he buttered her a roll. Joe had a thing about feeding her. He liked to offer her bits of his food and make her take them from his hand, or give her bites from his wedge of pizza. Eileen found this little quirk endearing. It was almost as if by feeding her he was providing for her, a modern version of killing an animal and laying it at her cave door. She accepted a bite from the roll. It was loaded with sun-dried tomatoes and basil and tasted heavenly.

"Oh, my," she said, putting a hand up to her mouth to catch the crumbs. "You should have a bite of that."

"So tell me how you knew he was killed," Joe asked again, and took a big bite out of the roll.

"Well, he was laid out flat on his back with his arms and legs straight," Eileen said, ticking the reasons off on her fingers. "Nobody lands like that after they've put a bullet in their head. Second, although he had powder burns on his hands, he had the gun *in* his hand. Most guns are thrown from the hand after the shot, when the victim is falling. They usually don't hang on to the gun. Third, there were blood trails from his mouth."

"Blood trails?" Joe asked, buttering another roll. His aunt was a nurse and had lived with his family for years. She shared tales of work with Joe's mom, stories that Joe and his brothers had listened to with fascination. Joe had an iron stomach to be envied, another reason why Eileen enjoyed his company. She never had to edit what she said.

"Blood trails," Eileen smiled, and took another bite from Joe's roll. "Going from his mouth to his chin. And from his mouth to his ear. And going from his mouth up his cheek-bone."

Joe considered this while chewing.

"Not possible," he said eventually. "Unless the man rolled around after he'd shot himself."

"And then they would be spatters, not trickles," Eileen said in satisfaction. "Yes, the man was moved after death. Blood trails don't run out of someone in different directions. And here's the last thing. The man had shot himself in the eye."

"In the eye?" Joe grimaced.

"In the eye. Do you know how many suicides shoot themselves in the eye socket?"

"None?" Joe guessed.

"None," Eileen said. "Nobody shoots themselves in the eye. Your eye is too fragile, too sensitive, too—"

"Too icky," Joe offered solemnly.

"Too icky," Eileen laughed. "All of this is circumstantial, but all of it tells me Jim Leetsdale didn't kill himself. I'm going to find out why someone wanted me to think it was a suicide, then I'm going to nail the one who did it."

"Supper," Joni said, setting down plates and whisking away without another word. Joni picked their meals for them and they were always her best dishes.

"Poor bastard," Joe commented, eyeing his plate with relish.

"Who, Leetsdale?" Eileen asked.

"No." Joe smiled wolfishly. "The one who's going to be behind bars in a week. The bastard who killed him."

Best Western Motel, Alamosa, Colorado

"The scene is completely sealed," Marcia repeated. She had the makings of a tremendous headache. Why hadn't she taken pictures? Her pity for the poor dead girl had blinded her to the reality of getting actual pictures of a human mutilation.

The motel room was steamy and warm. Marcia had soaked her sprained ankle, and the rest of her too, in the motel bathtub. Drying off with the regrettably thin towels the motel supplied, she'd prepared the double bed just the way she liked it; all four pillows piled against the headboard, extra blanket, television remote, glass of ice water, her journal. Dressing in her warm, clean sweatpants and a thick pullover, she finally felt clean for the first time that whole exhausting day. She'd settled herself in the bed and started making phone calls.

"Don't feel bad, Marcia," Robert said in her ear. Robert Carter was the head of Colorado Mutual UFO Network (MUFON), and he was asking questions she couldn't answer. He'd called her back on his encrypted line, because Robert never discussed anything unless he was on an encrypted line. What was the position of the body with regards to the compass? Was the woman burned? Did anyone see any lights the night before, as well as hearing the Taos Hum?

"I just can't believe I didn't take any pictures," Marcia wailed. She rubbed her temple fiercely, fighting a desire to weep.

"I'm sorry I've been pushing you. I would have done the same thing, really," Robert said. "Particularly when we've just been through the first earthquake in Colorado in who knows how long. This is why we have such trouble with proof. By the time people are calm enough to do some scientific research, the government has moved in and the scene is sterilized. Your descriptions have been remarkably good."

"Thanks, Robert," Marcia said. She still felt miserable. "I

just didn't think about taking pictures. She was so pale and—oh, young."

"Have they identified her body yet?"

"Not that I know. She's at the morgue now, but no one has stepped forward. With any luck, the coroner's report will be made public."

"I'm sure it won't," Robert said grimly. "An autopsy is going to reveal all the classic symptoms of abductee mutilation—cooked tissue, missing organs, lack of blood. They won't print that."

"Alamosa is a pretty small place," Marcia said. "Let me talk to some people and see what I can find out. People talk, you know." She massaged her leg and flexed her ankle.

"Make it quick," Robert said. "I'll see who we can send down from MUFON. If we send the wrong types, we'll shut the locals up like clams and we'll never find anything out. Hopefully, the Rabble won't find out too quickly."

Marcia grimaced. The Rabble was the serious UFO community's name for the fringe elements. The Rabble were people who believed they themselves were space aliens, or who believed Nazi Germany colonized Mars, or who believed the special effects in the *Star Trek* shows were actual shots from the Galactic United Nation's ships. The Rabble was also heavily infected with government agents, disinformation agents who did their best to discredit the entire organization.

"If we get Rabble down here," Marcia said, "we'll be in real trouble."

"They'll come before a week's out," Robert said grimly. "The government will send them in, to trample the truth and make sure no one in Alamosa will ever talk to anyone."

"I'll see what I can find out before then," Marcia promised.

"Marcia," Robert said, then stopped and cleared his throat.

"What is it?"

"Well, just be careful. You might get a visit from men in black. Or—god help us—they might abduct more."

Robert always sounded apologetic when discussing actual

danger, Marcia thought numbly, realizing for the first time that she might actually *be* in danger.

"I'll be careful. Nobody even knows what I am," she promised. "They think I'm just some retired schoolteacher who stumbled across the body."

"Good," Robert said. "Keep it that way. And keep safe."

"You bet I will," Marcia said.

She sat for a few moments after hanging up the phone, absently massaging her warm and flattened ear. She'd been a teacher and a researcher her whole life. She observed, she didn't act. Now she was in the middle of an event—an Event—and it was hard to get her mind around that, to swallow it and make it hers. If she were foolish, she might end up on the sand as dead and bloodless as that poor girl.

"And I wouldn't make nearly as pretty a corpse," she said to herself. Marcia had to chuckle at that. She reached for the remote and turned on the television, settling back into the softness of the pillows and brushing her clean hair back from her forehead. She would cope.

6

The Williams's Ranch, San Luis Valley, Colorado

Alan Baxter woke with a start. For a moment, he couldn't remember where he was. Then he remembered. The Williams's Ranch. Earthquake. Cattle. Bright sunshine poured through the guest room window that had been a black square the night before. The sunshine laid a bright band across the bed, picking out the white sections of the quilt that covered him. The morning air was chilly, even though it was August, so it must still have been early.

Alan stretched luxuriously under the covers, feeling his muscles give little creaks and sighs. He was a fit sixty-five, even if he was sixty-five. A fly fisherman has to have good balance and a lot of strength to wade across swift-flowing streams. If an angler was a particularly good fisherman, he developed well-muscled arms from fighting fish and bringing them to the net. Alan hunted new streams every year, and that often called for long hikes. He would be a little sore after spending a day working with cattle, but that would be all.

Rising, he dressed quickly and took time to shave and wet down his unruly white hair. He'd gone to bed with his hair still wet the night before so now his head looked like Einstein's. Time for another haircut, he thought, and perhaps he should do that before he met Krista.

Thinking of Krista sent a pleasurable tingle down his spine. She was such a fascinating woman. Too bad there were so many years between them. Alan gave a last rueful glance at his own silly, infatuated reflection and left the bathroom. He swept the covers back and made the bed quickly and neatly. Years of fishing had left him a well-behaved guest. The better the fishing, the better he was as a guest. A professor's retirement salary didn't leave much money for motels, so Alan did his best to make his hosts feel little pain.

Beth Williams was in the kitchen, dressed in a house robe and flipping pancakes. Beth was a handsome woman, large-boned, with enormous curves that looked just right on her frame. Her skin was as fresh and clear as an apricot, and only showed her age in the lines of her neck and her hands. Her brown hair was clipped back in a ponytail with an enormous, colorful elastic band that matched her robe.

"What a beautiful guest room," Alan said from the kitchen doorway. The Williams's house had a country kitchen, a large room with a huge table that could seat fifteen without a problem. The floor was pine, lacquered to a high gloss and easily cleaned of mud and grime, of which there was always plenty on a ranch. Beth turned at his voice and beamed at him. Her smile was as pretty as her skin.

"Why thank you, Alan," she said. "I tried to make it nice for you. Did you sleep well? Here's some coffee. What do you take?"

"Cream only," Alan said, "and I can get it myself."

"Thanks," Beth said, returning to her pancakes. "I'm trying to get a mess of these on the table, and some eggs too, for the kids. They're going to have a big day today, too."

Alan opened the cabinet above the coffee machine and found an entire array of coffee mugs. None of the mugs matched, and they were all from tourist spots: Yellowstone, Disneyland, Grand Canyon, New York City. Alan laughed and picked out a mug from Mount Rushmore.

"Do you like my collection?" Beth smiled. "I get one

wherever I go. And Todd, he's our oldest, he sends them to me in the mail whenever he finds an interesting one."

"I'll send you one too," Alan promised, filling the mug with coffee and pouring in a generous dollop of cream. Beth finished with an enormous stack of pancakes and put them in the oven to keep warm. She started cracking eggs into a big bowl with amazing speed.

"So before you volunteer to help today, don't," Beth said, smiling at Alan. "You didn't come here to smear ointment on cows. We really appreciate the help yesterday, but today we're in the mop-up stages."

"I will help," Alan said, sipping at his coffee and sighing in pleasure. Beth knew how to make coffee. "I know you have a lot to do."

"Not so much," Beth said, whipping the eggs with a monster whisk. "Sit down and have some coffee and look at the paper, and then I'll throw a plate of cakes and eggs in front of you and we'll see what you do with those." She turned to her stove. Alan shrugged and ambled over to the table, feeling the glorious first rush of hot morning caffeine. He sat down at a sunny spot of the table and peeled off the rubber band from the paper. The smell of scrambled eggs began to compete with coffee and pancakes, and Alan's stomach rumbled pleasantly.

The headline, in huge type, declared, "Earthquake." It was the story under the fold that brought Alan's thoughts and his breath to a stop.

"Body Found in Great Sand Dunes," the title read. The woman was as yet unidentified but she was between twenty-five and thirty years of age and had blond hair and blue eyes. The type blurred as Alan's hands began to tremble. It couldn't be, could it? How many young blond women were there in the world, anyway? Too many to count. But Krista had been investigating the recent high pollution levels in Medano Creek, the odd stream that flowed under the Great Sand Dunes and surfaced at the edge as a rippling shallow creek. How many young blond women were at the dunes this week? Alan told himself he was just being paranoid, thinking that Krista Lewis was dead right before they met. Yet as Alan asked permission from Beth to use the phone, something in the lowest part of his guts was already telling him that his fears were true. His gut was telling him that the dead girl was Krista.

Special Investigations Bureau, Colorado Springs, Colorado

"We'll do a complete search of his office today," Eileen said to Dave Rosen. "Then we wait for the coroner's report." The morning office was already at a dull roar. The coffee machine barely finished filling the pot when it was emptied and started again. Someone had brought in a couple dozen donuts and the empty boxes sat by the coffee machine. An occasional late-comer would stop to peer in the boxes, then sigh and move on.

"You can finish up those earthquake reports while you're waiting," Captain Harben said dryly. He was walking from the coffee machine with a deep black cup of joe that could fell a horse in its tracks. "And what is *that?*"

"This would be a latte, boss," Eileen said, giggling. Captain Harben was Eileen's idea of a perfect boss. He was cynical and outwardly morose but as nurturing as a mother duck. He liked his people to laugh.

"If you fail to solve this case in your customary week, I'm putting you back on straight coffee," Harben said, eyeing Eileen's foamy drink. He walked toward his office, stopping at every desk for a moment or two.

"That's a super mocha, two shots of espresso, by the color," Rosen observed, looking into her cup. He had perched one haunch on her cluttered desk. His own desk was already pin neat.

"Joe has corrupted me," Eileen said mournfully, taking a long sip of her drink. "If Harben makes me stop drinking this, I'll have to drink eight cups of coffee in the morning just to start my heart."

"Caffeine," snorted Rosen. He sipped his distilled water and stood up from her desk. "Let's go see what Jim Leetsdale left in his office."

"We're going to a stage set," Eileen said, picking up her

keys and her latte. "Someone wanted to make this a suicide. Want to bet on a suicide note?"

Rosen said nothing as he signed them out on the board, and they headed for the stairs. Only when they were in Eileen's Jeep and heading for Peterson did Rosen speak.

"I bet lunch there's a note," he said thoughtfully. "But I think there's going to be something else. He died hard. He left us a message."

"Rache," Eileen murmured. She was thinking of "A Study in Scarlet," the Sherlock Holmes story where a murderer leaves a mysterious word on the wall. The word, Rache, turns out to be German for "revenge."

"Revenge!" Rosen said, making Eileen jump.

"Damn, is there anything you *haven't* read?" she complained.

"Well, I've read Sherlock Holmes," Rosen said scornfully. "Who hasn't?"

"Did you read the unedited versions?" Eileen asked. "The one where he's always getting down the cocaine bottle and the needle at the end of the story?"

"Nope, my versions always had him smoking his pipe," Rosen said. "I was an adult when I learned he was actually shooting up."

"I'll lend you my copy. You'll have to read the real reason why Jefferson Hope killed Enoch Drebber," Eileen said smugly.

"For love of a woman," Rosen said flatly. "Who needs the details?"

"Love of a woman," Eileen said softly, looking out the windshield and not really seeing the flow of traffic around them. Lori Leetsdale was dead a year when Jim Leetsdale was killed. Who wanted to kill this man? And why did they try so hard to make it look like a suicide? Or were they wrong this time, and Jim Leetsdale killed himself?

Major Bandimere looked somewhat frazzled today. She was waiting in her government Jeep at the entrance to Peterson. Her hair lay limply against her cheeks as though it had refused the curling iron. Her face was paler than usual and her lipstick was dry around the edges. Eileen pulled up and parked her Jeep, and she and Rosen got out.

Yesterday's threatening weather had blown over toward Kansas. Today was fresh and beautiful. The sky was blue and serene and the trees and grass were a vibrant rain-washed green. The precise lawns and pruned bushes of the Air Force base looked great in the dazzling morning sun.

"Good morning," the little major said, handing a badge to Eileen. "I hope Mr. Mitchell doesn't show up today."

"If he gives me any crap today, Deanna, I'll throw his ass in jail," Eileen said comfortingly. "And you can tell everyone how you tried to make me stop."

Bandimere giggled jaggedly and then bit the sound off with a hand to the back of her lips.

"Sorry," she said. "You don't know what I've been through today already."

"Explain," Rosen said economically, failing to evade her little hands as she clipped his badge to his shirt.

"Let's talk while we're going through Major Leetsdale's office," Bandimere said. She climbed back into her Jeep without another word. Eileen looked over at Rosen with raised eyebrows when they were seatbelted into her own Jeep. Rosen gave a tiny shrug.

Building 12-E looked just the same, although there were more cars in the parking lot. The hill by the cannon was empty now, both of the body and of the sentry. Eileen drew a last deep breath of piney summer air and followed Bandimere into the entrance of Government Building 12-E.

Leetsdale's office was cluttered and untidy. The room was fairly small but was stuffed with filing cabinets as well as a battleship gray desk and chair. Papers spilled over the top of every available surface as well as the floor. A computer sat, screen dark, on Leetsdale's desk.

Eileen stood in the doorway and looked around, seeing Leetsdale's personality in the shape and the focus of his room. His desk faced away from the door, where windows would be if there were any. In a classified building like this one, there were no windows. His computer keyboard was grubby and well used. Some dandruff and hairs speckled the back of the chair. There were heel marks on the left side of the desk surface. Leetsdale liked to stretch back in his chair with his feet on the desk and think, or type on his keyboard, or perhaps doze after lunch.

"Shall we go in?" Bandimere said nervously.

"All right," Eileen murmured. There was nothing obviously out of place, but she expected that. Whoever had killed Leetsdale had done a careful job, just not careful enough.

Huerfano County Sheriff 's Office, San Luis Valley, Colorado

Marcia Fowler was waiting patiently. She was reading the local paper, paying careful attention to the local police blotter and the social columns. A latte steamed at her side, sleeved into a cardboard ring that allowed her to hold the hot drink without burning her fingers. She hadn't even tasted it yet, she'd merely sniffed it. The local coffee shop was down the street from the sheriff's office, where she waited for Sheriff Reg Gonzalez to see her. Marcia had already learned that Reg and his wife Conchita had been blessed two weeks ago with their fifth child, a girl, named Maria Elena Gonzalez, weighing in at seven pounds, eight ounces. A healthy size, at this altitude.

"Pardon me," a man said. Marcia looked up from the paper, realizing the man was speaking to her. He was just taking a seat next to her, and he was her own age or close to it and he was unexpectedly handsome. He was tall and rangy and his eyes were a light-colored brown, almost golden, like a lion. His skin was weathered but healthy, reddish over the cheekbones and nose as though he spent a lot of time in the sun. His hair was white and thick and brushed back from a deep widow's peak. He was wearing a light blue shirt and a pair of ancient khakis.

Marcia realized she was staring, and blinked. How long had it been since she'd met a good-looking older man who wasn't on a movie screen?

"Yes?" she said, and breathed an internal sigh of relief when her voice came out normally.

"I was wondering where you got the coffee," the man said. "Is that a cappuccino?"

"A latte," Marcia corrected with a smile. And he liked coffee, too! The internal girl in her, who would never be anything more or less than twenty-five years old, tried to get her to smooth her hair. She refused.

"I'm waiting to see Sheriff Gonzalez," the man said. "The clerk told me it might be a while. So I thought I'd get a coffee."

"I'm first in line, I think," Marcia said, her focus suddenly returning. "Why are you here to see him?"

"The girl they found on the dunes," the man said, his expression suddenly desolate. "They—"

"Ma'am?" the clerk called from the desk.

"Yes?" Marcia said, getting to her feet and unable to help her hands from smoothing down her skirt, her brain buzzing with unexpected surprise.

"Sheriff Gonzalez will be another hour or so. Are you sure you want to wait?"

Marcia took a breath and turned to the man in the chair.

"Want to get a coffee down the street?" she asked. The man stood up and shrugged, still looking bleak.

"Might as well," he said, and held out a hand. "Alan Baxter."

"Marcia Fowler," Marcia said, shaking it. Was he MUFON? Rabble? Or a goddamned government agent? A goddamned gorgeous government agent. She was going to find out.

Peterson Air Force Base, Colorado Springs, Colorado

"We'll call you this afternoon," Eileen promised as she buckled her seat belt. Another homicide, in an apartment close to the Citadel Mall. She and Rosen had to go clear the scene.

"Shall I clear the office for Mr. Mitchell?" Bandimere asked. "He wants to get Major Leetsdale's files."

"If he means computer files, he's going to be disappointed," Eileen smirked. The computer's main processing unit sat in the backseat of her Jeep along with a box of disks. They also had Major Leetsdale's briefcase, his uneaten lunch, the contents of his desktop and a yellow Post-it Eileen had found pasted to the underside of his desk, all carefully marked and logged as evidence. Of the lot, Eileen was most interested in finding Krista Lewis, whoever she was. That was the name on the little Post-it note, and the location and the jagged look of the writing gave Eileen a little buzz at the base of her spine. The note might lead somewhere.

"I don't know what he wants," Bandimere said. "Can I let him into the office?"

"Sure," Eileen said. "We'll return the items within the week, if Mitchell wants to know."

"Thanks," Bandimere said, but she still didn't look very happy. She gave a little wave as they drove away.

"She is spooked as hell by that guy," Rosen said. He had Leetsdale's briefcase on his lap and was methodically going through the contents.

"I don't like him," Eileen said. "Even though I don't like Bandimere either. I pretty much don't like any of this."

Rosen nodded absently and Eileen grinned. She was lying, and Rosen knew it. This was going to be a fascinating homicide, a puzzle as interesting as they'd had for a long time.

The new homicide was close to the mall. It was messy. Eileen and Rosen met Officer Hetrick at the door to the apartment building. Shelly Hetrick was as tall as Eileen but almost Rosen's size. Her breasts strained the buttons at the front of her uniform. Her belt cinched in to a narrow waistline but her pants strained over an enormous bottom. Some people didn't notice that Hetrick's buttocks didn't jiggle, that her curve of belly was as hard as stone. Hetrick could bench-press nearly two hundred pounds. She wore her hair in a complex series of braids, held back by a huge clip.

"Welcome, guys, this one should be simple," Hetrick said

without preamble. She shrugged her ample shoulders and led the way into the building, talking as she went, jingling and creaking with handcuffs and leather holster and belt. "Young female, Carol Campbell, working in the kitchen while her two kids, aged two and ten months, take a nap. Perp enters the apartment through the front door, which is not locked. Grabs the woman at the entrance to the kitchen, is in the process of raping her when—" Hetrick looked down and consulted her notepad. "When neighbor Charlie Washington shoots him in the side of the head. Thirty-eight caliber, we've got the gun and Charlie. And here we are."

Hetrick stopped in the hallway, then stepped aside to let Eileen and Rosen by. Eileen caught the stink of blood and human waste before she walked through the door. There was a dead man on the kitchen floor in a pool of blood. There were murmurs of voices down the hallway, the querulous voice of a young child, a hiccuping sob.

"Janine is with them," Hetrick said from the doorway. Officer Janine Johnson, as fair-skinned as Hetrick was dark, had a knack for comforting victims. She was the least motherly looking person Eileen had ever met. She was thin and tall and had wispy white-blonde hair and a bony face. Her eyes were pale gray. Even her eyebrows were white. She looked like she could play the Fairy Queen in a movie, or maybe the Lady of the Lake. Yet Johnson had incredible skills when it came to negotiation. She could walk into a pile of arguing drunks and send them on their way within a few minutes. Domestic assault victims practically fell into her arms. Johnson had a knack.

"Good," Eileen said. "She's doing her usual?"

"Excellently as always," Hetrick said with a grin. Eileen grinned back. Janine Johnson couldn't hit the o-ring on a target to save her life, and everyone knew it. She barely made her certification each year and Eileen suspected someone was helping her out. Perhaps by turning in a faked target sheet from the shooting range? But what did it matter? As long as Captain Harben kept Johnson and Hetrick together, Janine's shooting skills didn't matter. Hetrick was deadly, with gun or fists or feet.

"Where's Washington?"

"He's in with Janine and Carol. He's an old guy, good friend of Carol, plays with the kids. Apple pie grandpa type."

"So tell me, Rosen," Eileen said. "Is the story a true one?"

Rosen looked at the dead man, eyed the splintered apartment door, and looked down the hallway.

"Yep," he said.

"Why?"

"Don't make him talk too much, he'll get a sprain," Hetrick said with a teasing smile.

"Door is splintered properly for exterior blows. Kitchen floor is not a typical place for consensual sex. Blood spray consistent with story, perp had his pants down when the neighbor shot him but he still had them around his ankles. If they were lovers, he probably would have taken them all the way off."

"He didn't put a condom on," Eileen observed, squatting by the dead man to take a look. "Sometimes they do." She suppressed a quick, vivid shot of Teddy Shaw, with the same dead expression of surprise as the rapist, lying on the black grass in the darkness. "Did she know him at all?"

"She says not," Hetrick said.

"You going to advise her on shades and dog?"

"Yep," Hetrick said, mocking Rosen's laconic tones. "And, for starters, to lock her front-damn-door."

"Shades?" Rosen asked.

"Shades," Eileen said. "And dog. The shades clinch the story for me. Women who are raped by strangers overwhelmingly have no window coverings and no dog. If you have those two things, the chances of what happened to her today go down substantially. With a big dog, to practically nothing."

"We'll tell her," Hetrick said. Rosen nodded, looking at the uncovered windows, filing it away in his computer-like brain. Eileen stood up and stretched, feeling her back crackle pleasurably. She flipped open her notepad to take a few brief notes. This case was their bread and butter, the kind of homicide investigation that made up ninety percent of their workload. The victim and the perpetrator clear as glass, and only the details and the forms to be filled out. The puzzle of a Jim

Leetsdale was tantalizing and frustrating, without any of the obviousness of the crime in front of her. Who had killed him, and why? Why did they take such care to make it look like a suicide?

"Do you want to talk to Charlie Washington?" Hetrick asked, interrupting Eileen's thoughts. She blinked and turned to Hetrick.

"No. He'd be embarrassed because I'd kiss him right on the lips," she said with a grin. "I don't see any reason to impound his gun. We'll write this up as citizen defense."

"Okay, then," Hetrick said with a laugh. "Thanks for coming by so quick. Nice doing business with you."

As they walked back down the apartment hallway, Hetrick shouted after them.

"Hey, Rosen, good job. But you should shut up once in a while!"

7

**Alamosa County Sheriff 's Office,
San Luis Valley, Colorado**

"I know I'll be held for questioning," Alan Baxter said worriedly. He and the schoolteacher, Marcia Fowler, were once again sitting in the hard plastic chairs of the sheriff's office waiting room. Alan put his arms on his knees and leaned forward, massaging his face with his hands. His mouth tasted like milky coffee, and he realized he was going to have to find a bathroom soon.

"I'll be happy to help you if I can," the schoolteacher said kindly. She had already told him her version of events. Running into the person who found the body on the sand dunes was not so remarkable considering how small Alamosa was, and how someone like Marcia Fowler would be interested in finding out the identity of the young woman. Marcia was a teacher, or had been, just like Alan. Curiosity came with the itch to teach, and it never really died.

She was his own age, or near to it. Her body was as trim as a girl's, although she was quite short. Her gray hair was cut close to her head and swept back, and her eyes were the dark color that told Alan her hair used to be black.

"If they arrest me, call Sam Williams at the Williams's Ranch," Alan said with a sigh. Did he have alibis for the past three or four nights? He lived in Pinedale, Wyoming, and it had taken him three days to drive down. Luckily, he had stayed with friends in Laramie and Pueblo. They would be able to vouch for him. He was still trying to get his mind around the fact that he would have to identify the body as Krista's. Alan repeatedly tried to contact her through her Internet mailbox before he gave up and drove his Bronco into Alamosa to talk to the sheriff. Krista had promised to meet him for dinner tonight. She would have contacted him by now.

"I'm very sorry. I hope it isn't your friend," the woman said.

"Marcia Fowler?" the clerk called, opening the doorway to the inner offices. She held a clipboard and she looked tired. "Sheriff Gonzalez can see you now."

"I think he wants to see Mr. Baxter first," Marcia said. "I can see him afterwards, if that's okay."

The clerk shrugged and wrote on her clipboard.

"Fine by me," she said.

"Thank you, Ms. Fowler," Alan said, holding out his hand to shake hers. "I'm glad we had a chance to talk."

"I hope we can talk some more later, and it's Marcia," Marcia said. There was a half-embarrassed, half-determined look on her face. "There's more we need to talk about."

Alan was barely listening. He nodded to her and followed the clerk into the inner hallway. His gut was twisting, and he really needed to find a bathroom now. He knew what he would feel if he discovered that Krista was dead. He would feel relieved, because not knowing was worse than knowing, just like his ex-wife. He hadn't heard from her in thirty years, and then he found out, when he qualified for social security, that she would not be getting a portion of his benefits because she hadn't used her social security number for twenty-eight years. People changed their names, but never their social security numbers. She might be dead. She might still be alive. He would never know now.

"I'm sorry, ma'am," he mumbled to the clerk. "I need to use the bathroom."

"Right here, next to the sheriff's office," the clerk said kindly, her tired face breaking into a smile. "I know how it can take you sometimes."

"Thank you," he said.

"Just knock on Reg's door before you walk in," the clerk said. "I'll let him know you'll be a minute."

When Alan knocked on Reg Gonzalez's door a few minutes later, he felt much better. He was still nervous, but at least his system wasn't threatening to blow in all directions.

"Come in," the sheriff said. Sheriff Gonzalez was sitting behind his desk typing rapidly at a computer console. He was a big man with black hair and eyes and swarthy skin. His hands were huge. He looked up as Alan approached his desk. His fingers kept typing away, as though they knew what they wanted to do and were independent of his brain. "Sit down. Alan Baxter, yes? What can I do for you?"

"I might know the girl you found on the dunes," Alan said. "I'm not sure, but I was supposed to meet her here tonight for dinner and she hasn't answered her e-mail. She was supposed to contact me before today and she hasn't."

The fingers stopped typing and hovered over the keyboard. The sheriff's face showed nothing.

"What does she look like?" he asked.

"I've never seen her in person," Alan said, feeling his face grow red. "She and I wrote to each other over the Internet. But she sent me a picture once. She was blonde, with blue eyes. Not large, but not tiny either. That's about all I know."

The sheriff looked at Alan for a few long moments.

"Hmm," he said finally. "The body is at the hospital morgue. Let's go down and take a look, shall we? I'll ask you some questions on the way."

Alan, who had not sat down despite the sheriff's request, nodded and sighed heavily. Just like that, he was going to find out.

"I hope it's not her," he said.

"We'll see," the sheriff said. He got to his feet, and he was more than big. He was huge. He topped Alan's own six feet by at least five inches, and he was as thick around as a barrel. "Let's take my cruiser, it's out the side door. I want to keep things as quiet as I can for as long as I can."

"Quiet?" Alan asked. "What do you mean?" Sheriff Gonzalez led him down a short hallway and into the blazing bright day. A big four-wheel-drive Ford Expedition sat next to the door. It was white with a few streaks of rust. A county seal was pasted brightly to the passenger side door.

"Get in," the sheriff said, unlocking the doors. Alan clambered into the big vehicle and belted in, wincing as his fingers touched the hot metal of the seat buckle. The car was explosively hot and smelled like old shoes. Litter was packed between the seats and the back floor was covered in old fast-food wrappers. A gym bag sat on the backseat, unzipped. The old shoe smell was thus revealed. The sheriff got in and started the engine. Within a few seconds, cool air blasted from the vents.

"Ahh," Alan said gratefully.

"Because there's rumors around town that this girl was abducted and killed by UFOs," the sheriff said calmly, engaging the gears and backing out of the parking space in a swirl of gravel. "I'm hoping she's your girl and you're the killer, come to see if I can figure it out." The sheriff eyed Alan, who was trying hard to breathe normally and look innocent, and smiled. "Or maybe not. We'll just have to see."

Twenty minutes later, Alan stood before a white shape under a sheet, and he wasn't sure if he was going to see Krista Lewis or the face of his wife. Nothing seemed quite real, not the cold dead smell of the brand-new morgue or the sad expression of the coroner. Sheriff Gonzalez laid a huge paw on his arm, and the warmth and gentleness of this touch was almost more than Alan could stand.

"Are you ready?" Gonzalez asked gently.

"I'm okay," Alan said, and took a shallow breath. "Okay, then."

The coroner gently folded back the sheet and Alan let out a miserable little cry of pain. He'd never met Krista face to face, but he knew this poor, forlorn shape was her. What was left of her. She'd sent him pictures over the Net—funny poses of her with fish she was examining for her work and once a scholarly pose when she'd been published in the *Journal of the American Medical Association*. Now her face was drawn tight, showing the fine bones of the skull beneath. Her eyes were open and filled with sand, giving her a calm statuesque look, as though this were only a marble casting of Krista and not her remains.

Alan couldn't speak. He nodded, and bent his head, and heard the swift rustle as the coroner folded the sheet back over her.

"Come this way," Gonzalez said gently, and led Alan back down the hallway where they'd come in. Behind them, Alan could hear the oiled sound of the drawer sliding back into the refrigeration unit. He drew shallow breaths and tried to seize control of his horribly spinning brain.

"What happened to her?" he asked, as Gonzalez showed him to a chair in the coroner's office.

Gonzalez got a paper cup of water from a bottled-water dispenser and handed it to him, then drew one for himself. Alan drank gratefully and thirstily, feeling ashamed that the water tasted so good, so pure and sweet. Krista would never drink water again.

"Before we talk about that, let's talk about Krista," Gonzalez said, settling into the coroner's office chair. The morgue was in the basement of the hospital, so the coroner's office had no windows. He'd done something both amusing and soothing to his wall, hanging a real window frame with a poster of the Sangre de Cristo Mountain Range behind it. A little flower pot with silk daisies sat on the sill of the frame. Gonzalez flipped open a well-worn notebook and picked out a pen.

"Okay," Alan said huskily, suddenly feeling afraid. Just because he was innocent didn't mean he wouldn't spend time in jail. His brave words to Marcia the schoolteacher now sounded foolish.

"I know you talked to Miz Fowler, the lady hiker who found Krista on the dunes. Did she tell you how she found her?"

"Yes," Alan said. "Was that incorrect?"

Gonzalez smiled unexpectedly. "You sound like a teacher. What do you do?"

"I was a professor at Laramie County Community College, in Cheyenne, Wyoming," Alan said. "I retired two years ago. I taught English."

"Where do you live now?" Gonzalez asked. He led Alan through name, social security number, address, phone, and all the other identifying tags that would tell the world who Alan Baxter was. Alan explained how he'd driven down to see Krista and fish the Rio Grande, and who he'd stayed with in Laramie and Pueblo. When he described the earthquake, Gonzalez straightened up in surprise.

"The rest stop's gone?"

"Half of it," Alan said. "The half I wasn't standing on."

"Well, shit and shinola, that's in my jurisdiction," Gonzalez said. "I haven't had any reports, and I've been working this goddamned homicide. Come with me, Mr. Baxter. We need to get back to my office."

Gonzalez gave a wave and a shout down the hall to the coroner, who mumbled something back, and he and Alan worked their way out of the basement and back into the moldy shoe smell and the icy blast of the Ford's air conditioner. Gonzalez got on his radio immediately and sent out a deputy to the rest area. He ordered the man to bring a camera and some police tape to rope off the site so no silly tourists would kill themselves by looking at the damage.

Gonzalez then blew a deep sigh and swiped a hand across his forehead.

"What a hell of a mess," he said, putting the Ford in gear. "We're going back to my office, Alan. We'll finish up there and check your alibis."

"Okay," Alan said humbly.

"You're going to come clean, I think," Gonzalez muttered. He looked furious. "At least we know who she is now. I got a strong feeling you weren't the one to end her life, Mr. English Professor. Although I'm still hoping I'm wrong."

The Ford scattered gravel as they left the parking lot, and Alan leaned back in his seat and let Gonzalez, and events, carry him.

8

Briargate Subdivision, Colorado Springs, Colorado

When Joe Tanner opened the door, he looked surprised. Eileen smiled at him over the computer she held.

"For me?" he asked, putting a hand theatrically to his chest.

"Kinda," Eileen said. "Quick, take these Zip disks."

Joe snagged the toppling little pile of disks from the top of the computer and put them on the table by his door. He then lifted the computer from her arms.

"Thanks," she said with a sigh.

"I'll take this to my office," he said. "Get the disks."

The television was on in the background and the smell of quesadillas was in the air. Joe thought that quesadillas, flour tortillas folded in half with cheese inside, were the world's most perfect food. He put various things in: cheese, mushrooms, chicken, and spinach, and whatever happened to be around.

Joe's house was a three-bedroom family home, a place he'd bought for tax purposes. One spare room was empty and bare and the other one held Joe's sport's equipment—camping gear and skis and bike parts. The basement, never used, was full of dust and empty boxes. The study off the master bedroom was a bewildering array of computer equipment spread over four desks and a series of small tables. This is where Joe brought the computer he'd taken from Eileen. He set the computer on the carpeted floor since there was no room on the desks or the shelves.

"What did you bring me?" he asked, turning to Eileen and putting his arms around her. She laughed and shifted the Zip disks so she could put her arms around him. She kissed him briefly, then sagged against him as he refused to break the kiss. He forced her lips apart with his tongue and cupped a breast with one hand. His other hand slipped deliciously to her bottom and pressed her against him. He was already most of the way to an erection.

"Wait, let me put these down," she said breathlessly. Less than a minute inside his door and he was already trying to strip off her clothes.

Joe took the disks from her and set them carefully on the top of the computer she'd brought. Then he turned to her with a look of such leering anticipation that she started laughing helplessly.

"Come on, Joe," she protested, as he picked her up, managing to get one hand on her other breast as he did so. He shifted her with a grunt as her shoulder holster dug into his chest. "We had sex last night, remember?"

"That was yesterday," Joe said with an incredulous look. "That was hours and *hours* ago." He carried her into the master bedroom and dumped her with an undignified bounce onto the bed.

"Well, okay," Eileen said, in mock reluctance. She reached up and pulled him down across her on the bed.

San Luis Valley, Colorado

When Sheriff Gonzalez hung up the phone on his last call, he shrugged his shoulders and turned to Alan Baxter, who was sitting in the corner chair of his office. The calls had taken an hour and a half. The rest stop was the first order of business and then Gonzalez had worked his way through calls to the Pinedale Police, Alan's friends in Laramie and Pueblo, and finally Sam Williams. As Gonzalez spoke to Sam Williams, he waved Alan to the corner chair.

The corner chair was a comfortable wingback affair upholstered in a plush fabric. The chair in front of the sheriff's desk, where Alan had started that day, was a straight-backed wooden chair. Alan felt like he could breathe again once he'd settled into the embrace of the nonsuspect's chair.

"You're clean, once I have the local cops check out your alibi," Gonzalez said. "I didn't expect different." He leaned back in his chair and stretched powerful arms above his head. Alan distinctly heard the big man's neck crackle. "From here on out, we're going to backtrack Krista Lewis. Every move she made, every place she's been."

"She's an—she was an environmental engineer. She specialized in river pollution. I know she was investigating that *E. coli* outbreak in Medano Creek."

"That's right," Gonzalez said. "Some kids got sick from playing in the water, and that never happened before."

"That's right. The contamination was found where the river rose up from the sand, and that water should have been all but distilled. So she said she was backtracking the contamination, trying to find a source in the sand dunes or in the water drainage from the mountains. That's all I really know, except we were going to meet for dinner—tonight? I think so. Tonight," Alan said miserably. Now that the enormous weight of being a murder suspect seemed to be easing, he could feel the first real stirrings of grief. He dropped his head into his hands, massaging his forehead with his fingers.

"She worked for the government?"

"No, a private company called Riverworks. She worked with the government a lot, though. I guess you'd call Riverworks a government contractor. State and federal, wherever the work took her," Alan said. He lifted his head and looked at Gonzalez, who was taking notes.

"Family?"

"Her parents are alive, and she's real close to one of her sisters. I don't know about other relatives."

"What was her job here in the dunes? Federal? Tell me it's federal."

"Federal, I think. She was working with a guy up in Colorado Springs, some Air Force officer. I can't remember his name, though."

"Federal," Gonzalez said cheerfully. "You know what this means?"

"No," Alan said.

"The FBI, if we're lucky," Gonzalez said with satisfaction. "With any luck, I'll be shoved aside by the Bureau kids and they'll take care of this."

"You want to be shoved aside?" Alan asked carelessly. But Gonzalez was not angered. His grin broadened.

"Shoved aside is good, if I care about finding Krista Lewis's murderer. I don't have the resources to work a murder like this. I have my hands full, Alan, and I don't have any detectives. The last murder here was four years ago and it was real easy to solve, since Vic went straight to the bar and started drinking after killing his girlfriend. I'd have to work evenings and weekends on this, and I have a new baby."

"No time for a case like this," Alan said in understanding.

"Nope, and the FBI kids have lots of toys and lots of money," Gonzalez said. "They're also arrogant as hell, and annoying, and whatever else you want to say. But they'll work it, I hope, if I can get the right words said." Gonzalez paused and looked out his own window, a frame that showed the enormous sweep of mountains that made up the walls of the San Luis Valley.

"You'd work it anyway, wouldn't you?" Alan asked, smiling.

"I would, and I will, if I can't get the FBI to take this," Gonzalez said with a nod. "You're going to be at Beth and Sam's place for a while?"

"At least a week," Alan said.

"Don't leave without contacting me," Gonzalez said. "If the FBI wants to talk to you, make sure I'm with you. They have a tendency to forget little things like the Constitution when they get their boxers in a bunch."

"Okay," Alan said gratefully. "Thank you."

"Sam isn't a good judge of character, he'd bring home Ted Kasczinski if Ted asked him nice enough. But Beth, I know Beth. You wouldn't stay more than a night if you didn't pass muster with my Beth," Gonzalez said with a grin.

"Your Beth?"

"My big sister," Gonzalez said. "She got a dose of our Spaniard DNA, which is why she's got that light brown hair and light skin. Kind of a Mexican-lite."

"You look alike," Alan said, smiling for the first time since he'd seen Krista's body. Their smiles were the same, and the shape of the eyes, now that he knew.

"Except for the coloring," Gonzalez said with a grin. "Every once in a while the Gonzalez family produces a Spanish throwback. Sam was lucky to catch her."

Alan, who agreed, nodded firmly. "She's a great cook, too," he added.

"Well, stick around for her cooking," Gonzalez said. "I'll get a hold of you in a few days and we'll see where this goes."

Briargate Subdivision, Colorado Springs, Colorado

"Baby?"

"Don't call me baby," Eileen grumbled, mostly asleep. She was vaguely aware that Joe's weight had shifted on the bed, that he was no longer pressed against the length of her.

"I'm going to look at that computer you brought me," he whispered.

"Sleep," Eileen said, trying to put her arm out and draw him back to her side. The television was still on in the living room and she could hear the roar of a television audience in laughter. The late-night shows were on then. She wiped a sheaf of hair from her face and pried open an eye. Joe was sitting on the edge of the bed pulling on a pair of boxer shorts.

"I'm wide awake," he said softly, turning to her and kissing her on the cheek. "You sleep, babe."

Eileen tried to say something, tried to get up, but she couldn't seem to make the words come together in any particular order. The next time she drifted to the surface she heard the *Star Trek* theme music. The original *Star Trek*. Joe was a complete addict for all things *Star Trek*. Eileen did a sleepy calculation and realized that it must be one o'clock. She struggled up on one elbow and saw Joe through the door that led to his office. He was still in boxer shorts, a half-eaten cheese quesadilla in one hand, and his face was lit by the computer screen. His desk was angled so he could watch the television at the same time. This so he could see William Shatner say lines Joe already knew by heart. He saw the movement through the door and looked up.

"Go to sleep," he ordered. "You wouldn't understand what I'm doing anyway."

"Classified," she said sleepily. "Don't go on the Net with anything."

"Okay," he said with a smile. "I figured that one already. Go back to sleep."

Eileen wisely lay back down and curled up on her side. There was something immensely comforting about Joe working in the next room while she slept. Some half-sensed memory of sleeping while the grown-ups talked, perhaps, when she was a child. Whatever it was, she fell back into sleep so soundly she didn't wake until dawn flooded the windows with light.

San Luis Valley, Colorado

Alan drove straight back to the Williams's Ranch. He didn't try to fool himself about his motives. He was going home, or at least as close as he could manage. He longed for the warmth of Beth's kitchen, the merry eyes of Susan Williams, the comfort of his clean white guest room. He kept seeing the blank eyes of Krista Lewis, filled with sand. He kept smelling the morgue, the clean antiseptic smell that wrapped over the deeper smell of death like clear cellophane. How had he come to this place, this death?

The sun sank quickly over the range of mountains to the west, throwing the enormous valley into shadow. Alan spotted the turnoff to the ranch and slowed down, putting on his blinker and turning on his lights at the same time. There was no other traffic on the long stretch of highway and the air blowing through his open window was redolent with the smell of sage. Stars began to spring out over the sky. Venus appeared over the mountains, glowing with her bright and serene light. Sam had given him the combination to the gate so Alan didn't have to wait for someone to open it for him. Once he was on ranch property, Alan began to relax.

Then he saw the cluster of lights in one of the Williams's pastures. Alan turned toward the lights and boosted his Bronco to a teeth-rattling speed. Irrationally, he thought of Susan Williams, the same age as Krista Lewis. Not her, he thought. Not her, too.

As he bumped to a stop over the pasture, he breathed a gusty and trembling sigh of relief as Susan herself came running to his truck.

"Who's that?" she called. Her face was grim and pinched and she carried a very ugly looking shotgun in her left hand. The business end was pointed in Alan's general direction, which made the gun look even uglier.

"It's me, Susan," Alan shouted, waving his hand out the window. "I thought someone was hurt."

"Well, shit, Alan, you scared me," she said, coming up to the Bronco and leaning against the side. The shotgun now drooped toward the ground but was still held firmly in her left hand. She was wearing her work clothes, jeans and a sturdy patterned shirt. Her cowhide gloves were tucked in the pocket. "Nobody is hurt. But I'm sorry you didn't come any later."

"Why?" Alan asked. He got out of the Bronco and peered into Susan's eyes. He suppressed an urge to take her in his arms and hug her. He was not her father. But she looked forlorn somehow, weary and lost.

"Because you sure don't want to see this," Susan said, then breathed a gusty sigh and shrugged. "I guess you'll have to, though. You're here, anyways."

"The—what?" Alan asked. Here the sage was stronger, along with a whiff of girl-sweat from Susan and the ever-present smell of cattle. The sun was long gone over the mountain range and the twilight was deepening.

"Come with me," Susan said, with a touch of grim amusement. "Come and join the club, as it were."

Alan, mystified, followed her as she trudged back toward the headlights of the two ranch trucks. Frank gave a brief wave as he approached. Alan noticed without surprise that Frank was wearing two western-style holsters, crossed at the hips like a gunslinger, and that both holsters were full of what were assuredly not toy revolvers.

"Hey, Alan," Frank said. "Have a look."

Alan moved to Frank's shoulder and looked at what was in the glow of the headlights. He stared for an eternity, transfixed.

"Pretty bad, eh?" Susan murmured. She put her free hand on Alan's shoulder, her big callused palm warm through his thin shirt. "You gonna be sick, now?"

"No," Alan said numbly, looking at the bodies of the two cows. They were lying back to back, their heads thrown over at awkward angles. The flesh was stripped from the jaws of the cows, stripped so completely that half the faces were polished white bone. Where the udders and back ends of the cows were supposed to be there was nothing but gaping holes. Small circular holes were punched along the body of one cow, circles as big as a coffee cup and as black and gaping as the spaces where the udders were.

"There's no blood," Alan said numbly, and was grateful his voice did not tremble.

"And no ants or flies," Frank said conversationally. "Won't be, either."

Alan was suddenly aware of the immensity of the night that surrounded them. The sky was littered with stars, stretching from one end of the valley to the other. Alamosa was a feeble glow in the distance. There were no other lights, no car lights or streetlights or traffic lights. The night seemed to press against him.

"I wish I had a gun," he murmured plaintively. Frank surprised him by throwing back his head and roaring with laughter. Susan, too, giggled madly. She and Frank staggered into each other, laughing, and the night seemed to recede a bit from Alan.

"You are so funny!" Susan finally gasped, wiping her streaming eyes with a grubby hand. "You don't even ask about what did this, you just want a gun. You're my kind of guy, Alan."

"Thank you," Alan said. "So what did this?"

"Predators," Frank said, his laughter gone in an instant. His eyes were angry. "Predators, Alan. We don't report UFOs at the Williams's Ranch. We don't report cattle mutilations, no matter how often they occur. This was done by predators."

Alan looked silently at the dead cattle, at the surgical precision of the circular holes punched into the tough hide, at the polished bone of the jaws.

"My granddad reported one of the first series of cattle mutilations, back in the seventies," Susan said. She held out her shotgun to Alan, who took it automatically. "You know how to use one of these? Safety? Yes? Good. First he was ridiculed, then he was harassed, then when everyone was having them, he was the first to shut the hell up. The insurance company began to refuse payoff on a cow lost to little gray men from saucers. So now we have predator attacks."

Susan picked up a shovel from the truck bed and began to dig in the sandy soil. Frank, after a sincere look at Alan's hands on the shotgun, took up another shovel and joined her. Alan was afraid they were planning to bury the two big beasts, but then realized they were digging a trench around the bodies.

"Firebreak?" he asked.

"We burn them," Susan said. "It's my dad's idea. First we take pictures, which the insurance company requires. I don't know what they do with them, and I don't care. They pay up, that's what matters. Then we burn them. Like poisoning meat for a coyote, which of course we never do because it is illegal, of course, to poison the beautiful and lovely coyote." She grinned at Alan, her face lit like a Halloween pumpkin by the glow of the truck lights. "Anyway, if they want to come back and—dine, or practice their surgery, or whatever the fuck they do, well, we try to deny them the carcass."

"Coyotes won't eat 'em anyway," Frank said. "No predators will touch a thing like this."

"How often does this happen?" Alan asked, looking away from the headlights into the darkness and trying to see if anything moved out there. His skin crawled into gooseflesh. The roof of the sky was suddenly enormous, deep, stretching over his head. There were pinpoints up there that were galaxies. It was then he realized how scared he really was.

"Don't be too scared; they never attack humans," Frank said, his trench joining Susan's. With well-practiced movements, the two cowhands threw their shovels in the back of their trucks and both took out containers of diesel fuel. They poured the fuel on the carcasses without stepping close to the bodies, an awkwardness that would have seemed comical without the look of the stripped faces beneath them.

"Some people who touch kills get funny burns on their hands," Susan said, capping her fuel can and setting it back in her truck. "I don't plan to get funny burns on my hands."

Susan got into her truck and moved it to a watching distance from the fire. Frank moved his next to Alan's Bronco.

"You want the honors?" Frank said, dusting his gloved hands together.

"Not today," Susan said. Frank nodded and touched a wooden matchstick to the palm of his glove. With a soft whump and a bloom of light, the cattle went up in flames. They turned off their lights and the three of them settled on the tailgate of Susan's truck. Susan and Frank's calm was soothing.

"We'll stay until it's done, then we'll bury the ashes," Susan said. "There's not much wind, but we need to keep a watch the whole time. We'll miss dinner but Mom will keep plates hot for us. Hey, does she know you're out here?"

"No, I drove straight here," Alan said. "I thought—well, I thought someone was hurt or something."

"Okay," Frank said. He reached into his shirt pocket and flipped out a small black gadget. He pressed a few buttons. "Hi, Beth, it's Frank. We're at a little bonfire and we've got

Alan Baxter with us. He helped us out. We'll bring him in
when we're done. Yes, he did. No, he didn't. Yes, you're right.
Bye." Frank grinned at Alan. "That Beth, she likes you. She
knew you'd be fine with it. Hey, what about your friend? She
okay?"

"No," Alan said heavily. He remembered everything about
Krista again all in an instant, and his head drooped. "She's
dead. She's the girl they found on the dunes."

"Oh, Alan, I'm sorry," Susan said. She put an arm around
him and hugged him against her side.

"What a bitch," Frank said. He nudged Susan and handed
her a flask. She took a deep gulp and handed it on to Alan. He
took a good mouthful and felt Wild Turkey cannon down his
throat and light a fire in his belly. It felt very good.

"You have good taste in medicinal whiskey," he said
hoarsely, handing the flask back to Susan.

"We only chug the best Kentucky bourbon when we deal
with UFOs," Susan said solemnly. Then they were all laughing, leaning against each other in the darkness, their eyes lit
by flames from the pyre of the cows, and Alan knew that this
was okay, this was right. This was another way of understanding Krista's death, and his own eventual death, and the
death of everything that lived and moved and breathed under
the hard sprawl of the stars above them. The flames danced
and crackled, and when Susan handed the flask back to him,
he took it gratefully.

9

Briargate Subdivision, Colorado Springs, Colorado

"Hi, baby," Joe said as Eileen opened her eyes. The good smell of coffee filled the air. He was standing in the doorway wearing sweatpants and a ragged T-shirt and he held a steaming cup of coffee in his hand. "The coffee is for you."

"You're calling me baby," Eileen groaned. "I hate that." She rolled over in bed and stretched.

"I've been up all night," Joe said. He sat on the edge of the bed and carefully handed her the hot mug as she sat up. "By the way, have I told you that you are absolutely beautiful when you wake up?"

Eileen grimaced and took the coffee. A glorious mouthful lit a warm fire in her stomach and radiated in all directions. "Ahh. That's good. Have I told you how gorgeous you are when you stay up all night?"

"That deserves a kiss," Joe said, and leaned in to capture one. Eileen balanced the coffee mug and kissed him thoroughly, knowing that she wanted this man, this morning, forever. She almost said so, just like that, and then she couldn't.

Joe hesitated, as though he were going to say something,

then he didn't. Eileen caught a sudden flash of Teddy Shaw, dead forever, and a sudden bleakness filled her soul. She had told Joe she loved him over a year ago, the first time they had slept together. He'd said he loved her too. That was the last time they'd said the words to each other, and Eileen couldn't figure out why. She wanted to hear the words from him. Maybe he wanted to hear the words from her. But she was afraid, afraid that a cop wife wasn't what any man wanted, particularly now that she was a cop who'd killed a man.

"Let me tell you about Jim Leetsdale," Joe said, leaning back from her. His dark green eyes were grave, as though he'd been reading her thoughts.

"He's my homicide," Eileen said, taking a quick gulp of coffee and glad to be on safer ground.

"I figured. Well, the guy had an okay system as far as security goes. He used PGP, Pretty Good Privacy, as an encryption method."

"Which is?"

"A public domain encryption scheme. The guy who created it put it out on the Net and the government went after him. Said that he was hurting national security, or whatever," Joe snorted. "They don't like it because it's unbreakable."

"Except to you?" Eileen asked.

"Oh, I can't break it either," Joe laughed. "Unbreakable in the classic sense, as in un-freaking-breakable."

"So how'd you break it?"

"He wrote the encryption key down on one of his Zip disks," Joe grinned. "He scratched it on the back."

Eileen put the mug between her knees and clapped her hands, grinning.

"So next I looked at his files, then I looked at his Zip disks, and then I did some thinking, then I looked some more," Joe continued, scratching his uncombed hair. He rubbed his eyes, which were tired and red. "Something made this guy get whacked by people who wanted him to look like a suicide. So maybe I found something."

"I'm all ears," Eileen said, finishing her coffee.

"I found some pictures," Joe said. He scratched an armpit. His face flushed a little in embarrassment. "Girl pictures."

"Oh," Eileen said, frowning. "Like pornography?"

"Yeah," Joe said. "Like pornography. Not too bad, really, girlie pictures like you'd see in a magazine."

"So what's significant about girlie pictures?" Eileen asked.

"That's what I wanted to know," Joe said, brightening. "You can go on the Net and find any pictures you want, anytime day or night. Why bother storing data images away when you can look at them for free? Plus, storing girlie pictures is a good way to get fired. We had some people get fired that way out at Schriever Air Base. They were storing dirty pictures on government equipment."

"A no-no," Eileen murmured.

"A big firable no-no," Joe said. "Plus this guy had these images stored three times, on two hard disks and one Zip disk."

"Three times?"

"Three times, same images."

"Can I see them?" Eileen asked, looking for her clothes.

"No," Joe said. "You shouldn't. Waste of time." He flushed again. "Besides, they're—well, they're girlie pictures."

Eileen put her mug down and swarmed out of the sheets. She thumped into Joe's chest and knocked him backward on the bed. Kissing him, she smelled all the work of the night in his breath and on his body. He was sweaty and unwashed and his breath was stale, and she didn't care.

"You are such a gentleman, Joe Tanner," she said. "Thinking that I shouldn't be seeing girlie pictures." Joe grinned underneath her and began caressing her naked body.

"Stop this, because I'll make love to you again and forget everything I want to tell you."

Eileen put on a pout and flounced out of bed.

"Follow me to the shower, then," she ordered, "and tell me why I shouldn't see these pictures."

"Okay," Joe said amiably, following her to his bathroom, watching her with an unabashed smile of appreciation. "But I'll have to explain what a digital picture is. You ready?"

"I'm ready," Eileen said, turning on the shower.

"Good. Okay then, each picture that you see is composed of a grid of pixels. Each pixel, or point on the picture, is a color. The color is stored on the computer as a digital code—you know, ones and zeros that tell the computer what color to display on the screen. All the pixels make up a picture of colors and you have Wanda displaying all her charms. Right?"

"Right."

"Okay, then, next interesting point. Color codes only take up part of a computer word. Colors are easy. Therefore in a picture map, each word is a color, which takes up only a part of the word, and a bunch of extra space."

"He put stuff in that extra space," Eileen said, cupping her hand to test the water. Still cold.

"Excellent! You're so quick," Joe said, clapping his hands. "This isn't new, of course. People have been hiding data in pictures for a long time, ever since the Net made picture transmission possible. Once I realized these pictures were valuable to the dead guy, what's his name—"

"Leetsdale," Eileen said.

"Leetsdale. Once I realized he'd stored them multiple times, it was a matter of dumping the data hidden within the words."

"How'd you do that?"

"I wrote a little program," Joe said modestly. "Took me a few hours but I did it. Now comes the interesting part." He paused and looked at her with a smile.

"The numbers look like simulation points."

"Simulation points?"

"Yup. My field, simulations. Now I'm sure another programmer could have figured it out eventually, but I saw it immediately. Simulation points, each one time-marked and set for a geographic location. Looks to me like maybe a traffic simulation, or a weather simulation. I'll know by tomorrow, maybe, or the day after."

"Wow," Eileen said slowly. "Why tomorrow? Not that I'm pushing, of course. You need to sleep today?" She put a hand on his arm, feeling like she'd just insulted him. Joe, to her relief, didn't appear to be insulted at all. The shower, forgotten, began putting out a cloud of steam.

"No way, I just need to catch about three or four hours is all," he said. "The reason I'll know tomorrow is that I need to get out to Schriever with this data and put it through our big simulator."

"Will they let you do that?" Eileen asked.

"They won't know about it," Joe laughed. "You know Nelson, he doesn't really care what we do. Nobody else will be around. We're in between war games right now, and I'm improving the simulation speed anyway."

"Okay," Eileen said. "Nothing else in the files? No confessions, love letters, anything?"

"Nothing," Joe said. "Just some e-mail from his wife, over a year ago, which he saved. You going to get in? Can I get in too?"

"This is not efficient," Eileen smiled, adjusting the water temperature. "We take twice as long this way."

"But I always get that long, gorgeous back of yours completely clean," Joe said innocently, stripping off his shirt. Eileen stepped into the shower and let the water cover her. In the few seconds before Joe crowded in next to her and coherent thought was lost, she thought about Leetsdale and the care he took to hide whatever it was he was working on. The next thread she had to follow was to find Krista Lewis, whoever she was.

Great Falls, Virginia

"Eileen!" Lucy Giometti said. "It's so good to hear from you."

"You too," Eileen said. "And how is Hank? Sleeping okay?"

"Sure," Lucy lied brightly. "Sleeping like an angel. And I'm in such good shape that *Sports Illustrated* is using me as a swimsuit model this year."

"Well, of course," Eileen said. "They called me first, though. I had to turn them down so they called you."

"Why did you turn them down?"

"I hated that leopard thong bikini."

"Oh, you kill me," Lucy laughed. She rubbed Fancy's ears and waved at Hank. He'd had a good night's sleep last night, the first one in days. At dawn Lucy had found a new white

tooth poking up through his pink gum. With the pressure and
the pain over, Hank was a different baby. He sat in his playpen
and examined brightly colored toys with the seriousness of a
research scientist. After he'd looked one over minutely,
he would toss it aside and look at the next one. Lucy wondered what he was looking for when he played this toddler
game. She hoped he wouldn't find it soon. When he was in
this mood, he'd play until his morning nap.

"I do have a reason for calling," Eileen confessed. Lucy
raised her eyebrows. Eileen didn't often ask for help.

"Whatever I can do," Lucy said. A cup of decaffeinated
coffee steamed next to her computer. She took a quick hot
mouthful and sighed. If she pretended it had caffeine in it, she
would almost feel like a human being again. Hank couldn't
tolerate caffeine in her breast milk. Yet another reason to
wean the little fiend.

"Okay, then. We had a murder at Peterson Air Force Base;
a guy named Jim Leetsdale. Major. He was working on a top-
secret project that's headed by a guy named Jacob Mitchell."

"Congressman Mitchell?" Lucy asked, typing quick notes
on her computer. "Ex-congressman, one of the crowd that ran
for President last election?"

"That's the guy, I guess," Eileen said. "I don't pay much
attention to politics."

"Well, I'll see what I can find out," Lucy said. "You caught
me at a good time. I actually got four hours sleep last night."

"I'd be dead," Eileen said. "I can go without sleep for a
couple days, but you haven't been sleeping for a whole year."

"You get used to it," Lucy said. "When you nab Joe and
marry him and start a baby, you can call me up and complain
about morning sickness and not sleeping. I'll be sympathetic."

"Oh, now," Eileen said nervously. Lucy teased Eileen
every chance she got about Joe Tanner. She wanted to be the
matron of honor in a Colorado wedding, she told Eileen.
Mostly, she wanted another friend to call and talk to when
motherhood got to be too much. She figured Eileen would be
a great mom. Mostly, she wanted Eileen to be as happy as she
was. The lack of sleep, the extra weight, the loss of freedom,

were meaningless compared to the bliss of having a family. Lucy wanted Eileen to come in out of the bleak single life and into the warmth of marriage and home and children. She knew what she had wasn't for everyone, but it was for *mostly* everyone. She thought Eileen needed Joe. Lucy had the matchmaker urge, and she had it bad.

"Any other names?"

"Oh, yeah, one. Krista Lewis. We don't know anything about her, just her name. She might work for this project, she might not. Whatever you can find out would be great."

"I'm the oracle," Lucy said. "Ask and I shall find out."

"Thanks," Eileen said.

"So, how are you, anyway? Sleeping okay since the whole Teddy Shaw thing?" Lucy asked cautiously. Eileen had told her about Teddy but most of the details came from the police report Lucy grabbed off her secure computer link. Eileen wasn't talking much about it yet. Lucy knew how she'd feel if she shot someone. She'd feel awful and she'd feel glad and she wouldn't know how to feel, all at the same time. Her friend would cope, and Lucy wouldn't pry. Eileen would talk in her own good time.

"Sleeping fine. They're making me see a psychologist. That's no fun."

"Female?"

"Female. Gerri Matthews, you'd hate her like I do. Little, cute, not an ounce of fat on her body. Seriously, she's okay."

"Call me anytime," Lucy said. "I'm always up with Hank. If you can't sleep, *call* me."

"I will, girlfriend," Eileen said with a smile in her voice. "Thanks."

Lucy turned to her computer and rubbed her hands briskly together. She was supposed to be researching a new religious cult that was springing up in northern Afghanistan but this was much more interesting. Time to find out about Jacob Mitchell and his secret project.

"Here we go, team," she said to Hank and Fancy. Fancy panted and Hank gravely threw a Big Bird toy over the edge of the playpen. Lucy grinned and took a gulp of coffee and connected to the Internet.

Kim's Place, San Luis Valley, Colorado

"I'll sit at the bar, thank you," Marcia told the waitress, a young girl with a tortured hairdo and the bored, sullen expression of someone who watched far too much television. Her young skin was covered with a heavy layer of makeup, and the curves of her eyelids were painted bright blue. Marcia gave an inward sigh, wishing the girl would listen to some advice. Advice about her skin and her hair and her pretty eyes, and how the center of the world is wherever you are, be it the San Luis Valley of Colorado or a cornfield in Iowa or the city of Los Angeles. But this girl, like so many of her former students, believed that there was some place just like the world seen through her television, a place she could reach. A place where boredom and unhappiness and acne would vanish, never to appear again.

"Okay," the girl said. Her nametag read "Kay," though Marcia was sure she'd rather be called Melindra or Tori or whatever movie stars in Hollywood called themselves nowadays.

Marcia picked a spot in the middle of the diner's bar and Kay placed a menu, a clean glass of ice water, and a cup for coffee in front of her. Marcia gave the girl a grateful smile and a nod. There was competence behind the makeup.

"Are you a senior this year?" Marcia asked.

"No, I'll be a freshman," Kay said, breaking into a surprised smile. Marcia tried to look suitably astonished. Children wanted to look older, and grown-ups wanted to look younger.

"Well, I'm sure you'll love high school," Marcia said.

Kay walked a round of coffee to the tables in the restaurant. Marcia had picked her seat deliberately; there was a table full of locals right next to her. As she sipped her hot coffee and looked at the menu, she heard the four men at the table greeting a newcomer. He had just walked in. He was young, in his early thirties, and he held a bicycle helmet under his arm. He had the lean body and the overdeveloped calves of a serious bicyclist.

"Hey, it's Grantham," one of the men said.

"Sit with us, Daniel," another one said. "We were just talking about the girl they found on the dunes yesterday. She wasn't one of your students, was she?"

"I don't think she was from around here," Daniel said, stripping off bicycle gloves and taking a seat at the table.

"I'm not sure she was from this time, much less from around here," the first man said solemnly. The teacher, Daniel, was frowning at the other diner, but in a way that suggested he was a friend of the other man.

"Now Tony," he said.

"Now what?" Tony said. He was older than the teacher was but not as old as Marcia. He looked like a rancher, or perhaps a local businessman, in for breakfast and some gossip. He had large hands, scrubbed pink, curled around his coffee cup, and a weathered face that had seen rough work in cold weather. "Like we all don't know that this was going to happen someday."

"What was going to happen someday?" the fry cook asked from behind the counter. He was tall and round—was that a law, that all fry cooks have to be fat, Marcia wondered—and he was red-faced from the heat of the grill or, perhaps, anger.

"That they were going to kill a person, and not just horses and cattle," Tony said triumphantly. "You know, Hal. You've seen my cattle with their legs stripped to the bone and their eyes—"

"That's enough of that, Tony," Hal said calmly. "I'm serving breakfast."

"I'll have pancakes and eggs, scrambled, no bacon or sausage," Marcia murmured to the waitress.

"Yes, ma'am," the waitress said, and took the menu away.

"Just because you lost some cattle to our local vandals—"

"They're not local, and they're not vandals," Tony said contemptuously. "You telling me those lights you saw six weeks ago were just jets from the Air Force? Jets that can cross the valley in four seconds, stop, turn around, and go the other way? What kind of jets can do that?"

"I heard that some people heard the Taos Hum," another rancher said in a low voice.

"I heard it! I heard it!" Kay said in a near whisper, nearly sloshing coffee from her glass pot as she spoke. "Did you hear it?"

"Yes," Tony said.

"Maybe vandals," Hal murmured to his grill, flipping an enormous pancake with one hand and cracking eggs with the other.

Marcia knew all about the San Luis Valley and the plague of cattle and horse mutilations. The first and most famous mutilation was in fact Snippy the horse, found dead with no blood, no predator tracks around the body, and stripped of flesh from legs and face. This was in 1967, twenty years after the supposed crash landing of a UFO in Roswell, New Mexico.

Snippy was actually a young mare named Lady, a beloved pet of a woman named Nellie Lewis. Snippy, her sire, had such an evocative name that the press couldn't resist attaching the name to Lady. Few people knew the story of Nellie and her own mysterious death. Marcia did. She'd read about the San Luis Valley for months before her trip. The valley averaged at least one mutilation a month, sometimes more. Many people reported fast, silent lights, orange or white or blue, zipping across the high night. Often military aircraft screamed after the intruders, though the Air Force always denied any activities.

The most interesting aspect of the UFO stories surrounding the valley was the mutilations. Here was evidence, actual physical evidence, unexplainable. The mutilated animals were found with no blood. Their reproductive organs were removed with cuts so precise the cell walls showed cauterization under a microscope. Sometimes the facial skin and tissue were removed as well, like the hapless Lady. Often the bodies showed no insect life, no small animal predation, and no sign of decay. All Earth's creatures, even flies, shunned the bodies.

After a great deal of adverse publicity, what Marcia would categorize as disinformation from government agents, cattle mutilations seemingly stopped. The reports of mutilations had gone underground. The local ranchers reported their livestock losses as predator losses. Insurance companies would then pay their fees and not hassle the ranchers with talk of UFOs and little gray men.

"So I heard the lady on the dunes was found the same way as the cattle," Tony the rancher confided.

"But they never take people," the other rancher said. Marcia knew them by face as well as voice now. This one was younger than Tony, about the same age as the schoolteacher Daniel Grantham.

"That's not true," Tony said. "I read up on the Internet last night. Did you ever hear of a man named Bill English?"

Marcia, who had, sipped her coffee and stared into the distance as though she weren't listening to every word at the table at the end of the bar.

"He was part of a Special Forces investigative team that went in to retrieve a downed B-52 bomber in Laos back in seventy-one. The plane had gone off radar after sending some very strange transmissions, something about a large light and 'under attack by a UFO.' "

Tony had the table's rapt attention now. Marcia noticed Daniel's distressed look. He knew this story too.

"So they found the plane, intact, and crew, not intact at all. They were all dead, all mutilated just like my cattle, and when Bill English tried to reveal this information, he was discharged from the military and his reputation was ruined. He's been trying to tell his story ever since, and no one listens."

"Not exactly," Daniel murmured.

"Then there's Jonathan Louette," Tony continued. "He was a sergeant in the Air Force at the White Sands Missile Test Range back in 1956. An Air Force major witnessed his abduction by a 'disk-shaped' object at two o'clock in the morning while they were searching for missile debris after a test. He turned up several days later, dead, his eyes gone, blood removed, and his privates—"

Tony cut off abruptly. Hal was leaning over Tony with a heavy spatula in his hand, glowering.

"Well, you know what I mean," Tony said to his coffee cup, and Hal turned back to his grill.

"The Internet," Daniel sighed, speaking to Tony's fascinated audience. "What used to take months of research now takes minutes. But Bill English's story of the B-52 pilots is just rumor, Tony. Sergeant Louette's story was told by a guy named John Lear and it has never been corroborated either."

"And the Guarapiranga mutilation down in Brazil? That dead guy, he's a rumor too?"

Marcia blinked. That was an interesting mutilation, heavily suppressed by the Brazilian government. A man was found by the Guarapiranga reservoir in 1988, apparently a victim of a Jack-the-Ripper kind of sadistic killer. The doctors who autopsied him were not cattle mutilation experts, so they didn't recognize the signs of a UFO-style mutilation. The removal of organs, the lack of signs of struggle, and the precise and bloodless cuts puzzled them. The man's eyes and genitals were missing as well as many of his internal organs and parts of his brain, all through tiny circles punched through various parts of the victim's body.

The detectives who were assigned to the case—which was never solved—were fascinated by the strangeness of the murder, and eventually the pictures were bootlegged onto the World Wide Web. From there, the UFO community came to full alert.

Nothing happened after that, of course. The Brazilian government sat firmly on the evidence and declared that it had never happened. Once again, a chance for proof was hidden away.

"So now we have one right here, after years of my poor cattle being ripped apart and nobody wants to listen," Tony was saying.

"I have a strong feeling, Tony," Daniel the teacher said solemnly, "that you're not going to like it when people *do* start to listen. You really want *Hard Copy* making you look like some stupid country yokel with a UFO story?"

"Somebody has to listen. Whoever this girl was, she's dead now. I don't want my daughter to be next."

This sent a chill through the people at the table. Hal, briskly cooking eggs and bacon and hotcakes, paused with spatula in hand. He eyed the busy, bustling restaurant, then turned and walked to the table.

"Well, folks, we just have to be careful. Whether it was

UFOs or some ordinary killer, it doesn't matter much, now does it? We have to watch our kids and our wives and be careful."

With this calm assessment, Hal returned to his eggs. As the waitress placed her breakfast in front of her, Marcia looked at the schoolteacher. She knew what he was. When she left, she placed a slip of paper neatly under the brake line of his bicycle. On it was her phone number and a brief message.

10

"This was not what I ordered, Roger," Jacob Mitchell said pleasantly.

"He almost killed Scott," Roger Bennett said, as relaxed as a cat. He was sprawled in Mitchell's office chair. Bennett had gray hair but the rest of him was built like a twenty-year-old weightlifter. His face had the odd, flat look of a habitual steroid user. He'd been turned down by the Marines, long ago. Mitchell had seen the report; Bennett had failed the psyche board, not the strength requirements. Bennett, unaware why he failed, spent two years in bodybuilding only to fail again. His bodybuilding frenzy intensified. He failed enlistment in every branch of the military, the FBI, and the Colorado Police Academy. Eventually, he'd ended up in a security firm as a bodyguard. Mitchell saw a kindred spirit in Bennett as soon as he first saw him standing quietly outside his Congressional office at the Capitol. Mitchell could sense the simmering bitterness behind the stony face.

Bennett held a can of soda pop in one hand and took a long

drink before he went on. "He smacked him with a file cabinet drawer. A *drawer*. He could have killed him."

"Really," Mitchell said. He rubbed the corner of his jaw with one hand. His muscles there were bunched tight as marbles. Any member of his staff, seeing that gesture, would shrink into themselves and find something to do that took them as far away as possible.

Mitchell was a powerful congressman—well, had been a powerful congressman—and he led a stressful life. He didn't smoke or drink. He knew he was highly intelligent and clever, and he was blessed with craggy good looks and a gorgeous voice. He'd been born with good looks; one only had to look at his baby pictures to see that. After a brief period of terrible acne in high school, he'd come into maturity, with height and breadth and looks enhanced by the pits the acne left.

But the stupid voters had turned him out of office, the fools. He'd been orchestrating a political life since middle school, and when he had achieved the position of Colorado Congressman, he thought the White House was only a few years away.

He was beaten by an aw-shucks opponent, a man whose campaign was based on his experience running a remodeling business. Mitchell didn't look back, not for long. His goal was to be President, of course, and there was more than one former President who'd lost a few campaigns before taking the highest office in the world. When he was assigned Secret Service protection during the Presidential primary race, he felt completely at home. This was what he was born to do. This was what he was born to *be*. That was four years ago. His Secret Service protection was withdrawn after it was clear he would not win the primary. The past four years had been spent on an alternative plan for his lifelong goal.

Now Roger Bennett, his strong right arm, had endangered the whole plan. It was disturbing.

"Did Scott leave any blood in Leetsdale's office?" Mitchell asked, still rubbing at his jaw like a philosopher contemplating an interesting question. Bennett finished the soda pop and dropped it into Mitchell's wastebasket. He took out a stir stick and twirled it in his fingers. Bennett was never without his supply of plastic stir sticks, his one nervous habit. He would chew them methodically, mangling them with his teeth until they were wadded balls of plastic. Then, like a chain smoker, he would take out the next stir stick before he spat the first into the wastebasket. His soda pop done, he was ready for a stick.

"No, he caught him with the flat part so Scott just has one hell of a concussion," Bennett said. "Anyway, Leetsdale had Scott down and was coming right at me so I shot him." He put the stick in his mouth and gave it an initial chomp. Mitchell folded his hands carefully, containing his rage.

"In the eye," he said coldly.

"In the eye," Bennett admitted. "I missed. But we did everything else perfectly. I loaded low powder bullets so the back of his head didn't blow. We rolled him in the rug we brought and placed him by the cannon and left the gun in his hand. I even left the other low-powder bullets in the gun. No prints, no evidence, a clean suicide."

"Except nobody shoots themselves in the *eye*," Mitchell shouted. "You fucked up! The little skirt, Bandimere, already told me that the Colorado Springs detectives think it was a murder. That skinny bitch and the fucking Indian, they're looking for evidence."

"They won't find it," Bennett promised, his eyes like angry pinpoints.

"If they do, you might have to take care of them, too," Mitchell said. "And it will have to look like an accident."

"Killing cops?" Bennett said doubtfully, taking the mangled stick out of his mouth. "Sir, killing cops is never a good—"

"I'll tell you what's a good idea or not," Mitchell said. "Shooting a man in the eye, that's a bad idea. We'll just wait and see if these two are any good. If they are, they're going to be very dead."

"Yes, sir," Bennett said stiffly. "I'll come up with a plan."

"Good," Mitchell said with warmth. His voice was instantly soothing, calm and reassuring. Time for honey, after the sting. "I need you, Roger."

"I know," Bennett said with a smile in his voice. "You won't be disappointed."

Mitchell turned to look out his window, rubbing the clenched muscles of his jaw. Bennett left the room as soundlessly as a cat.

This was only a setback, he told himself. Leetsdale was dead. O'Dell was dead. Everyone else on the project was his, body and soul.

Mitchell sighed and stretched. Sometimes he felt that Bennett was more than his right-hand man. Bennett was his other half, his shadow set free on the world. Bennett hadn't batted an eye when Mitchell reluctantly ordered him to kill O'Dell. Mitchell emptied a bottle of whiskey the night O'Dell had died. He was stricken, unable to bear the thought of kindly, pudgy O'Dell no longer a living, breathing creature. Bennett wasn't bothered by O'Dell's death, even though he himself had blown a neat hole in the computer programmer's chest. O'Dell had begged for mercy, Bennett reported casually, but he didn't trust a man's word under the round eye of a gun.

Then there was Lori Leetsdale, killed by accident in the Burbank earthquake. And Jim Leetsdale, a year later. Victims, both of them, victims like O'Dell. But they had died for a cause much greater than they knew. There was so much riding on his shoulders right now. So many lives depended on him, millions of lives. He couldn't let anyone stand in his way now. Not when he was so close.

San Luis Valley, Colorado

Halfway to the Rio Grand River, Alan suddenly remembered the name of the Air Force officer with whom Krista had been working. The day was just beginning. Sam Williams insisted he go fishing this morning. Beth had agreed, which sealed the decision. The last thing Alan Baxter needed to do was hang around and feel depressed about his poor friend Krista, they decided. The best thing would be some fine trout, an early morning hatch, and a healthy communion with nature. Perhaps because he wasn't thinking about Krista right then, the name sprang into his mind.

"Leetsdale!" Alan exclaimed, and gave the steering wheel a little smack with his fist. "Major Leetsdale. I'll have to call the sheriff when I get home." Then Alan reconsidered. Would Gonzalez mind if Alan took a quick trip up to Colorado Springs and talked to Leetsdale? With his workload, Gonzalez might appreciate a little amateur help. Alan immediately shook his head at the thought. Gonzalez was a professional and wouldn't appreciate Alan Baxter, elderly amateur detective, messing with his case.

But maybe he would do a little harmless snooping. He couldn't go back to fishing when Krista's murderer still walked free. And Colorado Springs was only a few hours away. He picked a spot on the highway to turn around, and he put on his blinker.

Gaming Center, Schriever Air Force Base, Colorado

Joe Tanner sat alone in the Gaming Center, his feet folded comfortably beneath him. The computer screen in front of him was lit with a picture of the earth from a low orbit. At this height, only a tiny slice of black space showed beyond the curve of the planet. The atmosphere swirled with clouds.

"No clouds," Joe muttered to himself. He typed rapidly. The clouds disappeared from the screen, leaving an earth that looked blue and brown instead of blue and white. Brown for land. Brown for dirt.

"Let's take the dirt view," Joe said. He often talked himself through a difficult problem. Art Bailey, his old friend, had taught him that trick. When Art and Joe were in their frenzied last days before a major war game, an observer would have thought they were crazy. Each one would talk to their screen, ignoring the other one. It was a strange sort of three-way conversation among Art, Joe, and their supercomputer.

Art was dead over a year now, and Joe still missed him fiercely. Particularly when he had a difficult problem like this one. What were these coordinates all about? They were larger than citywide but less than countrywide, he'd determined that already. They were time-driven. Each one had a stamp and each coordinate progressed in location as the times progressed.

Joe had spent the entire day inserting the data Eileen had given him into his war-game program. It felt strange to see the earth without missile silos or submarines or country boundaries. He'd gotten rid of all of them one by one as he determined that the data had nothing to do with military transport or weaponry.

"What now?" he said, but the back part of his brain was already supplying the answer. He'd color coordinate the time-stamped data, so that the colors would correspond to the coordinates as they changed with time. That would tell him what was going on. Maybe.

Joe worked for the next two hours without lifting his head and thought he'd been working only fifteen minutes. Computers were like that. You sat down for a little while and when you stood up you were sore all over and you had to pee so badly your eyes were crossed. He sighed and strapped on his sandals. He jogged to the bathroom and then took a quick run to the stairwells to pick up a can of soda pop, working his way through submarine-style doors and coded doorways and back again without noticing his surroundings.

When he returned, his code had compiled and was ready to run. Joe opened his can of soda pop and sat back in his chair.

"Illuminate me," he said, and pressed the return key.

Special Investigations Bureau, Colorado Springs, Colorado

"You're sure this is a murder?" Harben asked. His face was expressionless as always but his hands were clasped on top of his spotless desk. For Harben, this was the equivalent of a screaming fit.

"Positive," Eileen said. She was worried, though. The evidence was all circumstantial at the moment. The autopsy was still being done. Without a good piece of corroborating evidence, they wouldn't be able to get a verdict of murder at the inquest. She and Dave Rosen were sitting in Harben's office in the late afternoon, and that was worrisome. Harben's clasped hands were even more worrisome. Before Eileen could express her thoughts, Rosen did it for her.

"Where's the pressure coming from?"

"The police commissioner. The mayor. The general in charge of Peterson Air Force Base. I'm expecting a call from the Governor, the President, and, possibly, God."

"Make sure you ask Him who killed Leetsdale," Eileen said dryly.

"Mitchell's putting the pressure on," Rosen said.

"He was a Colorado congressman for two terms," Harben said. "And he's running a big government project out at Peterson. And he's the district-wide FEMA director."

"The what?" Eileen asked. "Isn't that for floods, or whatever?"

"FEMA is the Federal Emergency Management Agency," Rosen said, his eyebrows raised. "This district would mean the entire western states, wouldn't it?"

"Everything but California, Oregon, and Washington State," Harben said. His eyes glittered. "Of course in the western states we mostly have blizzards and the occasional tornado. Mitchell doesn't have a whole lot to do as a FEMA director, which is why he's got himself a job at Peterson. Still, the FEMA director carries a lot of clout."

"Why?" Eileen asked. She was honestly puzzled. She'd grown up in Wyoming, a place where disasters were dealt with at a very local level. The only time she'd ever seen anything to do with FEMA was when they rescued people out of trees during midwestern floods. Seemed pretty harmless to her.

"The FEMA director can suspend the Constitution and impose martial law, did you know that?" Rosen said. "They control all police, fire, ranger, and National Guard units during the duration of the emergency, whatever that might be."

"So if the earthquake had been really severe, Mitchell might be our temporary boss?" Eileen found the thought horrifying.

"I find it horrifying as well, Eileen," Harben said dryly. "But Colorado is a place where natural disasters on a large scale just don't happen. So Mitchell has a pretty title and not much else. The FEMA association doesn't worry me as much as his power with the state government. And he's bearing down hard on us right now."

"Can you hold them off?" Eileen asked. "And for how long?"

"I can keep this open for three days, detectives. You'd better have a tight case by then."

"Deal," Rosen said. "We'll have it for you, boss."

"See to it," Harben said. He waved a hand at them to shoo them out of his office, and turned to his computer. Eileen and Rosen shared a look, then heaved themselves up and exited quickly.

"Are you pissed?" Rosen said conversationally, as they headed for their desks.

"I *am* pissed," Eileen said. "I hope being pissed off is enough to get us what we need."

"What about Joe?" Rosen asked. "Did he let you know anything about the disks?"

"Still looking at them," Eileen said. "Hey, you know if Harben got pressure from the commissioner, you think the coroner might change his verdict on Leetsdale from murder to suicide? There wasn't much doubt to me, but—"

"Good thought," Rosen said. "I think I'll pay a visit to Doctor Durland. If he's getting pressure from one side, I'll apply it from the other."

"I'll get Joe on the line," Eileen said. "We'll see what he says."

"Detective Reed?" the secretary asked. She was holding out a slip of paper. "Major Bandimere called. She said she got a call from a man who wants to talk to Jim Leetsdale. He's coming into town and she wants to know what to do."

Rosen looked wolfish. "Go gettum," he said. "I'll go twist Doc Durland's arm. Be careful, et cetera."

"Of course," Eileen said absently, looking at the slip of paper. The name was Alan Baxter, which sent an odd shiver down her spine. It was a perfectly ordinary name, and nobody she'd ever heard of before.

"He said he'd be into town at six o'clock or so, and he'd call after he checked into a motel," the secretary said. "That's about half an hour from now."

"I can tell time," Eileen snapped, and turned toward her desk. She felt bad about the snap even as she walked away. She felt worse after getting Joe's answering machine at work and at home. He was probably in his chair in the Gaming Center, his hair bristling on end and his eyes red, lost to the world. She wanted him desperately right now, not for his work on Leetsdale's files but simply because he was Joe, and he was hers, and he was good. She sighed and looked out the window at Cheyenne Mountain, then heaved herself to her computer screen and started working on her earthquake reports.

The phone rang promptly at six.

"Hello, this is Detective Reed," Eileen said crisply.

"This is Alan Baxter," a man's voice said. "I'm calling about Jim Leetsdale. I called his office and they referred me to you."

"Why did you want to speak to Jim Leetsdale?" Eileen asked.

"Well, it's hard to explain," the man said, hesitating. "My friend Krista Lewis was working—"

"I think we need to meet, Mr. Baxter," Eileen interrupted, feeling a jolt run up her spine. Krista Lewis! Right in her lap.

"Should I come to the police station?"

"Where are you staying?"

"At the Rodeway Inn, off Bijou Street."

"There's a Perkins right across the street. I'll meet you there in fifteen minutes," Eileen said, glancing at her watch.

"Okay," the man said doubtfully. "Will you be in uniform, ma'am?"

"No," Eileen said, amused. "Just find a seat and I'll find you."

Eileen hung up the phone and found herself twisting a lock of her hair with her finger, a nervous habit from her childhood. She thought she'd broken the habit long ago. Odd. And there was no reason to be this nervous, either. Even odder.

11

Crestone, San Luis Valley, Colorado

Daniel Grantham's house was agreeable, obviously built from a log home kit and added to over a period of years. The large center room was open to the ceiling, with a stone fireplace at one end and a bank of windows at the other. The furniture, huge and overstuffed, looked comfortably used. A television sat unapologetically atop a set of bookshelves crammed tight with books. Books in stacks surrounded the television. Two stacks of library books were piled on top of the set itself. More books sat in untidy piles on the floor. The air held the tang of woodsmoke and the smell of some sort of evening stew. In one corner a staircase rose to the second story where Navaho rugs hung over the railings. Marcia was examining the rugs with pleasure when she saw a flash of movement behind one. A little figure suddenly darted down a hallway and disappeared. Marcia flinched, startled.

"That's my daughter, Sara," Daniel said, stepping from the kitchen with two glasses in his hand. He shrugged. "She might come down later. She's going through a shy period right now. Or maybe she's playing at being a super spy. It's hard to tell, with Sara."

"Might we sit down, Mr. Grantham?" Marcia asked, smiling. "Do you have some time?"

"Time enough for conversation and supper, too, if you don't mind stew," Daniel said, gesturing to the couch. "We have stew a lot. My lady Jane is a weaver and she doesn't cook. She's in Alamosa tonight, so she won't be back for supper."

"She did the rugs?" Marcia asked, settling herself on the couch. It embraced her with well-worn cushions. The edge of a paperback rose out of a crack as her weight pushed the cushion down. Marcia picked it up and set it on the side table.

"Yeah. She doesn't make a whole lot of money or anything, but they are really beautiful. And it makes her happy."

"They are beautiful," Marcia said. "Is Sara yours, hers, ours?"

"Originally hers, mine too since she was two," Daniel said without offense, drinking from his glass. "Crestone attracts people, Miz Fowler. Some people feel the call when they get here, some when they read about it. Jane was here when I came here, with little baby Sara and her loom and not much else. She was staying with some friends, and we met at a party the school held for me. Took me a year to romance her, never have gotten her to agree to marry me." Daniel frowned. "Eight years now, and she's my Lady Jane and our Princess Sara and that's all that matters to me. So what enchantment do you have, ma'am, to make me tell you these things?"

"I'm nothing but an old schoolteacher," Marcia laughed. Then she stopped smiling, wanting to be honest with this lean young man, wanting to convince him that she was worthy of trust. "I wanted to find out about you, Mr. Grantham. I'm willing to tell you all I know about the girl on the dunes. I need to know if you'll be open with me, too."

Daniel nodded gravely. "Done. First of all, I'm Daniel, not Mr. Grantham."

"Marcia," Marcia said, and they nodded heads. It wasn't even a handshake, but they didn't need to shake hands or sign documents. They had made an agreement, and it would bind them both as though it were written in blood.

"Tell me about the girl, first," Daniel said. Marcia took a deep sip of her water, and started.

"I was trying to see the dawn from the dunes," she said. "I'd been hiking for about forty-five minutes when I thought I saw something on the sand . . ."

When she finished, the water was gone from her glass and her voice was a little husky. Her ankle throbbed a little, as though remembering the pain from her story. She'd soaked it well and wrapped it tightly in an Ace bandage, but it was grumbling.

"More water?" Daniel asked, and Marcia nodded. When he left, Marcia leaned back in the couch and stretched her arms above her head, feeling her back crackle a little. She worked the ankle in circles and rotated her head backward to relieve the stiff tension in her shoulders.

She stared directly into a pair of wide brown eyes, peering at her through the banister.

"Hi," she said softly.

"Hi back," Sara said, in a deliberately scornful voice.

"Your stew smells delicious," Marcia said, and Sara broke into a surprised grin.

"It's elk. And I put morel mushrooms in the broth, and carrots that we grow in our garden. Potatoes, too. Dad makes biscuits, but they're pretty heavy." She stood up, revealing herself as a compact little girl of ten or so. Long brown hair spilled down her back. She was dressed in jeans and a thick wooly sweatshirt that contained a swirl of so many colors it hurt Marcia's eyes.

"You listened to my story," Marcia said. "I hope you're not upset."

Sara's scorn intensified.

"Not me," she said. "Dad gets all the calls from the valley. He keeps all the information. Cattle and horses all chopped up, and lights and fireworks and the Grays and the jets."

"So you hear about it."

"Yeah, and when he gets a live one we go out and see if we can spot it, too. Lots of times we do. We always see the jets come screaming by, trying to follow." Sara was all the way down the stairs now, her face animated. She wasn't shy at all, Marcia realized. Her father's second guess must have been the correct one. Sara had been playing some sort of espionage game, with Marcia as the target. The game now forgotten, Sara strode into the room.

"This must be yours," Marcia said, picking up the book she'd recovered from the couch cushions.

"Hey!" Sara said in delight and sat down with a solid thump at Marcia's side. Sara was no pixie of a girl. Everything about her was steady, as though she could break down walls by walking right through them. She was going to be a formidable woman in a very few years.

"One of my favorites of all time," Marcia said, handing Sara *The Black Stallion*. "But I never owned a horse in my life."

"I have a horse," Sara confided. "His name's Dusty. He's not like the Black, of course. He's a quarterhorse, and Mom and Dad never let me ride without a helmet. But he'll take a carrot out of my hand. You want to help me feed him?"

"After supper, Sara," Daniel said from the kitchen doorway. He was wiping his hands on a dishtowel and looked very satisfied. "I put some biscuits in to go with Sara's stew. About fifteen minutes. Marcia and I need to talk some more before supper."

"Make sure you tell her *all* the parts," Sara said, heaving herself up from the couch and stomping from the room. She was not angry. Stomping was her way of walking. She held her recovered book in one hand and when she'd disappeared upstairs, the lights seemed to dim a little.

"Wow," Marcia said. "What a girl."

"I know," Daniel said smugly, and happily. He tossed the dishtowel over his shoulder and settled into his chair.

"I don't like to talk about the Big Picture over supper," he began, "so let's get right to it. First of all, you've read about the SLV?"

"The SLV?"

"What we call the San Luis Valley."

"Okay," Marcia said with a nod. She leaned forward. "I

know there are a huge number of sightings in the San—the SLV. Lots of cattle mutilations. The Taos Hum, the mysterious Great Sand Dunes that may not have been here as little as ten thousand years ago. That's about it. Not a very coherent picture."

"I'll give you a list of books to read," Daniel said. "Here's the short version. The SLV is the largest alpine valley in the world. Mountains border it. The only entrances into the SLV are over mountain passes—Poncha Pass in the north, Cochetopa in the northwest, Wolf Creek to the west, and La Veta to the east. All of them close during heavy snows, which we get often during the winter months. The southern part of the valley closes up down in New Mexico. There are hardly any roads down there."

"I came over Poncha Pass," Marcia said. "The north. It was breathtaking to see the ranges on either side, opening out into the valley."

"One of the best ways to come into the SLV," Daniel said approvingly. "When you came in, the Sangres were to the east—your left. To the right was the San Juan Mountains. Over the San Juans is approximately twelve million acres of national and state forests. You could get lost in there for months and never find your way to Gunnison or any other town. To the east, over the Sangre de Cristo Mountain Range, there is another deep valley, quite small, and then the Wet Mountains. Over the Wets you hit civilization—Pueblo, Colorado Springs, Interstate 25, and then the plains spreading out on into Kansas."

"I see," Marcia said. "Two mountain ranges to the east, wilderness to the west. You're pretty isolated here."

"A big empty playground," Daniel agreed. "Now, I hope you're not going to take this wrong, but I believe most of the playing down here is done by the U.S. government."

Marcia raised an eyebrow.

"I know, I know," Daniel said, raising his hands. "There are cattle mutilations that defy any explanation. There are abductions and lights that travel across the SLV at better than a thousand miles an hour, silently. Those are inexplicable to me and fit the category of a UFO. However, there's a big Army base up north, Fort Carson. There's Peterson, and Schriever Air Force Base, which we believe is not a weather station at all but some sort of missile defense base. There's NORAD, of course, which is extremely interesting to us not only in terms of what they do, but who they work with. NORAD—the North American Air Defense Command—works with every branch of our military and they act as the early warning system for the free world. So, in sum, we have a very large military presence to the north, and a very isolated valley with a small, rural population down here."

"Missile defense?" Marcia said, puzzled. "I never even heard of Schriever Air Force Base. And wasn't missile defense cancelled—"

"We don't think it was," Daniel said. "And we believe some of their technology comes from either bartered or captured alien spacecraft. Plain old American military pilots fly some of the craft that we see in the SLV. We knew all about the Stealth fighter long before the Gulf War. They flew it down here and over the San Juans, to try the fighter over something other than Area 51 desert terrain."

"What an interesting aircraft that is," Marcia murmured.

"Here's a tidbit for you," Daniel smiled. "The designers of the Stealth knew that it was going to work when they started seeing dead bats in the hangar. Every morning they would have to clean up dozens of bats." He paused and looked at Marcia expectantly.

"The radar deflection is passive?" she guessed. "The bats couldn't see the plane and ran right into it."

"Bingo," Daniel said. "We've got some pretty amazing technology without ever adding in Grays. I think that perhaps ninety percent of what we see is plain old American know-how."

"And the rest?" Marcia asked, knowing the answer.

"We know the rest," Daniel said. "Most UFOs are spotted close to or by military bases, sites of military activity, nuclear power and weapons plants. They aren't here to gather soil samples. Military presence generates UFO presence, which generates more military aircraft, and so on. I'm surprised we don't see them chasing each other in big circles in the sky."

"The girl I found," Marcia said. "What does her death mean?"

"I don't know," Daniel said soberly. "The Grays are usually much more careful in abductions. They usually don't leave bodies behind. But the girl you saw was mutilated."

"Large, rectangular cuts on her shoulder and arm." Marcia said. "I didn't try to roll her over and see if there were any underneath her, though."

"Odd thing about muties," Daniel said. "You always see mutilations on the up side of the animal. Hardly ever on the down side. As though they aren't big enough to roll the creature over once they get it down." He grimaced and Marcia hunched her shoulders. The image was all too clear—childlike Grays, with their instruments and probes in their three-fingered hands, and the rolling frightened eye of the doomed cow.

Marcia collected herself and swallowed past a dry throat. "These clues seem to point toward a human being, then."

"Which is even more frightening to me," Daniel agreed. "A human implies a sociopath, a psycho, someone who enjoys killing women and cutting them."

Into the silence, the buzzer from a kitchen timer went off. Sara came striding out of the upstairs hallway, her book in one hand. She thumped down the stairs two at a time.

"Supper!" she yelled. "I'm starving! Come on, you guys. Marcia needs to taste my stew."

Daniel met Marcia's eyes as they stood from their chairs, and the fear in Daniel's eyes was as apparent as a shout.

Perkins Restaurant, Colorado Springs, Colorado

Eileen Reed was nervous. For no reason. Something had lit up the lizard part of her brain and it was frantically alert. This reminded her of her one bungee-jumping episode, back in her teens. She'd had no problem going up in the balloon, and the tightness of the cuff on her feet was reassuring. She pushed off the platform built along one side of the balloon's wicker basket and that was okay, too. The falling, though, woke the lizard part of her brain. No matter how much she tried to tell herself that she was safe and on an adventure, the ancient part of her screamed in fear and poured adrenaline into her body until she saw spots in front of her eyes. Her heart raced and her mouth filled with a coppery taste as a field of grass beneath her raced to meet her. Then the cord tightened around her ankles and she was jerked abruptly skyward. She shook for an hour after she was safely down, laughing in delight and fear.

Now the coppery taste was back in her mouth and the adrenaline pounded in her bloodstream. At Perkins? She shook her head. This was ridiculous. The restaurant was roaring with the dinner hour, six o'clock. The scent of greasy frying and the tasty smell of baking and roasting food drifted in the air. The evening was warm and still and the sun was just settling down towards the Front Range.

The restaurant was just off Interstate 25, surrounded by trees and residential housing. The houses were beautiful small Victorians, built for the middle-class workers of the eighteen hundreds. Across the highway and down in the valley stood the grand Old Dames, the priceless Colorado Springs Victorians with twenty rooms and cupolas and gingerbread so elaborate it looked like Battenburg lace. The smaller Victorians were once crumbling and in disrepair, but a whole generation of young couples had discovered they could afford them. Eileen could see half a dozen people with paint or shingles or lawn equipment, working on their houses in the warmth of the evening. A beautiful time, late August, heading into the incomparable days of Indian summer.

She took a breath and resolutely entered the door of the restaurant. There were two couples waiting for a table and a family taking care of their check at the cash register. A teenage host stood behind a little podium, working on the restaurant map. The carpet was clean. Eileen remembered this place as well-run and tidy.

"May I help you?" the host asked with a credible attempt at dignity.

"I'm looking for a friend," Eileen said. "A man, Alan Baxter? Is he here?"

"Oh, yes, this way," the host said. "Please." His face was spotted with acne and his ears seemed too big for his head, but his eyes were bright and quick. He was trying hard to sound like a grand maitre d'. Eileen nodded gravely back, silently applauding the effort, and followed.

Alan Baxter had managed to get a booth, Eileen saw, in the nonsmoking section. His back was to her, but he was a tall man, white-haired, wearing a clean blue shirt. He stood up as the host appeared at the table and turned, and the turning seemed to take forever because Eileen recognized him.

The hair was white now where it once had been brown and the skin was weathered and wrinkled where it once had been smooth and fresh, but a three-year-old's memory of her father does not go away. Besides, looking at Alan Baxter was a bit like looking in a mirror.

"Daddy?" Eileen said, in a tiny little voice. The man who stood in front of her, his eyes widening, the color draining from his skin, was her father. Until now, she hadn't known his name.

"Oh my god," the man said. "Eileen? Eileen?"

Then he stumbled a little, pitched forward, and Eileen barely had time to get her numbed arms up to catch him. His head narrowly missed slamming against the plastic of the booth as Eileen eased him to the carpet.

The teen host, his face dismayed and shocked, yelped and dropped the menu he'd been carrying for Eileen.

"Don't fret, he's only fainted," Eileen said, her cold fingers feeling for the pulse in the old man's neck. There it was, steady as could be. "Get me a cold cloth." She noticed the sudden silence, the lack of conversation. All around her, people sat with forks in hands or bites of food in their mouths, still and staring.

"It's okay," she said loudly, with a forced amusement, to the restaurant at large. "He's just fainted and he'll come around in a minute. Don't worry."

Around her, the noise rose again like someone turning on a switch. People were generally very nice, Eileen thought. They were curious, and that sometimes made them appear mean, but they were mostly just nice. The man stirred under her hands. She became aware that she was smoothing the hair back from his forehead, and stopped. She told herself she didn't feel at all like fainting. Time slowed and stretched. She could feel her heartbeat, thudding firmly. Her father's name was Alan Baxter, and he was alive. She took a deep breath. She told herself she felt fine. She told herself that Alan Baxter meant nothing to her, that what really mattered was Jim Leetsdale and Krista Lewis and what information this man might carry. She knew she was lying to herself but that didn't matter now. She had to get through this moment. Beneath her hands, Alan Baxter opened his eyes.

"Just stay still for a minute," she said, more harshly than she intended. "I've got a wet cloth coming for you."

"Did I pass out?" he said in a wondering voice, and Eileen nodded calmly. She recognized the voice now, too. It hadn't changed a bit.

"You fainted," she said. The man, Alan Baxter, blinked hard a few times. His eyes cleared.

"What a stupid thing to do," he said. "I want up off this horrid carpet, please." He sat up gingerly, then got to his feet. He brushed at the seat of his pants. Eileen rose silently next to him and brushed at her own pants. The carpet wasn't really that bad. Alan Baxter looked better, though very pale.

"Let's sit down," he said, not looking at her. "I'm not sure if I look at you I'm not going to pass out again."

Eileen sat down and watched as Alan Baxter slid carefully into the other seat of the booth. The teenage host bustled up with a cold cloth and two glasses of ice water, his face still frightened.

"You okay, sir?" he asked, his voice cracking. "You sure scared me."

"I'm fine, thank you," Alan Baxter said. "Such a silly thing to do. Thank you for the cloth." He took it and wiped his face, then handed it back to the boy with a smile.

Such a nice seeming person, Eileen thought. He looks like a nice person. The nice person raised his head and looked at her.

"Are you really Eileen Baxter?" he asked.

"I'm Eileen Reed," she said, trying to sound level and calm. "Funny for us to run into each other like this."

"I can't believe it," he said hoarsely. "After all the years I looked—"

"Look," Eileen interrupted. She felt icy calm and completely in control. "Whatever happened is in the past now and I don't want to talk about it. It was a long time ago."

"But I'm your dad," Alan Baxter said in a bewildered voice.

"I already have a dad," Eileen said.

Into the silence the waitress arrived, coffeepot and cups in hand.

"Coffee for you too, ma'am?" she asked, and poured expertly at Eileen's nod. She filled a cup for Alan Baxter as well. "Feeling better, sir? I'll give you a minute to look over the menu."

Off the waitress went. Eileen met Alan Baxter's eyes levelly. He nodded at her, his own expression smoothing out. It was eerie to see a face that looked so much like her own, controlling emotion the same way she did. Her calmness wavered like water for a moment and she forced it back.

"All right," he finally said. "Let's not talk about the past. I'm glad to meet you, though."

"Okay," Eileen said. The man (*her father,* her mind whispered) stirred cream into his coffee and took a healthy sip.

"We met to talk about Major Leetsdale, Miss Reed—er, is it Miss?"

"Detective Reed," Eileen said, and felt a thin trembling in her stomach. Could that be pride? How ridiculous.

Alan Baxter smiled at her, an uncomplicated smile of happy pride, pride that he had no right to feel or express. He must have seen her reaction because he stopped smiling and took another sip of his coffee. Carefully, he opened his menu and gazed at the contents.

Eileen opened her own menu, knowing that she couldn't choke down a bite of food. She picked a chicken salad and shut the plastic menu with a snap.

"Why do you want to talk to Major Leetsdale?" she asked. "Is Krista Lewis with you?"

"Krista Lewis is the reason I want to talk to Major Leetsdale, and no, she's not with me," Alan Baxter said grimly, closing his own menu and setting it carefully on the table. "She's dead, Eilee—Miss Reed. She was murdered in the San Luis Valley. She was a friend of mine, and she was working with Major Leetsdale up here in Colorado Springs. I thought I might be able to talk to him—"

He stopped, and Eileen saw the calculation and the conclusion in the widening and narrowing of his eyes. She was a police detective, and she didn't know Krista Lewis but she did know Jim Leetsdale. Ergo . . .

"He's dead too, isn't he?" Alan said.

"Murdered, Mr. Baxter," Eileen replied. For a moment, her relationship to this man forgotten, she contemplated him over the rim of her coffee cup.

"How interesting," he said dryly, and picked up his own cup. His hands were shaking enough to slosh the coffee back and forth in the thick restaurant mug. "You wouldn't have a murder suspect, would you?"

"No," Eileen said.

"Would you—would you tell me about Major Leetsdale? I'll tell you about Krista Lewis in any case, but I would like to know about Leetsdale. Sheriff Gonzalez is going to want to know—"

"Gonzalez? You're working with the sheriff's office?" Eileen interrupted. "What do you do, Mr. Baxter?" He couldn't be—was he a police detective too? That would be too much, she thought remotely. It just couldn't be true.

"I'm a retired English teacher, Miss Reed," Alan said apologetically. "I'm not a deputy or anything. I ended up talking to the sheriff because I identified Krista's—Krista's body." He swallowed hard and finished his coffee.

"Oh. Okay. Could you tell me about Krista Lewis, then? I'll tell you what I can about Major Leetsdale."

"That's a deal," he said.

"Ready to order?" the waitress said brightly, startling them both.

"Ready," Alan said.

"Ready," Eileen said.

12

"Hey!" Joe said in surprise, as Eileen thumped solidly into his chest. She wrapped her arms around him and buried her face into the curve of his neck. For a moment he was sure she was weeping, but when she lifted her face for a kiss, her eyes were dry. "Well let's get inside and close the door, at least. The neighbors, you know."

"Very funny," she said, her voice not entirely all Eileen-sounding. Joe frowned but knew better than to pry. He wondered if this had something to do with that Teddy Shaw guy, the psycho child-killer that Eileen had shot. Joe desperately wanted to talk to Eileen about this, to give her his opinion on child-killers and what should be done with them, but she wouldn't talk to him. It was frustrating.

He loved her. He'd loved her when he told her, over a year ago. Eileen loved him back, he was certain. At least, he knew when they were in bed together. When they were making love she was entirely there, entirely open, entirely his. At other times she would cloud over, turn away, and hold him away with her words. He'd realized months ago that he felt like the girl in their relationship, which made him laugh at the same time it made him furious. He was determined to make her trust him, not just with the fragile length of her glorious body but with her heart and mind. It would happen eventually, and then he could stop biting back his "I love you." When she was ready, she would be ready.

"Talk to me," he said, making his voice light and teasing. "Tell me about your day."

"Rough day," Eileen said. She allowed herself to be shuffled down the hallway so he could close the door.

"If you're going into barnacle mode, we're going to have to sprawl out. Bed okay?"

"Sure," she murmured against his chest. He was certain her eyes were closed. He picked her up—that would be twice this week—and carried her to the bedroom. When he collapsed on the bed with her, her head bounced on his chest.

"You okay?" he asked, seriously this time. She nodded, still limp against him, and he shrugged. When she was ready, she would be ready. After ten minutes, her weight became heavy and her breathing slowed. He eased her to his side and waited, grimacing, for his left arm to come back to life. Then he cautiously reached out and snagged the television remote. As long as she was sleeping, he could catch up with preseason football.

At the end of the third quarter, he realized Eileen's eyes were open. She was watching the game.

"They've got a good linebacker prospect," she said, in a very Eileen-sounding voice.

"And a new receiver too," Joe said. He picked up the remote and turned off the television. "But it's preseason, so who cares. Talk to me, my woman. It is the price I demand for watching football with me."

Eileen sat up and smoothed her hair back with both hands.

"It was a tough day," she said. "I met this guy at Perkins, over off the Bijou exit, and he knew Krista Lewis. The late Krista Lewis."

Joe flipped the remote in the air and caught it. Then he gently set it down. When she was ready, he reminded himself.

"Was she murdered too?" he asked.

"Yeah. She was found down in the San Luis Valley, two days ago. Same day Jim Leetsdale was snuffed. Hers didn't look like a suicide, though. According to Mr. Baxter, this guy I talked to, she was laid out like one of those cattle mutilations they get down there."

"Cattle mutilations," Joe said darkly. "Was this guy one of those UFO freaks?"

"I guess not," Eileen said. "He was visiting some friends down in the valley. Anyway, he says the whole place is about to boil over with talk of alien abduction and UFOs and stuff like that."

"Oh, great," Joe said. "Just what you need to screw up your case."

"You don't believe in UFOs?" Eileen asked with a teasing little smile. When she smiled like that, it made Joe want to leap right on her and lick her like a big ice cream cone. A *strawberry* ice cream cone.

"UFOs?" he said, bringing his mind back with an effort. "No way, man. UFOs are for sad, stupid people with nothing better to do. What a bunch of idiots."

"So what about your simulations?" Eileen asked. "Have you figured out what Leetsdale does—er, what he did, yet?"

"I think so," Joe said. "Maybe. I'll know tomorrow morning."

"Why tomorrow?"

"I can't tell you," he said. At 4:40 A.M., to be exact, he was going to know if the incredibly crazy theory he'd developed was correct or just a bunch of UFO-like hot air. "So if you don't have anything better to do tonight, you want me to order pizza? You want to work up an appetite for it?"

Eileen's eyes went so dark for a moment he was sure he'd said something wrong. Then she grinned like a little girl.

"You betcha," she said. "I've got lots of things to do tonight. But nothing better than you."

"That's what I want to hear," Joe said, loving her so fiercely he didn't care if she ever told him she loved him back. He picked up the phone and hit the speed-dial number for pizza.

La Veta, Colorado

Alan Baxter pulled into the Texaco for gas and sunflower seeds. Sunflower seeds kept him alert and awake while driving, even though they made the sides of his mouth sore after a while. Tonight, he didn't care. Every inch of him felt sore.

After his daughter had left the Perkins parking lot, Alan had sat in his Bronco for almost half an hour, unable to move his hand to start the engine. Everything in him was paralyzed with exhaustion. She looked just like him. That was the thought that kept returning to him. He'd comforted himself for years with the thought that his daughter would look just like Linda when she grew up and would probably act just like her too. That her loss was inevitable and predetermined from the moment he married Linda Doran.

He had slowly leaned forward until his forehead was pressed against the plastic of the steering wheel, there in the Perkins lot. It felt good against his hot skin, like a warm hand. She looked just like him. The height, the shape of the eyes, the cheekbones that made him handsome had made her absolutely beautiful. The only touch of Linda in her was her dark red hair, a beautiful sweep to her shoulders. She'd had it cut indifferently, which only made her more outrageously beautiful. Alan wondered if she'd gone to her high school prom, and the thought sent a spasm through him so sharp he clutched his middle with both hands.

The spasm passed. Eventually, he found the energy to start his Bronco. He had told his daughter he was staying at the Rodeway Inn, but he was planning to register only if he had to. The place he wanted to be right now was the Williams's Ranch. Pulling into the bright glare of the Texaco station in La Veta, he found himself longing for his white bedroom, for Beth Williams, for Susan and Frank. How strange, that the Williams's Ranch was so much like home. His spare little two-bedroom house in Pinedale, Wyoming seemed like a relic from another life.

At the Texaco station he walked slowly into the store, trying to stretch muscles that were stiff from tension and exhaustion. The interior of the building smelled like boiled coffee and smoke, a nauseating mix that almost made him decide against a cup of coffee to help the sunflower seeds. The clerk was settled deep into his chair with a thick fantasy novel, something with swords and cloaked soldiers and ram-headed monsters on the front. He didn't look up when Alan put his credit card on the counter, but Alan saw the man was holding the book with only one hand. The other was under the counter, probably resting comfortably on a shotgun fully chambered with the safety off. A veteran night clerk.

"I'm going to fill up, pump six," he said. The clerk nodded, eyes on his book. Alan loped out to the Bronco and filled the tank, trying not to think about Eileen Reed. If the clerk had decided to shoot a hole in his belly the size of a dinner plate, he could have tried not to think about that either.

A few minutes later, a wad of sunflower seeds in his cheek and a hot cup of coffee steaming in his cup holder, he pulled out of the station and accelerated down the highway.

If Beth Williams asked, he was going to tell her, he decided. Perhaps he could tell Beth and Susan and Frank about his daughter, and Linda Doran, and what happened thirty years ago. Maybe they could help him decide what to do. The one thing he wasn't going to do, he knew, was lose his daughter again.

Peterson Air Force Base, Colorado Springs, Colorado

"I checked on the stocks of water in Rapid City," Mitchell's administrative assistant said, her face tired and resentful. She'd been there much later than usual, and she was on salary and didn't get overtime.

"Sorry about this, Greta," Mitchell said. He knew his own face mirrored hers, with sympathetic lines of tiredness and impatience. "I want to be home with my family just like you do. But we have to make sure we're prepared."

"Yes, sir," she said. She lifted a piece of paper from the stack she carried in her arms. "We're fully stocked with food and clothing for a major Colorado earthquake reaching into

Wyoming, Montana, Nebraska, and Idaho. We have tents, first-aid supplies, names and numbers of doctors and nurses from the entire FEMA area. We also have National Guard Armory locations and access codes for call-up from each governor. The governors prefer to call up their own guard and then pass it on to the FEMA director, but since our area has never had to call up the guard for a natural disaster, they were willing to pass on the codes. We won't need them, probably?"

"Probably not," Mitchell said warmly. She was the administrative assistant for his FEMA directorship. With a staff of close to fifty, her responsibilities were enormous, and after the earthquake she'd been working nonstop. He had to force his face away from a smile. Fifty people, and only three of them knew what was going to happen. The others would believe, and follow, and adore the man who saved them all. "After all this preparation, the Colorado earthquake illustrates the importance of the work we're doing."

"Mr. Mitchell," Bennett said from the doorway, a half-chewed stir stick in his mouth. That spelled some sort of trouble.

"Thank you, Greta," Mitchell said. Greta disappeared through his office door like smoke, deftly managing to avoid touching Bennett as she went. She'd never liked Bennett and he knew it. He contrived to bump into her constantly, lightly, and never quite offensively. Mitchell didn't care, as long as Bennett didn't tease her into quitting.

"We may have a problem," Bennett said as soon as he'd closed the door. "We traced a call into the Alamosa sheriff's office from the Colorado Springs Police Department, Special Investigations."

"Krista Lewis," Mitchell said immediately. He could feel his face darkening with rage. His teeth clenched together. "This is terrible. How?"

"My guess is the homicide detectives," Bennett said reluctantly. He moved his stir stick from one side of his mouth to the other. "The Indian and the girl. There's a guy down in Alamosa, named Alan Baxter, identified the dead girl. He took a trip up here and now they've connected Leetsdale and Krista Lewis."

"Get a picture of Alan Baxter. Then you know what to do," Mitchell said, relaxing back in his chair.

"Sir, Alan Baxter is no problem, but the detectives? I still don't think we should kill cops, sir—"

"My decision, Bennett," Mitchell said. "My responsibility. Do you have a plan for it?"

"Of course, sir," Bennett said.

Special Investigations Bureau, Colorado Springs, Colorado

"Murdered," Rosen said without expression.

"Murder," Eileen said, taking a deep sip of her double-shot mocha latte. Despite her evening with Joe, she hadn't slept well. Her dreams had been tangled and full of desperation. She'd slept at her own apartment because Betty needed to be fed and she was afraid of what she might say while she was sleeping. Joe wanted to know about her, parts of her that would drive him away. She couldn't bear to lose him. Not *him, too,* whispered a part of her mind.

"We should contact this sheriff," Rosen said. "Is Alan Baxter still in town?"

"No, he had to go back to the valley. He's not a suspect but he knew the victim, so Gonzalez wanted him to stick around."

"Is Baxter a potential suspect?"

The question hung in the air a lot longer than it should have. Eileen knew the answer but it still took an eternity to force it out of her mouth.

"I guess so. We'll have to check his alibis for Leetsdale's murder. Evidently he's solid for Lewis's murder. According to Sheriff Gonzalez, which is according to Alan Baxter."

"So we'll check him out," Rosen said.

"Of course," Eileen said, taking another sip of her coffee. "We'll start with—"

"With your appointment," Harben interrupted. He had appeared, as always, with no warning whatsoever.

"Damn, sir!" Eileen yelped. "I just about dumped my coffee."

"That's not coffee, that's some sort of government conspiracy," Harben said grimly. "You've got an appointment with Gerri Matthews this morning."

"I don't have time for that," Eileen said. "I've got—"

"You've got to tender your badge and your gun if you don't go," Harben said. "That's policy, Detective."

"Oh, jeez," Eileen mumbled.

"I'll follow up on Alan Baxter. Don't let her shrink you too much," Rosen said. He hardly ever made jokes. Peter O'Brien, already at his computer console, overheard and laughed far too loudly for Eileen's taste.

"That's a great one, Dave!" he roared.

"Ha, ha," Eileen said, and punched the keys on her computer to lock up her machine. She gathered her car keys and jacket and left, refusing to feel anything but numb. Refusing to feel at all.

Gerri was as relaxed and shapeless as ever when she opened the door to her office. She was wearing pottery-red pants and a baggy shirt of a no-color beige. She looked terrific, of course. She smelled of fresh rose soap. Her hair was shiny, and the whites of her eyes had the clarity of a child. Eileen had finished her latte on the way over and carried a glass of water from the small service area off the waiting room, an area that had originally been the family kitchen in the old Victorian house. Eileen knew her own eyes were bleary and tired. She felt exhausted just being among the battered women and the stiff unhappy couples waiting their turn with one of the six therapists who worked there.

"Hey, Eileen, come on in," Gerri said, opening her office door and dimpling into a smile that was as fresh as her eyes. Eileen walked past her and dropped into one of the comfortable armchairs Gerri kept in her office. Gerri's office breathed comfort, from the quiet prints on the walls to the plants that grew happily around the windows. A thick wool rug covered the glow of a pine floor. Gerri settled into the other chair and picked up a clipboard. It was stacked with papers.

"Okay, I'm here," Eileen said, trying to sound neutral instead of grumpy.

"Nick told you he'd take your badge, didn't he?" Gerri laughed. "That's usually how I get officers for their second appointment. Nick uses threats. Intimidation. What a guy."

"Nick?"

"Nick Harben. Nick to me, and to you, in this office," Gerri said. "He wouldn't send his people to me until he'd talked with me and made sure I was acceptable. He's a good boss, your captain."

"He's a great boss," Eileen said absently. His name was *Nick?* The image was almost unthinkable, the emotionless Harben sitting in this very armchair, talking with Gerri Matthews. Harben, drinking tea? "Did he drink tea when he came here?"

"That is a secret between Nick and myself," Gerri said serenely. "Just as I will never reveal that you drink Red Zinger with honey. It's all confidential."

"Right," Eileen sighed. "So what do you want to know about today? Do you want to hear about Teddy Shaw again?"

"Nope," Gerri said, consulting her clipboard. "Let's get really Freud and talk about your childhood."

Eileen clutched the chair arms convulsively. Her stomach squeezed into a ball of ice. For a moment, she could see nothing but the face of Alan Baxter.

"Okay," she said, forcing calm. "What do you want to know? I grew up on a ranch in Wyoming. My parents love me, they're still married, I had a great childhood."

Gerri looked up from her clipboard. "Funny," she said. "Because your personal records show you were adopted at the age of four. Plenty old enough to remember what happened before."

Eileen was up and at the doorway in four quick strides, fumbling at the door handle with trembling hands.

"You know department rules, Eileen. You'll lose your badge and your job," Gerri said mournfully, not moving from her armchair. "You'll never work in law enforcement again. Is this what you want?"

Eileen stopped trying to turn the doorknob. She leaned her

forehead against the wood panels, smelling a clear odor of Lemon Pledge. She couldn't leave this room. She couldn't give up the career that she loved with all her heart. She felt like she was being torn in two. Weren't adoption records *sealed?*

"Sealed as to content, but not the fact of adoption itself," Gerri said calmly. Eileen didn't realize she'd spoken aloud.

"Fine," she said, rolling the hotness of her forehead across the smoothly polished wood of the door. "I'll talk to you about what I remember, Gerri. If that's what it takes, I guess I can do that."

"I've said this before, but I'll say it again, Eileen. Nothing that goes on in this room goes outside. Have you noticed my filing cabinets are all made of metal?"

Eileen shook her head, still leaning against the door, still struggling not to tear open the door and run.

"They're metal because if somebody decides to violate the Constitution and grab my records, I can burn them without burning down this beautiful house." Behind her, Eileen heard a click and the unmistakable sound of a lighter. "I don't smoke, Eileen." There was a click as the lighter went off. "Does this convince you?"

"Sure," Eileen said. Her stomach was lurching inside of her. She wondered if she were going to throw up. "What do you want to know?"

"I want to know why you think adoption is such a horrible thing. Do you think if people knew you were adopted they would stone you in the streets? Laugh at you? What?"

"My mother didn't love me," Eileen said, and grinned a mirthless grin at the door. "Isn't that clear enough?"

"She loved you enough not to abort you, Eileen," Gerri said, implacable as a field of snow sliding downhill. "She loved you enough to bear you, which I hear is pretty difficult and painful to do. She loved you enough to give you up for adoption—"

Eileen laughed wildly at this, and turned around. She didn't know if she were going to throw up or try to kill Gerri, and she didn't care.

"She didn't give me up for adoption, Gerri," she snarled.

"The last thing she did was try to unbuckle my seat belt, after she picked a long straight road and a bridge to hit. After she'd downed enough alcohol to drown a horse, after she had a little bonfire at a campground where she burned every piece of identification we had, she floored the car and aimed at the bridge and tried to unbuckle my seat belt. She missed, and lost control, and flipped the car before she hit the bridge, and I stayed buckled and I lived. That's how much my mother loved me, Gerri."

Eileen covered her face with her hands and sank to the floor, her shoulders quivering. She did not cry. Tears had been burned out of her a long time ago, perhaps even before she was three years old. But she curled up in a ball and wrapped her arms around her legs and buried her face into her knees, and she shook. She wished she were dead. Anywhere but here.

A hand touched her shoulder, a hand as light and soft as a dandelion seed.

"Don't touch me!" she shrieked into her knees. "Don't look at me!" She hunched away, trying to curl herself tighter. Her ankle gun pressed painfully into her thigh.

"Well," Gerri's voice said from right next to her. "Aren't I a great big turd."

There was a long silence.

"Yes, you are," Eileen said. There was more silence, and the sense of Gerri's body sitting right next to hers. Gerri wasn't touching her, but she could smell the light scent of the soap Gerri used. Eileen started giggling. She couldn't help it. The image of Gerri, a great big turd, sitting on the floor next to her. She giggled harder, unable to stop, her face pressed into her knees.

"I'm sorry, Eileen," Gerri said sadly. "I've got this—blind spot, I guess, about adoption. I had an abortion when I was twenty-two, just out of school. I was married, but my husband and I weren't ready. He was in law school and I was starting my master's degree in counseling work."

Eileen's giggles trailed off. She scrubbed her face against her knees and was surprised to see dampness there. Gerri continued, her voice calm.

"So it turned out I had a condition called endometriosis. It's a fibrous growth in the uterus and fallopian tubes. Sometimes it causes very painful periods; sometimes it's absolutely silent. In my case, it was silent. But by the time my husband and I decided to have children, my tubes were scarred shut and my uterus too damaged to bear a child."

"Oh no," Eileen said.

"Oh, yes," Gerri said. Eileen looked at Gerri and saw a flood of tears down Gerri's pretty face. She was sitting right next to Eileen with her back against the door. Her eyes were red and her cheeks were flushed, but her voice never changed. "That baby I aborted was a miracle child, the only one we would ever have. And we never knew it, until it was too late."

"I'm so sorry," Eileen said. She reached out a hand and touched Gerri's hand, which lay limply on her knee. Gerri squeezed back. Gerri's hand felt like a little bird, all lightness and fragile bones.

"I'm okay," Gerri said. "I'm a therapist, after all. My husband and I, we love each other very much. We didn't know what we were doing. But I've got this wad of scar tissue in my heart, and it makes me make bad mistakes sometimes."

"So I guess you're pro-life, right?" Eileen asked.

"Not always," Gerri said. "I believe abortion is the only answer in very rare situations. But I counsel waiting, and thinking, and understanding your options. Nobody told me that pregnancy is a miracle, that stopping this baby was stopping the potential for an entire life. Abortion is such a fiercely protected right they don't bother to tell you what could be the result. This abortion meant more than a life." Gerri blew out a breath in a resigned sigh. "The cure for endometriosis, you see, is a baby."

"Oh, no," Eileen said, and realized she was gripping Gerri's little hand far too hard.

"Oh, yes," Gerri said. "I've told this story lots of times, Eileen. The pain does go away, mostly. If you carry a baby to term, endometriosis is cut back, in many cases never to return. So if I'd carried this baby and given it up for adoption, I could have had more children, when I was ready."

"That's why you talked about my mother loving me enough to have me."

"That's right. But I had the adoption hat on, instead of the abused child hat on, and I made a great big turd out of myself. Not for the first time, as you now know," Gerri said, grinning a little girl grin at Eileen. Eileen smiled back, still holding Gerri's hand.

"Now we have to get back to me, don't we?" she said, and Gerri dimpled into a smile.

"You are a very, very intelligent woman, Eileen Reed," she said. "Yes, I do have to earn my pennies. If we keep talking about me, I'll end up paying you. Let's get up, and sit back down, and start all over. Okay?"

"Okay," Eileen said. "But I don't think I can tell you my story the same way you told me yours."

"You haven't had the practice I've had," Gerri said grimly. She scrambled to her feet and dusted off her narrow bottom and held a hand out to Eileen. "Let's get to it, shall we?"

"Right," Eileen said, taking Gerri's hand. She unfolded from her crouch and stood up. It was harder than it should have been, to stand straight as though she were unafraid. She walked to the armchair and sat down and took a sip of water as Gerri settled into her own seat. Gerri took a tissue and blew her nose with a very unladylike honk. She wiped her eyes and took up her clipboard and grinned a one-sided grin at Eileen.

"This job sucks sometimes, eh? Tell me about what happened after the accident. You survived? Where was this? Take a deep breath first, then—just tell me."

Eileen took a deep breath and held on to Gerri's courage as though it were her own. She knew that Gerri had told her the story of her aborted baby so that Eileen would feel that she could open up, too. But it still took incredible guts to use your own horrible mistake as a way to help your patient. If Gerri could talk, so could she, no matter how much it hurt. And it hurt plenty bad.

Eileen took a deep breath, and told her.

"I was about three and a half, I think. I remember my mom packing me up and putting me in the car late at night when we first left. She woke me up when she buckled me in the car.

She forgot my Raggedy Ann doll and I cried the whole next day. But she wouldn't go back."

"You were on the run because of your father?" Gerri asked.

"I guess," Eileen said doubtfully. "I don't remember him ever hitting her, or anything like that. I was only three, hardly old enough to remember anything but the way he—the way he smelled and sounded, and I remember him rocking me in a big rocking chair. So I had good memories of him. But something made my mom take off. I wish I knew what it was." Eileen blinked hard, realizing that maybe she could find out now, if she wished. Her stomach gave another huge lurch, and she gulped some water. Gerri didn't seem to notice her hesitation.

"What do you remember about the accident?"

"We were in Rapid City, South Dakota. It had taken us a long time to get there because she spent some time in Las Vegas, a couple of months I think. I think I must have been born in California, but I'm not sure. It just seems that Las Vegas to South Dakota makes sense if you started out in California. Anyway, I remember all the lights in Las Vegas, how the lights made the night seem like day. She bought me a new doll in Las Vegas but she burned it at the end, the last day."

"She was erasing your identities?"

"Yeah, I guess that was the idea. One night we drove to a campground and she burned everything except our clothes."

"License plates?"

"Buried them, I guess, or hid them somewhere. So we were in the car and she was crying, and humming, and then she'd sing a little bit and then cry some more, and I kept telling her I was hungry, and she told me I wouldn't be hungry soon. She was dressed in jeans and a T-shirt that was a very pale pink, I remember, and she had red hair like mine and she just looked beautiful, and wild, and, and—"

"Crazy," Gerri commented. "You can say crazy. What you mean is that she was very ill, Eileen."

"Yes," Eileen sighed. "She was ill. I know that now. I took a course in college, psychology, and there was a chapter on manic-depressives and—Pow!—there was my mom, staring me in the face. Everything I remembered about her fit the profile."

"Any signs of that illness in you?" Gerri asked, voicing Eileen's worst fear in the most casual tones imaginable. Eileen laid a hand across her belly, but apparently her stomach had decided that throwing up was not going to happen this morning. Her stomach gave another lurch, and that was all.

"None that I've seen," Eileen said, trying for the same even tone. "I had the psych tests done before I entered the Police Academy. So far, I think I dodged the bullet."

"That's a relief," Gerri said neutrally.

"I'll say," Eileen said fervently.

"So, your mom managed to kill herself but not you. How long before you were found?"

"Less than five minutes," Eileen said. "My angel was watching over me, that's what Mom—my adoptive mom, now, not my birth mom—says."

It was like an angel had sent them, Paul and Tracy Reed of Wyoming. They picked up their mail in Belle Fouche, South Dakota, because that was the closest town to their ranch. But their baby was in the hospital in Rapid City, their little boy slowly dying in an incubator. They'd both gone home for a day to look after the ranch and to try to come to grips with what was going to happen, something their doctor had talked them into after their third dreadful week at the hospital. There was no way to know that little John Reed would be born with transposition of the vessels of the heart. The condition was a simple blunder of nature, a mix-up where fresh oxygenated blood circulated through the lungs, and old, used-up blood circulated through the body. The doctors had put a shunt in his chest and had operated twice. A transplant heart was the only option in John's case, and there wasn't one available. So John Reed slowly slipped away, and Paul Reed wondered if he were going to lose Tracy along with John. She was mad with grief and helplessness, and even one day away from his side was too much for her. She'd insisted they leave that evening, not wait until morning.

So there they were, two people with broken hearts, and they saw the dirty sedan flipping and corkscrewing through the air, and the abrupt star shape in the windshield that meant that someone had probably just died. The night had been quiet and still and warm, with the fragile scent of early spring in the air and the stars so thick in the sky the Milky Way itself was visible, hanging over them like a shroud. Tracy had the window down, her hair blowing back in the breeze, and she smelled the black scent of burning rubber and the sharpness of the spilling gasoline as the car passed them, tumbling into the ditch by the side of the road.

Paul stomped on the brakes and their truck skidded to a stop, adding their own stink of rubber to the still night air.

"Oh my god, Tracy," he gasped. "Hang on." He reversed the engine and backed up the road, tires squealing, and came to a stop next to the silent wreck. They both sat there, paralyzed, looking at the crumpled thing that had been a car. One wheel spun crazily, upside down.

Then, from a thousand miles away, it seemed, they heard the tiny wail of a child.

"Oh," Gerri said, her pen forgotten in her hand. "They found you."

"They found me," Eileen said, and shrugged her shoulders. "Their child was dying and God dropped me into their arms. I was trapped in the wreck, but I wasn't badly hurt. A piece of glass cut my arm. They were afraid of a head injury, of course. They were Wyoming ranchers, and they'd seen wrecks on rural highways before. So Dad stayed with me and Mom drove into town to get the ambulance and the police."

"That's odd. Why Tracy, instead of Paul?"

"Because Dad worked at the hospital when he was in college, learning Agricultural Engineering. Actually, he told me later, most of his training came from the veterinary courses he took. So he wormed his way into the wreck and put a towel around me and immobilized my head, just the way he'd been taught. Then he put his socks over the cut on my arm, and laid his head right next to mine and talked to me nonstop until the ambulance got there. Mom went screaming into town and brought back, well, everybody, I think. Fire truck, ambulance, police."

"And your birth mom?"

"Dead just the way she wanted," Eileen said without emotion. "Painlessly, I think. Dad said she was completely still, not a sign of life. I couldn't see her in the wreck, which was a mercy."

"I was a difficult problem for the police, as you might imagine. Dead woman, living child, not a clue as to her identity. The only thing they found was my first name, and that didn't turn up anything. Evidently my father hadn't filed a missing persons report."

"Maybe she killed him before she left," Gerri mused.

Eileen bit back a response and nodded as though thinking that idea over.

"At any rate, your brother died, is that right?"

"Within a few hours after I got there. While I was in X ray, and they were deciding I didn't have a head injury. As though he were waiting for me to come so he could go ahead and go." Eileen swallowed past something in her throat. If there was an angel in her life, his name was John Reed, she thought, and gave a silent little prayer up for him.

"So how did they end up adopting you? Were you in foster care?"

"They *were* my foster care," Eileen said. "This is rural South Dakota. They don't even have much of a social services department there. They had a bureau of Indian affairs office that dealt with foster kids, but since I was definitely not Indian, they didn't want anything to do with me. The police had no clue what to do. So Mom and Dad stepped forward and said they'd be happy to take me home until things got worked out."

"As simple as that," Gerri murmured.

"As simple as that," Eileen smiled. "Like taking home a lost puppy. Once they had me in Wyoming, South Dakota was happy to wash its hands of me. So after searching for a year, the state declared me free for adoption and I think it took about five minutes for the paperwork to go through. They didn't change my name, though. It was the only thing I carried out of the wreck, and they wanted me to keep it."

"Wow," Gerri said, her face alight. "You are one lucky woman, Eileen Reed."

"I know," Eileen said. "I know I am. And that's what I want to *be*, Gerri. Daughter of Tracy and Paul, sister to John. I don't want to be some little girl by the side of the road, next to the body of her crazy dead mom."

"You are their daughter, Eileen, and you always will be," Gerri said firmly. "But you are also your birth parents' daughter."

"I know," Eileen said. Gerri fixed her with a stern look, and Eileen wilted back in her chair. "Okay," she mumbled. "Maybe I don't know so well."

"Eileen, I'm not just a sponge, you know. I'm here to give you tools. To arm you, as it were, just like your guns and your badge. We aren't just going to pick at our old wounds and admire the scar tissue, we're going to get beyond them."

"I want to forget all about it," Eileen said. "Why can't I just forget about it?"

"Because it's a part of who you are. Do you know how many parents kill their children every year?"

"How many?" Eileen asked with a sigh.

"I don't know," Gerri said promptly, and dimpled into another infectious laugh. "I pretend to be a fountain of knowledge, but I actually have a cheat sheet on my clipboard. Guess what my cheat sheet is all about today?"

"Adoption," Eileen grinned.

"Adoption. Next week, I'll have a great slew of facts and figures for you. Just let me arm you with this today. Lots of parents kill their kids, every year. Hardly any of them kill themselves along with their children. They drown them, shake them, burn them alive, strap them into car seats and let the car coast into a lake. But they don't kill themselves along with their kids. They walk away and try to get away with murder. Your mother, crazy as she was, didn't do that."

"So what's better about killing herself along with me?"

"Do you think she hated life? Hated her condition, hated what was becoming of her?"

"Definitely," Eileen said without hesitation. She could re-member her mother's black fits of depression, the hours she spent staring into a mirror without moving, the crying, and the maniacal laughter. She remembered being held by her mother, nearly crushed in her arms, as though Eileen weren't a child but a comforting teddy bear.

"Then take this with you today, Eileen. She wanted a re-lease from a life of hell for herself. And she tried to take you away from that hell, too. She had no idea that the whole world wasn't just the way she thought it was. She tried to release you as she released herself."

"She tried to kill me out of love?" Eileen tried for a cyni-cal laugh and it stuck in her throat like a fish bone.

"She loved you, Eileen," Gerri said earnestly. "She was sick and she was confused and she abused you horribly, but she loved you. It was a broken love, but it was still love. Think about that, just take it with you. Next week, we'll talk again."

"Time to go?" Eileen asked shakily. "I don't know if I can stand up."

"I'm sure you can, girl," Gerri said. "Me, I'm meeting my husband at home for lunch, and I'm going to cry and cry and make him hold me. He always knows when I tell my own story. He can see it in my face. So I need to go, too."

"Thank you," Eileen said, and was surprised to find she meant it. She stood, and managed it without wobbling. "I feel like going home and sleeping until next week."

"It's called catharsis, my dear," Gerri said. "Fixing what's wrong doesn't come easy. Now out with you, before we get all weepy and girlish with each other." Gerri shepherded Eileen to the door and waved her out after giving her a firm, no nonsense hug. It wasn't motherly or girlish, and it felt just right.

"Next week, okay," Eileen said numbly. "I will think things over."

"Just let it simmer. And remember, I carry a lighter. No one on this earth will know a word of your story, not my husband, not anyone."

"Okay," Eileen said. She walked out through the waiting

room and into the brightness of a beautiful late August day. The grass was overwhelmingly green, like something out of a drug scene in a movie. Nothing seemed quite right. The angles of the buildings seemed a little out of true, and the cars in the parking lot were too shiny. Her own Jeep was blazing hot and stuffy inside when she opened her door. She sat down anyway and started the air conditioner, looking at the windshield instead of through it. She noticed the clarity of the new glass, replaced shortly after Teddy Shaw blew out her old windshield. There were already several tiny pits in the glass, catching the noon sun and blazing like tiny diamond chips.

Eventually the cold of the air conditioner and the reassuring comfort of her Jeep brought her back.

"What a morning," she said to herself, blinking her vision into focus. Suddenly she remembered what Rosen was doing while she was getting her guts hung up to dry by Gerri Matthews. He was doing a background check on Alan Baxter. The man who could answer questions that she didn't know if she had the courage to ask.

"Gerri," she said to herself as she drove out of the parking lot. "Gerri, I met my father yesterday." She laughed, thinking of Gerri's owl-eyed response. She spotted a sign for a sub shop and her stomach awoke and growled at her. She was hungry, ravenously hungry, as though she'd run a marathon with Gerri instead of just sat in comfortable armchairs and talked to each other.

"I'd rather have run a marathon," she said to herself, and pulled into the sub shop parking lot. She felt hollowed out with hunger, but she could feel her energy rising back inside of her. It was over. She'd told a stranger the worst story of her life and she'd survived it. Time for a sub sandwich and a huge iced tea, and then back to work.

13

Great Falls, Virginia

"Okay, this is what I've got. It might not be much good," Lucy warned Eileen. She had just bathed Hank and he was sitting in her lap chewing on a squeaky baby toy. Drool ran down his chin, and he smelled wonderful, a clean warm baby scent that was the finest thing Lucy had ever smelled.

"Tell me," Eileen said. "I hope you have something new."

"First of all, Krista Lewis is dead. You knew?"

"Not when I first called, actually. But I do now. Who was she?"

"She was an environmental engineer. She worked for Riverworks, a government contractor enviro company. The head of Riverworks is Walter Albrose. You probably don't know him, but he swings a lot of weight in D.C. Former head of the EPA, lawyer, golfing buddies with every President since Bush, apparently. But as far as I can tell, Riverworks isn't corrupt. Powerful and political and dedicated to a clean environment, but not corrupt. I'm going to have Krista's autopsy online here as soon as the Pueblo medical examiner puts it out. Do you want it?"

"Yeah," Eileen sighed. "She was murdered. It wasn't an accident."

"That's what I've read. Walter Albrose is on fire out here, trying to find out what happened to her. She was a good, solid engineer with good instincts. She was working on some kind of stream pollution in the Great Sand Dunes National Monument. That's where she was found, right?"

"Yup."

"And every other hit I get on the Internet on her name is on the UFO nets. There was something very strange about her death, and the UFO guys are going crazy."

"I don't think it was UFOs," Eileen said doubtfully.

"Okay," Lucy said. "I'm not up on UFOs."

This wasn't precisely true. Four years ago Lucy let her top-secret clearance and her computer snoop in every government archive looking for information on the so-called saucer crash in Roswell, New Mexico. She'd seen a UFO documentary on The Learning Channel and it made her ravenously curious. She found some interesting documents that were so cropped they were gibberish. She found some files that were locked so tightly even she couldn't pry them open. She got nervous after a while and stopped looking. Whatever the government had about Roswell, not even a CIA agent with top-secret clearance could take a look.

The only other time Lucy had become nervous about her government snooping was when she found out what happened to Eileen's friend Bernie Ames, a pilot who'd crashed herself and her A-10 combat plane into a mountain. She thought she'd get the government reports on Bernie's crash without any trouble, but after her second attempt to access the Office of Special Investigations database, she'd received a stiff e-mail asking for an explanation. She talked her way out of trouble but it was obvious she wouldn't be allowed access.

So she used a virus. When the Office of Special Investigations bureaucrat sent her the e-mail, she sent him an e-mail apology card. The card was animated and adorable, a little puppy who barked and ran in circles and held up her spotted paw. The puppy said she was sorry and could they still be friends? Hal Blackwell, the OSI bureaucrat, had mailed her back a cheerful response accepting her apology. Lucy almost felt guilty at his response. When Hal had opened the animated card, he'd started up two computer programs that were contained in the same e-mail. One program was the spotted puppy. The other program was a virus that examined the logging data of the OSI computer and found passwords. At the end of the day, Lucy had her own account in the top-secret OSI computer and the virus had vanished without a trace. No tracking system could find her now; she had her own perfectly legal account on the computer. She used it and kept the account. After all, she might need it another time.

She delivered the information to Eileen personally, at Hank's baptism. She sat with Eileen in the back guest room while the party roared down the hall. Eileen bent her head over the sheets of paper, her hair swinging down over her face.

"I'm sorry," Lucy said, putting her hand on Eileen's shoulder.

Eileen sighed and let the sheets fall to the coverlet of the bed.

"It could have been me," she said. The report, still classified, had been about a malfunction in Bernie's oxygen equipment. The mixture had been fouled and Bernie had gone into a delusional state where her abilities were compromised.

"Compromised," Lucy said bitterly. "She was hypoxic and dying, and she did her best to land her plane anyway. It wasn't her fault."

"They fixed the oxygen equipment failure," Eileen said. "I remember when they came around and did that. They didn't even ground us. They said it was just a routine upgrade of the equipment."

"Didn't want to scare the pilots, perhaps," Lucy said.

"Or the contractor who made the equipment was a big political contributor," Eileen said bitterly. "What's the reputation of a single pilot, a woman pilot, compared to a scandal?"

"Now you know," Lucy said. "What are you going to do?"

"Nothing," Eileen said. "I didn't get this officially, and I don't want to get you in trouble."

"Thank you," Lucy said with a sigh. She'd support her

friend however she could, but she was afraid her hacking would be discovered if Eileen tried to bring the information to the public.

"It's good to know," Eileen said at last, smiling a grave and lovely smile at Lucy. "A mystery is solved."

"There are always more," Lucy said, crinkling her nose and bumping her shoulder into Eileen's.

"Always," Eileen said, grinning.

"Let's go get some of my father-in-law's homemade wine and get snookered," Lucy suggested.

"A fine idea," Eileen said. And they did.

"*What about the* other two people?" Eileen said into her ear.

"Let's move on to Jacob Mitchell. This guy is as sanitized as a brand new baby diaper. Every hit on the Internet looks like a public relations piece. If I do hits on 'mitchellsuxs. com' or 'mitchellblows.com' I come up with a glossy Web site that tells me all about Jacob Mitchell, the man who should be President. He's got some savvy computer people working for him, I know that much."

"Any dirt at all?" Eileen said.

"Yes, of course, I am a relentless snoop," Lucy said smugly. She shifted Hank to the other side of her lap and moved the phone to her other ear. "He divorced his first wife and his second is as glossy and shiny as he is. The first is where the dirt comes in."

"I'm all ears."

"She called 911 twice during their marriage, both times for domestic assault, and both charges were dropped. She had a very good lawyer during the divorce and got a substantial settlement. According to sealed police documents—sealed except to me, o' course—she had pretty good proof that he beat her up."

"How nice to hear," Eileen said in a voice both satisfied and hungry.

"Yes, it does make one interested in where he was the night

Krista Lewis was murdered. However, you can't use this information to bring him in since—"

"It was obtained illegally, yeah, I figured," Eileen said. "But it's good to know anyway. What about Jim Leetsdale?"

"He's clean but in a different way. Clean, as in ordinary. He went to Rolla University, got an undergraduate in Geology and a Masters in Computer Science, joined the Air Force, traveled around, ended up at Peterson Air Force Base where he was killed."

"Do you know what they were working on? The project?"

"I don't," Lucy admitted. "I feel awful about it. I might take Hank up to the Pentagon and do some strolling around. Sometimes you have to talk face to face. Whatever this project is, it's hidden well. I'll keep looking."

"Thanks, Lucy," Eileen said. She sounded tired and strained. Lucy jiggled Hank on her lap and frowned.

"You okay?"

"Doing okay," Eileen said, and laughed in a way Lucy didn't like at all. "I'm just having a hard day."

"Take it easy, okay? I know you won't, but try."

After Eileen promised with a total lack of sincerity that she would definitely take it easy, Lucy sat with the phone in one hand and stared into space. There was something wrong with Eileen, something different. Hank dropped the toy in his hands and lunged at her computer mouse.

"No way, kiddo," Lucy laughed, pushing the mouse away from his grasping fingers. "Let's find some other toy that won't get wrecked by a good soaking in drool."

The Williams's Ranch, San Luis Valley, Colorado

Alan Baxter walked into Beth Williams's kitchen to see Sheriff Reg Gonzalez having lunch. His lunch was a huge steak and egg breakfast. His sister was working her way through a salad. Both looked up as Alan walked through the kitchen door, and both smiled identical smiles. Despite their coloring, they looked enough alike to be twins. Alan had left for the Rio Grande before dawn, too wound up to sleep more than a few hours and too polite to wake his sleeping hosts. Instead he'd left a note, put on his fishing waders, and headed for the river.

"H'lo, Alan, how was the fishing?" Beth asked.

"I hooked one, landed one, spent a lot of time looking at the water and the trees," Alan said. His fishing gear was stowed neatly in his Bronco and he'd changed out of his waders and muddy wading shoes, so all he needed to do was wash his hands. He headed for the sink as Gonzalez washed down an enormous bite of steak with a swig of Beth's coffee.

"I whipped up breakfast for Reg because he loves my steak and eggs, but we have some of that leftover meatloaf and some salad in the fridge," Beth said. She started to get up, and Alan waved her back down with his hands still dripping water.

"I can rustle up my own lunch, if you don't mind me rummaging in your fridge," he said.

"You can't use my stove, that's my only restriction," Beth said. "She's an old gas beast, and I don't like letting amateurs near her."

"I'll make myself a meatloaf sandwich and have some of that salad," Alan said with a smile. Beth relaxed back into her chair.

"Not that I like eating salad for lunch," she grumbled, spearing a carrot with her fork. "But if I eat like Reg, here, I'll be as wide as he is and look like a beer keg."

"I don't look like a beer keg," Gonzalez protested mildly, putting another chunk of beef in his mouth.

"I'm only half your height," Beth said crisply, and bit into her carrot. Alan grinned, his arms full of supplies from the fridge. They talked like siblings, too. He felt much better this morning, after spending time in the river. Fly-fishing was the best therapy he'd ever had. The peace and the calm of the rushing water, the solitude, the sharp jerk of a fish taking the fly, these took every problem out of his mind. Even the horrible memories of Linda that were brought up by meeting his daughter, the nightmare of his marriage, was soothed and flattened by his time in the river. Everything would work out. He had found his daughter, and whatever else happened, he would hold on to that for whatever time he had on earth. He'd found his daughter.

"You going to make that sandwich, or just stare at it?" Beth asked from behind him. He jumped, and started assembling ingredients.

"Sorry, I got lost there for a minute," he said sheepishly.

"Thanks, sis," Gonzalez said. Alan turned around with his sandwich on a plate to see Gonzalez's plate polished clean. "I needed a break from town. And my little Maria Elena, if I go home right now I won't be able to think."

"Reg goes all goo-goo eyes around his kids," Beth explained to Alan, still working on her salad. "He goes home and his brain melts. So he comes out here to take a think-break."

"And to talk to my favorite senior-citizen homemade detective, Alan Baxter," Gonzalez said with heavy sarcasm. Alan, with his sandwich halfway to his mouth, froze. "Captain Harben called me this morning. Krista Lewis was working with Major Jim Leetsdale, who was killed the same day she was, or near enough. Luckily your alibis are sound, or I'd be herding you into our facilities right now."

"I'm sorry, Sheriff," Alan began guiltily, his sandwich still in the air. "I just remembered, all of a sudden, so I thought I'd drive up and talk to him, then come down here and tell you—"

"You're not a deputy, you're not a detective, and I don't need your help," Gonzalez said. "Are we clear about this, Alan?"

"We're clear," Alan said. He felt awful. "I'm sorry."

"Okay then," Gonzalez said. "Now, eat your sandwich and tell me what you found out."

Alan gaped at him, and Gonzalez gave him a wicked grin. "Just because I don't need your help doesn't mean I won't use your information. Since you deputized yourself, Deppity Baxter, I want a full report."

"Okay," he said, and put down his sandwich. "I met a detective in the Springs. Her name is Eileen Reed. She's working the case, and she told me everything about Major Leetsdale."

"As long as you told her everything about Krista, right?" Gonzalez said unhappily, and Alan nodded. "Oh well, that's what I expected. Shit. Go ahead."

"First I need to tell you something. Eileen Reed is—well, she's my daughter."

"Your daughter?" Gonzalez asked.

"My daughter," Alan said. He blinked heavily a few times, then took a large and determined bite of his sandwich. He chewed and swallowed. Gonzalez looked confused while Beth looked stunned. She knew something about Alan Baxter's past, and there had never been a daughter there before.

"And I'm glad you asked," he said, "because I've been wanting to tell somebody about this since it happened. But I don't want to take the sheriff's time with a family issue when he needs to get back to work—"

"Right now I've got CNN, Fox News, CNBC, MSNBC, and the Sightings people in town," Gonzalez said, turning his empty coffee cup around in his hands. "I have UFO investigators from all over the country making reservations at every hotel, motel, and trailer court. I have a call in to the FBI but they haven't given me an answer yet. Tonight I'll be busting up fights when drunken journalists pinch local barmaids' bottoms, and I'll be giving out speeding tickets to UFO fanatics trying to get here before the mothership lands, or whatever the fuck they believe. I believe right now I'm going to have another cup of coffee and listen to your story, Alan."

"Alan, you didn't tell your daughter about—our cows, did you?" Beth suddenly spoke up, her eyes worried. Gonzalez gave her a sharp look, groaned, and started rubbing his forehead.

"No, I didn't," Alan said, bewildered. "I didn't think— they aren't connected. Are they?"

"Not unless you believe in UFOs," Reg said grimly. "How many, Beth?"

"Two. We burned them. Alan helped Susan and Frank."

"Grantham might have seen the fire," Reg said heavily. "Has he called you yet?"

"No," Beth said. She put her fork in the remains of her

salad and stood up. She started cleaning up the dishes with a distracted air.

"Who's Grantham?" Alan asked.

"Daniel Grantham. He teaches math at the high school. He also writes books on the San Luis Valley. He's brilliant, and very dedicated, and as hard to shake as dogshit from your shoes when he's on to a story."

"Books?" Alan asked. Beth set a big cup of coffee in front of him, creamed and stirred just the way he liked it. She sat down with a mug of her own.

"UFO books. They sell well. The San Luis Valley has a lot of sightings, strange lights, abductions, crap like that," Gonzalez said. He held out his mug to Beth who threw him a withering glance. He pouted, then got up and poured himself another cup of coffee.

"Cattle mutilations," Alan said.

"That too," Beth said grimly. "We aren't wealthy, Alan. We can't let the insurance company get away with denying our claims because some of our cattle are killed under mysterious circumstances. Susan told you about this, didn't she?"

"She did," Alan said, sipping his coffee. "I wonder if Krista's death has anything to do with all of this."

"CNN, Fox News, MSNBC all seem to think so," Gonzalez said heavily, sitting back down. The afternoon light was just starting to come in through the kitchen windows. It would be dark in less than nine hours, Alan thought, suddenly feeling a touch like a cold hand at the back of his neck. Something was out there, something that had killed Krista, and maybe Jim Leetsdale, and the cows that lay so forlornly with the holes gaping in their sides . . .

"Creeps you out, doesn't it?" Gonzalez said with a nasty grin. Alan barked out a laugh at being caught with his thoughts on his face.

"Your daughter," Beth said. "This has to be all connected. I want to know about your daughter."

"Okay," Alan said. "Maybe this does all tie in, somehow. I married when I was thirty-two. I lived in Los Angeles and I was a salesman, can you believe it? I sold data storage, big tape machines for the big computers we had back then. I made a lot of money, and I fell in love with this young girl at Lockheed. She was the desk receptionist as I was finalizing a big deal with the aerospace division at Lockheed, and she was beautiful and full of energy and her name was Linda Doran." He took a sip of coffee to clear a throat suddenly dry and scratchy with memory.

"So we had a short engagement and we married, all within six weeks, and I took her to Hawaii for our honeymoon and when we got back she was pregnant. Life was perfect, you know. Then she changed. She got depressed, really depressed, and I took her to the doctor, and they thought it was pregnancy-related. They thought she might just have mood swings because of the hormones. So we struggled through, and our little girl was born, and we named her Eileen."

"Eileen," Beth said with a smile.

"Eileen. So six months after she was born, Linda got better, then she got worse, then she got better again. I think she was manic-depressive, what they call bipolar nowadays, but I never got her to the right kind of doctor. She thought I was going to have her committed because I wanted to have her evaluated." Alan looked down at his coffee and it was sloshing around in his cup. He was trembling a little with the memory, even though it was thirty-three years old. Funny, that a memory so old could hurt so much.

"So she took off. I got back from an overnight business trip up in San Francisco and she and Eileen were gone. She took all our cash from the bank account, packed the car, and left."

"When did you find them again?" Gonzalez asked.

"Yesterday," Alan said, and nodded at the stunned expression on their faces. "Yup."

"Oh my god," Beth said.

"I thought she'd killed them both, because I never found them. Not the car, not a record, nothing."

"Like they dropped off the face of the earth," Beth said. "Did your daughter tell you anything about it?"

"She was about as upset and surprised as I was," Alan admitted, remembering again the odd look of her face, so much like his own, shutting down like someone putting on a mask. "She said she didn't want to talk about our past, and I re-

spected that. She's a detective with the Colorado Springs police, and she's—she's just beautiful." Alan took a last gulp of
his coffee and set the cup down.

"Wise, to go slow," Reg said. "Who knows what her
mother told her about you?"

"Nothing good, I fear," Alan said sadly. "But I know she's
alive, and she's my daughter. At least we can keep in contact."

"She's on Leetsdale's case?"

"She's a homicide detective," Alan said, and smiled at
Beth who was grinning at him. "Nothing I can take credit for,
of course. But I'm still proud."

"I know Harben," Gonzalez said. "I'll give him a call later
today and talk to him about Leetsdale and Krista Lewis. If
they're related, this could help everyone."

"Can I go back up there and talk to her again?" Alan asked,
as Gonzalez stood up and adjusted the mile of black leather
around his waist. Gonzalez fixed him with a baleful eye, then
shrugged his shoulders.

"You are a strange duck, Mr. Baxter," he said. "You've
been here three days and you've got the most important
women in my life treating you like a long-lost uncle. If my
wife falls in love with you too, I'm just going to have to shoot
you."

Beth giggled and stood up. She gave Gonzalez's shoulder
a hearty punch.

"You big softy," she said. "Go spend some time with Conchita and your little Maria Elena."

"Call me a softy tonight when I'm throwing Mr. Important
Journalist in the drunk tank," Gonzalez said wryly. "Hopefully I won't be scraping his puke off my shoes at the same
time."

"I won't talk about Leetsdale or Krista," Alan promised. "I
just want to talk to her."

"Well, whatever," Gonzalez said. "If she lets anything slip
about her case, you trot on back here like Deppity Dawg and
unload it, hear?"

"Deal," Alan said with a grin. "And thanks."

"Don't thank me, thank your loyal brigade of supporters,"
Gonzalez said, putting a huge arm around his sister and hug-

ging her. "Thanks, Sis. I'll call you with any news. I wouldn't come in to town for dinner for a few days. It's going to be a circus for a while."

"We'll stay away," Beth promised. "If some journalist pinches Susan's bottom, you'll be picking up pieces of him all over Main Street."

"I know," Gonzalez sighed. "So keep her here."

"I'll try," Beth laughed. "But I haven't been able to tell her what to do since she was ten. She's just like I was." She opened the kitchen door and waved her brother through, then came back and started cleaning her massive stove. To Alan's eyes, it already looked spotless.

"I'm making roast beef enchiladas for supper, Alan," she said. "I could sure use some help grating cheese."

"You bet," Alan said. "I think I'll head back up to the Springs tomorrow morning, and see if I can get an appointment to see Eileen."

"Good idea," Beth said, setting a block of cheese and a grater in front of Alan. "Now, grate. And tell me about Eileen. You haven't told me what she looks like. What happened when you met? Is she married?"

Alan grated cheese, and waited for Beth to stop talking so he could answer her questions, and hoped that things would be well, all things would be well. The kitchen was safe and warm with sunlight and the smells of cooking. Alan tried to avoid thinking about the emptiness beyond the windows and the coming darkness.

14

Crestone, San Luis Valley, Colorado

Marcia Fowler was huddled over Daniel Grantham's computer when the door to his tiny study burst open. She looked up in surprise to see a fantastic creature standing in the doorway, fierce green eyes glaring at her. Marcia gaped. The creature resolved itself into a woman after a few blinks of her computer-blurred eyes, a woman wearing a wild shawl of a hundred colors, fringed extravagantly.

"Hello," Marcia said uncertainly. "Are you Lady Jane? I mean—er?" She felt like a fool, but it seemed the right thing to say. The woman's fierce glare dissolved into a grudging smile.

"That's me, although the Brits wouldn't like me claiming a title just like that," she said, in a rich, throaty voice. Her voice was beautiful, like music. "Daniel told me he's lent you the spare room."

"I hope that's all right," Marcia said uncertainly. "I had planned to camp for this vacation, and the motels are so expensive this time of year . . ."

"Oh," Jane said, and the line of her shoulders relaxed a trifle. She came into Daniel's study, filling it to bursting. She had her daughter's solidness, draped in that wildly woven shawl, and as she came into the light, Marcia realized she wasn't a whole lot younger than herself. She was perhaps fifty, with the radiant skin of a woman who'd spent a lot of time outdoors, with no makeup at all. Lines bracketed her eyes and mouth, lines of a life well lived. Her hair was a pumpkin orange shot with gray, rich and coarse and spread over her shawl like a cloak. She was absolutely beautiful, and Marcia understood instantly why Daniel Grantham loved her. And perhaps why Lady Jane wouldn't marry her young and handsome schoolteacher.

"I can go back to the motel, if you feel uncomfortable," Marcia offered. "Truly, I don't want to be a bother."

"You'll have to get a motel in Pueblo, if you want one," Jane said dryly, dropping into an ancient armchair wedged into the corner. "The Rabble's here."

"Oh, shit," Marcia said. "Er, I'm sorry."

"No problem," Jane said, with a shake of her head and a wave of a sturdy hand. "I mean real rabble. The news organizations. Sightings. *The Skeptical Enquirer.* And every MUFON member who can get some time off work."

"Because of Krista?" Marcia asked. "This is awful. Daniel and I think we've determined this isn't UFO-related. That's what I was reading about, news reports of rapes and murders in the Front Range. I didn't—"

"Daniel told me you found the body. You really did, didn't you?"

"Yeah," Marcia said, and then understood. "You thought I was a reporter, didn't you?"

"Yes," Jane said. "But I can see you're not now. Daniel is a brilliant man, but he lacks the cynicism he needs in his chosen field of . . . expertise. I was prepared to bounce you out on your arse if you'd fed him some cock-and-bull story just to worm your way in here for a story."

"Why do you think I'm real?" Marcia asked, fascinated.

"Your aura. Your honest face. Your politeness. I'm the true cynic in this family, Miz Fowler. I make judgements based on a thousand clues and call it intuition. But I'm never wrong."

"I'm glad I'm not a reporter," Marcia said humbly, and Jane laughed. She laughed the way she looked, a full-bellied lioness roar that brought Sara stomping to the doorway.

"Hey Marcia," she said happily. "The whole town is going nuts. Did you see?"

"I'm clueless," Marcia sighed. This was going to be much more difficult now that someone had tipped off the media. Who it was, she'd like to know. That might point in a direction that would be interesting. She clicked off her Web browser and disconnected from the phone line.

She'd traveled back to Daniel's house early that morning after checking out of her motel room, not stopping for breakfast. She was right in her guess; Sara had fixed breakfast for her, an enormous plate of eggs and toast. The eggs were scrambled badly and were rather rubbery, but the toast was hot, and Sara provided homemade chokecherry jam. Thus she had missed what was undoubtedly the beginning of a media circus. She'd spent the whole day buried in Daniel's books and computer. She hadn't turned on the little television at all. Daniel took himself and Sara off to school not long after her hoped-for breakfast. She was amazed and gratified at his trust in her, leaving her alone at his house all day. She'd have to leave the valley, otherwise. She lived off a pension and limited social security, and she really couldn't afford to spend nights in a motel and eat at restaurants all the time. Not if she still wanted to make that trip to Stonehenge at Christmas.

"So what's that in the oven?" Sara demanded. "Did you make supper, Marcia?"

"I cobbled a lasagna together," Marcia said. She'd taken a lunch break earlier that included making lasagna for supper. There were no lasagna noodles, but there was an old bag of egg noodles, so she used those, along with some deer burger and mozzarella cheese and canned spaghetti sauce. It wasn't real lasagna, more like Italian food in layers. "I hope you don't mind. I thought I could fix you dinner."

"Fine by me," Sara said. "Have to do homework. Later." She left, and Marcia heard every step as she thumped her way upstairs. She looked at Jane and smiled at the bemused look on the other woman's face, a look of love and exasperation and happiness.

"You couldn't make me do homework when I was her age," Jane said with a shake of her head. "I had to be dragged. My room was always a disaster. Sara's room looks like a magazine photo. If she hadn't come from my body right in front of me, I'd think the fairies brought her."

"Very solid fairies," Marcia remarked. Jane grinned.

"Exactly!" she said, but her look faded quickly into worry. "Daniel told me a few things, enough to send me back from Maria's house without finishing the weave. We talked a Navaho weaver into coming up from the reservation, and we've spent the last week working with him. I'll just have to catch him some other time, if ever," she said, and chewed her lip.

"Krista was murdered by a human," Marcia said firmly.

"Daniel is sure of it," Jane replied. "After he spent the evening with you, and listened to your account, and after sleeping on it, he's sure. So I drove Sara home today instead of letting her catch the bus."

"Can Daniel talk to the principal? The administration?" Marcia asked, then bit her lip as Jane gave her an I-thought-you-were-smarter-than-that look.

"Of course, and he has, and he'll be talking to Sheriff Gonzalez today. A very nice pig, as pigs go," she said. "Even with Beth, that fat, pampered witch of a sister he's saddled with. He doesn't believe, but he'll work with Daniel. Grudgingly. Maybe not so grudgingly now, since he's not talking abduction but some kind of bad human."

"Very bad human," Marcia said, her mind supplying her with a fresh image of Krista, crumpled and dead on the sand.

"So," Jane said, standing up in a swirl of shawl and hair, "let's go open some wine to go with that lasagna, which smells wonderful. You can tell me about yourself, and I'll tell you about myself, all those girlish things. And if Serial Killer comes through the door, I'll be Scarlett O'Hara and shoot him in the face, and you can be Melanie and faint in the doorway."

"Melanie didn't faint in the doorway," Marcia said primly.

"She'd gotten that god-awful heavy shotgun and she was ready to use it. Besides, why do you get to be Scarlett?"

"Because I'm bigger than you," Jane said, as solidly as her daughter. Marcia giggled like a girl and followed Jane to the kitchen.

Briargate Subdivision, Colorado Springs, Colorado

When the doorbell rang, Joe realized he hadn't brushed his teeth all day. And they'd had garlic on their pizza last night, and he'd sweated right through his T-shirt at least twice, leaving dried salt rings under his arms and down the front of his chest. He jumped for the bedroom and grabbed a fresh shirt, snatched his toothbrush from the bathroom and tried to stick the toothbrush in his mouth while pulling his old shirt over his head. The doorbell rang again before he untangled himself. Cursing under his breath, he pulled the fresh T-shirt over his belly and opened the door with his toothbrush still in his mouth.

"Hey, Joe," Eileen said, smiling. She looked tired, more tired than he'd seen her for a long time. There were shadows under her remarkable blue eyes and her mouth looked pinched. She was gorgeous.

"Hey," he said, "Let me finith with my teef." Eileen followed him inside. He gestured at his computer study and rinsed his mouth in the bathroom. He quickly swabbed at his armpits with his deodorant, much like pouring perfume over a great big dead skunk, but it was worth a try.

"Wow, what's this thing?" Eileen asked. The Thing was sitting on his second desk, and was the reason he smelled like roadkill and hadn't brushed his teeth. He hadn't eaten today either, he suddenly realized. Well, whatever. The Thing was an old laptop personal computer, re-wired extensively and running Linux, the personal computer version of Unix. Extra battery packs were duct-taped to the bottom along with an extra hard drive. A special fan he'd salvaged from a very old Macintosh whirred off the rearranged guts of the back end. It was portable still, barely, though he wouldn't try to take it on an airplane. The extra battery packs made it look like a computer timing device wired to a bunch of C-4 plastic explosives.

"This is Frankenputer," Joe said. "And you are going to love what she's going to show you tonight."

"Your theories were correct?" Eileen asked eagerly.

"My theories were correct. Let me show you," Joe said. "You are not going to *believe* this. I don't believe this, and you know what I do for a living."

"Yes I do," Eileen said absently. She sat down in his guest chair. Joe took his own well-used office chair and put his arm around her. She did not smell like roadkill. She smelled faintly of apricot soap and faintly of something which was really just Eileen. She was warm and soft, and he kissed her temple.

"You okay?" he asked. "Want to get right to it, or do you want food? Water?"

"Let's get to it," Eileen said, making Joe adore her all the more. Unlike most female types, who seemed to have to go through elaborate dances of drinks and snacks and conversation, Eileen could cut directly to the point. Food, sex, work—she knew what she wanted.

"Here we go, then," he said, and hit the Enter key with a flourish.

The screen, dark at first, changed to a globe, almost exactly like the simulation globe from the War Gaming Center. Eileen, who'd seen her share of war simulations a year ago, gasped in surprise.

"This is from Schriever?" she said. "Isn't that illegal? I mean—"

"This isn't all from Schriever," he said dryly. "I pirated certain parts to get my world display, but only the unclassified ones. I suppose I'd get in trouble if I tried to sell this as some sort of commercial package, but I'm not violating any rules. So don't worry. I like my job too much to risk it."

"Good," Eileen said. "That's a relief. So—why did you need to do this?"

"I had to build this laptop today to power my software," Joe said. "Incredibly complicated stuff, simulations. I have eight CPUs working in here and a different operating system, Open Linux, that makes your usual personal computer operating system look like garbage, and—well, I won't go into boring, computer-geek detail. Let's just say I've got a good simulation of the earth, right here."

"Okay," Eileen replied intently. "Show me."

"Here we go," Joe said, clicking on a pull-down bar that showed a series of names. "Here are all the girlie pictures that Jim Leetsdale took such care to store on his disks. I'm going to click on this one, Tia." He did so, and the pull-down bar disappeared. "Here we go." He clicked on another series of controls that dropped their point of view from a near-earth orbit down to an airplane-level view of Central America.

On the earth in front of them, a rainbow band of colors appeared on the green and brown tones. The colors were jagged and thickly drawn, like paint strokes. Suddenly the color bands moved, bumping against each other and sliding up and down on the map. The colors stopped moving. Joe let out his breath. He hadn't run the simulation enough to know if it would run perfectly every time. Usually software decided to go belly-up when it was first demonstrated to a new person.

"Wow," Eileen said. "Okay. What the hell was that?"

"An earthquake," Joe said. "That was an earthquake that took place in Colombia this morning at 4:40 A.M. Mountain Standard Time. A 4.2 on the Richter scale, not a big one. I looked it up on the Internet."

"An earthquake," Eileen said.

"Yes indeed. Jim Leetsdale's girlie pictures are all earthquake simulations. Now let me show you an interesting one." Joe pulled down the menu of girl's names and clicked on "Celeste." He pulled his world angle back to a low earth orbit and then dropped toward the United States. He hovered over Colorado, and felt Eileen go tense and still next to him as the strange pattern of colored lines appeared. The lines humped and crawled and then disappeared.

"The Colorado earthquake," Eileen said.

"Our earthquake," Joe agreed happily.

"So his girlie pictures are earthquake simulations. That tells us what the project is all about, I guess," Eileen said heavily. She leaned into him, slumped against him, really. She really was tired. She hadn't made the connection.

"Leetsdale was killed the morning of the Colorado earthquake," Joe said gently.

"So he was—oh!" Eileen straightened. "He knew it was going to happen?"

"He knew it was going to happen. He didn't simulate earthquakes that had occurred, he simulated earthquakes that were going to occur. That's why I had to wait until 4:40 this morning."

"The Colombia earthquake."

"The Colombia earthquake," Joe said. He grinned at her. "I can think of lots of ethical reasons why a project like this would be kept a big secret."

"If they can predict earthquakes, why don't they warn people?" Eileen asked.

"That's the ethical dilemma, yes. If you warn a population of an impending earthquake, do the resulting deaths from panic outnumber the deaths from the quake itself?"

"So logical," Eileen murmured, scrubbing at her forehead. "But so true."

"Maybe Leetsdale couldn't handle the pressure of watching people die in earthquakes he knew about in advance. What if he decided to go public with this?"

"They'd fire him and discredit him," Eileen said. "The government doesn't make hits on people and stage suicides. They can just make him appear to be mentally unstable, crazy. Or they'd arrest him before he had a chance to get his information out."

"Well, maybe," Joe said. He held his own opinions on what the government was capable of doing. "But he hid a bunch of very interesting data in a bunch of girlie pictures. Why, if he wasn't going to go public with it?"

"It's a good premise," Eileen said. She reached forward and slid her hand under Joe's, which was still resting on the little touch mouse pad on his laptop. The feel of her hand under his palm sent forks of electricity down his arm. He wanted to make love to her immediately.

"Let me try one," she said. She pulled down the menu of

girls' names and picked one halfway down the list. Juanita. The date of the file, which Leetsdale had changed to mean the date and time of the earthquake, appeared on the upper left corner of the screen. Eileen looked, puzzled, but there were no jagged lines.

"We don't know where this one is," Joe said, and moved her hand on the mouse like a father guiding a child's hand. He adjusted the picture so that their view rose and hovered at earth orbit, and he ran the simulation again. The squiggles appeared, very faintly, in the middle of North America. Joe dropped them towards the earth with tapping motions on the mouse pad. They were suddenly hovering over the Midwest of the United States, Missouri perhaps. The squiggles appeared roughly along the Mississippi River.

"Wow, those are big," Joe said. He felt a small chill, different from the one he felt when Eileen's hand crept under his palm. This one was centered in his back and was cold.

"They're really big," Eileen said. "But there's no—is there a fault line in the Mississippi Valley?"

"Let me consult the machine," Joe said. He spun around in his chair and duck-walked himself and the chair over to his main computer desk. He ran an active Web site from his home, so his computer was always on and always on the Web. With a few quick keystrokes, he opened a search window on his computer screen.

"Earthquakes, fault lines, Mississippi," Eileen murmured, duck-walking her chair over and reading his rapid typing.

"Let's see," he said, leaning back and putting his arm around her. She nestled into his chest with a sigh and closed her eyes while the machine hummed. Joe began to think of food for the first time that day. Would Eileen mind pizza again? A big wheel of pepperoni and mushroom would taste just right . . . his stomach awoke and growled furiously, right below her ear. She sat up straight and started laughing. "You're hungry," she said. "Did you eat today?"

"No, I forgot," he said, thinking that if he had a choice between lovemaking with Eileen and a pizza, he would be hard-pressed.

"Let's order a pizza," she said. Joe pressed both hands to his heart and rolled his eyes.

"My woman! You read my mind."

"No, I didn't," she said dryly. "Pizza is the only delivery food out here, and we're not leaving for a while."

"Nope," Joe said, "you are correct. But I still adore you."

Eileen laughed and leaned forward for a quick, hard kiss. Then she spun her chair around and reached for the phone.

"Hey, it's coming up," Joe said, as Eileen speed-dialed the pizza.

"The usual," Eileen ordered into the phone. Their pizza service knew their address from caller-ID on their phone, and knew their usual order from their computer system. Joe loved that. He supposed there were pizza ingredients other than pepperoni and mushrooms, but he couldn't imagine what they might be.

Joe forgot the pizza as he scanned the first of the Web sites that contained information on fault lines in the Mississippi Valley. The first site he'd chosen was the University of Missouri's library system. There, a master's thesis from a geology student was available. The title of the thesis unhinged Joe's jaw and brought his hands limply into his lap. Eileen rolled over and read over his shoulder.

"A Nation Split in Two; Ramifications of a New Madrid Fault Line Earthquake," Eileen read aloud. She scanned the first few paragraphs.

"Early in the morning on December 16, 1811, the residents of New Madrid, Missouri, were awakened by a sound like distant thunder. The thunder intensified, accompanied by a strange smell, like sulfur. Then the ground began to shake. The ground heaved wildly, floors cracked and broke apart, cabins fell into piles of lumber. Mixed with the sound of rumbling were sharp explosions and a loud whistling and hissing sound. For the sailors on the Mississippi River, the earthquake was even more deadly. Ancient trees shot from the bottom of the river and exploded from the surface. Whirlpools appeared and raced upriver, swallowing small and large craft alike.

Banks along the river began to crumble and fall into the water. The very course of the mighty Mississippi River was changed.

The New Madrid earthquake had begun. For a series of months, the Mississippi Valley was shaken by earthquakes that would measure today somewhere around 8.4 on the Richter scale. The tremors were felt in twenty-seven states, from Colorado to Virginia. Few people lost their lives because the Mississippi Valley was sparsely populated in 1811. Fewer than four thousand people lived in the whole region.

In the beginning of the twenty-first century, we see a heavy population in the most fertile stretch of land in the world. From the industrial centers of Chicago, Illinois, and Gary, Indiana, to the port city of New Orleans, people live and work in blissful unawareness of the potential for cataclysm underneath their feet."

Eileen turned horror-filled eyes to Joe. He found that his hands were clenching hers too tightly and he forced himself to loosen them. He remembered what it was like, seeing Ralph Morrison bellowing in his Jockey shorts, feeling the earth writhe and crawl underneath him like a huge slug. Colorado's was a baby earthquake, just a minute or so in duration, and Joe didn't think he'd ever forget what it had felt like.

"How big is this earthquake?" Eileen said, voicing his thoughts.

"Let's see," he said, and they rolled together back to the laptop Frankenputer. He hit the replay button on his simulation and they watched the deadly squiggles appear along the Mississippi River. "Oh, my god," Eileen said faintly.

"Eight oh," Joe said, leaning back in his chair. "Is that possible?"

"When?" Eileen asked. Joe leaned forward again with a jerk, peering to read the numbers off the digital window.

"Three days," he said numbly.

"No, this isn't right," Eileen said suddenly. "This has to be a mistake."

"What do you mean?" Joe asked. He couldn't get his mind

around the idea that an earthquake could—was going to—strike in three days that would leave millions of people dead. It just couldn't be.

"No, not that it *shouldn't* happen," Eileen said. "But it *wouldn't* happen. If the government knew this, there would be massive National Guard call-ups. A few days are plenty of time to evacuate the towns around the Mississippi River. Hurricanes strike in less than a couple of days, and they evacuate everybody. No government agency—oh, shit."

"Oh, shit, what?" Joe said. Eileen was frozen, her eyes wide and empty. She was obviously rummaging for a memory and had turned herself inward. She blinked and her eyes focused. It was an eerie thing to watch. Joe had seen it several times. She reminded him of a robot when she did that. Eileen could abandon her body and go searching through her skull, as though her body were nothing more than a brain-support system and she'd left the controls for a few minutes.

"I got it," she said. "The guy, Jacob Mitchell. He's Leetsdale's boss, and he's the FEMA director for the whole Rocky Mountain Region. FEMA mobilizes the National Guard in an emergency."

"No, that would be the state governors," Joe said. "The National Guard is called out by the governor, not by the FEMA weenies. Besides, this earthquake isn't the Rockies. This earthquake is in the Midwest. Wouldn't that be a different FEMA?"

"Oh, that's right," Eileen said, frowning. "And he only gets to take over the National Guard if there is an emergency. But he can't do anything before. So—well, now I'm not sure what to think. Are we sure this earthquake will happen?"

"Hey, no, we're not," Joe said. "Let's check on the rest of the earthquakes that should have happened. If any of them didn't happen, we can hope."

By the time the pizza arrived, they'd found two that were duds. Charlotte and Odetta were beautiful girls with enormous breasts, as Joe recalled, but they both contained earthquakes that hadn't happened.

"Oh, thank you," Eileen breathed when Odetta refused to put out. Joe answered the door and paid the deliveryman and danced back to the study with the pizza box held high in the air. He spun around and around, doing a Snoopy dance of joy.

"Beer, my woman?" he asked.

"Just don't call me 'baby,'" Eileen growled.

"Hey bay-bee, beer me and be quick about it. I won't grant you the pleasures of my body later if you don't hop to," Joe grinned. Eileen narrowed her eyes at him and smiled dangerously, then fetched two beers and a pile of napkins as Joe piled cushions on the floor next to the coffee table and dug out the television remote. There was no need for utensils or plates. They dug in, and the food was glorious and the beer was fine and foamy and just right. And later, when she held his shoulders in the act of love and ground her face into his neck and muffled her cries against his skin, and when he shuddered and surrendered everything to her as he came, he knew that there was no more he wanted than this, ever.

Then it was late, and she was picking up her clothes by moonlight, and he lay in bed and pretended to be asleep and felt the icepick of loneliness and fear digging into his guts and his heart. Why wouldn't she stay? Why was she going? After the door clicked closed behind her, he turned over and dug his face into her pillow and the bed was too large and cold. Cold.

15

Westside, Colorado Springs, Colorado

Eileen, wide awake, turned off her lights and cruised in darkness the last few blocks to her house. Despite what had happened the last time she cruised without lights, despite Teddy Shaw and everything he seemed to have brought down upon her, she still enjoyed the silence and the motion. It was very late, two thirty, and she tried to soothe herself with darkness. Why had she left Joe? What was so wrong about spending the night with him, many nights, a lifetime?

Her small apartment building had no parking lot, so she pulled into an empty spot on the street two blocks from home. The night air was warm and fresh, and the stars filled the sky in the slice she could see between the trees that lined the street. She got out and stretched and tried to fake a yawn, keyed up as tight as a wire, trying to think of nothing at all and succeeding only in remembering Teddy Shaw. Damn. This night, like that one, was clear and beautiful and full of danger. There was a movement in the darkness.

A man was walking toward her from her apartment building. He had a friendly stride and was not hurrying and had his hands bent at the elbows like he had them in his pockets, but he didn't have them in his pockets. Eileen wasted no time peering at the man's chest to see if he had a gun held flat to his chest, because she knew he did. She hurled her body into a rolling fall over the grassy lawn to her right and drew her pistol as she fell. He was settling into a full-armed firing position, quick as a snake, as she came up into her own firing position and it was luck, really, that she shot first. First, and only, because he was less than twenty feet away, and that was better than any dusty Western shoot-out at high noon. He flew backward just like Teddy Shaw, and because she was using the heavier caliber Sig Sauer instead of her Ladysmith, she didn't have time to take a second shot before he fell backward on the sidewalk. He bounced once and lay still.

Eileen got to her feet, pistol held straight and steady, her mouth and throat filled with acid and dismay. She'd just killed *another* guy? She was going to have to see Gerri Matthews for years. Pete O'Brien was going to roast her like a Thanksgiving turkey. Captain Harben was going to be so angry—

A pair of headlights flipped on like eyes coming open in the night. A car engine roared and tires squealed. Eileen took one eye blink to decide that she didn't want to try to take on a car with an unknown number of occupants and guns. Her neighborhood contained a mixture of town houses and small apartment buildings. Lights were already clicking on in windows. The Sig Sauer was no Ladysmith; the sound of her shot was loud enough to wake people from their sleep. She clicked the safety on her pistol as she ran for the nearest fence. She reached the fence in five strides and scrambled up and over like a cat chased by a dog. Once over the fence, she ran straight for the back fence and scaled that one, too, taking out a pottery urn filled with flowers as she went and setting off a fusillade of barking dogs within the house. Two turns and she was behind the building and running along the carports, listening to a fading scream of engine and tires. The dogs barked for a few moments more, then settled down.

Eileen realized she had no breath left. She was panting and trembling and hot. A tiny early morning breeze touched her cheeks and her sweat-soaked hair. It took almost more courage than she had to make the final turn back on to the street where her car was parked. Gun still in hand, ready for the car or another hurrying figure, she stood silently and listened. Nothing. The dogs had quieted and the night was silent. There were lights in several windows, and far in the distance Eileen could hear sirens. As soon as the police arrived, the awakened neighbors would venture out in bathrobes and slippers, but for now the street was silent and deserted.

She walked carefully down the block, hugging the fence line and trying to avoid shrubs and more pottery. It would be just her luck to be shot by a homeowner right before she finally reached her Jeep and was safe. There was something missing. Eileen stood still and tried to calm her racing heart. What was it? She stood next to a bush that was heavy with late summer blossoms. The air was thick with the scent of roses.

Then she had it. The body was gone. The man she'd shot. He was gone. She slithered as quickly as she could to the spot where she'd shot him, looking for the pool of blood that had to be there. There was no blood. The sidewalk was clear. Eileen stood with her mouth open, staring at the ground. This wasn't possible. She pulled the clip from her gun and felt the cartridge weight. She'd shot a round. There was no way she'd imagined this. She'd hit that man in his chest and had seen him bounce backwards onto the sidewalk. But there was nothing there.

She turned and walked back to her Jeep. Her skin started to crawl with goose bumps as she fumbled out her cell phone and called in. Whatever she'd shot, it wasn't human. It was a dark man-shape, and it walked like a man, but it hadn't been a man. She waited for the patrol to come to make the night less hugely empty and menacing, to give her company, and she started to shake.

Briargate Subdivision, Colorado Springs, Colorado

Joe awoke when the door opened, and knew it was Eileen even before she called his name. The blinds that covered his bedroom window glowed with the approach of dawn.

"Come to bed," he said. He turned over and opened the comforter after she'd hurriedly stripped off her clothing. She put her knee on the mattress, and he asked no questions as she swarmed in next to him. She was naked, and her skin was cold, and she smelled funny. Like she'd been lighting off firecrackers. She shivered against him for a few minutes. He was already mostly asleep, happy that she was there, but knowing without asking that this wasn't what he wanted and needed. She was there for some other reason than love. Whatever. She was with him.

Alamosa, Colorado

Marcia spotted Alan Baxter as he left the Daylight Donuts shop, his arms full of fragrant donuts. She was waiting in the line that snaked out the door. The Rabble was here, and they were hungry. It was six o'clock and the morning sun had just sprung over the mountains to the east. A huge mountain stood like a sentinel at the end of the Sangre de Cristo Mountain Range, its snowy peak catching the sun rays—Blanca Peak, one of Colorado's famous fourteeners and a tough one to summit. Marcia was looking at the staggering view and observing the line of Rabble at the same time. Alan Baxter saw her at the same time she saw him.

"H'lo, Miss Fowler," he said, stopping.

"Good morning," Marcia said, smiling too widely in return and cursing herself internally. He was damn good-looking, but she was far beyond reacting to a good-looking face. "Picking up some donuts for your friends?"

"Yeah, you too?" Alan asked, shifting the boxes to one arm so he could dig out a set of car keys with the other. Marcia got a good waft of chocolate and hoped there would still be some chocolate donuts left when she got to the counter.

"Me, too," Marcia said, which was not precisely true. There was going to be a very quiet MUFON meeting at the Alamosa County Library this morning. Robert Carter had reserved a room yesterday and the morning's breakfast selections were going to include donuts, coffee, and Marcia Fowler. She was incredibly nervous about the meeting. Some of these people had dedicated their lives and fortunes to the paranormal, and she had no illusions about the grilling she was going to receive. She hoped the gift of donuts would help. That, and MUFON members were generally very nice people. Tough, but not mean.

"This is amazing, isn't it?" Alan said quietly. He didn't cut his eyes toward the slow-moving line and didn't have to. The Daylight Donuts sat on the highway that ran through Alamosa and the street was lined with vans festooned with colorful logos and radar dishes. There was even an enormous RV parked along the street with a forest of dishes and antennas growing from the top like weird hair. Kim's Place, the diner where Marcia had breakfast and saw Daniel Grantham, had a line out the door nearly as long as the one at the Daylight Donuts.

There were people in the streets, even this early, people with avid looks on their faces, searching looks. People who were attracted to trouble like moths to a light. Some of those people were paid for what they did; television reporters and camera crews and print journalists. Quite a few of those types were waiting patiently in the lines at Kim's Place or for morning donuts. Marcia had already abandoned the idea of trying for a latte.

"Can we get together later today?" she asked him quietly, breathing a sigh of relief when he stepped sideways so she could keep her place in line. "There's some things I think you need to know."

"Not today," Alan said, his brow furrowing. "I'm going up to Colorado Springs to work on something up there. Maybe tonight? Tomorrow morning?"

"You're working on something?" Marcia asked, and could

feel a flush climbing in her cheeks. She wanted to leap forward and grab him by his nicely pressed shirt lapels. He knew something, he did!

"Maybe," Alan said quietly, and took another step sideways with her. Now his own face looked flushed, across the nose and cheeks. "And you?"

Marcia nodded, and then she couldn't help it—she cast her eyes left and right. She was terrible at this spy business. Alan stepped forward immediately and bent his head down next to hers, as though he might give her a kiss. She caught a clear whiff of Dial soap and some light shampoo and ruthlessly stomped on her interior girl.

"Looks like human, not alien," she whispered, barely moving her lips. "Daniel Grantham thinks he might find his victims out in the dunes. They lost two hikers there five years ago, young women, never found."

Alan stepped back and nodded with interest, as though she'd told him nothing more important than the cheapest place to gas up his automobile. There was so much Marcia wanted to tell him, but she couldn't say anything here. For all she knew the murderer was the broad back of the man in front of her, stolidly waiting his chance at the chocolate donuts.

"We'll get together tonight," Alan said casually, but his eyes were blazing and intent. "Do you have a phone number where I can reach you?"

"Sure," Marcia said brightly, and dug her address book out of her purse. She quickly copied Daniel's number to a blank page at the back. She ripped the page out and felt her face grow terribly hot and flushed. She couldn't help it. It looked like a pickup.

Alan suddenly grinned at her, understanding. He dropped a broad wink at her and tucked her phone number into his back pocket with a satisfied little gesture that telegraphed to anyone watching that he was putting a "hot score" right into his pocket. Marcia giggled a little and put her hand up to her mouth, and she wasn't acting. She was a terrible actor. She couldn't help the giggle any more than she could help smelling the fresh scent of his skin. She couldn't help her wrinkles and her gray hair and the funny saggy places at her knees and elbows, and she couldn't help that what lived within her aging body was eternally dancing and light and young.

She remembered Krista Lewis the same time he did, she saw. His face drooped and he nodded and turned away without another word. She watched him go, and shuffled forward another pace in line, and tried to stiffen herself against a wave of loss and despair. Krista Lewis never had a chance to feel like this, a young thing somehow caught in an old body. After a while, Marcia convinced herself that Krista was the one to be pitied.

Special Investigations Bureau, Colorado Springs, Colorado

"You're not crazy," Rosen said economically as Eileen approached her desk. He was working on a report, and the remains of a lunch salad sat next to his terminal. The office roared with afternoon business. She sat in her chair and uncapped her latte. Her watch said twelve thirty. She'd slept through the morning with Joe, who had happily lazed in bed next to her. When she woke she found he'd sneaked a book into bed and was reading it quietly. It was titled *Earthquake,* and the cover screamed in lurid tones of red and orange. Joe's library of books was amazing. He picked up hardbacks at garage sales and used bookstores and piled them into bookshelves he'd built everywhere in his house. His choices were random and sometimes based on nothing more than the size of the book, or the color of the cover, or the good condition of the dust cover.

He'd put the book down when she awoke and showered with her. He'd kissed her and gone off to work at the same time as she. He came and went as he pleased. Just as long as he produced miracles every game time. Which, he allowed modestly, was never a problem.

"Why am I not crazy?" she asked Rosen, after taking a sip from her latte.

"Because there was hair and traces of blood on the sidewalk where the skull of your 'man-in-black' bounced after you shot him," answered Rosen. "Because we didn't find a bullet."

"My 'man-in-black'?"

"Harben's idea," Rosen said. "He's been on the phone to Sheriff Gonzalez down in the San Luis Valley about the Lewis homicide. Evidently they've got a UFO frenzy going on."

"Men-in-black should be appearing in the valley, not up here," Harben said. As usual, Eileen hadn't seen him approach. "But since your mysterious gentleman appeared to be able to absorb a nine-millimeter bullet in the chest, I felt some humor was in order."

"At least I'm not crazy," Eileen said in relief.

"But you do appear to have attracted some attention," Harben continued. "That was quite clearly a hit, and I'm quite sure it originated on Planet Earth. We checked your apartment but there were no signs of entry or explosive devices. I'd still prefer that you stayed away until we figure out what went on last night. Your neighbor, Maria, took your cat to her place. She says she takes care of her when you're away."

Eileen nodded and took an enormous gulp of her cooling coffee. *Explosive* devices? "Okay," she said weakly.

"You and Rosen will work Leetsdale, also this side of the Lewis homicide. I've assigned Peter O'Brien to your case, Eileen. Try to put it out of your mind." With that, Harben was gone.

"Put it out of your mind," Rosen said soberly as Harben disappeared into his office.

"Ho, ho," Eileen said heavily.

"What about Joe?" Rosen asked. "Did he crack those files yet?"

"Oh, yeah, I forgot to tell you!" Eileen said. "He did. He put together a—"

"Hold it," Rosen said. "Let's keep that thought until we're in your Jeep."

"Where are we going?" Eileen asked.

"No questions," Rosen said. Eileen shrugged and recapped her latte.

* * *

"What's up?" she asked crossly, as soon as they'd buckled into her Jeep. Rosen hadn't said a word the whole way to the parking lot. This kind of silence was extreme, even for Rosen.

"Let's cruise up in Garden of the Gods," he suggested. "It's a nice day."

The Garden of the Gods was a spectacular natural rock formation in the midst of Colorado Springs. The rocks were sheer and vertical, hundreds of feet high and sometimes no more than a few feet apart. Their bright red color and the deep green of the trees and shrubs that surrounded them made for breathtaking views from any angle. The garden was crisscrossed with sandy trails, perfect for a run or a leisurely hike. It was a lovely place.

The drive to the garden was only a few minutes. Rosen said nothing at all the whole time. Eileen stubbornly refused to try and make conversation. Rosen would talk when he was ready.

The parking lot at the entrance to the park was nearly full. A couple of women with a flock of brightly clad children were struggling with two double strollers. They inserted babies and bottles into one and older children into the other and strode off with expressions of exasperation and triumph as Eileen pulled into an empty slot.

The afternoon was hot and still as Eileen got out and closed her door. The air was full of the smell of pines and sun-warmed rock. In the distance, the chattering of the double-stroller moms was tiny and meaningless, like the conversation of geese.

"Beautiful day," Eileen said to Rosen. "Shall we walk? Does this mean you'll talk, now?"

Rosen's eyes glittered. He tucked a water bottle into a pouch at his belt and gestured toward the first trail. Eileen sighed. Whatever.

As soon as the trees closed in around them and the parking lot was gone, Rosen worked his big shoulders in a circle and took a swig from his water bottle.

"Here's the why for the cloak and dagger," he said. "Who can take a nine-millimeter bullet in the chest?"

"I don't know," Eileen said. "But I get the feeling you do."

"A cop can," Rosen said grimly.

There was silence. They continued walking. The stroller moms had taken another path and now there was nothing on the trail but themselves and a man with a dog, further ahead.

"Kevlar vest?"

"Something like that. That's the worst option, is a cop. Here's another one. Who else has Kevlar?"

"The military," Eileen said. The day was hot and she was sweating, but the sweat suddenly felt chilly on her forehead.

"I'm not sleeping at my place tonight either," Rosen said. "Harben and I had breakfast this morning. I'd gotten most of the way there, but he had more arguments than me."

"This has to do with the Leetsdale case," Eileen said. "And the Lewis case."

"That's what Harben thinks. Me, too. So here's the next question, if supposition number one is true. What did you do that makes you worthy of a hit?"

"I didn't do anything," Eileen said.

"You tied together Leetsdale and the Lewis girl," Rosen said. "Water?"

Eileen took the bottle and drank it gratefully. The late August sun felt like the height of summer. There was no wind and no thunderstorm clouds along the Front Range. This was a certain sign of a change in weather. By tomorrow there might be a solid bank of rain clouds to the west. Or it might snow a foot by midnight. Indian summer was unpredictable.

"I found out something else, too," she said. "Or at least, Joe did." She explained the earthquake simulations in a few minutes. Rosen stood motionless, his face calm and remarkably unsweaty. When she explained about the New Madrid earthquake, Rosen shifted and blinked his eyes.

"This is not good," he said after she finished.

"No, it isn't," Eileen said. "Though we found a couple of duds among the pictures Leetsdale stored. I think this one has to be a dud, too. We still don't know why Leetsdale died. But how could anyone know what Joe's discovered? How could they even know about Joe?"

"Nobody knows about you and Joe but Harben and me," Rosen said. "And Lucy Giometti." This was true. Eileen, as discreet as a cat, didn't discuss her lover with anyone in the department. Not even her friend Gary Hilyer knew Joe Tanner's name. Hilyer, who'd been a reporter longer than Eileen had been alive, knew she had a lover. He'd tried mercilessly to find out who was putting that creamy, satisfied expression on her face, as he put it, but even he had been unsuccessful.

They crested a mild rise on the trail, coming into an open space amongst the scrub oak. The rise held a breathtaking view of the spires of the garden. The man with a dog had paused here and was sitting on a bench with a sketchpad on his knee; his face turned dreamily to the view. Eileen looked at him suspiciously as she and Rosen walked by, but he didn't move his head.

"So it's probably Lewis and Leetsdale, which sounds like a floorwax," Eileen said. "If that's true, then—"

"Then your contact, Alan Baxter, might also be in danger," Rosen said casually. "Harben got a hold of Gonzalez. Evidently Mr. Baxter is on his way up to see you, so he'll be in town sometime tonight. We'll talk to him then. What's the matter?"

Eileen stood still, her hands clenched together. The view from this vantage point, further down the slope from the dog man and his sketchpad, was still stunning. She saw nothing beautiful in it. She wanted to turn and run for her car, to find her father and make sure he was safe. And if she did so, she'd have to explain to Dave Rosen about the real Eileen Reed. The abandoned Eileen Reed, the adopted one, the one who was so worthless her own mother . . .

She made a strangled sound in her throat. Rosen stood calmly, watching her. She cursed Teddy Shaw in her heart, cursed him for bringing her to Gerri Matthews, for breaking her eggshell of a life into a thousand pieces that couldn't be brought back together again. She had to stop trying to paste all the ruined pieces into some sort of covering. The thought brought a certain relief, in the midst of roaring embarrassment.

"Oh, shit," she said, when she could get spit back into her mouth. She looked Rosen squarely in the face and met his undemanding eyes. "I have to tell you something."

"He's related to you, isn't he?" Rosen said immediately.

Eileen burst into laughter. She covered her mouth with both hands, but the laughter kept coming. Rosen stood without smiling, waiting for her to stop. She felt sure that if she started weeping hysterically, he'd slap her with the same level demeanor. That more than anything caused her laughter to dry up to a stream of giggles.

"Sorry," she said finally, wiping tears from the corners of her eyes. "I just was all prepared to tell you this incredible secret, and—"

"I saw his picture from the background report I did. He looks just like you," Rosen said. "Is he your dad?"

This, on top of everything else, was too much. Eileen held up her hand politely, then turned and stumbled behind the nearest shrub. There she threw up everything in her stomach, her latte, her breakfast cereal, what appeared to be last night's pizza. She wouldn't have been surprised to see a lunch from grade school.

Finally, an endless time later, she sank back onto her heels and spat a couple of times to clear her mouth. Rosen nudged her elbow and handed her the water bottle. She rinsed her mouth and then drank gratefully. She handed the bottle back to him and scooped dry, reddish soil over her vomit.

"Sorry," she said, standing up.

"It's okay," Rosen said, with a shrug of his shoulders. "We should go back, though. We need to make sure we get Mr. Baxter into safety as soon as he gets here."

"Let's keep him Mr. Baxter to everyone but you, for now," Eileen said. "I'm not ready for more than you."

"Well, Harben knows I think," Rosen said. His dusky face suddenly looked darker, and Eileen realized he was flushing. This was a first. She looked at him curiously, then understood.

"You were talking about me!" she accused him. He looked down and blinked rapidly and the flush increased. She laughed again, but this was her old Eileen laugh, a good one from the belly. "Gossiping like girls. What did you talk about?"

"Nothing, except that Alan Baxter sure isn't your dad from Wyoming. Harben met him, remember, when you got promoted to detective."

"Oh, yeah," Eileen said, and felt a longing like a pain for her mom and dad. They'd been puffed up like spring mushrooms when she got her new badge and had insisted on taking her to dinner up in Denver at some fancy place in LoDo they'd discovered on one of their trips to the National Western Stock Show. The dinner was extravagant and enormously expensive, and she drank too much champagne and spent the whole trip home sleeping on her mom's shoulder.

"They're my adopted parents," she said sadly. "I never knew my dad. I thought he was dead, or something. My mom took me away and never told me how to find him before she died. It was a big weird coincidence that we met that way."

"Stuff like that happens sometimes," Rosen said. His face had lost his unexpected flush. He held out the water bottle again and she took it and drank deeply. She handed it back and nodded without a word. The water was his version of a hug, a reassurance, and an entire conversation that they would never have about the subject of Eileen and her father. Rosen would never pry, never tell Peter O'Brien over a few beers at the pub about Eileen's past.

"Thanks," she said, and knew she needed to say nothing else.

"Let's get back and find Mr. Baxter," Rosen said, and turned to walk back up the trail.

"Where are we going to take him?" Eileen thought to ask, after they passed the man with the dog. She could see the parking lot at the end of the trail ahead of them. The stroller moms' van was still in the parking lot but many of the other cars had gone. The lunch crowd had gone back to work.

"I think we should take him to Joe's house," Rosen said. "If you can handle it. I want to see Joe's simulation. And nobody knows about Joe except us."

Eileen tried to shrug nonchalantly. She felt like an iron bar had just been driven side to side through her shoulder blades.

"Great, I'll just get this all over at once," she muttered, and Rosen surprised her with what sounded suspiciously like a snort of laughter.

16

"Hey, Eileen, take a look at these—" Joe Tanner stopped abruptly. She wasn't alone. There were two additional people on his pocket-sized porch. One of them he recognized; Dave Rosen, her partner. The other was a much older man, tall and white-haired and somehow familiar-looking.

"Hi, Joe," Eileen said. Her face was pale. When she was very tired or very stressed, he could see freckles scattered across her nose, remnants of a childhood spent outdoors.

"Come on in," Joe said. He dropped the books he had in his hands to his mail-collector table and put his arms around her as she stepped inside. She came into his arms woodenly, but she didn't push away. He didn't move from his doorway. She smelled of breath mints, which she usually scorned, and oldish Eileen-sweat. Something had happened today.

"Can we come in, Joe?" Rosen asked. "Somebody tried to kill Eileen last night." As usual, Rosen said a lot with very few words. The tall white-haired man flinched in surprise and his mouth dropped open.

"What?" he said, too loudly. "You didn't tell me!"

"Let them in, Joe," Eileen said, pushing away from his shoulder. She had spent only a second or two hugging him, but her color was back and the freckles were gone. Joe backed up, and in a few seconds Rosen had closed and locked the front door. Joe's mind was still full of earthquakes and the Mississippi and the New Madrid fault line. He had trouble coming to grips with what Rosen had just said.

"I was grilling brauts for supper," he said stupidly. "Can we still do that?"

Eileen laughed and the good color came back even further into her face.

"We sure can," she said. "Let's go into the kitchen and break out some beer and we'll all fill each other in."

"Somebody tried to *kill* you?" the white-haired man said. Eileen's color was good but this man's face was paling. Joe wondered, not for the first time, who the hell he was. Then what he was saying sank in.

"Somebody tried to *kill* you?" he said, turning to Eileen.

"Yeah, that's one of the reasons we're here," she said, shrugging her shoulders as though the topic held little interest for her. "But first things first. We need to sit down and talk. Then eat, because I'm starving."

Joe led the little group to his kitchen. The table, a slab of oak, sat in what would be a breakfast nook in an ordinary person's house. He'd paved one blank wall with shelves so *that* side was a solid mass of books. Two other sides of the nook faced into his mostly unused kitchen and the family room. Sliding glass doors led to his deck and a smallish backyard. His propane grill was on and smoking off the remains of the last thing he'd cooked. Joe believed a good grill scrubbing consisted of turning up the flame really high and waiting fifteen minutes. The smoke from the grill spiraled into the late afternoon air, hot and still as a held breath. There would be a change of weather later, he was sure of it.

Tonight, he was planning to grill fat Polish brauts and smother them in sauerkraut and mustard. He'd also picked up some potato salad at the deli and some green salad ingredients that he hoped Eileen would want to assemble into something good. After days of pizza, he wanted to make it up to her.

Luckily, he always bought his food in family packs. What he didn't eat tonight he was planning to freeze for later. He'd be able to feed his guests.

"Beer?" he asked the strange man, opening the refrigerator. He fetched beer and brought out a bottle of distilled water for Rosen without asking. He still had the remains of the last six-pack Rosen had brought over. If Rosen hadn't been Eileen's partner, he supposed he could be friends with the man. But he was certain Rosen was secretly in love with Eileen. Joe couldn't imagine any man failing to fall in love with Eileen. He handed the distilled water to Rosen and sat down with his own beer. The other man, still unnamed to him, sat down.

Eileen took a healthy swig of her beer, eyes closed, as though she were taking medicine, and seated herself. Rosen opened his distilled water and headed toward Joe's back deck.

"I'll check on the grill," he said, and disappeared neatly out the door.

"Okay, then," Eileen said. She took Joe's hand in her own and looked into his eyes. Her freckles suddenly stood out on her face again. "This is going to be the hardest part for me, so I'll just get it out of the way. This is Alan Baxter, and he's my father."

"But," Joe said. He realized Eileen was gripping his hand far too hard.

"I met him two days ago, and I've never seen him since I was three," Eileen said. Her voice was small and husky and determined. "I was adopted when I was four and all I've ever wanted to be was my mom and dad's child."

"You still are," the man—Eileen's father—said in a calm voice. Joe looked at him and saw the resemblance, the feeling that he knew this man suddenly understood. Alan Baxter had Eileen's cheekbones and the way her eyes were placed, although his eyes were a disconcerting yellowish-brown color and hers were blue. The height, the long and sensitive hands, all were hers as well.

Eileen stared at the man—Alan Baxter—levelly. "I know," she said coolly.

"How did you meet—wait, is this Krista Lewis's friend? The one who wanted to talk to Jim Leetsdale?"

"Yeah," Eileen said, and grimaced. "I should have told you then, but I couldn't believe it myself. I'm sorry, Joe."

"It's okay," Joe said automatically, squeezing her hand. That's what one said, anyway, when someone apologized. It's okay, even if it's not. Even if it means that the person you love with all your heart doesn't love you enough to seek your consolation, your understanding, your help. It's okay, but it's not. It hurts like hell.

"So Mr. Baxter and I found ourselves involved in different sides of the same case," Eileen continued with a rush, obviously relieved to move to safer ground. "He's been visiting friends in the San Luis Valley and we've been working our case up here."

"Then someone tried to kill you?" Alan Baxter asked. "My God, what happened?"

Rosen slid the glass door open and observed the grouping at the table. He nodded at the plate of brauts Joe had set on the kitchen counter.

"Brauts," he said.

"Someone tried to shoot me when I went home last night," Eileen said, standing and fetching the plate. She gave it to Rosen who disappeared toward the grill. Joe also stood and moved to the refrigerator. He started pulling out condiments and side dishes.

"They must have been waiting for you," he said. "You left here late."

"I think they were," Eileen said. She started collecting plates and napkins and flatware with the easy movements of a person who knew where everything was stored. Joe glanced at Alan Baxter and saw a flat, speculative look in his eyes. Alan was looking directly at him. For a moment he felt absurdly like flushing.

"Anyway," Eileen continued. "A man came along like he was just out for a walk, which would have worked at ten or so but not at two a.m. I think he was going to shoot me with a silenced gun, then they were going to bundle me into the car they had waiting and drive off. But I saw his gun and startled him enough to outdraw him, and shot him right in the chest."

She set her dishes down at the table with a clatter and looked down at her hands. "So I spent the next second or two wondering how it was I ended up shooting two men inside of two months, and then his friends came roaring down the block in a car. I jumped a fence near me and circled the block, and by the time I worked my way back to my Jeep, the whole crew was gone, including the guy I shot. There had to be two, I know that. I don't know how many more there were."

The sliding glass door opened, sending in a gust of grilling braut that sent the juice into Joe's mouth in an instant.

"Captain Harben thinks someone put a hit on Eileen because she tied together Jim Leetsdale and Krista Lewis," Rosen said, sliding the door shut behind him. "So if they wanted to hit her, they might want to hit me too, and maybe Mr. Baxter, here."

Joe set a pot of potato salad down on the table.

"But nobody wants to hit me?" he asked. "No, of course not. Nobody knows about me, do they?" He looked at Eileen. Something heavy suddenly went rolling off his chest.

"I didn't want—" she said, then stopped abruptly. She didn't have to say anything. For once his Eileen's face was as open as the sky. He would bet his life, that moment, that she loved him.

"Could someone have followed us?" Alan Baxter asked. Eileen's expression closed like a set of blinds rattling down.

"That's why we're in a division car," she said. "Rosen and I left our cars at the motor pool. We're having your Bronco towed there, too. Harben is having all three swept for bugs."

Alan flinched and his eyebrows drew together.

"They're going to search my car?" he asked. "I didn't give permission—I mean, I don't want them to do that!"

"Drugs?" Rosen asked. "Should we have asked?"

"No drugs, for godssake, just my shotgun and my .357," Alan Baxter said. "Is that illegal in Colorado? Do I have to have permits, or something?"

"We have reciprocity with Wyoming," Eileen said easily.

"I know they have Vermont-style carry there. You don't have the .357 in a spring-loaded clip or anything, do you?"

"No, but it's loaded," Alan said miserably. "And I have hundreds of flies—for my fishing, you know. Thousands, probably. They're all sorted and I tied them all and if you open any of my boxes in a breeze, they'll blow away."

Joe started laughing. He couldn't help it. Sometimes one thing or another just struck him as funny and not a thing on earth could keep him from laughing. Alan, Eileen, and Rosen all turned to look at him. He struggled for a moment, trying to stop.

"They're going to sweep his car for bugs," he explained, and then he was off, laughing like a fool. Nobody laughed with him. They looked at him like a panel of solemn judges, and that made him laugh harder. "Let me check the brauts," he offered, and ducked out the sliding glass door before he really lost control.

Outside, in the still afternoon air, he kept on laughing. The brauts sizzled and popped on the grill. Rosen had placed them neatly in a row, too close together for Joe's taste. He took the fork and moved them apart, checking to make sure the fat juices didn't start a fire and char the food. Suddenly, he wanted a dozen ears of butter and sugar corn, still in their green jackets, to lay on the grill. That would have made a perfect addition to his little feast. The door slid open behind him and he didn't need to turn around to know it was Eileen.

"They smell delicious," Eileen said awkwardly.

"Of course they do, they are my specialty," Joe said grandly, turning around and waving his barbecue fork in the air. Eileen shut the door behind her and stepped towards him on the deck.

"I have more to tell you about, well, me," she said.

"Okay," Joe said evenly. "I wish you trusted me enough to tell me."

"I couldn't," she whispered thickly, not looking at him. "I will now, I promise. But not now, and not here. Can you wait for me?"

Her words hung in the air, as still and moveless as the barbecue smoke. Eileen's face reddened and then paled again.

She looked tired and unhappy and grim. Joe lowered the barbecue fork and held his free arm out to her. She came into his
arms as neatly and quickly as a nesting bird.

"I'll wait for you," he said, holding her and keeping the
tines of the barbecue fork out of her hair. "Don't worry about
me, my love. Never worry about me." For a moment her
shoulders trembled under his hands and then she was still.

"Thank you," she whispered into his neck. "I can't lose
you. I just can't."

"Not a chance, woman," Joe said, with mock ferocious-
ness. "I would make love to you right here, but people would
talk. The neighbors. Your partner. Your dad. And the weenies
would burn."

Eileen loosened her arms and let him go. He turned to
check on the brauts with his barbecue fork. She stood next to
him, and he stole a quick glance. She looked tired still, but her
color was high and her eyes were bright. Joe Tanner magic, he
thought smugly, and flipped a braut so exuberantly he nearly
tossed it onto the deck.

"Wanna make a salad while I finish these?" he asked. "I
bought the ingredients but I haven't had time today."

"I will," Eileen said. "We've still got a lot to talk about. So
hurry in."

Joe turned his brauts and contemplated the depths of his
grill and listened as the door slid open and shut behind him.
Things would be well, he thought to himself, all manner of
things would be well. A man should always quote Robert
Burns while grilling weenies. He began to whistle.

Peterson Air Force Base, Colorado Springs, Colorado

Jacob Mitchell sat quietly, words and figures on pieces of
paper in front of him. He sat with his hands on them, his face
turned dreamily to the open window where the stillness of late
afternoon made the sky look like a depthless lake of blue.
Everything was ready. Everything was prepared.

"Martial law," he said to himself, relishing the sound of his
own voice in his ears. He had an incredible speaking voice, as

smooth and rich as butter. He'd need every talent he possessed in the coming days.

He'd been working to this day, this coming moment, all his life. He understood the joke in the phrase *public service* as soon as he started reading history at the age of seven. Politics in this country, America, was the only path to real power. Some of the smarter Presidents had shown quite clearly that laws did not apply to them, even the most ordinary ones.

All of the Presidents, however, bent their necks to the Constitution and meekly walked out of office after their time of service, leaving the country to flounder through an election and a new administration. Mitchell knew an administration with twenty years of experience would achieve remarkable prosperity. All it took was for one man, one President, to provide stable leadership. The country desperately needed it.

Mitchell was the man to help his country, and he knew it. His staff knew it. The media seemed to know it, too. He consistently received favorable, even fawning, press. Yet America persisted in their silly bread-and-circuses elections, where the stupid electorate voted again and again for the wrong men.

"Martial law," he said to himself. That was the answer, of course. There was no voting during martial law. There was no Constitution. There was no court system, no due process, no free press. During martial law, there was something as good as a king in America, a man whose very word was law. That man was the FEMA director. And the Western District FEMA director was Jacob Mitchell. All he needed was a disaster. A disaster large enough to require martial law. Once imposed, there would be no turning back.

His hands moved on the papers. Here, under his hands, was the plan that would catapult him into the highest office in the world. He knew it would work. And nothing on earth could stop him.

Briargate Subdivision, Colorado Springs, Colorado

"They didn't open anything in your Bronco," Rosen said, pressing the off button on his cell phone. "They did an electronics search only. Jean says thanks for the warning about the guns. No bugs in any of the cars. No bugs in our apartments."

"These guys are very careful," Eileen mused.

They were all seated in Joe's living room. Eileen was stuffed full of brauts and potato salad and sauerkraut and now all she wanted to do was take a nap. She was on the short couch leaning back into Joe's shoulder. The other couch, the longer one, held Rosen and Alan Baxter. They too had the look of serious food overload. The beer hadn't helped. The sun was nearly at the edge of the Front Range and rays flooded the kitchen and laid bars of gold on the living room carpet. The weather hadn't broken yet; if anything, it was even more still and breathless than an hour ago. Eileen struggled to keep her eyes open.

"I'm going to make coffee," Joe announced. "Then, when we all wake up, I think you guys should see my simulation. I've been doing some reading too. Maybe everything will start fitting together."

Eileen sat back into the couch cushions as Joe went to the kitchen. Joe selected his furniture the same way he chose his clothing, with regard for maximum comfort. Eileen had glanced at the tag on the sofa once, a long time ago, and noticed a very expensive brand. The side tables were junk, though, wood veneer over particleboard and already peeling up at the edges. No need for coasters in Joe's house.

The sharp whir of the coffee grinder made Alan Baxter jump. Eileen looked at him, and for a moment his image wavered. She lost her grip on Alan Baxter, interesting subject in a homicide investigation, and saw her father sitting on a couch not five feet from her, looking back at her. Something filled her mouth like water, a taste that felt exactly like fear. But it couldn't be fear. What did she have to fear from this man?

"I'm staying at Sam and Beth Williams's ranch this week," Alan said. "I might have something interesting to add to Joe's simulation. I talked to a local—no wait, I don't think she's local. She's a schoolteacher like me, retired, and she told me the local opinion is that Krista was murdered by someone inside the dunes."

"Raped and murdered," Rosen said. "Got the preliminary coroner report today. No semen, bastard wore a condom. Maybe he thought that would save him, but they found a couple strands of hair that weren't hers, and she showed rape injury. So if we find the guy, we might be able to nail him."

"Raped," Alan said, in a lost and horrified voice. "Oh, Krista." He put his face into his hands and bent over his knees. Joe's coffee maker gurgled in the kitchen and Joe walked back into the room, looking cheerful.

"Coffee soon," he promised, then looked at Alan in concern. "What's wrong?"

"Sorry," Rosen said to Alan. "I forgot you knew her."

"Krista Lewis was raped before she was murdered," Eileen said flatly.

Joe bent next to Alan and put a hand on his shoulder.

"I'm sorry, man," he said. "Hang on."

"I'm okay," Alan said, his voice muffled. "It's just a shock, that's all."

Eventually he sat up and took his hands from his face. His eyes were reddened and looked tired. He nodded at Joe, who patted his shoulder and moved back to the kitchen. Eileen sat on the couch and felt both awkward and cruel. But she simply could not get up and go to this man and give him a hug or even Joe's reassuring pat.

"Coffee," Joe announced. "Hot as hell and loaded with caffeine."

"That's the wrap," Joe said, borrowing an Eileen phrase. He drained the last swallow of coffee from his cup. "The New Madrid fault line, a subject in which I am swiftly becoming an expert. Did you know the Mississippi actually ran backward for a period of hours, right near the fault?"

"That's hard to believe," Alan Baxter said, his cup held carefully in both hands. He and Rosen sat in kitchen chairs. It occurred to Eileen that since Joe's laptop was portable they could view his simulation anywhere, but she didn't suggest moving. Joe's study contained his Web machine as well as what seemed like an endless array of other machines, mostly computers. Books lined the walls in every direction and stood in stacks on the floor. If a house had a heart, this was it.

"There's lots more, stuff I can hardly believe myself," Joe said. "I got a bunch of books from the library today. Let's take the San Andreas, for example. Everybody knows about Los Angeles and San Francisco, right?"

"Right," Eileen murmured.

"Well, turns out San Andreas is a less dangerous fault than the New Madrid. The San Andreas is fractured, like a plate with cracks all the way through it. The fractures of the San Andreas fault run right under downtown L.A., it's true, but they also act as an absorber for earthquakes."

"An absorber?" Rosen asked.

"A buffer, I guess I should say. The earthquake breaks up into the fault lines and doesn't continue its large-scale wave-form. Like a wave hitting a series of rocks. It breaks up the power so the wave that moves through the rocks is disorganized and weak."

"There's no break in the New Madrid?" Alan Baxter asked.

"No small fractures. When the New Madrid went off in 1812, people in Boston lost china from their shelves. In Denver, water sloshed out of those pitchers everyone used to have in their room. You know." Joe made curving motions with his hands, trying to trace a shape.

"A pitcher and basin for washing, like in the Old West movies," Alan said. "In *Denver?*"

"Denver. At the fault line, in New Madrid and Little Prairie, entire homes dropped into cracks that opened up in the ground. The river boiled and turned dark in seconds from all the silt and mud. Trees that had sunk to the bottom of the river shot up into the air like they'd been wired with explosives." Joe pushed the button that made the New Madrid happen in bright cheerful colors on his little laptop screen.

"Trees fell. Lots of people scrambled onto the trees since they were large enough to span the cracks that were opening in the earth. There was a groaning sound, and shrieks, and sulfur fumes filled the air. What an incredible night that must have been, right? No television, no radio, just townspeople running away from the riverbanks and trying to hold on to trees. People were sucked into quicksand that opened up near the river, and all sorts of small boats were pulled into whirlpools or buried by collapsing riverbanks.

"Hey," he continued, still staring at the laptop screen. "I could probably figure out how many people would die today, just the way we figure deaths from nuclear blasts. There were only three thousand people living in the Mississippi Valley in 1811. I don't know how many today. Millions, though. I need to program in the intensity at ground zero, and decreasing rings of intensity as the distance from the quake increases. This could tell us where the worst damage would be . . ." Joe trailed off and tucked his bare feet under him.

"Wait a minute," Alan said. "Let's get back to the topic, here. How does this affect Krista Lewis?"

"Leetsdale was going to expose the earthquake prediction project, that's what we think," Eileen said. "And somehow Krista was a part of that."

"Krista and the Great Sand Dunes," Rosen said.

"Hey, Joe, was there anything in Leetsdale's files about the Great Sand Dunes?"

Joe, staring raptly at his laptop screen, started in his chair. "What?"

"Leetsdale's files. Great Sand Dunes," Eileen said, with amusement. Joe would be gone for hours if they let him, and when he came back he'd have programmed the computer to show damage in three-dimensional color.

"No, not that I can remember," Joe said. His eyes were drawn back to his laptop screen as though he were hypnotized.

"What about anything odd, anything out of place?" Rosen asked patiently.

"Oh, yeah, hey," Joe said. "There was one thing. Leetsdale kept one picture that wasn't a simulation description at all."

"What was it?" Alan asked.

"Well, it was kind of weird. Among all those girlie pictures he had a black and white image of a guy named Nikola Tesla."

"Who's Nikola Tesla?" Rosen asked.

"He's a famous guy here in Colorado Springs, and he

should be famous around the world. He was an inventor. He invented AC power, did you know that?"

"That was Thomas Edison," Alan said.

"Nope," Joe replied. "Edison invented the lightbulb. Tesla and Thomas Edison were huge rivals. Edison invented DC and Tesla invented AC, and now everybody uses AC power. And whom do people know? Edison. Tesla sold his patents to Westinghouse so he could beat Edison Power. He did, but he died broke and unknown in some fleabag hotel in New York City."

"Was he from around here?" Alan asked, looking bewildered. "Or was he from the sand dunes?"

"No," Joe said, his laptop forgotten. "He was born in Croatia and emigrated to America when he was young. He spent a summer here in Colorado Springs in 1899 doing experiments. That's why they had the Tesla museum here. I wandered in one day and became an instant Teslaphile."

"A Tesla *file?*" Alan asked.

"A Teslaphile, with a p-h," Eileen said with a grin. "As in, the opposite of a phobe. A really big fan."

"Tesla was very strange, I mean *very*." Joe laughed. "He blew the entire power structure in the city one night with his experiments. He used to invite people over for these crazy experiments with electricity. I've seen a picture of him sitting in the midst of a tiny lightning storm that he created. He's reading a book, calm as could be. Anybody else would be afraid he would become a crispy roasted critter, but not Tesla."

"What does this have to do with the earthquake simulations?" Rosen asked. "Why did Leetsdale put Tesla's picture in his files?"

"His picture, his name, and a latitude and longitude point," Joe said. "Hey, I have some books on him that I bought at the Tesla Museum. They were those kind of off-the-wall books, you know, published in somebody's basement. I never got around to reading them. Let me see if I can find them." He rose from his chair and left the room, coffee cup in one hand.

"So what does this have to do with the Great Sand Dunes?" Alan asked.

"I don't know," Eileen said slowly, feeling a tingle run like a cat's paws up her spine.

"Hey, Joe," Rosen called out. "Where was the lat and longitude point?"

"I didn't plot it," Joe shouted back. From his voice, he was somewhere in his breakfast nook, rummaging through his wall of books. "I would have, but I got sucked into this New Madrid thing."

"Can we plot it?" Alan asked.

There was silence from the other room.

"Joe?" Eileen called. There was no response, and the total silence made the hair on Eileen's arms brush up in an instant. "Joe?" she called again. She started to stand up, her hand going to her gun, when Joe appeared in the doorway.

His face was dead white, pale as if he'd not only seen a ghost, but become one. The handle of his empty coffee cup was clenched in his hand so tightly the knuckles stood out in sharp relief. He was holding some documents in his hands, all large and unwieldy and dusty. They were obviously home-printed, with cheap binding and faded colors.

"What's the matter?" Alan asked.

Joe said nothing. He turned the top document in his hands around so that it faced Eileen, Rosen, and Alan.

After a few moments that felt like an eternity, Eileen found her voice.

"Nikola Tesla's Earthquake Machine," she read calmly.

"It's getting dark outside," Joe said. He was standing at the edge of his study window, looking through the blinds. He was looking for strange cars, or people behaving oddly, just in case Eileen, Rosen, and Alan had been followed after all and the killers were waiting for darkness for their strike. The sun had set over the Front Range long ago, and the long twilight was starting to draw down towards full dark. The weather, still and breathless until now, was beginning to change. Little puffs of air, like breaths, were starting to gust in the trees. The temperature was starting to drop rapidly. If Joe had been alone, he would have had the television on long before now,

watching the weather reports. As it was, he felt out of touch. There was a big storm coming, and he wanted to see the satellite pictures.

"I feel like those vampire hunters in Dracula," Alan said. "Worried about the dark."

"I *am* worried about the dark," Eileen said. "If we're right about this, we're dealing with something very dangerous."

"Big enough for the Government to send in assassins?" Alan asked soberly. "Like what happened to Eileen?"

Joe shook his head, still staring out the window.

"I don't think so," he said. "The Government, big-G Government, doesn't really exist. You could no more order some Fort Carson soldiers to come kill us than you could order Eileen and Rosen here to go kill someone. Special Forces, SEALs, Delta Force, they're professionals. They don't kill Americans on command, they are Americans. They have a code of honor as long as your arm."

"Well, what about the CIA, then?" Alan asked stubbornly. "Or the FBI? Like what they did to those religious dialogues at Waco, Texas. That sure wasn't friendly. Or honorable."

"It was a total fuckup, is what it was," Rosen said. Eileen was nodding in agreement, Joe saw.

"*People* in government can screw up," she said. "People can be bad. Our government can do bad things by stupidity or accident, like a big, dumb kid. But there are too many good people in government for anything really bad to happen, at least not for long."

"Japanese-Americans during World War Two," Rosen said.

"Sure, and slavery, and the eradication of the buffalo to starve the American Indians," Eileen said. "Really bad things happen. But we aren't bad by design, like the Nazis or the Communists. Eventually, things get straightened out. There are enough good people to fix the bad things."

"I wish I had your optimism," Alan said. "So you don't think your men-in-black were government men?" Eileen was already shaking her head.

"No, actually, I think they *are* government men," she said.

"Okay, now I'm totally confused," Alan said.

Joe left his place by the window and came to sit by Alan on the long couch. He saw the remote control to the television and suppressed the urge to pick it up.

"I agree with Eileen, I guess. Big Government can't do this," Joe said, clasping his hands in front of his knees to keep them away from the remote. "But little government can. A small project could get away with murder. Or a small project could do something really, really good." He looked over at Eileen and saw her looking gravely back at him. She didn't smile. They'd saved the world, Eileen and he and some little government people. No one would ever know, except for a tiny few, what they'd done.

"True," Eileen said. "You can keep a huge secret if you have a small enough group."

"The Manhattan Project," Rosen offered.

"The Roswell saucer crash," Joe said.

"Yes, and the missile defense program," Alan suggested. "I heard that it was really already deployed—are you all right?"

"Must have swallowed a bug," Joe said, choking. He cleared his throat and sat up. "Where did you hear *that?*"

"From Krista," Alan said sadly. "She thought that there might be something in Colorado that dealt with missile defense, because of NORAD and all. She read some Internet stuff that suggested we might really be able to shoot down nuclear weapons in flight. But what she was looking for was environmental pollutants any way she could find them."

"Well," Joe said with an effort, "I think if our earthquake people are responsible for Krista Lewis and Jim Leetsdale, then they might be a government-funded project."

"A top-secret, special-access-word project," Eileen said. "Small enough to hide murder, if necessary."

"Rape and murder," Alan reminded them. His face flushed across the cheekbones and the bridge of his nose. "And I don't know why we're still just sitting here talking. We need to get up and go there."

"Where?" Joe asked in puzzlement.

"There," Alan said angrily, pointing with his finger at the Colorado map Joe had spread across the coffee table an hour before. Directly in the middle of the Great Sand Dunes, at latitude 37 degrees, 47 minutes and 50 seconds and longitude 105 degrees, 33 minutes and 20 seconds, Rosen had drawn a small and careful X. The latitude and longitude points stored in the picture of Nikola Tesla.

"And what do you propose to do there?" Eileen asked gently. "Have us walk in and arrest these people, if they're there? For what?"

"For murder," Alan said. "You said you had hair from Krista's murderer. Arrest everybody and DNA everybody and then you have your killer."

"Not a bad plan," Rosen said, deadpan.

"Yeah, if we lived in *China*," Eileen said. "We can't do that, Mr. Baxter. We have to have some sort of probable cause and we have to have a warrant. We might be able to get one from the sheriff down there, Gonzalez, but—"

"We can get one, I bet," Alan said. "He's a friend of mine."

"First of all, we have to figure out what they're doing. Then we can figure out why they've decided to kill people," Joe said patiently. "I still think they're causing earthquakes with a Tesla machine."

"I still don't know about this Tesla machine idea," Rosen said. "I can't figure out why nobody knows about the earthquake thing. If it really exists, everybody should know about it."

"You didn't even know about Tesla until an hour ago," Joe said with a shrug. "And we're sitting under electric lights powered by his invention. We run our *world* on AC power, invented by Nikola Tesla. And not one of you knew that."

"So call it the Edison Earthquake machine," Rosen said reasonably. "Why doesn't the world know about it?"

"I think I can answer that," Alan said.

Rosen made a go-ahead gesture.

"Because Tesla's documents got into the government's hands, somehow," Alan said. "That's the answer. That's why this is a government project."

"So what about these home-published books?"

"Based on rumors about the earthquake machine," Alan said. "Just like the books you can read about the Roswell saucer crash. No proof, just rumor."

"I can't believe a government project would be assigned to create earthquakes," Eileen protested. "Anyway, why? They're not holding anything for ransom, they're not making money or advancing any kind of agenda. What would be the point?"

"I don't know," Joe said stubbornly. "It's a gut feeling sort of thing. I'm going to check my printer. Maybe there's something in the reports I'm printing out."

Joe's ancient laser printer, beloved and reliable, was also as stinky as a very old dog. When he started to print documents from the Web on the sand dunes and Nikola Tesla, the whole group had fled his study. No one seemed inclined to go back to the hard wooden chairs after sitting on Joe's couches.

When he returned from his study, a thick handful of papers in his hand, the television was on.

"Hey!" Joe said happily. "I wanted to do that hours ago."

Eileen shrugged her shoulders guiltily and patted the couch next to her. The nine o'clock news was on and the headlines were all about the Colorado earthquake cleanup. From there the newscasters moved on to the adorable baby eagles at the Cheyenne Mountain Zoo, then to a birthday celebration of a one hundred-year-old woman in Nebraska.

"Slow news day," Rosen said.

"The Great Sand Dunes are made of ground quartz, did you know that? And they didn't exist ten thousand years ago?" Joe read from his papers. "Wow. There's some talk here about something called the Taos Hum, or something. It's this weird noise, supposed to originate in the dunes, or maybe down in New Mexico, nobody knows."

"Probably the earthquake machine," Eileen said absently, her eyes on the television. "It's got to make some sort of noise to trigger an earthquake."

"Weather," Rosen said. Everyone shut up and leaned towards the set.

Joe felt a sense of satisfaction, seeing the long comber of clouds approaching the Front Range. A huge front had moved in from the California coastline and was making its way across the country. Often this meant sunny weather in the Front Range and a Midwest buried in rain or snow, but sometimes the front combined with a wet low-pressure system moving up from the Gulf of Mexico. This front swept up from New Mexico and had a nickname that sent a shiver down every Coloradan's backbone.

"An Albuquerque low," Rosen, Eileen, and Joe said at the same time. The weatherman gave a wolfish smile on the television screen.

"It's an Albuquerque low, folks," he said. "Get up early tomorrow. Give yourself plenty of time to get to work in the morning, and be sure to check our listings for closures."

Joe clicked the remote and the set went dark.

"What's an Albuquerque low?" Alan asked.

"Big storm, heap big snow," Joe said. "My gut has been telling me all day there's something coming in. I hope there aren't any summer campers left in the woods."

"Good thing it's Wednesday and not Saturday," Rosen said. "Or we'd lose some hikers."

"I still want to go to the sand dunes," Alan said stubbornly.

"Not tonight, you don't," Joe said. "Where do you live?"

"Pinedale, Wyoming," Alan said. "It's a nice little town at the foot of the Wind River Mountain Range and yes, I know all about snow. You guys live in the tropics compared to Wyoming. What's a little snow? I want to *do* something."

"I do, too," Rosen said. "Because they almost got Eileen, and next time they might get her. Or me."

"Believe me, we're not going to relax about this," Eileen said. "We just need to know more, or we'll be shoving our heads into a trap."

"Speaking of knowing more," Joe said, "here's about four hundred pages of articles. If we each take a stack of papers, we'll get through them that much quicker."

"Oh, no," Eileen groaned, but she was smiling. She took a stack of papers from Joe. "I hope you gave me some interesting ones."

"They're all interesting," Joe said. "Somewhere in here is our answer. It has to be."

17

Briargate Subdivision, Colorado Springs, Colorado

Two hours later, snow began to blow through the wind. Joe perched himself next to the window with his stack of documents. He watched the first swirls appear, little gusts of snow travelling quickly down the street as though they had urgent business.

"Eileen, come watch this," he said quietly. Eileen jerked her head upright and blinked owlishly at him. She'd been dozing over her papers. Joe grinned at her and she smiled guiltily back. She swept her hair back from her forehead and massaged her temples with her narrow hands. Joe suppressed a wave of desire, a need so sharp it was almost pain, to take her to bed and hold her and love her. She looked so tired.

"Snow?" she said softly.

"Snow," he said.

Alan Baxter was frankly asleep, his head pillowed in the couch and his mouth open. Rosen, who apparently needed no sleep at all, also got up and joined Joe at the window. The three of them watched the thin rags of snow grow heavier and heavier, until the window was a horizontal blur of white. The window rattled under a gust and sent a swirl of flakes against the glass. The sound was sly and secretive and unfriendly, as though the storm knew they were inside, dry and warm, and resented the walls that kept them safe.

"No killers in this," Rosen said, and Joe saw his shoulders drop a tiny bit. For Rosen, this was remarkable.

"You were really worried, weren't you?" Joe asked.

"I'm still worried," Rosen said.

"I need sleep," Eileen said. "I can't read this stuff any more. I'm not getting any of it inside my head. It's all just words. Listen to this guy." She took a page at random from her pile of papers and read out loud.

"There were a lot of trucks that were leaving with government files, specifically IRS and tax files, moving them to the eastern parts of California and into Arizona. So, I think that the Northridge quake was somehow artificially induced. And that the quake was induced specifically to relieve the kind of pressure on the San Andreas fault that so many people have been talking about, to relieve the nine-plus megaquakes that were building along the San Andreas up in Lancaster, Palmdale, all the way up into Parkfield and Cloverdale."

Eileen stopped, her mouth open in surprise.

"Holy shit, that's it!" Joe said.

"I didn't see this one," Eileen said. "I hadn't read this one yet."

"What's that one from?" Rosen asked.

"This is from a conspiracy newsgroup named Truthnet. This person was talking about a conversation they heard on *The Art Bell Show.*"

"Hey, I listen to him sometimes," Joe said. "AM Radio. He's the night owl's friend."

"Some of it might be true, evidently," Rosen said dryly. "What else does it say?"

Eileen read through the paper, bright flags of excitement in her cheeks, her tiredness erased.

"Now, for the last couple of years there've been very mysterious hums. One is called the Taos Hum in Colorado and New Mexico, where many people are hearing these very, very odd radio frequencies that some people can hear, that other

people cannot. There's another interesting thing that was reported on CNN, which they call the Monterey Heartbeat. And that there is a thumping, pounding, heartbeat sound that's being heard directly off the coast of Monterey. And one of the reasons I was able to pinpoint the Northridge quake is because, in my meditations with the Grays, I kept getting 'man-made, man-made, man-made.' That word kept flashing across my mind."

Eileen trailed off. One of Rosen's eyebrows was raised exactly like Mr. Spock's on *Star Trek,* and Joe couldn't help it. He started laughing like a fool.

"Hey, this guy has got something," he said, raising his hands as Eileen looked at him with a thunderous expression. "It's just, you know, Monterey, and meditations, and communicating with the *aliens* . . ."

"He gets this way sometimes," Eileen said coldly to Rosen. This only made Joe laugh harder, so he flapped his hands at Eileen and Rosen and headed to the kitchen. It was far too late for coffee or a soda pop, so he snitched one of Rosen's distilled water bottles from the refrigerator. The cold, tasteless water soothed his throat and dried up his laughter.

When he came back in, Eileen and Rosen were still at the window, watching the snow. There were already a couple of inches on the streets. It was going to be a big one, a fall storm that would break tree limbs and paralyze city services for a day or so. Then the sun would come out and everyone would whoop and laugh and throw snowballs at one another. A few men would drop dead of heart attacks shoveling the heavy snow, like modern sacrificial offerings to the storm, then a few days later, the snow would be gone and people would wear shorts to the parks. That was the Front Range for you.

"Okay, I'm better," he announced. "Want some of Rosen's water? He'll be pissed when we're stuck here for three days and he runs out because I drank it all."

"I have more in the car," Rosen said evenly. Joe grinned at him, feeling a bit friendlier towards him. Rosen had a sense of humor after all.

"So who cares if this guy got his information from the

aliens," Joe said. "It doesn't really matter, does it? It puts everything together."

"You're right," Eileen said, smoothing the paper with her fingers. "It is bizarre, but there's the Taos Hum, and the Northridge earthquakes, and a plausible reason for setting off a Tesla earthquake."

"Not only plausible, but heroic, really," Joe said. "If you can keep a fault like the San Andreas from hitting an 8.0 level, you can save thousands of lives."

"Heroic," Alan said from behind them, startling them all. He was blinking and rubbing at his eyes. "Maybe they started out that way, but then they killed Krista. Why, because she found the place where they set them off? They killed her because she stumbled on to something she shouldn't have? What kind of heroics is that?"

"Not heroic at all," Joe said evenly. "They killed Jim Leetsdale, too, you know."

"We know who heads the project," Eileen said in a musing, thoughtful voice. Joe looked at her sharply. She was looking at Rosen, who gave a very small shrug to his shoulders.

"Jacob Mitchell," she said to Joe. "We met him the day we investigated Leetsdale's murder. This man practically had 'bad guy' tattooed on his forehead."

"We saw his worst side," Rosen said. "There must be other sides to him. He's got a lot of power."

"Do we have enough of a linkage to get a DNA sample from him? For Krista?" Eileen asked. Rosen was already shaking his head.

"Not enough," he said. "Not yet."

"Why not?" Alan asked, clearly exasperated.

"Because privacy laws make DNA sampling a very tricky issue, Mr. Baxter," Eileen said coldly. "Private citizens have a right to keep their DNA to themselves, and that's the way I like it. We can't take a sample from Jacob Mitchell without his permission, or unless we have some very good circumstantial evidence that he's committed the crime we suspect him of. We don't have those things."

"Damn it," Alan said.

"Can't have it both ways," Joe said, and grinned at Alan to

take the sting from his words. "We can't complain about government assassins and then allow Detective Eileen to go taking blood samples from innocent citizens."

Alan flung his hands out, then laughed ruefully. "You're right," he said. "I admit it. So how do we get evidence? Find our killer over the next dead body?"

"No," Eileen said. "Particularly not since the next dead person is likely to be one of us."

"Lucy?" Rosen asked.

"She's working on her side. I'd call her right now with what we've found but she's definitely sleeping. Remember the time zones make it even later there."

"Let's send e-mail," Joe suggested.

"Encrypted," Rosen said abruptly. "If someone is searching for keywords in e-mail, they could find Joe."

"Who's Lucy?" Alan asked.

"A friend of ours," Joe said after a moment. "She works in Washington, D.C."

"Let's do it, then get some sleep," Eileen said. "We all need it."

"Do we need to set watches?" Alan suggested. "I was just thinking perhaps we shouldn't all sleep at once."

"Good idea," Joe said. "I'll take first watch. I'm still wide awake. I'll send Lucy e-mail. Do you have a regular password with her, Eileen?"

"Yeah, it's 'peckish,' " Eileen said. "Lucy picked it. I hope she has something else for us."

"Me too," Joe said, and briskly rubbed his hands together. "Ready for bed? Alan, why don't you take the couch? Rosen, I have a camping mattress in my second bedroom. And Eileen, you take my bed for now." Joe tried very hard for nonchalance and avoided looking at Alan.

"Sounds good," Eileen said. She leaned into Joe and kissed him, then disappeared toward the bedroom without another word. In a very few minutes, Joe was alone in his study with the door closed. He could hear the wind-driven snow beating against the side of the house. Little hoots and howls screamed around the corners of the eaves, making sounds like a hundred masked killers sneaking towards the house. Joe wasn't afraid.

He knew what it was like to be out in weather like this; buffeted and blinded, freezing cold and unable to breathe through the wind that snatched your breath away or stuffed your mouth full of flying snow. It was not a night for anyone, much less human killers.

"Hey, Lucy," he typed. "It's Joe. I've got some interesting stuff for you. First of all, let me fill you in on what's happened here the last few days . . ."

Crestone, San Luis Valley, Colorado

"I love Albuquerque lows," Daniel said.

Marcia grinned at Lady Jane and took a sip of her spiced tea. It was spiced with more than herbs; Jane had tipped a generous slug of brandy into each glass. Marcia had no idea if the brandy was expensive or not. Probably not, considering Daniel's salary as a teacher. But Marcia had never had any money to develop a taste for fine brandy. The herbal tea, the roaring fire, the company, and the enormous white blizzard made the brandy taste as fine as anything she'd ever had.

The wind roared around the little cabin. The big sheets of glass at the front of the great room were white and blind with snow. The panes rattled occasionally and sent icy little drafts to make the flames dance in the fireplace. The wood stove in the center of the house was delivering the real heat, but Daniel had lit the big stone fireplace with a roaring fire.

"For effect," he'd said with a grin.

"Feeling better?" Jane asked. "Or should I make the next one mostly brandy?"

"Feeling lots better," Marcia said with a sigh. "The MUFON team was very nice, actually."

"Liar," Jane said comfortably. "They would have spread your guts out on the table and tried to read the future in them if they could."

"Jane," Daniel said. "That's horrible."

"I know," Jane said. "But I'm right. They want an alien murder and they've only got a standard one, and it's bugging them."

"I think you're right, but you can't blame them. I mean, us," Marcia said. "I'm one of them, you know. MUFON is a very meticulous group. They'll come out tomorrow with an official announcement, and hopefully that will be it."

"Too late now," Daniel said. "The Rabble is here in force and the media always pay attention to them. The MUFON announcement will be ignored because that would lend too much credibility to the UFO-investigation movement."

"I'll say the Rabble is here," Jane said. "When I went into town to pick up Sara today I could hardly believe it. There wasn't a parking place to be had. I saw a guy walking down the street in a cowboy hat with ping pong balls glued all over it. He'd covered them with aluminum foil. *Green* aluminum foil."

Daniel and Marcia sighed in unison. Marcia drained her cup and tilted the empty cup toward Jane with an inquiring look. Jane gave her an evil little grin and disappeared toward the kitchen teapot.

"Just bring the bottle, Hon," Daniel called after her. "I think I'm going to need it too."

"Nothing from the cops?" Marcia asked. Daniel shook his head.

"Nothing from Gonzalez. Except I think there might have been another cattle mutilation somewhere in the valley. Something in the way he was avoiding my eyes. Maybe on his sister's place, maybe somewhere on the Baca Ranch. Wherever it was, they didn't call me, so that narrows it a bit."

"People call you?" Marcia asked.

"I photograph, I document, I take them seriously, and I never talk to insurance companies. This allows ranchers to have someone to express their fear and anger to, and also a way to collect on their losses. So far, only a few ranchers have been really hostile towards me."

"Gonzalez's sister?"

"Beth Williams," Jane said flatly, returning with teapot and a brandy bottle from the kitchen.

"She and Jane have never seen eye to eye, you might say," Daniel said.

"I think she's a big-arsed snooty bitch," Jane said.

"Oh, Jane," Daniel said with a smothered grin. He tilted his teacup to Marcia and addressed her. "She came into the valley with her beautiful baby girl and her gorgeous everything else and I think Beth was a little jealous, that's all."

"Huh," Jane snorted. "Calling me a barefoot slut of a hippie chick doesn't sound like jealousy."

"Trust me," Daniel laughed. "It was."

"Enough about *her,*" Jane commanded.

"Okay, so what now?" Marcia asked. She took the cup from Jane, and the buttery smell of brandy wafted up to her nose. The tea was nearly all liquor, this time. She needed it. The MUFON meeting had gone as well as could be expected, but it was exhausting. Marcia had reacted as a normal person and not a field agent, and her lack had been pointed out to her multiple times. This, even though everyone had finally come to the conclusion that there was nothing in the murder of Krista Lewis to suggest anything but a natural, human predator.

"Luckily, I don't think we have to worry about another murder tonight," Daniel said. He pointed toward the windows with his teacup. The windows roared with snow. The whiteout was total, blind, and beautiful to watch.

"Not a night for murder," Marcia sighed, and felt her shoulders relax even more. The brandy was setting up a nice glow in her midsection, tingling her fingers and toes and making her lips go slightly numb. It had been a long time since she'd drunk anything more than an occasional glass of wine with dinner.

"Not tonight," Daniel agreed. "I was thinking, though . . ." he trailed off. Jane frowned at him immediately, obviously sensing something bad.

"What?" Marcia asked.

"I was thinking that after this storm finishes, there's going to be a lot of snow over the dunes. For a few days, anything that moves out there is going to leave a trail. A big one."

"You're going to go hunting for this guy?" Jane asked, and snorted angrily. "Are you crazy? Who do you think you are, Jackie Chan?"

"No," Daniel said patiently, "Although I'm not sure I like

what you're suggesting, love. What, I'm a wimpy, geeky math teacher and anybody could knock me over with a feather?"

"No," Jane backpedaled immediately. "I don't mean that at all. But this is a murderer, Daniel. You should leave this to—oh." She stopped, and gave Daniel a small and rueful grin. "Sorry. You were going to suggest that Gonzalez go out there, weren't you?"

"I was," Daniel said. "I really don't care to shoot someone, or whack them about with karate chops, or whatever. If this girl were you or Sara, I would feel differently."

"I should think you would," Marcia said through her increasingly numb lips.

"It's something to think about," Daniel said. "A nice carpet of white. Maybe he stalks the dunes a lot, maybe he only comes once in a while. If he's still out there, though, we could get lucky and the storm could get him."

"I hope it does, the bastard," Jane said viciously, and raised her glass in a toast to the rattling windows. "To the storm. May it kill the killer, tonight."

"Tonight," Marcia said, and raised her teacup at the windows.

"Tonight," Daniel said, but his eyes weren't hopeful.

Great Falls, Virginia

"Nikola Tesla? Who the hell is he?" Lucy asked Hank. It was two o'clock in the morning. Hank was starting another tooth, which made Lucy weep with frustration. What was God thinking, making teeth come so quickly in a little baby? Couldn't he have taken a break from designing octopuses or leopards or something and made teething better?

At least she had something interesting on her e-mail. Hank was nursing sleepily at her breast. The pain medication was starting to kick in and he'd finally stopped wailing. Lucy hated late-night television, even though the armchair in the family room was her favorite place to nurse. Nothing seemed to be on but infomercials and horror movies. So she had car-

ried Hank to her basement office and her second best armchair and logged on to the Internet.

"Wow," she said, reading Joe's e-mail. No wonder Eileen
was strained. Joe wrote logically and well. His e-mail letters
were like computer programs: first this, then that; if this is
true, then that must be true.

Lucy grasped immediately the concept of a government
program to set off bleeder earthquakes. She could understand
the logic of such a concept, and how it could go terribly
wrong. There were lots of examples of good ideas gone bad
in government programs. The swine flu vaccine. The welfare
system. Helium reserves. Mind control experiments. The list
was long and full of sometimes fatal blunders. These earthquake games sounded reasonable. Wrong-headed, but reasonable. What was really interesting was Nikola Tesla.

"Let me see what I can find out," she said. Hank gave a
snort and a sigh and let go of her nipple. She looked down and
saw that he was fast asleep. "Tomorrow," she sighed to her
computer. "Tonight, I'm going to get some more sleep."

Briargate Subdivision, Colorado Springs, Colorado

Joe blinked owlishly over some sketchy drawings of what
Nikola Tesla's earthquake machine might look like. It was
very late, nearly three o'clock in the morning. He should have
woken Alan Baxter over an hour ago. But like a program that
was almost but not quite running perfectly, the pieces of the
Tesla puzzle refused to come together.

He thought he had the general story right. A secret government project created small earthquakes to bleed off pressure from major fault lines. They did this using a Tesla device,
nothing supernatural or alien about it. Rumors of Nikola
Tesla's plans for an earthquake machine have been floating
around the conspiracy-minded population for years.

Joe's smudged book on Tesla's earthquake machine
seemed simple enough. Evidently Tesla made a device that
would create sonic vibrations. His machine would tune these
ultra-low frequency sound waves until the waves matched the

natural frequency of whatever was interesting to him. The waves would build naturally within the building or the bridge or the fault line until it destroyed itself. The drawings of the Tesla machine were poor. Joe couldn't even tell how big it was supposed to be.

He looked at the second book in his lap. The book was open to pictures of the Tacoma Narrows Bridge, a perfect example of a natural Tesla effect. Joe had seen the film of the bridge, along with everyone who took high-school physics. The destruction of the bridge was incredible and, best of all, caught on film. The wind currents down the Narrows in Puget Sound, Washington State, made the brand new suspension bridge vibrate. The vibration became an uncontrollable, spectacular sine wave. The bridge was totally destroyed within a matter of days.

So that was the essence of the Tesla machine. It made a thing vibrate at just the proper frequency, and the thing would shake itself apart all on its own. Earth, buildings, bridges, people even, could be destroyed by this thing. Theoretically, anyway.

Someone, Jacob Mitchell perhaps, headed up the government project to use the machine to help ease pressures on fault lines. A scientist lost his wife and unborn child in one of the bleeder earthquakes and decided to go public with the project. Someone panicked and killed him. A woman stumbled on the location of the project and she, too, was killed. Probably by the same someone, who was now willing to commit murder and perhaps had a taste for it. Detective Eileen Reed, too close to tracking down the killer, was marked for assassination. The killer had to keep killing to cover up each death.

All of this made sense and fit perfectly. There were only two problems, and these two puzzle pieces had Joe Tanner blinking over a dusty book and trying fruitlessly to find a place for them.

First, why the New Madrid earthquake? It was due to go off in two days. It was an 8.0 earthquake, a massive human killer and certainly not a "bleeder." None of the other simulated earthquakes in Jim Leetsdale's files had the magnitude of the New Madrid. The only explanation Joe could come up with was that the New Madrid was a simulation only, an earthquake that was not going to be set off by the earthquake people.

Maybe the New Madrid was just one of their worst-case simulations. Joe loved fighting virtual nuclear battles with his missile defense system, shooting down incoming nuclear bombs. Sometimes, though, his job as a war gamer called for fighting a losing war. In these games everyone died. He hated them. He understood the necessity of fighting for the last scrap of breathable air in Australia, the last penguin in Antarctica, the faint potential for human life to continue on the planet after a nuclear holocaust, but he still hated it. He hated fighting a war game and using every last brilliant pebble, every single ground interceptor, every patriot battery, and then sitting helplessly while the final missiles fell like deadly rain.

Perhaps that was the New Madrid. An earthquake game that wasn't supposed to ever happen. But it still didn't quite fit right, it didn't feel right. Why would Jim Leetsdale have included this game in his selection of secret pictures?

Joe moved on to his second worry, the second puzzle piece that lay on his imaginary table. Why hadn't a Tesla machine been built and used before now? Terrorist groups had existed in the United States since the American Patriots had kicked the English out and declared themselves a country. There were labor riots in the twenties and thirties, coal strikes in the West in the twenties. Then there was George Metesky, the Mad Bomber, who terrified New Yorkers from 1940 to 1957, an astonishing seventeen years. Joe had seen a late-night documentary on Metesky and was amazed when he saw the plain, ordinary face of the madman who had injured so many people with his bombs. Wouldn't George Metesky have shaken down buildings with a Tesla machine if he could? Perhaps Metesky just wanted to see things get blown up.

But what about the sixties? Joe knew about the dark side of the sixties, more than most children of his generation who'd only read the sanitized flower-power history textbooks or seen the vapid television shows from the period. His father was a Vietnam veteran and an insurance claim adjuster after his tour of duty. He worked a lot of claims from universities, hospitals, and government buildings that were bombed and vandalized by the "love generation."

He had, in fact, done some paperwork on the Patty Hearst case, the dreadful story of the kidnapped newspaper heiress who'd been tortured and raped by the Symbionese Liberation Army back in 1974. Beaten and psychologically terrified, she'd been compelled to join their bank-robbing gang. Joe, who'd heard about Patty Hearst from his father, remembered how disgusted his father was that she was put on trial as a gang member when the SLA was finally captured.

So if Donald DeFreeze, the SLA leader, had access to a Tesla earthquake machine, wouldn't he have used it? Joe blinked again, realizing his thoughts were slowing and stretching like taffy. He was starting to fall asleep. Yes, Donald DeFreeze would have happily slaughtered hundreds to spread his message of peace and love. Maybe the dark man, the legendary terrorist who somehow slipped away before DeFreeze's death in fire, knew about the earthquake machine and they just hadn't built it yet.

Then there was the Oklahoma City bombing, and there was a dark man there too, wasn't there? John Doe Number Two, the one so many witnesses had sworn seeing with Timothy McVeigh before the truck bomb had gone up and the building had come down. He had escaped somehow, just like the dark man from the SLA, escaped so completely that finally the FBI declared that he didn't exist, that only Timothy McVeigh had parked the truck and set off the killer bomb.

The print blurred in front of Joe's eyes. He was tired, but he was spooking himself out, too. Somehow he was imagining the dark man as Stephen King had written him in his stories, the walking dude with his rundown bootheels and his jolly mad grin. Joe thought of hiking into the dunes, tomorrow or next week or next year, and finding latitude 37 and longitude 105, and there would be a man with no face sitting cross-legged on a dune crest, his arms cradling a metal device drenched in blood, his smile as sharp and mindless as the grin of a shark.

There was a tapping on the glass behind him. Joe whirled

around, the books on his lap falling to the floor, his heart giving a tremendous horsekick. For a second he saw a face, crazed and madly gleeful, framed in the black and the snow whirl of the window. Then it was just snow, and the tapping was a branch from his tree that had torn in the relentless wind.

"Ah, jeez," Joe said to himself, putting a hand to his heart. If he were twenty years older, he was sure he'd be dead right now.

"Hey," Alan said from behind him, and Joe whirled again. Alan was standing in the doorway to his study, hair frowzled, eyes red, scratching at an armpit and frowning at Joe. "You were supposed to wake me up at two."

Joe started laughing and clapped a hand over his mouth to muffle it. It sounded wrong, too high and too scared. He had succeeded in completely weirding himself out. Two cops in the house with guns and a blizzard outside so he had to go inventing himself a supernatural monster.

"I got carried away," he said. "I was trying to fit all the pieces together and I just can't do it."

"Like how come Ted Kaszinski didn't use a Tesla machine to bring down civilization?" Alan asked. He rubbed his eyes and stretched.

"Yeah, the Unabomber, exactly," Joe said, feeling foolishly happy that someone, anyone else was awake. He didn't want to be the only one awake right now. "Except with me it was Timothy McVeigh, the Oklahoma City bomber."

"Yeah, I was thinking maybe because there's something missing from your drawing," Alan said, pointing at the Tesla book spread open on the floor. "Maybe the government took the real drawings and locked them up, and these are ones that don't work right."

Joe bent down and picked up his books, feeling a new respect for Alan Baxter. That would make sense. And the earthquake gamers, they were a government agency, weren't they?

"The killers, they're a government agency, so maybe they could get the good drawings," Alan said, voicing his thoughts. "But you guys all seem to think the government is a good guy, an impression I really don't share. Hey, would you mind making me some coffee before you go to bed? I didn't sleep so well, and I don't know where your stuff is in the kitchen."

"I'd be happy to," Joe said automatically, his eyes still on the drawing. He was searching for the missing piece, the part of the machine that looked unfinished or strangely incomplete. It wasn't obvious to him. He surprised himself by yawning, a huge jaw-creaker that made his eyes water.

"Make me some coffee before you fall over," Alan said with a smile. Joe nodded and rose to his feet. He was going to make Alan Baxter some coffee, and then he was going to go in and snuggle up next to Alan's sleeping daughter. He'd be damned if he were going to sleep on his couch because of the measuring look in the old man's eyes. Still, after making Alan coffee, he went to the bathroom first and brushed his teeth far too long. Alan was safely in Joe's study when Joe opened the door and walked carefully to his own bedroom, feeling foolishly as though he were sneaking.

But all guilt was forgotten when he slid carefully under his covers. Eileen was divinely warm and heavy with sleep, curled up on one side with her hair half covering her face. He slowly moved closer until they were spooned together, and within a few seconds, he was sound asleep.

18

"I see you made it through the night," Harben said. Eileen
grinned around a mouthful of latte. She was still half frozen,
exhilarated by the glorious morning world. The wind had
blown all night, sculpting the heavy snow into enormous
white drifts. The storm itself was now moving ponderously
over Kansas and into the Midwest, feeding from the warm
Gulf moisture and storming heavily where it went.

Colorado Springs had woken to a lovely hard blue sky and
a moveless world of glittering white. Because the storm had
brought winds with it, the snow had blown from the trees before they could build up enough of a covering to crack
branches and send old, weak trees to the ground. Therefore,
everyone had power and hot water and, with the exception of
icy streets, a harmless aftermath to the storm.

"We made it," Eileen said. "But you'll notice we're wearing the same clothes as yesterday. I'm hoping to get some
fresh stuff soon."

"We've got a bag for each of you," Harben said. "I forgot

about it yesterday. Sorry. Hetrick packed a bag for you, Eileen, so don't worry about O'Brien going through your underwear."

"I have very unexciting underwear," Eileen said. Her cheeks started to sting a little in the warm air, and her nose suddenly regained its sense of smell. Her latte suddenly came alive with chocolate and she took a heavenly warm gulp. "But thanks."

"Alan Baxter wants to head back to the San Luis Valley this morning," Rosen said. "We couldn't talk him out of it."

"He should be safe at the Williams's Ranch," Eileen said unhappily. Harben looked at her sharply, and she nodded her head slightly. That was enough, for Harben. Harben, like Rosen, would not discuss Eileen's parentage with her unless she wished him to.

"No reason to hold him here," Harben said. "But let's go into my office. I'd like to know what you came up with last night."

"Some interesting things," Eileen said. This was going to be fun, laying out the different information they'd discovered and seeing if Harben bought their way of piecing everything together. Breakfast that morning had been far too early but more fun than Eileen expected. Joe had dug a huge bag of pancake mix from his cabinet and what seemed like a five-gallon jug of pancake syrup. He continually surprised her with what he considered important. Who would think, pancakes? He made them superbly: thin and steaming and with a crisp crust at the edges that crunched beautifully under her fork.

The morning sun was striking in dazzling spears through the windows as she followed Harben to his office. Eileen knew the storm was going to be more bark than bite, today, for the police. The drifts would be a trial for the snowplow drivers and an education for the military personnel from points south of Colorado who'd never tried to bust a snowdrift before. This would bring lots of business to the body repair shops and a few stitches at the local hospitals. Who would think that such a lovely light thing like snow could make a drift that would crumple a car so completely? The dangerous driving conditions would exist for the next few days, as the melting snow froze into glare ice each evening. That would be a problem, but a problem the department handled each winter.

This morning, the ideas that everyone had come up with during the night were handled and examined and set aside or placed in what they all thought of as the explanation. Someone in Jacob Mitchell's organization, perhaps even Mitchell himself, had killed Jim Leetsdale and Krista Lewis. They had done this to keep their secret project under wraps, which meant that they probably received funding from black money and their project would be shut down if they were exposed.

Black money was fragile stuff. The military had a budget that they spent on items so secret not even Congress knew where the money went. This money, nicknamed "black," was legitimate but dicey. Only successful black projects, like the Stealth bomber, were ever revealed. The unsuccessful ones disappeared. But no project, however secret, had permission to murder people. Area 51 had UFO nuts practically tunneling into it, and the worst that happened to the nuts was the confiscation of their cameras and a quick escort out of the area.

"Mr. Baxter wants his Bronco cleared," Bob said from his station near Harben's office. He was holding a hand over the phone receiver, a habit that irritated Eileen to no end. Why didn't he ever put anyone on hold? Bob was the office manager, and he and Eileen had never gotten along.

"Clear it," Harben said. Then when they were in Harben's office with the door shut, he seated himself and folded his hands calmly. "Let's hear it," he said.

The Williams's Ranch, San Luis Valley, Colorado

Alan Baxter drove carefully past the destroyed rest stop. Gonzalez or one of his deputies had wound orange tape around the entrance sign and put traffic cones across the entrance to the parking lot. The cones were half buried by snow thrown up by a plow. The roads were actually quite good, plowed and sanded and now nearly dry after a half-day of brilliant sunshine. Alan caught only glimpses of the valley as he negotiated his way down the pass. The snow had fallen here, too, frosting the tops of the mountains and turning the tan stretch of the sand dunes into a glittering prism.

He didn't care to breathe in the beauty, today. He wanted to get to the Williams's Ranch, to rest, to decide what to do. He had to call Marcia Fowler, he knew that. Perhaps they should meet. He had the feeling Marcia had the same distrust of government organizations as he did. He hadn't made any promises to keep the information he'd learned a secret. In fact, he'd promised Gonzalez that he'd come back to the valley and tell him everything.

The ranch turnoff was neatly plowed. Alan could see tire tracks leading into the pasture where the cattle were kept. Susan and Frank, undoubtedly, feeding the cattle or making sure they were okay, or whatever they did after a snowstorm. He took the main road to the ranch house and parked next to Sam Williams's truck.

"Well, hello, Alan," Beth said. She was, as always, in the kitchen. This time she was seated at an old-fashioned pull-down desk. The front was down, revealing a powerful looking laptop. Beth was typing rapidly as Alan entered with a quick, country-style knock, a double rap of the knuckles that announced entry.

"Hello, Beth," Alan said.

"Coffee if you want; let me finish this up and I'll join you and we'll catch up," she said, her fingers rattling over the keys. Alan found hot coffee in the pot but chose the teakettle instead. It was steaming, on the edge of a boil. He made himself some mild hot tea and sat down at the empty kitchen table and thought for a moment that if Eileen were here right now, he'd be the happiest man alive. Even if she looked at him without love, even if she mistrusted him.

"Accounts," Beth said balefully, closing her laptop and her pull-down desk. She stretched and stood up, knuckling the small of her back. "I make myself keep up, or I have to spend days making all the numbers work. How are you, Alan?"

"I'm fine, now that I'm here," Alan said, and smiled guiltily. "I hope that doesn't sound wrong."

"Not to me," Beth said. She poured herself a cup of coffee

and stirred in milk from the refrigerator. Sitting down, she curled both hands around her cup and looked directly at Alan. "Tell me all. Did you see your daughter?"

"I saw her," Alan said. "She has a boyfriend. He's a good man, I think. But I still want to punch him in the nose. Isn't that strange? She's thirty, and I disapprove of her having a boyfriend."

"The last time you saw her she was just out of diapers," Beth observed with a wry smile. "It takes time, I think. Though it's not easy for me, even now."

"Susan?" Alan asked.

"She's—well, she's what she wants to be, I guess," Beth said. She gave a small, pained shrug to her shoulders. "She's the same age as your Eileen. Thirty. Time to get married and have kids, and she acts like she's twenty. But who am I to drive her life? My mom tried to drive mine, and I ran in every direction but the one she wanted me to go in."

"I don't want to drive her," Alan said sadly, sipping at his tea. "I just want to get to know her. I think I made a little bit of a start yesterday. I don't know. But there's more than Eileen to all of this."

"Krista Lewis?" Beth asked. "Your friend Marcia Fowler called last night. She thought you might be able to get out for dinner, but I told her you'd be back today. Is she involved in this too, this Marcia?"

"She's the schoolteacher who found Krista's body on the dunes," Alan said. "We met at the donut shop the other morning and I thought we should get together. Does your brother know anything more?"

"More than getting no sleep last night and throwing a dozen half-frozen drunks in his jail?" Beth said. She threw up her hands in a little gesture of disgust. "Early fall snow is bad enough without adding a bunch of out-of-towners. Reg wouldn't know anything more about Krista unless the murderer tapped him on the shoulder and confessed. Poor guy. He's going to have to ask the county to give him another deputy. At least we didn't have any fatalities last night. Couple of fender benders, but no big wrecks."

"So the roads are okay today?" Alan asked. "They were

good coming into the valley, but I wasn't sure how much you'd gotten."

"They're fine," Beth said dismissively. "Little bit of blowing, six inches or so of good fall snow. Susan and Frank are out in pasture two looking at some of the cattle, but they'll be back soon. My Sam is working in the barn; he's got a tractor he wants to fix before it gets really cold. Spring storms are the real killers. That's when we lose the babies. Calves, I mean. Don't forget to scrape your shoes the next few days, it's going to be muddy."

"I won't," Alan promised. "I better call Miz Fowler and find out if she still wants to talk to me."

"She'll want to talk to you," Beth said, laughing. Alan, puzzled, looked at her for an explanation, but she waved a hand at him and raised her bulk to her feet. "Got to get the roast in for supper. You go on and call Miz Fowler."

The Pentagon, Washington, D.C.

Lucy felt strange without a stroller and a diaper bag. She locked her car and swung her tiny, light handbag over her shoulder. The morning was humid and hot. She'd left Hank with Ted, who'd agreed to take a day off work. School hadn't started, but most teachers were already putting in full days in meetings and administrative work. Ted was happy to miss a day of that. He'd swung Hank to his hip and declared that they were going to visit the Washington Zoo. Hank giggled delightedly. He loved his daddy.

Suddenly, Lucy stopped still, wondering if Ted had put sunscreen on Hank. Was he wearing a hat? Did Ted have enough diapers? She blinked and forced her feet, feeling funny in brand new shoes, onward.

She was wearing a good suit, one that used to fit her perfectly. Now it strained. Only seven pounds separated her from pre- and post-pregnancy weight, but it all seemed to be in her hips and breasts. Her good shoes simply did not fit her. None of her dress shoes fit her. She made a quick call to her sister-in-law, Carolyn, who was up and sipping hot tea and reading the morning paper.

"Yeah, your feet got bigger," Carolyn laughed. "The ligaments relax during pregnancy and your feet get a little bit bigger. Plus, they get ornery and unwilling."

"Unwilling?" Lucy said, dress pumps clutched in her hands, her suit buttons straining over her breasts, her curly hair, still wet and uncombed, nearly standing on end with frustration.

"Yeah, unwilling. You used to squinch your feet into those horrible girl's shoes, but you're a mom now. So are your feet. They're not going to put up with being squeezed. Throw out those horrid things and go get a sensible pair of low heels in a size bigger."

Her feet did feel better. She'd found a pair of cushioned pumps with low heels in a good color in five minutes at the local shoe store. So she shouldn't feel so nervous. She realized she was feeling very nervous about seeing people, not about her shoes. For an entire year her whole life had been her computer and her baby boy. She was feeling *shy*.

"I gotta start getting out more," she muttered to herself. She smoothed her curly hair and hitched at her jacket. The Pentagon was where she had to go. She'd found a marker for Nikola Tesla in the FBI weapons database. There was no information, only the marker that stood for a classified box in the Pentagon basement files. She'd never been to the Pentagon basement. The basement, carved out during the renovation ten years ago, was now an archive. The Pentagon covered over six million square feet, which made the archive enormous. Lucy hoped there was someone who could help her look, or at least point her in the right direction.

Everyone knew about the National Archives and the Smithsonian, but few people knew about the Defense Archives. Lucy didn't know if her CIA credentials would get her into the files. She was going to give it a try, though.

Twenty minutes later she'd worked her way through metal detectors and guards at the Pentagon. She'd been to the Pentagon many times and she knew the routine of entrance, the way the Pentagon sloped at odd angles and smelled like old, dusty paint, the way the guards checked not just badges and faces, but eyes. Her eyes were nervous but evidently not nervous enough to capture the guard's interest. At ten thirty the largest office building in the world was stuffed with people, but most of them were at their desks. A goodly number of people walked the halls on business from one place to another, most carrying documents or notebook computers. Nearly half were dressed in civilian suits just like hers. Lucy fit right in.

She got on the elevator and pressed the down button. When the doors opened on the basement level, she walked to the staircase and headed down one last flight of stairs. She'd called a friend at the CIA and gotten directions. What she was doing was perfectly legitimate, but she still felt that any moment security guards were going to burst from a doorway and hold her at gunpoint.

When she opened the door at the bottom of the stairs, she found herself in a large room. Two desks sat facing each other, both topped with huge computer terminals. A water cooler with a blue bottle stood against one wall and a big copy machine stood against the other wall. Facing her from across the room was a vault door with a big spin lock like the helm of a pirate ship. Two men sat at the desks, both intent on their computer screens. They both looked to be of medium height. One had sandy blond hair and pale skin and the other was bald and had dark skin. Except for the hair and the color of their skin they could have been brothers, so alike were the sharp profiles of their noses and chins.

"Hold on," the bald one said in Lucy's general direction in a Southern accent.

"You die now," the sandy blond one said, with satisfaction. He was hunched over his keyboard. Suddenly he sat up straight and back from his screen, wincing. "Damn!"

"Left your flank exposed," the bald one said. He took his hands off his keyboard and massaged his fingers. He turned to Lucy and smiled. "May I help you?"

"Lucy Giometti, I'm with the DIA," she said. "I'm an analyst and I'm doing some research and I was wondering if I could get some information from the archives."

The two men exchanged glances. The sandy-haired one massaged his fingers and left arm and regarded her levelly.

"DIA never comes here. Usually when we get fake DIA they're really CIA. Is that what you are?"

"Depends," Lucy said. "What are you two party animals? The guardians of the gate? Or are you just minimum-wage security guards?"

"We're archivists," the bald one said with a grin. "So that makes us very much guardians. Tate Webster. Doctor Webster. Tate to my friends."

"Randy Streeks," the blond one said. "Doctor Streeks. No jokes about the name, please. I'm sensitive. You can call me Randy."

"Lucy Giometti, from-another-bureau-but-I-have-to-say-DIA," Lucy said, and held out her hand. "I'm Lucy. Nice to meet you."

They both stood and shook her hand.

"What brings you here, Miss Lucy?" Tate asked.

"I'm trying to find the archives on a man. Nikola Tesla. Have you heard of him?"

"I've heard of him," Randy said. "Yeah, he's the guy who invented the whole missile defense program, right? Death rays, and all that. I heard he was the one who caused the huge explosion in Tungus, Siberia, in 1908. That's him?"

"Well, I'm not sure about that," Lucy said, blinking. *Death rays?* "I wanted to see his file box. I've got the tag number from the FBI database."

She dug in her purse, well aware of their interest in her legs and breasts and curly hair. After a year of nothing but Ted and Hank and family, it felt pretty good to be seen as a female, not a mommy.

"Oh, yeah, and he invented AC power too," Randy said. He stood up from his desk and took the slip of paper from Lucy's hand. "We can find this."

"Want to go with us?" Tate said abruptly. Randy glanced over at his friend with a slight, quickly suppressed frown.

"I'd love to," Lucy said instantly. She held out a foot with a brand new, navy blue sensible shoe. "Look, I wore comfortable shoes."

This seemed to tip the scales. Randy laughed and shrugged.

"Tate has a nose for bullshitters," he said. "He's never been wrong yet. Come with us, then, Miss Lucy. Prepare to be amazed."

Five minutes later Tate spun the vault door shut behind Lucy. The three of them were wearing masks, jumpsuits, and booties. Tate and Randy looked like a couple of deranged surgeons. Lucy had no idea what she looked like, with her skirt crumpled on each side of the big jumpsuit and a paper hat on her unruly hair. Probably like an overweight clown.

In front of her the files began, piles of boxes that blocked her view in almost every direction. The boxes were stacked on metal shelves and the shelves were set close to one another, at a distance that would send a claustrophobe into a panic attack. She saw shelves stacked randomly as far as she could see. She knew the archives were large, but now she understood how big they really were. The air was hushed and still and she sensed the enormity of what she stood in. In Mammoth Cave, Kentucky, as a girl, she'd stood and felt the same weight in the cool air against her face.

"What are you doing?" she asked Tate. He had taken a spool of twine from a hook by the vault doorway. The twine was heavy-duty plastic cord, and one end was tied securely to the hook, which was a big steel affair bolted to the metal frame of the door.

"This is our trail of bread crumbs," Tate said through his mask. "We wear these lovely outfits to protect the archives from us. The twine is to protect us from the archives."

"Getting lost, you mean," Lucy said. She looked at the maze of shelves in front of her and gave a tiny uncontrollable shiver. The air was still in here, cool like a basement or a tomb, and the quiet was absolute.

"Yes, getting lost," Randy said. He scratched at his armpit through the paper jumpsuit. He picked up a folder that sat on a small table under the hook. "Here is our raison d'être, Miss

Lucy, our life's work, I'm beginning to believe." He flipped the notebook open and Lucy saw a geometric drawing.

"A map!" she said.

"A map," Tate nodded. "Government types have been shoving papers in here since the twenties. Well, not here, exactly. The Pentagon basement was set up ten years ago and all the archives were sent here from different defense organizations."

"Like Roswell," Lucy said immediately, and bit her lips behind the mask.

"Hey, a believer!" Tate said instantly. She could see his smile behind his mask. "You don't know how much I want to stumble over some alien mummies in here."

"Me, I want to find the Ark of the Covenant," Randy said. "Remember that final scene in *Raiders of the Lost Ark?* The government worker is putting the box in with a million other boxes in an archive? This is where it should be."

"That was fiction, man," Tate said. "Roswell, Roswell was real."

"Roswell was fiction, you freak," Randy replied. This had the flavor of an old argument, well maintained.

"How do you expect to find Tesla's file in this?" Lucy asked.

"Because we already found it," Tate responded absently. He tested the knot on the twine with several sharp tugs on the line. "It's a fairly recent file, you know. Nikola Tesla died in—what, 1943? We found it two, three years ago."

"Looking for Roswell," Randy said derisively.

"Gives me a reason to go on, my friend," Tate said. "Organizing this mess is going to take more than our miserable lifetimes. Let's go. I'm sick of this suit already."

Tate struck off ahead and Lucy followed. Randy walked behind her because the stacks were so close together. He could have managed a brush at her breasts or her bottom at every turn but he kept a foot or so away, talking nonstop as Tate walked from stack to stack. He was a sweetheart, Lucy decided. All man and very interested, but polite.

The mask began to chafe and her skirt clung to her legs under the paper jumpsuit, but Lucy appreciated the protection as the twine unrolled behind them. Paper dust hung in the air, dust as fine as powder. Even through the mask the smell of moldy paper was pervasive.

"Did you know there really was a curse of King Tut's tomb?" Randy asked conversationally as they passed through two stacks of dark brown boxes piled to the ceiling.

"Trying to scare me?" Lucy asked, peering in every direction she could see. Wanting to see shriveled alien feet, of course.

"Nope," Tate said. "One of my favorite stories, too, since we're working in a version of a pharaoh's tomb."

"Lots of people who were at the opening of King Tut's tomb began to die," Randy said behind her. "Lady Evelyn Herbert, the diggers, Arthur Mace. Over thirteen people were dead by 1929. This was the genesis of the 'curse of the mummy.' "

"Turns out anyone who worked with mummies also got sick, sometimes fatally," Tate continued. He stopped at a junction and consulted his map. Lucy stood waiting as patiently as Randy, trying not to think of the lights failing and leaving her in the dark. Once the thought had crossed her mind, of course, she could think of nothing else.

"Yeah, and it was only years later they discovered a spore. Sometimes it was in the mummy's wrappings, sometimes in the paintings on the tomb walls. One woman died after touching the wall of the tomb with one finger. It's called *Aspergillus niger,* and it infects the lungs, fills them with fluid, until you suffocate. Thus the mummy's curse," Randy finished. Tate turned left. The stacks began to look more and more disorganized, paper spilling from overpacked boxes and wrapped shut with twine instead of tape. The smell got worse, more moldy and awful.

"Smells like a mummy *is* in here," Lucy said. "Either that or a cat got loose."

Tate barked out a laugh and Randy chuckled behind her.

"Worse than cats, I'm telling you. Some of this stuff was stored in places where rain got in, mice got in, chipmunks, cats, whatever. We wear more than this paper stuff when we open a new crate, I'll tell you."

"So these masks will protect us from airborne spores?" Lucy asked. "Keeping us safe from the mummy's curse?"

"We think so," Tate said with horrible nonchalance. "Hey, here we are." He stopped along a wall of boxes, each one taped and marked with black pen. The other side of the narrow corridor was piled high with crates, stenciled carelessly with numbers and letters that made no sense at all. At the top of the pile of boxes, Lucy saw a chain of wooden beads painted in bright colors, something that would go on an old-fashioned Christmas tree. A section of the beads were stained dark brown, a substance that looked suspiciously like very old dried blood. She instantly wanted to know the story of the beads. She *craved* to know.

"Aren't those interesting?" Tate said, following her gaze.

"All of a sudden I think I wouldn't be bored by this job," Lucy said, looking at the bright colors of the beads.

"Treasure, yeah, the best kind," Tate said approvingly. "I dream of breaking open the right box, someday."

"Somewhere in this stack, right?" Randy said, stepping down the stack, fingers trailing along the boxes.

"Tesla," Tate said. "Help us look. But don't let go of the twine, please."

"Not on your life," Lucy said fervently.

19

Special Investigations Bureau, Colorado Springs, Colorado

"Bad news, team," Harben said, his hands folded together. He'd appeared between their desks while they were both at their computer screens, and as usual, Eileen didn't see him coming.

"Don't tell me," Eileen began, and Harben raised his hand slightly. She shut up like he'd thrown a switch.

"Durland changed his verdict to suicide."

"They got to him," Eileen said quietly, swallowing past acid in her throat.

"Mitchell must have leaned on someone," Harben said. "I am very disappointed. I don't believe Leetsdale was a suicide."

"So what do we do?" Eileen asked. She glanced at Rosen. His face was dark and his lips were pressed tight together. He was absolutely furious.

"Look at Krista Lewis. That *is* a murder and we have an arrangement with Sheriff Gonzalez. That's the only link we have open. Sorry." He turned and walked back to his office.

"We'll have to prove he killed Krista to get to Leetsdale."

"That might be difficult," Rosen said. He had been looking through the autopsy report on Krista Lewis.

"What is it?" Eileen asked. She was beginning to think about lunch before Harben came by. The office was still at a post-snowstorm roar. The light outside, tending toward noon, was blindingly bright with reflected snow. The snow was already melting rapidly, which would make driving after dark an incredible hazard.

"Looks like the time-of-death of Lewis's body was revised by the Pueblo coroner. The Alamosa coroner put her in a twelve-hour time slot, but the Pueblo office revised upward at the autopsy."

"The Alamosa coroner didn't do an autopsy?" Eileen asked.

"He doesn't handle murder very often. He didn't want to screw it up, so he did the prelims and sent the evidence and the body on to Pueblo. Good people there."

"Good coroner in Alamosa," Eileen commented. A good decision. So much evidence could be lost in a botched autopsy that a conviction could be lost as well.

"Anyway, the Pueblo coroner said that she might have been dead more than twelve hours, given the state of the body and the location."

"The sand dunes," Eileen said. She was thinking of latitude 37.47.50 and longitude 105.33.20. Was that spot where Krista had met her death? The light outside seemed even more blinding for a moment. Eileen realized she was developing a headache. From hunger, perhaps.

"Maybe we should have a talk with Jacob Mitchell," Eileen said. "Really find out his alibi for Krista's murder. Maybe my little incident as well."

"If Harben will let us," Rosen said doubtfully. He turned to her and held up the autopsy report. Then he set it down. Then he picked it up again.

"What is it?" Eileen asked. Rosen was never unsure. He certainly never hesitated to speak his opinion, if he had one.

"It's just that there's another person involved," Rosen said slowly. "Whose alibi might not cover the twenty-four-hour period of Krista's murder time."

Eileen heard a rushing sound, as though a large airplane had passed over the building. She realized it was her heart, pounding sickly and heavily against her temples. Spears of light from the windows seemed to strike into her eyes. She took her hands from her keyboard and touched her temples lightly, to steady herself.

"I see," she said. "Alan Baxter."

"I can't believe it," Rosen said. "I don't believe it. But—"

"Of course we know it could be true," Eileen said sharply. "Murderers can look like anybody. Just because he seems like a nice person doesn't mean he's not our murderer."

Rosen rustled the autopsy papers in his hands, then set them down at his desk and smoothed them awkwardly with his hands.

"This would disconnect our two homicides," he said slowly. "Which would complicate our story."

"But they could be disconnected," Eileen said. "Perhaps we can't tie this all together because it isn't tied together."

"So we should talk to Alan Baxter again," Rosen said. Eileen looked directly at him and saw distress in his eyes. She had no idea how she would handle the reverse situation. Discussing a person's father as a potential murderer was difficult enough without the person being a cop, and your partner.

"I'm okay, you know," she said.

"We can check his alibis with Gonzalez," Rosen said, picking up the autopsy pages and scanning them. Eileen knew he wasn't reading a word.

"Okay. I really need some food." She stood from her chair and reached for her coat.

"I'll go with you," Rosen said immediately, starting to rise from his own chair.

"No, don't bother," Eileen said. "I'm just going to run down to the sub shop. Why don't you get on the phone to Gonzalez and clear this up? I hope."

"Okay," Rosen said doubtfully, sitting back down.

Eileen wrapped her coat around her and put her gloves on. The rushing sound was back, like the way her A-10 jet airplane used to sound at idle, the way it sounded before takeoff. It was called the Warthog, the ugliest plane the Air Force had, and she loved it. Warthogs cruised very close to the ground, carrying heavy antitank cartridges in a chain gun that ran the length of the plane. Eileen had never seen combat, and was glad. She loved to fly, but she'd never loved to shoot. She'd never wanted to kill anyone.

"What was that?" Rosen asked.

"Nothing," Eileen said, trying to keep a small, hurt smile from her face and failing. "I was just thinking that it would only make sense."

"What would make sense?" Rosen asked, real concern flaring in his eyes.

"That my father would turn out to be a murderer too," Eileen said bitterly, and turned to find her way to the stairs. She could hardly see, the light from the windows was so mercilessly bright and glaring.

While she was warming up her Jeep, there was a knock at her window, nearly scaring her to death. It was Rosen, and he was pointing at the other side of her car. He wanted to get in. She smiled and gave him a friendly wave, and pulled away from the parking lot and out into the street with what she hoped was nonchalance. As she drove away, she caught a glimpse of Rosen standing, coatless, staring after her.

His figure receded in her rearview mirror, receded like the events of her life, as though being a detective were a dream she had once before she woke up. She felt nothing but the roaring sensation, heard nothing but the pounding blood in her ears. She made a slushy, muddy turn onto the entrance ramp to the Interstate, and headed south toward Pueblo and, eventually, the San Luis Valley.

She was going to confront her father. She was going to learn the truth. And if it killed her, if he killed her, then that was okay too. Her whole life felt like a dream, the dream of a dying three-year-old child, perhaps, as the wheels spun in the crushed car and her mother lay dead beside her. What lay between that moment and the coming one was unimportant, as meaningless as a mote of dust drifting in the air. As she accelerated onto the nearly dry highway, she began to hum tune-lessly.

Kim's Place, Alamosa, Colorado

Kim's Place was almost deserted in the hush between lunch hour and the dinner rush. Alan saw Marcia Fowler immediately. She was sitting in a booth with her back to him. A tendril of steam rose from a cup of coffee in front of her.

"Have you been waiting long?" he asked, sliding in to sit across from her. She looked up and smiled and tilted her cup toward him.

"Just poured," she said. "I nearly got stuck getting out of Crestone. The roads are dry here, though."

"Menu?" the waitress asked. Alan noticed that her nametag said "Kay." She was a hard-looking teen but she carried a glass of water, a cup of coffee, and a menu with competence. Marcia smiled at the girl as though she were a fresh-faced country girl with rosy cheeks instead of a pale-faced thing with too much makeup.

"Yes, please," Alan said, taking the menu. His body was settling down and he was ready to refuel. "Coffee, too, thank you."

"So tell me all and I'll tell you all," Marcia said with a smile that didn't reach her eyes. Alan realized for the first time that she was pretty, with curly gray hair framing a face that carried lines that all curved up, as though she'd spent a lifetime being cheerful. Her eyes were dark, framed by lashes as black as soot. They were poker eyes, those, revealing nothing. Her hands, older than the rest of her, rested quietly around her coffee cup.

"I remembered the name of the Air Force officer that Krista was working with up in Colorado Springs," Alan began. "So I drove up to the Springs to talk to him, and found out that he was dead, too . . ."

Alan talked through two glasses of water and a turkey and Swiss cheese sandwich. Marcia was a good listener, her dark eyes intent and interested. She lost her poker expression when

Alan finally got to Nikola Tesla and the earthquake machine. Her eyes widened and she mouthed something that looked to Alan like "arp."

"What was that?" he asked.

"Nothing," she said, waving her hand. "Finish your story."

Finally he wound down, poking his french fries one by one into his ketchup and eating them as he finished with his own lonely vigil in Joe Tanner's house. No murderers attacked, no assassins tried to stage suicides, no explanations came to Alan Baxter as he read through Internet pages spit out by Joe's smelly laser printer. Nothing tied the whole story together for him.

Marcia, who had ordered a piece of pie somewhere during his story, stirred the crumbs with her fork after he stopped.

"Well," she said. "That certainly explains a lot."

"What about you, then?" Alan asked. He felt confused all over again. Telling about the events of the past few nights didn't seem to make much sense now. People were setting off *earthquakes?* It was fantastic, impossible.

"Don't go running away screaming, now," Marcia said. "I don't want to be left with the bill. I'm on a fixed income, you know."

"I won't run away," Alan said, smiling.

"Okay, then," Marcia said calmly. "I belong to MUFON, the Mutual UFO Network. So I'm one of your friend Joe Tanner's freaky alien believers. I was convinced that aliens murdered Krista Lewis when I first saw the body. There was a lot that seemed similar to cattle mutilations, but a lot that didn't seem similar as well." She glanced up beneath her black eyelashes to gauge his reaction and must have seen something in his face. "What?" she asked.

"The cattle," Alan whispered. He swallowed hard, seeing the cattle in his mind's eye with perfect clarity. The round brutal holes punched into the tough hide, the missing organs, the perfect blackness of the injuries, and the uncaring light of the night sky. He could almost smell the sage and the gasoline.

"You've seen a cattle mutilation?" Marcia said eagerly. "You have? Where? Was it here?"

"I can't tell you about it," Alan said, blinking the image

away. "But—I was told that Krista Lewis was raped. I saw those cows—" he stopped.

"You don't have to tell me," Marcia said, though she obviously wanted him to. "Our conclusion—MUFON, that is—is that this is a human murderer. The whole UFO frenzy going on is just a smokescreen. Your ideas make so much sense to me!"

"What do you mean?"

"I can tell you," Marcia said slowly. "If you want to hear."

"I want to hear," Alan said. He'd heard about UFO nuts and had watched television shows about aliens, but had never heard anyone explain the phenomenon in any coherent way. If someone could do that, it would be Marcia Fowler. He could hardly believe this very intelligent, sane-looking woman was a UFO believer.

"All right, then," Marcia said. "Here's the explanation in as few words as I can make it. You know about the 1947 Roswell, New Mexico saucer crash?"

"Sure."

"It was a crash, and there was a survivor. He was what we call a Gray, and they've been visiting our planet for a long time. The crash was an accident, and the original cover-up was just an automatic reflex, from a government that was essentially still in World War Two battle mode. But then the cover-up became something more."

"Why?"

"Because the Grays struck a deal with our government," Marcia said calmly. "They are a species on the way out, on the far end of their evolution. Their birth rates are almost nonexistent, their life-forms increasingly frail. They have incredible technology, though, far in advance of our own. So, more or less by accident, our captive became their emissary. Our government agreed to allow genetic testing of animals and limited, nonharmful abductions of humans."

"What for?" Alan asked. He took a long drink of water. The worst part of this was it sounded *plausible* to him. Who believed the Air Force when they came up with their lame explanation about Roswell? Alan thought the crash-test-dummies-in-balloons idea was hilarious. And ridiculous. And unbelievable.

"We share some parts of our DNA," Marcia said. "I'm a Christian, lots of serious UFOlogists are. God created us all, we believe, so why wouldn't we share a common ancestry? Anyway, the Grays believe they could re-infuse their species with our younger DNA. The deal was that the Grays give us technology, our government gives them some medical subjects who wouldn't be harmed, who wouldn't even remember that they'd had eggs harvested or sample materials taken—"

"That's horrible," Alan said thoughtfully, and Marcia nodded back gravely.

"Of course. But so was incarcerating Japanese-Americans, right? And the Tuskegee syphilis experiments on black men. It seemed like a pretty good deal at the time to men who were still reeling from World War Two and the rise of Communist Russia. Now here's the really horrible part."

"What's that?"

"The Grays reneged on the deal. They abducted far more than they agreed to, they harmed animals and humans, and they didn't deliver on the warp drive, or whatever it was they were supposed to give us humans. This, to me, is the part that makes the most sense. Why won't the government come clean on Roswell?"

"Because they'd have to admit they offered up their own citizens as medical guinea pigs," Alan said. "Of course."

"We're in a war, you know," Marcia said. "A very covert war, but a war just the same. That's what I believe. That's why you see Air Force jets trying to intercept UFOs; that's why they never admit that's what they were doing. And all of that has very little to do with Krista Lewis, except she doesn't fit into the pattern. She was raped. That's a human thing."

"So her murder has nothing to do with aliens."

"I don't think so," Marcia said. "But I do think there might be someone in the government involved. There's a lot of government activity in the San Luis Valley. That may or may not be why there is so much UFO activity here too. But when I found Krista's body I heard the Taos Hum, the tone, right before the earthquake."

"They set it off. They set it off right next to you," Alan said in wonder.

"Good thing it wasn't right next to me," Marcia said matter-of-factly. "Or I would be dead like Krista. But don't you see? The hum proves your story. The Tesla machine makes a *sound*."

"And it's gone off before," Alan said.

"Enough to have a name. Enough to attract the attention of the MUFON. It's going to go off again, Alan. Eventually, they're going to kill lots more people than Jim Leetsdale and his wife and baby and Krista Lewis. They're playing with forces they do not understand. This time they have to be stopped." Marcia stopped, breathing hard. Then she laughed and a blush climbed her cheeks.

"I sound like an idiot," she said.

"Not an idiot," Alan corrected. "Like a person who knows right from wrong. They don't, these earthquake people. They think it's okay to rape and kill. They think it's okay to set off earthquakes that might hurt more than they help. They can't have this kind of power."

"So how do we stop them?" Marcia asked. "Do you want to come back to Crestone with me tonight? There's some people you could meet—"

"No," Alan said. "I'll tell Sheriff Gonzalez what we know, and I'll let the Colorado Springs detectives know too. I think if we get the word out to the police, they might be able to handle the rest." He smiled at her, a great big reassuring smile, because he knew who was going to stop this madness.

He was. He hoped.

Interstate 25, Southern Colorado

Memories clamored outside the windshield like ghosts pressing against the glass. Eileen couldn't keep them out, not entirely. For a while she could concentrate on the road, on the slushy spray thrown up by the big trucks she passed, on the brilliance of the sun as it fell to the horizon. Then she would find herself remembering how it was to be hugged by Tracy

Reed, how it took her a year to allow herself to be cuddled and kissed without turning into a fearful wooden doll. She was four years old before she returned one of Tracy's carefully casual hugs. She remembered how Tracy had burst into tears when she put her arms around her adoptive mother's neck and gave her a tentative little squeeze. They'd been making cookies in the kitchen and the air smelled wonderful, full of vanilla and chocolate chips. Eileen had cried too, startled and afraid she'd done something wrong. Tracy tried to keep from weeping but she couldn't. So she sat down on the floor of the kitchen and rocked Eileen and held her until they were both calm. That was the beginning of trust.

Eileen put her turn signal on to pass a lumbering old Winnebago. She didn't want to remember any of that. She wanted to remember the ten-year-old Eileen. She hadn't hit puberty yet so she was slim and strong as a willow wand. She was chasing a cow that was trying to cut back out of the herd and head back to the creek bed, where there was shade and water. The herd had eaten all the grass in the area, so Eileen and her dad were moving them into the upper pasture. Eileen and her cowhorse, Redbone, had dashed after the cow, and when it abruptly disappeared Eileen had only a second to realize that the cow had fallen into a brushy, narrow ravine. Then she lifted herself over Redbone's haunches and lifted him into the air with all the force of her will. They'd jumped the ravine and saved both their lives, and even when Eileen had to put down the poor injured cow, she kept remembering how it felt to jump, how she knew she could leap over anything, anything at all.

She remembered the extra psychology courses she'd taken at the University of Wyoming, the extra reading she'd done to try and discover whether or not she would end up like her birth mother. She guessed her mother had been manic-depressive, or bipolar, in high school. She didn't know if she would end up like her mother. She didn't know who her father was or what he was, or even if he was still alive. She held herself back from humanity like a person in a glass jar. She always thought she was brave, but she wasn't. She was an enormous coward.

Now she knew who her father was. She was trying to find him, now, to find out if her father was a murderer just like her poor damaged mother. What haunted her, the thought that couldn't be kept entirely away, was Teddy Shaw. She was a killer now. Had Teddy Shaw's death brought her father out of the past like some ancient, unlocked door? Was her father a killer?

Once she knew, she would find a way to live with it, she promised herself. Not knowing was the difficult part. She had to know.

The exit for La Veta and the San Luis Valley loomed up in the distance. Eileen flipped on her headlights in the coming dusk and took the exit.

Briargate Subdivision, Colorado Springs, Colorado

"Okay, run that by me one more time," Joe said into the phone.

"Eileen's gone. I think she's heading down to the San Luis Valley after Alan."

"Who might be a murderer."

"Might be."

Rosen's voice was, like always, without emotion. Joe rubbed his forehead with suddenly cold fingers. He was sitting in his home office chair, where he'd been working all day on a refinement of his earthquake simulation. He'd had some ideas that he simply had to put into his program. Once Eileen, Rosen, and Alan Baxter had left, Joe had taken a seat in his chair and hadn't moved except for an occasional trip to the bathroom. It seemed as though Eileen had just left. Alan, a murderer?

"Impossible," Joe said flatly. "He couldn't be."

"I don't deal in impossibilities," Rosen said coldly.

"In other words, we can't take the chance that he could be the murderer," Joe said, feeling a sinking sensation in his gut. He couldn't, either. Could Alan be an imposter, a man pretending to be Eileen's father? As soon as the thought materialized in his head, Joe rejected it. You couldn't fake bone structure, placement of the eyes, the clever narrow hands. They were too alike to be anything but father and daughter.

But he could still be a murderer, Joe reluctantly admitted to himself. All murderers were someone's son or daughter, sometimes a father or mother or uncle. Just because Alan seemed as transparently good as a pane of clear glass didn't mean a thing.

"That's right," Rosen said, answering Joe's thoughts.

"Well let's go get her, then," Joe said.

"That's why I called," Rosen said. "Harben released me to drive down and find her. He contacted Gonzalez. It's my idea to bring you."

"Where are you now?" Joe asked.

"About two blocks away," Rosen said with infuriating calm.

"Well, shit, that doesn't give me any time," Joe said, and cast a glance at his Frankenputer. There was that one last change he wanted to make. Never mind. "Do you have hiking gear? Camping gear?"

"A change of clothes in a gym bag," Rosen said. "I can't go home, remember."

"Good thing I have two backpacks," Joe said, walking down the hallway toward what he'd dubbed his sports room. "And a tent. Knock when you're here, I've got to—"

"I'm here," Rosen said, and keyed off his phone.

"Get some stuff ready," Joe said grimly. He spun on his heel and hurried back to the front of the house. He caught a glimpse of his bedroom, and his bed, striped with late afternoon sunshine. He hadn't made the bed today and he could clearly see the imprint of Eileen's head on a pillow. He could almost smell her, the sleepy soapy fragrance that clung to every inch of her skin. Underneath that she always smelled a little bit wild, a strong musky scent that must come from her adrenaline-charged lifestyle. Joe loved her a bit sweaty, a little bit tangy, when her natural scent threatened to overwhelm all the civilized coverings of soap and deodorant. The way she smelled after they made love. He bit back a strangled curse and looked away from the bed. He couldn't lose her. He simply couldn't.

Rosen stood on the doorstep holding his gym bag and a six-pack of distilled water bottles that dangled from their plastic loops like little hanged men. Joe immediately wanted to punch him in the nose, and saw the tight line of muscles in Rosen's jaw. Rosen probably longed to punch him back.

"Come in," Joe said. "I haven't had time to pack. You can help."

Rosen said nothing. He followed Joe to the sports room and set his gym bag and the package of water on the floor. The room had been a nursery before Joe bought the house, and he'd never bothered to change the wallpaper. Banding the center of the walls was a happy collection of animals being loaded on a whole set of arks, with Noah and his wife cheerfully waving all the animals aboard. There were no clouds in the pastel blue wallpaper sky. Rosen contemplated the artwork and touched a gentle finger to the elephants. Joe felt a little less like hitting him.

Joe had arranged his equipment neatly on the carpeted floor. He had biking gear and his bike along one wall, his safety vest and helmet for whitewater rafting in one corner along with some climbing equipment that he had used only a few times. Climbing gave him no thrill at all, even though he gave it a few tries to really decide. He was simply scared and cold and mad at himself the whole time he was climbing, and tired afterwards. He had some fishing gear as well, but his hiking equipment was by far the most used of the lot. He had recently bought a new pack so he tossed his old one at Rosen. It still had his old sleeping bag and pad tied at the bottom. Rosen would probably get cold in his old bag, but right now Joe didn't much care.

He picked up his new pack and checked the contents. He had a propane camping stove, matches and a flashlight, toilet paper and bug spray, and sunscreen. He had a small set of cooking dishes and a plastic flask of Glenlivet Scotch. He had a ceramic water filter—but there was no water in the dunes. He left it in there anyway. He had a good first-aid bag with a snakebite kit. What else? Compass, but no map. Flares for bears that were useless in the sand dunes but might come in handy if they ended up anywhere in the San Juan Mountains.

Mountain lions and bears did not like the huge hissing noise and the bright red light of a road flare. Joe had never actually tried this out, he had merely read it on the Internet and decided it sounded like a great idea. He'd secretly wanted to encounter a bear ever since to see if it worked, which he knew was a very foolish idea. What if it didn't?

"Food and maps, and a set of warm clothing," he said to Rosen. "Do you have a GPS?"

"Yes, I do," Rosen said. A GPS module was essential if they intended to find latitude 37.47.50 and longitude 105.33.20 in the dunes. Otherwise they could stumble in circles for days and never find their spot.

"Alan has one, doesn't he?"

"Yes," Rosen said. "Is there anything I can carry?" He'd loaded his borrowed pack with his water and clothing, and it sat empty on the floor.

"Yeah, the tent," Joe said. "I'll carry most of the food and we'll split the water. Maybe we won't have to go in after them." He contemplated his newest sports room addition. It was a .357 handgun, polished steel, oily looking, and ugly. Eileen taught him how to shoot it, picked it out for him, showed him how to care for it. He still didn't like it much.

"You have a conceal-carry permit?"

"Yes, I do," Joe sighed. "Eileen made me get one."

"Then take it," Rosen said. "If you need it, you'll have it. Is that the tent?"

Ten minutes later they were out the door. Joe folded up his Frankenputer laptop and carried it with him along with his pack and an empty Thermos. He intended to fill it with hot truck-stop coffee when they refueled, somewhere between here and the San Luis Valley.

"I've got a division car," Rosen said. Joe had to smile. It was a full-sized Ford Bronco, old and battered. Originally a deep blue, the paint had faded over the years and turned a milky color over the fenders. It didn't look at all like a cop car.

"Does it work?" he joked.

"Yes," Rosen answered, and Joe rolled his eyes. That's right, Rosen had a very strange humor bone. The late afternoon was now definitely early evening. The sun was starting to set over the mountain range to the west, and Joe realized they would be driving over roads that were going to turn to slippery ice in a matter of hours. He stepped through slush to get to the back of the Bronco and put his gear inside, slush that was getting colder by the minute as the temperature dropped.

"I hope you're a good driver," Joe said.

Rosen shrugged, setting his backpack into the Bronco. Joe kept his laptop and his Thermos with him as he settled into the passenger seat. He put on his seatbelt and held his computer with both hands as Rosen muscled the Bronco into the street. They didn't skid on two tires going around the street corner, but Joe would have sworn he felt the tires lighten up on his side.

"Don't worry, I can drive," Rosen said, as he roared toward the interstate. Joe nodded and gave him a big smile. Rosen glanced over at him and Joe winked.

"Go faster," he suggested, trying not to clutch his laptop too hard. He'd be damned if he were going to let this cop out-macho him.

"As fast as we can," Rosen said. Joe found he could relax as they made their way to the interstate and accelerated up the on-ramp. Rosen was a very good driver. He pushed the limits of the Bronco but never exceeded them. Something about his driving seemed to reflect a hidden Rosen. His driving was flamboyant and arrogant. He took the car to the edge at every corner and squealed the tires like a freshly pinched girl at every stop. His driving was anything but emotionless. Joe decided he was starting to like Rosen. Maybe.

20

The Pentagon, Washington, D.C.

"What about Detective Rosen? Is he available?" Lucy asked. She'd kicked off her shoes the moment she got back into her car. Despite the fact that they were low-heeled and cushioned, she had blisters on the upper parts of both heels. The walk back through the archives and then her fast walk out to her car had broken one of the blisters, and it hurt like fury.

"One moment, ma'am," the administrative assistant said.

Lucy looked around the parking lot and saw no one close. She held her cell phone to her ear with her shoulder and reached under her skirt with both hands. She ripped a hole in her pantyhose pulling them down, but she didn't care. In a few moments she had the horrid things dangling from one hand, and her broken blister stopped throbbing so badly.

"I'm sorry, he's not available," the assistant said. Lucy remembered him, Bob. Evidently he was a whiz at administrative duties, but he hated Eileen and she disliked him right back. Consequently, he'd never been helpful to Lucy on the few occasions she called the Colorado Springs Special Investigations Bureau.

"Get me Captain Harben," she said, starting her car and slamming the door shut.

"He's in conference," the Bob voice said smugly. "I can take him a message."

"Tell him Lucy Giometti called for Eileen Reed. Tell him this has a material bearing on their current investigation. Tell him I have information that might save their lives. Can you tell him that, *Bob*?"

"I'll let him know, ma'am," Bob said. "Can you give me a number where he might reach you?"

Lucy relayed her cell phone number and started her car. She started the long drive home with the air conditioner blowing and her bare feet feeling strange on the pedals. She was on the beltway and moving slowly in the constant traffic jam when her phone chirped.

"Captain Harben?" she said.

"Mrs. Giometti," Harben said. "I wasn't aware your agency had any interest in this case."

"They don't," Lucy said impatiently. "This was a favor for a friend. As such, everything I say is off the record and unusable in court. But Eileen needs to know this. Is she there? I need to reach her."

"My detectives are on assignment," Harben said cautiously. "And this is a cell phone on your side?"

"Yes," Lucy said, and blew a sweaty lock of hair from her forehead. "We'll just talk in a roundabout way, then. Okay?"

"No way to get to a land line?"

"None," Lucy said, looking at the traffic. "Listen to me. I found the file that Joe asked me about. Certain information that was supposed to be there was missing. There was plenty there, but the file we wanted to look at was empty." Here Lucy had a memory of the open box with the files and the pictures and the ancient dead dove encased in plastic, the inexplicable white dove. "The—er, sanitized person that Eileen asked me about was the one who took the contents out of the file. So he took it, and he is using it, and I think he is more dangerous than she may suspect."

"How do you know?"

"He took the plans, but he left some of the other documents," Lucy said. "I know what he's doing, and it's *huge*." She had a copy of the folder but Tate and Randy had insisted on keeping the original. Her visit was unofficial and they were planning on taking the theft to their own highest level. They were incandescent with fury, even though the Tesla designs had been stolen before the box had arrived from the FBI. Randy had broken the FBI seal on the box to let Lucy look inside. Lucy was awed by Randy and Tate's command of curses in English, French, and what must have been medieval Latin when they saw the nearly empty folder.

"This could be difficult," Harben said slowly. "Your information isn't enough for an arrest warrant, and I don't have enough either. We could get a temporary for a few hours if my detectives find him in a compromising location."

The dunes, Lucy whispered silently to herself. Eileen was in the dunes with Rosen and she was going to try and find Jacob Mitchell.

"I have an idea," she said finally. "I have a contact with the FBI out there. I can get things moving on the FBI side to confiscate his—whatever it is, device, as material to an investigation here in Washington."

"We've been trying to get some action from the FBI on our side as well, since the young lady involved was a government contractor. So far, no luck."

"Let me try," Lucy said grimly. "I'll call you when I get some information."

"Thank you," Harben said gravely.

"Thank me when it's over," Lucy said, and hung up the phone. She tapped her bare toes on the gritty surface of her brakes and tried to think. She wanted to go out there. She wanted to get permission to fly out there, as she had once before, and meet up with Eileen and defeat the bad guys. She lifted her phone to call the travel agency. Then she put the phone back down.

She could not go. She could not. Hank was still a nursing baby. He needed her every four hours. She couldn't take him with her, either. What was she going to do, put him in a carrying sling? How ridiculous. The air conditioner spat cold air at her and the traffic shimmered through the heat waves and

Lucy started to cry. She cried bitterly for what she could not have, cried as inconsolably as a child wanting a toy that has been taken away. When she was done, she blew her nose one-handed and wiped her eyes, and then she picked up her cell phone and dialed the FBI.

The Williams's Ranch, San Luis Valley, Colorado

The main gate to the Williams's Ranch was closed and locked, an arrangement Eileen found curious. There was a button set into a pole at the gate, positioned for an easy reach from a truck. She pushed it, and waited. Eventually a tall woman in an enormous sheepskin duster arrived. Her name, Eileen learned later, was Susan, and as she approached, Eileen knew she was everything her own parents had hoped she would become. This was a woman, strong and tall and sunweathered, who would want nothing more than the land, the cattle, the horse, forever.

Eileen felt a piercing sorrow watching the other woman approach. She wanted nothing else, in that moment, but to be married to her childhood friend Owen Sutter and to live on a ranch in Wyoming. She wanted to be wearing a sheepskin duster and calfskin gloves and know nothing more of death than what happens to steers in the fall and lambs in the spring.

Susan was driving a pickup truck so exquisitely battered it could have been some sort of art sculpture. Or maybe it had just been rolled a few times. It was covered in icy mud, and the hood was wired shut with a twist of baling wire. Susan's expression was as chilly as the ice on her truck as she pulled up at the gate.

"Yes?" she said, then her expression changed into bewilderment. "Do I know you?"

"I think you know my father," Eileen said. "Alan Baxter. Is he here? Could I talk to him?"

Susan's face crinkled into a broad grin, changing her in an instant from sternness to merriment. "Of course, you're Eileen! I'm Susan Williams. You look just like him."

"Everybody says that," Eileen said under her breath as

Susan spun a combination lock and swung open the gate. Eileen had never seen a locked ranch gate before and it puzzled her. Why would you lock your front gate? What kind of visitors would you want to keep out of a ranch? In Wyoming, most people depended on their dogs to warn them of visitors. Visitors were rare where she was from. She drove through and pulled her Jeep over so Susan could take the lead after she closed the gate. This bit of ranch savvy elicited a raised eyebrow from the other woman.

Beth and Sam Williams's spread was instantly familiar to her, an arrangement of main house and outbuildings much like her own family home in Wyoming. At the main house, Susan waved Eileen to a parking spot in the slushy yard, then led the way to an enormous mud room where Eileen was shown a hook on which to hang her winter coat and hat. The floor was tile and it was covered in mud and dirt. Hooks and shelves and baskets held an astonishing array of coats, hats, gloves, and boots. Underneath a particularly large pile of mud-smeared clothing, a washing machine clanked and hummed busily.

Susan, shedding her duster and a shapeless wool hat, revealed herself to be younger than Eileen thought at first. She was Eileen's own age, but she topped Eileen by six inches of height and forty pounds of weight. There wasn't an ounce of fat on her; she was just large all over. She smelled strongly of horses, a scent that made Eileen draw a deep breath in nostalgia. Eileen used to smell that way.

"Horses," she explained to Susan. "I used to ride just about every day."

"I'm surprised you could tell," Susan said, brushing at her jeans and frowning. "I rode out this afternoon, but it was too muddy for Charlie so I came back and got the truck."

"You don't smell that strongly," Eileen said, sitting down at a handy bench and tugging at her shoes. "I just haven't smelled horse in a while, that's all."

"You could go out with me tomorrow, if you'd like," Susan offered. "My old mare, Origami, she's as gentle as a rocking chair. I don't ride her much since I got Charlie."

Eileen had to swallow before she spoke. What was *wrong*

with her? She wanted to accept; in that moment, it seemed as though she wanted nothing else.

"I don't know how long I'll be here," she said. "Is my father here?"

"No, he's in town having lunch with somebody who might know about Krista Lewis," Susan said, so casually it made Eileen jump. "He should be back pretty soon."

"You know about Krista Lewis?" Eileen said.

"Sure, and Jim Leetsdale too," Susan replied, shaking out her short brown hair. "Come on, Mom's got coffee and sweet rolls waiting. She's going to be really excited to meet you."

The kitchen, clean and warm and smelling of cinnamon and vanilla, was inhabited by a woman who could only be Susan's mother. She was as tall as her daughter but larger by far, with brown hair going to gray and light-colored eyes.

"I'm Beth Williams. Susan told me she was bringing Alan Baxter's daughter," she said, in a voice as warm as her kitchen. Susan patted her shirt pocket for Eileen's benefit. A cell phone.

Beth held out her hands and Eileen found herself being drawn into a hug. "I'm so glad you found each other," Beth whispered, for Eileen's ears only, then released her. Eileen found herself swallowing hard for the second time in five minutes.

"Coffee, and rolls," Beth said briskly, turning away. Eileen found a place at the big country table, watching as Susan poured herself a cup of coffee and rummaged around a cabinet until she found a package of what looked like hot chocolate mix. She dumped the powder into her coffee and stirred it with a spoon, then came and thumped down next to Eileen.

"Want one like it?" she offered. "It's my version of a hot chocolate. Hot coffee chocolate."

"Just coffee, thanks," Eileen said, grinning. She was starting to feel a bit less overwhelmed. The sweet rolls were very good, steaming and full of raisins and with just enough icing. She hadn't eaten lunch, she recalled, and she wolfed two of the rolls and finished a cup of coffee in just a few minutes.

"You look better now," Beth said, leaning back over her

own coffee and roll. "You were pretty pale. So why are you here?"

Eileen opened her mouth, and looked at the two women sitting at the table with her. Their hospitality was more than simple ranch manners, she knew. Her treatment was a reflection of the impact that Alan Baxter had made on this place. She knew what that was like. She liked Alan Baxter, too.

"I suspect he might try to find Krista's murderer on his own," she said, and before the words were out of her mouth she knew they were true. Either Alan Baxter was the murderer, or he was going to try and find the murderer. There was really no other explanation for what he was doing. In order to find out what he was, Eileen was going to have to play along with him. And it might get her killed. She'd known that, too, before she'd gotten into her Jeep. It was a risk that seemed acceptable. It still seemed acceptable.

When Alan walked into Beth's kitchen two hours later, Eileen was eating supper with Susan and Beth and Sam. Frank, Eileen had learned, was one of the hired men. He was out riding a fence line to make sure it was intact after the storm. The other ranch hands, Jenny and Mark, were married and had their own cabin. They usually ate supper at their own place. Alan stepped through the doorway and Eileen felt that peculiar humming sound again, the rushing sensation of her own blood through her veins.

"Eileen," he said, stopping abruptly.

"Hi," she said mildly, scooping a forkful of lasagna to her mouth. The delicious bite could have been sawdust for all she tasted it.

"What are you doing here?" he said. He looked stunned, guilty even, and Eileen's heart contracted fiercely.

"Some interesting developments," Eileen said. "So I came on down." She took another determined bite of food.

"We've been getting acquainted," Beth said with a grin. "I tried to get Reg to come out but he's at home with Maria Elena and won't leave. He said he'd try to come by tomorrow for lunch. I hope you're still here for lunch?" She looked anxiously at Eileen, who managed to nod and shrug her shoulders at the same time.

"We'll ride out in the morning, Eileen," Susan said with a wrinkle of her nose. "I promised Eileen a ride on Origami. *Before* you invited Uncle Reg."

"Are you hungry, Alan?" Beth asked. "There's plenty of food."

"I'm not hungry. I had a late lunch," Alan said, looking dazed. "Maybe Eileen and I could talk for a little bit?"

"Sure," Sam Williams said through a mouthful of food. "Use the living room, we hardly ever go in there 'cept for parties."

Eileen took a last bite and stood up. She carried her plate and cup to the sink, rinsed them, and stacked them in the dishwasher. She had no idea what she was going to say to Alan. Her father. When she shut the dishwasher door, it slammed more loudly than she thought it should. Then she realized someone was standing in the doorway to the mudroom, in coat and hat and muddy boots. The outside door had slammed shut at the same time as the dishwasher door.

This must be Frank, the hired man, Eileen realized. He was slender, not particularly tall, with black hair and eyes and a nose that would rival Rosen's. Frank would have been right at home in Lucy Giometti's very Italian family. If he were wearing a handmade suit and his hair were slicked back, he could have played an extra in one of the Godfather movies. Instead, he was wearing a sheepskin duster even filthier than Susan's. His hair was in disarray and his face pinched and white and wild. Eileen stood straight, and if she had coyote ears they would have come up into stiff, tall points. Frank looked upset. More than upset. He looked scared to death.

"There's two guys at the gate," he said, panting. "They were trying to get in and when I drove up they said—they said—"

"Take a deep breath," Sam said, standing from the table. "They didn't ring the bell." He took two steps and hooked an enormous shotgun from an alcove Eileen had not noticed. He calmly checked the load and clicked the safety off as Frank took a couple of calming breaths. Everyone else stood or sat as if electrified, and Eileen thought of a horrid movie she'd seen as a child, some late-night thing that scared her more than any bug-eyed radioactive monster ever did. The knock on the door, the jack-booted troops bursting in on a family at supper, and the long ride in the cattle cars to the concentration camps and horrible death.

But this wasn't Nazi Germany. Sam Williams's enormous shotgun was proof of that, if nothing else.

"They said they were from the DEFA, whatever that is, and they had badges, looked like FBI badges but different. They said they had a warrant to search this place and I had to let them in. They said they had an arrest warrant for Alan Baxter! I said I'd be right back and I kicked the Honda into top gear and I came right here."

"They don't," Eileen said into the silence. "I'm working with the feds and they don't have Alan as a suspect. They—"

"I think they shot at me," Frank said, and if everyone were silent before, the room was now as still as stone. "You know how the Honda can go, and I was going as fast as I could. But I heard something, like a backfire, and I swear something went right by my ear." He sat down on the bench in the mudroom, his face looking both lost and angry. "They *shot* at me."

Susan was kneeling at Frank's feet before anyone else moved, and as her arms went around Frank and she buried her face in his shoulder, Eileen saw a stunned look on both Beth and Sam Williams's faces. Then Beth's face broke into a grin of delight, uncomplicated and joyous. Evidently Susan was keeping a secret about the hired man. Beth, all thoughts of invaders at the gate gone, beamed at her daughter's back. Eileen could practically read "wedding" and "grandchildren" on the woman's broad forehead.

"Were they dressed in black, Frank?" Alan asked.

"Yeah," Frank said, bringing his face up from Susan's sleek brown head. She was still buried in his shoulder, hugging him hard. He looked at Beth and Sam anxiously. He was obviously more worried at the moment about the shotgun in Sam Williams's hands than the shooters at the gate. What he saw in their faces obviously reassured him. He blew a gusty breath out and his arms tightened around Susan. "How did you know? They were dressed in black. Black suits, like. Mafia suits, I'd call 'em."

"Men-in-black?" Sam Williams asked, his face even grimmer. Eileen looked at him with surprise. He didn't sound derisive, or doubting. Sam Williams sounded as though he believed in them. She shuddered, suddenly, and obviously. All heads turned to her.

"Just like the ones who tried to kill you, Eileen," Alan said calmly.

Eileen shrugged at the faces that were looking back at her. "I doubt my man-in-black was an alien. He was very upset when I shot him in the chest."

"But he survived," Alan said quietly.

"Evidently, he did," Eileen said. "But he might have been wearing body armor. And hadn't we better get out to the gate before your friends find a way through?"

"They aren't going to find a way through unless they have a tank," Sam Williams said with satisfaction. He was a big, rangy man, with muscles like old ropes in his arms and neck. The sun had weathered him to mahogany and put crow's-feet around his eyes that were as deep as cuts. His hair was mostly gone and what little remained was a brilliant, movie-star white. His eyebrows, white like his hair, were bushy and enormous, like wooly white caterpillars on his forehead. He smiled at Eileen.

"The ditch along the highway is too deep and broad for a truck to cross. The culvert where the gate goes is the only good place to get in. They can walk up here, but it'll take them a good hour or so. I got tired of reporters and those UFO types trespassing after our first set of cattle mutilations. So I fixed it."

"They might be on their way up on foot," Eileen said, thinking *cattle mutilations?* "They really might. These guys could be killers."

"Then we'll be ready," Beth said, focussing with an effort away from her daughter. "Frank, Susan, get Jenny and Mark up to the main house. Let the dogs out. I'm going to call Reg and get him out here as quickly as he can."

"You mean your cattle dogs?" Alan asked, as Susan and

Frank scrambled to their feet and rummaged in the mudroom. Eileen saw Susan come up with a handsome shotgun and Frank strap on a pair of revolvers fit for an Old West movie, and approved. They dove out the door as Beth dialed the sheriff's number.

"Yeah, the cattle dogs, and I'd hate to lose them," Sam said quietly. He turned off the kitchen lights and the room was plunged into gloom. The only light came from the gas burners on Beth's big stove. "They're mostly Border collie mixed with some German shepherd. You've seen them work. Damn smart dogs. They'll stay away from our friends and bark like mad, which is all I want. I hope they don't get shot at."

"Okay, Reg, just get here as soon as you can," Beth said into the phone, and hung up. She looked cheerful. "He's on his way with lights blazing. He said not to kill them, please, particularly if they're the fed agents he's been asking for. He said they probably won't send him any more if we shoot these guys."

"Better tell Susan," Alan murmured, his eyes sparkling. Eileen, too, felt much better. Perhaps this was all a mistake. Then she remembered that these men said they had an arrest warrant for Alan Baxter. Perhaps they *were* Feds, and they knew something that she didn't. So why did she immediately leap to Alan's defense when Frank burst through the door? She couldn't be losing perspective that badly.

"According to Joe's simulation, there's going to be an earthquake the day after tomorrow," Alan said abruptly. "I want to be at that spot in the dunes, that latitude and longitude, the day after tomorrow. And if I'm not here, and those feds are really feds, then you don't have to try and get them off your land. You can let them on and let them search when Reg arrives, and I'll be gone."

"You're going into the dunes? At *night?*" Sam gripped his shotgun and the wooly eyebrows drew together.

"Alan," Beth said gently, "we've had people go into the dunes in broad daylight and never come out. They're a strange place, and that was long before Krista was found. You could get lost. Really lost."

"Dead lost," Sam said.

"But he won't," Eileen said. "He's got a GPS system, and that's how he's going to find his X marks the spot."

"That's right," Alan said, "How did you know?"

"Because I have one too," Eileen said. "And I'm coming with you."

Sam shook his head and looked out through the curtains. "GPS systems go haywire in the dunes too. Sometimes they work great, sometimes they don't. Depends on sunspots, for all I know, or the UFOs that don't exist. All I'm saying is, you're taking a big chance."

"You can't go with me," Alan said to Eileen, as though they were the only two in the room. "I can't let you go with me."

"Because you might get killed?" Eileen said. "Because I might get killed? Because you might kill someone? This isn't some sort of revenge mission. We're going to find these people and talk to them, and if necessary I can arrest them."

"I wasn't planning on killing anyone," Alan said stiffly. "I just want to see who it is, that's all. And I'll tell Sheriff Gonzalez, and you, and whoever else needs to know—"

"I'm going with you," Eileen said again.

Alan threw his hands up in the air and his face suddenly crinkled into a twisted sort of smile. It was the strangest smile Eileen had ever seen. It looked like it hurt.

"You took your diaper off at two and a half," he said. "And you wouldn't put a diaper on again. You looked just like that when you told me you wouldn't wear a diaper anymore." He blinked furiously. Eileen's mouth dropped open in surprise. Beth looked at the two of them and shrugged her ample shoulders.

"I'd rather try and stop an avalanche with my bare hands than step between the likes of you," she said grimly. "And I'd prefer not to mess with real feds, if they're real feds. Let me get some grub put together for you. Sam, get your topographical maps out so these two can find the back way out of the ranch and to the dunes. You two get your gear on and we'll have you out of here before my brother arrives. He won't approve, so we'll just get you on your way."

Sam Williams's pocket chirped and he pulled out a cell phone.

"They're still at the gate? Good," he said. "Keep an eye out for others, just in case, Frank. Stay in pairs. Reg is going to be here soon."

"Let's go, then," Eileen said. "We don't have much time."

21

Peterson Air Force Base, Colorado Springs, Colorado

"We're ready, sir," Bennett said. Scott stood behind him, still slightly canted to one side.

"The ribs are healed?" Mitchell asked, his voice full of concern. He sat at his desk without an office light. The only light came from the dying day, behind him, and he knew he was silhouetted in the window. It was a fine dramatic effect and he'd used it before.

"Almost completely, sir," Scott said. The concussion, given to him by that traitor Leetsdale, was almost gone, but now the skinny bitch detective had broken two ribs through his Kevlar vest. Scott was loyal to the bone, though, however broken they might be. Mitchell almost giggled at the metaphor. Scott would take a bullet for him, he was sure of it. He would be secretary of defense in his new administration. Roger Bennett, of course, would be his chief of staff.

"I have a question, gentlemen," Mitchell said, bringing his thoughts back to the present. Here was the reason for the back lighting, the imposing outline of the Boss. He concentrated on their faces.

"Yes, sir," they said in unison.

"Did either one of you rape Krista Lewis? Did either one of you kill her?"

Both men, in the light where he was in shadow, reacted with innocence and surprise. Mitchell breathed a sigh of relief. He was afraid one of them had killed her. Killed her without permission, without orders from him. Killing without orders was unacceptable and dangerous.

When Krista Lewis had walked over a dune and into their encampment, no one had been more surprised than Mitchell. She was a tall girl with enough Swede in her to give her the vanilla blond hair and the bigboned look of someone who could walk up and down mountains all day. She was investigating an outbreak of *E. coli*–related illness among a picnicking church group at Medano Creek. The Centers for Disease Control investigators finally pinned the outbreak to the unpasteurized juice that was served at the picnic, but by that time Krista Lewis, working with the CDC, had discovered elevated levels of *E. coli* at the point where the waters of the creek rose out of the sand. Mitchell's group hadn't brought in latrines and they'd used the encampment for two years. Enough human waste had soaked into the sand to reach the ground water and create a trace of *E. coli* in Medano creek. Busted by their own shit, imagine that.

He'd known something like this could happen, of course. The Great Sand Dunes were the only location in the world for his experiments and they were public property. He couldn't arrange to have any part of them restricted. The edge of the dunes, where the roads and visitor's center were located, was crowded with tourists from June until September. Even the center of the dunes, his required location, saw an occasional hardy hiker or two. On top of the legal restrictions and the tourists, the dunes themselves were an almost impossible obstacle. The sand got into everything; equipment, tents, food, clothing. The device gummed up with sand after two or three experiments and had to be thoroughly cleaned before it could be used again.

The solution was obvious, though more vulnerable than Mitchell wanted. He'd finally agreed with his scientists; the

experiments had to be flown in and out. The base of opera-
tions, Peterson Air Force Base, was as secure as a locked
vault. But the experiments themselves had to take place in the
open, in the dunes, with nothing more than a few soldiers to
guard the perimeter. The team knew that someone like Krista
Lewis would happen. The irony was that she had been looking for them, following the telltale presence of their own
waste.

Krista hadn't been very impressed with his credentials and
his presence, but she'd allowed herself to be escorted away
from the area before they'd cranked up the machine. It was le-
gitimately top secret and she worked for a government contractor. She knew she had to leave the area. She made sure
they all knew they were busted, though, top secret or not. Environmental pollution was a trump card in the game of government bureaucracy and Krista knew it. They knew it, too. It
was infuriating to watch her stride out of sight, muscular
haunches flexing her Swede behind, knowing she would be
filing reports within the week that would require them to fly
in portable latrines with their experiments. Krista didn't have
to know what their experiments were. She obviously didn't
care what they were doing. Her job was to keep them from
polluting the environment and she had the power to do it.

Scott stood guard that evening to make sure she didn't
come back and see the machine with the tarpaulin off. They'd
spent the night, that night, as they sometimes did when they
had more than a single event to deliver. Any one of the three
of them could have crept away that night and followed her
tracks. But there was no need to rape her, to kill her, no need
to threaten the whole purpose of the project. Mitchell was le-
gitimately involved in a government project and by the time
her reports made it through Washington, it would all be over
anyway. There might not *be* a Washington anymore. Killing
her was a mistake. Raping her was stupid. There would be all
the rape in the world, if they wanted. But after, after. Not yet.

"Someone was very careless. The event is tomorrow," he
said coldly. "Let's not let our appetites get the better of us,
gentlemen. I don't really want to know which one of you did

it and endangered our entire program. I just want to warn you. Don't ever do anything like this again."

"Yes, sir," they both said, in unison again like the good soldiers they were. Then Bennett cleared his throat. Mitchell nodded at him.

"Yes?"

"Sir, it might have been someone else entirely," Bennett suggested. "We don't know that it was one of us. There are other people in the dunes. Maybe even that Alan Baxter guy, the one that identified her body. He seems like the most likely killer."

"This man?" Mitchell said, looking at Alan Baxter's picture in the file Bennett had created for him. This man didn't look much like a killer. The file also contained pictures and background sheets on Eileen Reed and David Rosen, the infuriating Springs detectives.

"That's right, it could have been that Baxter guy," Scott said, a bit too eagerly for Mitchell's taste.

"Perhaps," Mitchell said, and flipped the folder closed. "It doesn't matter now. Sit down. We need to go over the final plans one more time." He reached over and turned on the desk light. He gestured Scott and Bennett into the room, and as they took their seats, he spread out the first of the maps.

The Williams's Ranch, San Luis Valley, Colorado

"What do you mean, they're gone?" Gonzalez roared. His face was lit by the flashing blue and red police lights on top of his vehicle, and to Marcia Fowler he looked seven feet tall and as wide as a house and positively terrifying. She glanced over at Daniel Grantham, who sat with his arms wrapped around his chest. Daniel hadn't wanted to come with the sheriff. He particularly hadn't wanted to come to the Williams's Ranch with the sheriff. There was that big bad blood between Beth Williams and Lady Jane.

The two of them were in Gonzalez's office when Beth had called for help. Daniel was only part of the way through his idea of hunting the killer through the fresh snow of the dunes, and already Marcia thought they were losing the sale. Gonzalez looked thunderous at the start of their talk and only grew darker as Daniel continued. The only lightness to him was when Daniel explained the MUFON theory of a human, rather than an alien, predator.

"Well, okay, then," he muttered.

Shortly after that the phone rang, and now Marcia watched out the truck window as the ranch owner, who must be Sam Williams, talked to the sheriff. Gonzalez insisted they come with him to the Williams's Ranch. The Expedition had enormous heaters that kept Marcia warm even though the driver's side window was down, but she thought Gonzalez should be cold. He didn't look cold—he wasn't even wearing a heavy jacket, just his police jacket with his name sewn on the front and his badge of office on the sleeve.

Sam Williams didn't look cold, either, although both men were standing in six inches of snow. He was a big, rangy man, tall as Gonzalez but half as wide. An old baseball cap shaded his face, but Marcia could see his mouth and chin, and they looked capable and kindly.

"Come up to the main house," Sam said. "We'll tell you what happened. But I'm not happy having my gate open right now, to tell the truth."

Gonzalez glanced back at the Expedition then leaned forward and spoke urgently and softly to Sam Williams. Williams scrubbed at his face and adjusted his hat, then shrugged with a what-the-hell gesture. Gonzalez shouldered his way back into the truck and flipped his police lights off. Darkness fell abruptly. It was only then that Marcia realized how dark the night was out here, the absolute lack of any lights but those of their truck, Sam Williams's truck, and a lone approaching pair of headlights along the highway.

Gonzalez shifted into first gear and rolled the truck over the cattle guard and onto Sam Williams's property. Sam, who had stayed out of his truck to close the gate, straightened abruptly as the approaching headlights turned and lit him from head to boots.

"Oh shit," Gonzalez said, and was suddenly gone from the front seat. He was so quick and silent that Marcia was left with her mouth hanging open. How could a man that big move that fast?

Everything happened quickly after that. Sam Williams slammed the gate shut and shoved the lock into place. He stepped back from the gate, and as Gonzalez appeared at his side, he grew a pistol from one hand like some sort of magician's trick.

"Is that a gun?" Marcia asked in a silly high voice, then bit her lips closed. Of course it was a gun. And her own little .38 was stashed in her backpack at Daniel's house, where it was totally useless. She tried to shrink down into the backseat and wondered if she could run fast enough to hide herself in the vast blackness that surrounded them, if things went really wrong out there.

The headlights grew dazzling. The car pulled up and stopped at the gate. Marcia couldn't tell what kind of vehicle it was behind the glare from the headlights. Then the lights flicked down to fog lamps and a man jumped out of the driver's side.

"Hello," the man said. "Is this the Williams's Ranch?"

"Yes, it is," Sam Williams said, holding his pistol very casually in his hand. The man was mostly a shape to Marcia, a tall sort of shape. Another man climbed out of the other side and Gonzalez and Williams sharpened their stances minutely, like runners coming up to point before the starter's pistol sets them off.

"Oh, man, I hope you have a bathroom we can use," the other man said. "I gotta whiz like you would not believe."

"I'm Dave Rosen with the Colorado Springs Special Investigations Bureau," the driver shape said. "And this is Joe Tanner. Are you Sheriff Gonzalez? Did you talk to Captain Harben?"

Sam Williams's shoulders dropped in relief and his pistol disappeared as magically as it had arrived.

"Eileen thought you might come after her," he said. "And Alan told us all about you two. You're her partner, right? And you're the computer guy? Her boyfriend?"

"I'm the boyfriend, who has to go something awful," the

Joe shape said. "Are we all guys here? Can I just use your fence post?"

"Better water your truck wheel, my fence is electrified," Sam said with amusement. "Just a tickle, but it would give you a surprise in the wrong place."

"I'd like to see some identification before we open the gate," Gonzalez said stolidly. "I'm more suspicious thinking than Sam is."

"Sure," Rosen said. He stepped toward the gate and his shape resolved itself into a tall Native American with short hair and a neatly buttoned shirt and tie. He wore a roomy, puffy winter jacket that looked warm. He held out a badge, carefully not touching the gate. "Did you have some trouble here tonight?"

"He's sharp," Daniel whispered in Marcia's ear, making her jump. She'd forgotten he was sitting next to her, so absorbed she was in the drama playing outside their window.

"All better," Joe Tanner announced, coming out from behind the back corner of the truck. He saw Rosen handing his badge to Gonzalez and frowned, then his face cleared and he shrugged. Marcia liked him immediately. He was very young and had a big, impudent smile. His hair was bristly and dark-colored. He was wearing a soft blue jacket shell over a fleecy underjacket that was a swirl of colors, both of them well worn. Marcia had the same arrangement of cold weather gear, a fleece jacket with a waterproof shell that could take her from a desert night in August to a snow slope in December. This Joe was no stranger to the outdoors. He dug a dog-eared wallet from his pants and fingered through some slips of paper before he produced a driver's license. He offered it to Gonzalez and accepted it back from the sheriff with a nod.

"Let me warn Beth who's coming," Sam said, holding a phone to his ear as he worked the combination lock on the gate. "She'll put on some coffee and we'll get some chow for everyone and we'll get things sorted out."

"Is Eileen with Beth?" Joe asked. The brightness faded from his face as Sam looked at him soberly.

"We'll talk at the main house," Gonzalez said firmly.

"I want to get the hell away from the highway," Sam said, putting away his phone. "So let's go, people."

Great Sand Dunes, San Luis Valley, Colorado

Alan Baxter stopped at the top of a dune and looked around him. As far as he could see there were nothing but dunes, an endless rise and fall of them. Even the range of mountains had disappeared, the lovely Sangre de Cristos, buried by the mountains of sand. There was no wind but there were no clouds, either. The snow made the night seem colder than it was. The moon was thin, on the wane, which meant it was a horned moon. It gave enough light to see by, anyway, and he hoped the evil that a horned moon was supposed to portend was meant for the other guys, not for them. The rest of the sky was packed with stars, so thickly the Milky Way looked like a high, thin cloud.

"Are you cold?" Eileen asked. "Do you need to rest?"

Her voice was as cold as the snow they had slogged through for two hours. The wind had already blown the snow off the sand on the west-facing sides of the dunes, but the east slopes were deep with powdery snow. She was in fantastic shape. She made no attempt to show him that she could out-hike him. They both knew she could do that. She just wouldn't talk, that was all, and it pained him. He had parked his Bronco well off the little-used back road, hiding it as best he could in a fold of hills. A helicopter could spot it easily, but he hoped it would not come to that. Eileen assembled her gear and fell into an easy stride at his side. The road petered out to a trail, then disappeared into the sand. From then on, it was their GPS receivers and the stars.

"I'm not cold," Alan said. "But I think we should set up camp now. We're going to have to eat, and hide our tent, and that's going to take some time. Plus, look at our tracks." He waved over their back trail, and Eileen turned obediently and looked down the slope of the dune. Their trail stretched to the horizon, as clear and obvious as a pencil mark. Along each lee side of the sand dunes their footprints showed in snow; along the other slope their prints showed as a dragging, irregular line in the sand.

"Is there a morning wind?" Eileen asked, after contemplating their trail in silence.

"That's what Sam said. He said it picks up about three in the morning or so, and blows until five or six, unless there's a storm. Then it blows all day. That should help cover our tracks."

"Best to give it more time to blow our tracks away, then," Eileen said. "You said you had an idea how to hide the tent?"

"Something I picked up," Alan said. He carefully dropped one shoulder strap and set his pack down on the sand. Even in the cold, there was a curious smell to the dunes, a smell like some sort of obscure spice. It was a toasted smell, definitely, a well-baked smell, and elusive. Eileen set her pack down and took a long drink from the water bottle she carried at her waist. She had pulled her shoulder-length hair back and fastened it at her neck before they left. She was wearing a woolen watch cap. Her parka was a tan color and matched her khaki pants. They looked too light to be worn on a cold night like tonight, but she'd assured Alan with a chilly smile that she was wearing long underwear underneath and that she was plenty warm. Thank you.

He unsnapped his pack and removed his tent. The tent was a miracle. He simply removed it from its clever little container, holding it carefully, then tossed it into the air. The internal ribs sprang open and the tent came down onto the sand with a soft little thump, fully assembled.

"Nice," Eileen said with her first real smile. "That must have cost you a bundle."

"Worth it," Alan said. "I always come back from fishing when it's too damn dark to see, because I spent the last hours of the day casting to the evening hatch. I got tired of stumbling over equipment in the dark."

"So how do we hide this marvel?" Eileen asked.

"A trick from Afghanistan I read about," Alan said, which was a lie because he'd read about it in a science fiction book that was named, suitably enough, *Dune*. After he explained, Eileen nodded her head and pitched right in, digging a hole in the smooth slope of sand of a dune without snow. After they'd dug a ragged indentation, they pushed the tent into the hole. Alan watched apprehensively as Eileen scooped armloads of sand down the slope, spilling it over the smooth surface of the tent. The ribs of the tent held. After ten minutes of cold sandy shoveling, the tent was buried except for a person-sized opening.

"I think this is going to work," Eileen said, brushing sand from her arms and the front of her parka. She was smiling. He was sure of it; he could see the flash of her teeth in what was left of the moonlight.

"I think so, too," Alan said. He felt like cheering. In the daylight, after the breeze finished smoothing the rough marks their arms had made, their tent would be invisible, and so would they.

"Now if we can only avoid the worms," Eileen said, and hoisted her backpack to her shoulder. Alan straightened, seeing the blur of her face and the flash of her smile.

"Busted," he laughed. She'd read *Dune* too. "Let's see what Beth packed for us tonight."

What she had packed was plentiful, and it was very good. She'd made cold sandwiches of roast beef and turkey, loaded with mustard and cheddar cheese. She'd thrown in a baggie of black olives and a baggie of green ones, along with a tube of potato chips and a container of potato salad and some home-made chocolate chip cookies. Eileen dug a Thermos of coffee from her pack with a satisfied sound, her mouth full of sandwich. The tent was squeezed together on the inside by the pressure of the sand, so much so there was barely enough room for their sleeping bags and pads. They could sit cross-legged on their bags at the opening of the tent and share the food, which they did.

The sand was a good insulator. After just a few minutes, their body heat warmed the cold air and Eileen's shoulders dropped. Alan realized she'd been cold after all. He didn't say anything. Outside their tent door the sand spilled down to a little valley and then rose again to another dune, a tan flank that rose to the sky. A slice of the night stars was visible.

"At the top of the next set of dunes we should be able to

see outside to the Sangres," Eileen commented after she sipped her coffee. "The highest peaks of sand. Then we should work our way down into the center. I hope our GPS receivers work down there."

"It's worked so far," Alan said, patting his front pocket. The GPS had, in fact, performed flawlessly. Eileen checked her GPS with his at every stop and they had matched exactly. They'd also checked with the line of mountains they could see at the top of each dune crest. Alan also checked the North Star, though he wasn't very confident about his navigation skills by starlight. So far, though, everything seemed to be working. If everything went according to plan, they would be at the exact center of the dunes tomorrow by mid-afternoon.

"I was thinking we could set up the tent just as we have it now, if no one is at the spot when we reach it," Eileen said. "Then when our bad guys arrive, we can just sit tight and watch them. It might work a little bit better than trying to wade in there without knowing exactly what to expect."

"I think that's a good idea," Alan said. He had been thinking the same thing, but didn't want to say so. The meal was finished. They shared the cookies and the hot coffee and then it was time to settle into their sleeping bags. Eileen handled this as deftly as she did everything else. She removed her parka and khakis, revealing a fleecy top and a set of sensible long underwear, and rolled into her sleeping bag. She rolled her pants neatly and stored them inside the parka. The parka went under her head as a pillow and she was done. Alan clambered into his own bag with much less grace, feeling awkward and old. He settled his head on his jacket. Next to him was his daughter. He still had trouble getting his mind around the thought. But he could hear her breathing, the slow steady sound of it, and it was a wonderful sound. If he had nothing more from her, ever, he had that. He moved his head on his jacket, seeking a comfortable position, and closed his eyes.

The Williams's Ranch, San Luis Valley, Colorado

"We need to follow her," Joe said, his patience at the ragged edge. The sheriff, the Gonzalez guy, he was the one who was keeping them here. Rosen deferred to him, of course, since Gonzalez was the local law. If not for the big sheriff, Joe was sure he could have had them on their way by now, following Eileen and Alan's trail, maybe catching up to them. He wanted to be with her, not sitting in this kitchen jawing endlessly with the locals.

But since he had to sit here, he took another bite of coffee cake. That Beth, she made some incredible coffee cake. And the coffee to go with it was just as damn good. Joe took a swig of coffee from a big mug that was printed Monterey Bay Aquarium, and fidgeted impatiently at the table.

Dave Rosen sat at his left, then the big sheriff. Next to the sheriff was a younger, thinner version of Beth, her daughter Susan. Susan was merry and savage. Joe liked her. Next to her was a smaller guy, black-haired and wiry and with more than his share of nose. Frank. If Joe had been inclined to think little of Frank, the crossed pistol belts would have changed his mind. A man who would openly wear that kind of hardware was an actor, or a flake, or a man absolutely confident in his masculinity. Frank didn't look like an actor or a flake.

At the head of the table was Sam Williams, tall and rangy, white-haired, with "salt of the earth" practically stamped on his furrowed brow. Beth, his wife, was stirring something on the stove. She was fiftyish, large in a comfortable way, and was very worried about Alan and Eileen out on the dunes. Curiously, she seemed to lose her focus occasionally, as though she held some happy secret that would break out now and again like a light behind a flapping curtain.

The other ranch hands, Jennifer and Mark, had left long ago for their own cabin over the objections of Rosen. He wanted them to sleep in the main house, at least, but they insisted that with the dogs and their own guns, they would be fine. They were nice people, a matched set, dark-haired and slender and young.

The other two people at the table were still a mystery to Joe. Marcia Fowler, the older woman, sat composed and still with her little hands folded on the table. She had neat gray hair and deep dark eyes that were full of worry. She was dressed for the weather in a solid-looking pair of pants and a fleece jacket just like Joe's.

Daniel Grantham, her companion, was tall and thin. His hair was brown and his eyes were blue and he was hunched over his coffee like he wasn't sure if he were going to be offered food or thrown into the cook pot. Something about him and Marcia seemed similar, as though they were related somehow. They didn't look alike, but there was something there Joe couldn't put his finger on.

"I don't want to haul two sets of lost hikers out, or three," Gonzalez repeated, doing his own glaring, most of it at Joe. Some of it he shared with Daniel and Marcia, some of it was aimed at Beth, who evidently shouldn't have let Eileen and Alan head into the dunes, according to Gonzalez. Joe agreed heartily.

"Let's go in together," Rosen suggested. "Just you and me."

This set up an immediate chorus of protest around the table, which Gonzalez squelched by raising an enormous meaty paw.

"I can't go," he said reluctantly. "I'm supposed to have the FBI in here sometime tomorrow, and I have the valley to take care of. I have two drunks in jail tonight already. I can't go haring off into the dunes."

"I think we need to look at Joe's simulation," Marcia said. She had not spoken much so far. Her voice was warm and clear. It was the voice of a lifelong teacher and carried a little whip pop of authority. Everyone immediately turned to her, even Beth. "I think Joe's simulation might be the key."

"The key to what?" Susan asked.

"To the murders, of course," Marcia said, and looked around the table with her dark, intelligent gaze. "There's a pattern. I can almost see it."

"Yes!" Joe said. His laptop was sitting by his chair like a faithful pet. He reached down a hand and patted it. "The day after tomorrow if they set off the New Madrid, we could be talking about—"

"Millions of people," Gonzalez interrupted. "I know." He looked a little dazed, like he had the first time Joe had explained about his simulation. "I still don't get it."

"Let's look at this logically," said Marcia in her clear, carrying voice. "First, we have to decide if we think these earthquake people are going to set off the New Madrid tomorrow. If so, that's our first priority. We have to stop them, either because they don't know what they're doing, or . . ."

"Or because they do," Sam Williams said heavily.

"Yes," Marcia said. Joe found himself wishing she'd been at their impromptu information-gathering session the other night—was it last night? Yes, only last night. Twenty-four hours ago the snow had been howling outside his house and Eileen had been sleeping in his bed. No sense wishing things were different now. "If they think their earthquake is going to help prevent a large-scale disaster, then we have to convince them otherwise."

"If they know they're going to create this disaster, they're going to kill Alan and Eileen," Rosen said flatly.

"But why?" Beth asked, her eyebrows drawn together in distress. "Why would anyone want to do that?"

There was silence around the table. Everyone looked at Marcia.

"I can think of a half-dozen reasons right off the top of my head," she said dryly. "But I don't know that any of you want to hear them."

In chorus, everyone at the table disagreed. Marcia shrugged her shoulders, an oddly cynical shrug.

"Okay, then. Here's several. A New Madrid earthquake would cut the country in two. Set off a couple of earthquakes in Washington, D.C., or just blow a couple of canisters of anthrax virus. By the time you've gotten the mess straightened out, you have a new capitol in Washington State, or California, and another one in Washington, D.C. Two countries, just the way the South wanted us to be in the Civil War."

"A second Civil War," Rosen said thoughtfully.

"And we'd all be speaking Japanese pretty soon, or Chinese, or German," Daniel said. "As soon as they could figure out how to take over. But how about a revolution? A newly minted America with no taxes, no government, no bloated bureaucracy? Just a Constitution and a new Congress and no more of the old crap."

"Or a theocracy where homosexuals are hanged in public and attendance at church is mandatory," Joe said. "Just to balance out the concepts."

"It all sounds terrible," Beth said, wiping her hands slowly on a dishrag. She poured hot water into a cup and started rummaging around her cabinets. "What else can you think of?"

"How about the biggest bank robbery ever? Fort Knox, Kentucky," Marcia said apologetically. "Set off a massive earthquake as a diversion. Take a helicopter from here, kill anybody who's left there, grab all the gold you can carry."

"Hell, just be ready to rob a few banks here or there," Sam Williams said. "How much currency could you get in a day, in conditions like that?" No one answered. Beth found a tea bag and stirred it around her cup, making small clinking sounds with her spoon.

"We could sit here all night," Marcia said. "I could come up with many evil reasons to kill millions of people, if you really want. I think we all know about evil." She stared around the table and Joe found himself dropping his eyes like a kid afraid to be called upon in class. "We have a chance to stop it. The question is, how?"

"Since we're not evil, we can't just go in and blow everybody away, just to be sure, right?" Susan asked. She sounded like she wanted to be convinced otherwise.

Gonzalez gave her a quick fond grin. "Not how it's done. We have to give them a chance to show us they're not going to set off this machine. Hell, we don't even know what it looks like."

"It'll look like a machine," Joe said. "In the middle of the dunes. I think we'll be able to figure out what it is."

"And when it starts, it's going to create a hum. If we're close, a loud hum. I figure about two minutes after the hum starts, it'll be too late," Marcia said.

"I can arrest anyone out there for the murder of Krista

Lewis, on suspicion," Gonzalez said thoughtfully. "Maybe I should go."

"I could arrest people, as your deputy," Rosen said. "Captain Harben wouldn't object."

"You realize that you probably will be arresting Krista Lewis's murderer?" Daniel Grantham said with a mirthless smile. "And Jim Leetsdale's, too. I doubt these people are going to be friendly. They're not going to allow themselves to be cuffed and hauled away."

"And if we don't get there before they meet up with Alan and Eileen, I wouldn't give them much chance of making it out," Beth said worriedly.

"Who's going to make it out?" Joe asked. "Depends on who sees whom first. But I still want to be there. She barely made it away from the last attempt."

"Let me call Paris," Gonzalez said. Joe thought he hadn't heard correctly, but he saw Marcia's puzzled expression. Daniel Grantham, however, was shaking his head.

"Oh, no," he said. "Save us all."

"Paris?" Rosen asked.

"You need to get out there fast. You need Paris."

"Paris Linsley is just a guy who lives in the valley," Daniel said, and rolled his eyes. "Just a guy. Right. He's an engineer, invented some kind of pollution sniffer device that every factory in America has to have on every smokestack. Now he's retired, and he invents other stuff that's mostly crap but occasionally makes him even richer."

"And he's only twenty-nine," Susan said, with a twist to her mouth. Joe had seen that look before on a woman's face. Paris Linsley had made a try for Susan and had been shot down in flames. She was obviously attached to Frank, nose and holsters and all.

"Why do we need this guy?" Joe asked. Rosen wasn't saying anything, but his eyebrows were drawn together.

"Because he owns Babe, his own personal hummer," Gonzalez said. "It's a two-hundred-thousand-dollar Humvee, outfitted for the sand and painted a color of purple that I have only seen on dead people."

"He helps with search and rescue," Susan added, with that

bit-into-a-sour-grape expression. "He loves to help with search and rescue."

"I'm going to call him," Gonzalez said, heaving an enormous sigh. "I'm going to send Detective Rosen, who will be my sworn deputy in about a half-hour, Joe Tanner, Marcia Fowler, and Daniel Grantham. No, Susan, you can't go."

"Why Marcia?" Susan all but wailed. "Why Daniel?"

"Because they might have a handle on things if they turn a direction that we haven't discussed openly," Gonzalez said heavily.

"What the hell does that mean?" Joe asked.

"It means aliens," Marcia said matter-of-factly, her face wreathed in a smile that made her look about sixteen years old. "Thank you, Sheriff. I'm sure we'll just be along for the ride."

"I hope so," Daniel said fervently.

22

Great Sand Dunes, San Luis Valley, Colorado

Eileen couldn't sleep. She was wire-tense. Her shoulders ached, not with the strain of the backpack but with the strain of lying a foot away from her father. He was unmoving, probably asleep, but she couldn't see his face. His interesting tent had an igloo-type opening and they'd left the flap open. Outside, the stars crowded the sky. The sand was still and moveless, so Eileen knew morning was still a few hours away. If, in fact, the morning wind blew. If it did not, they would have to come up with a different plan when they reached the center of the dunes tomorrow. They had to be completely hidden when Jacob Mitchell's people came, if they did come. She hoped one of them would have a bruised chest from her bullet. Eileen shifted a little in her sleeping bag. The sand was marvelously comfortable, as good as a mattress. She should be sleeping. She had to sleep. She was certainly not going to say anything. Certainly not.

"Do I have any brothers or sisters?"

"No," Alan said immediately, in a voice that told her that

he was as wide awake as she was, and was waiting for her to speak. "I never married again."

"Any older brothers or sisters?"

"No," Alan said, in a surprised voice. "We got pregnant on our honeymoon with you. Didn't she tell you? And Linda—that's your mother—she had those cycles."

"Bipolar cycles," Eileen said. Linda, she thought, through the sick pounding in her chest. My mother's name was Linda.

"Yeah, that's what I figure, but I couldn't get her to go to a doctor," Alan said. His voice was rough. He shifted a little in his sleeping bag and rose on one elbow. There was a faint gurgle of his water bottle as he drank. "I'm sorry. This is hard for me."

"No kidding," Eileen said under her breath. Alan chuckled rustily.

"Can you—tell me about your mom? Your adoptive parents? How did you end up in their care? I tried so hard to find you, and I never could."

"My parents called every state to see if a three-year-old and her mother had been reported missing, after Mom died. They never found any reports," Eileen said harshly, and louder than she intended.

"She's dead, then," Alan said, after a long silence.

"She's dead." Eileen took a long sip from her own water bottle, easing a throat that felt suddenly rough.

"I'm sorry," Alan said quietly.

"It's a long time ago," Eileen said with a shrug he couldn't see.

"I reported you both missing the minute I got home from my trip. The police never found anything. That's what they said. And—Linda knew where I was. I knew she could find me, if she wanted to. She never did. Now I know why."

"Maybe the police reports you filed never made it to South Dakota," Eileen said grudgingly. She was in police work. She knew how many things slipped through the cracks every day.

There was silence again, not as tense as before. Eileen could feel dampness at her hairline and down the line of her back. The tent was warm, even though there was snow not twenty feet from the entrance.

"I never knew she was dead, you know. I didn't know why she never wanted support of some kind, or a divorce. I—I missed you a lot."

"Really."

"Yeah, really," Alan said. His voice was rougher, and Eileen heard the gurgle as he took another sip of water. "Your mother wasn't right when I married her, Eileen. You know what she was. I didn't know, not for a long time. When we brought you home from the hospital you were so little and sweet. You had beady little eyes like some sort of wild animal baby, and it seemed like you were always awake. She nursed you, she would do that, but once you were done, she would just lie back and turn away. I had to burp you and change you and walk with you."

"She must have been in the low part of her cycle," Eileen commented. She had faint memories of digging in her mother's handbag and devouring crackers wrapped in crackly cellophane, crackers that seemed to taste like heaven, while her mother lay in a curled-up position on some motel room bed. She was sure there were more memories like that, if she dug for them. She didn't really care to dig for them.

"I know that she was, now. Then, I was just frantic. I had a job and a new wife and a new baby and nothing was turning out like I thought. I talked to my neighbors, thank the Lord for them. Maria Escobar came over every day while I was at work and looked after the two of you. She would fix supper and leave it on the stove, and I paid her in cash because she was an illegal alien, a refugee from Nicaragua. Her husband worked as a gardener with a big crew of mostly illegals. I would feed your mother and change your diaper and then I would rock you, for hours. We'd talk, you and I." Alan made a ghastly little chuckling sound. "I'd coo and say *hola* and hello and *guten Tag* and every other hello in every language I could think of, and you would look at me with those bright eyes and spit up on my shoulder. Then we'd talk some more. I loved my little girl. I was sure that Linda would pull out of it. The birth was so hard, you know. So hard on her."

"But things didn't get better," Eileen whispered, in a voice that felt like something run over in the road and left to dry in the sun.

"No, they didn't. So when I tried to have her evaluated, she thought I was going to have her committed, or killed. I should have waited until the manic phase of her cycle, but I didn't. My mistake."

Outside, the sand started to pick up in tiny swirls and drifts. There was a sighing sound. The toasted, burned smell of the dunes drifted into the tent.

"I think we'd better close the flap," Eileen said. She let Alan reach forward and fix the tent flap in place. Spatters of sand immediately began to strike against the entrance, and there was a mournful hooting sound as the wind began to pick up. The tent was now pitch dark inside, and a little stuffy. Eileen could smell some sort of soap smell from Alan, and a whiff of old-man sweat. The smell of her father. It didn't smell familiar to her, and for a moment she was swamped with a feeling of desolation. What was she doing here in the sand and the dark with this stranger?

"So I thought I'd got over hating her," Alan said hoarsely. "Can you tell me how she died, just to put my mind at rest? I know I have no claim on you, on your story. But I want to know what happened, where you went, how she died. I want to know why I couldn't—" he stopped.

"Couldn't what?" Eileen asked cruelly. She knew he was overcome with some strong emotion, but she didn't care. He owed her that much.

"Couldn't see you off to prom," he said, and laughed the laugh of a man who was trying very hard not to weep.

"Oh," Eileen said, feeling very strange, blinking in the stuffy darkness. Her prom had been like a checkmark in a series of things to do to graduate. Finish finals, get her graduation robe, go to prom. Owen Sutter was still trying to choose her instead of Molly although it was obvious to both girls that Molly belonged with Owen. So he took both of them, because there were always more senior girls than boys, and they'd smirked for the prom photographer and pretended they were a sophisticated, decadent threesome. Her mom and dad had taken lots of pictures of her in her pale green prom dress, and she supposed it was a fun night.

"I would like to know about your mother," Alan said simply. So Eileen told him. She told him about the little dented sedan and the failed run at the bridge and John Reed, her angel brother, sent to die so that she would live.

The near-total darkness made it easier for her to tell her story. The unseen weight of the sand pressing on the tent and the warmth of their sleeping bags, pressed shoulder to shoulder, made her feel curiously isolated and intimate at the same time. They lay curled close to each other like twins in a womb, sharing nothing but their warmth and their voices. And this was no stranger, assessing her flaws. This was her father, the only other person in the world who knew what it was like to live with the monster who had inhabited Linda Doran.

When she was done, there was silence. The sand scratched at the tent entrance like tiny hands, and the wind hooted against the flap.

"I'm so sorry," Alan said finally, in a voice so low she could barely hear him. "I couldn't save you from that. I'm your father, and I couldn't save you."

"I survived," Eileen said, shrugging in the darkness. "I was lucky, what happened to me. What—what did you do?"

"I survived, too," Alan said grimly. "After the first six months I gave up sales. I couldn't sell anything anymore. I used to be such a whiz, and it all turned bad. I quit before I got fired. Then I waited tables while I tried to decide what to do. I finally went back to school and got my master's degree in English literature. I know that sounds funny, but I didn't know what else to do. I was just drifting. Then I landed a job in Wyoming, at the community college in Cheyenne. That was pretty much it for me. I taught. I learned how to fly-fish. I learned how to love life again."

"But you never married," Eileen said.

"No, I didn't. I had a lot of girlfriends, if you want to know," Alan said, with a ghost of his old humor in his voice. "But marriage was poisoned for me, forever. I lost my wife. I lost my baby daughter. I wouldn't take that kind of risk again."

"Marriage is risky," Eileen whispered with an effort. She realized she was getting sleepy, which was insane. She should be asking him the careful questions that would let her know if Krista Lewis, recently murdered, was one of his girlfriends that he wouldn't risk marrying—if Krista Lewis had entered these dunes with him last week—and never come out. But it all seemed far away and silly, to imagine this man a murderer. He couldn't be.

"What was that?" Alan asked, from a long way away.

"I trusted Joe," Eileen said after an eternity. She thought she was explaining everything about Joe, how he was a suspect in her first big military case and how she couldn't believe in her heart that he was a murderer. How she'd been right, which was very good because if she'd been wrong he could have killed her and would have killed her. But she wasn't saying anything, she realized, surfacing for a last time. She was drifting down again, and across the now enormous floor of the tent she heard the measured, slow breaths of her father, asleep.

The Williams's Ranch, San Luis Valley, Colorado

"Thanks for sharing your room with me," Marcia said to Susan, trying to spot the best place on the floor for her mat and sleeping bag. The room was small, like most country bedrooms, small because most of the living was done outside the room and the space was truly meant just for sleeping. Susan had a large old-fashioned bed with a handsome oak headboard. Metal scrollwork curved along the top, flowers in iron. Very appropriate. She may have had an adolescent bedroom at one time, and a little girl's before that, but there was nothing left of that now. She had a big handsome quilt and two framed prints hanging over an oak dresser, a bedside table piled high with magazines, and a small carved chair. That was it. There wasn't much room on the floor.

"Not a problem. Don't look for a spot on the floor, there isn't one. You're about as big as a wet cat, so if you don't mind sharing a mattress, I don't," Susan said. She scratched her neck and yawned hugely and set her shotgun by the small nightstand. "I changed the sheets this past Monday and if you've noticed—"

"I noticed," Marcia said with a smile. Susan was in love with Frank, clear as a bell. So Susan wasn't offering to share her body as well as her bed. That was sweet, actually. Susan was a beautiful young woman and Marcia was older, so it should have been Marcia making the pass, not Susan, if she were a lesbian. Which meant—

"I have an eye for Alan Baxter, but don't you dare tell anyone," Marcia said firmly, and was powerless to control the blush. It was supposed to be a reassuring lie, but there was far too much truth in it. Susan grinned, and Marcia smiled back. The forms had been satisfied. They could now share a bed tranquilly. If their feet touched or someone shifted a warm buttock against the other one, there wouldn't be a sudden stillness from the other, and a quiet shifting away.

"You'll be getting an early start tomorrow," Susan said, and frowned. "I wish I were going. I'm a good shot."

"I wish you were going, too," Marcia said. "The more the better, I think. But the sheriff is just trying to protect you. And your parents are too."

"They just found out tonight about me and Frank," Susan confessed, stripping off her shirt. Marcia sat down on the bed and started stripping off her socks. She listened with real interest, but there was a part of her that was far away, in the wind and sand, waiting for the lights and the hum. Searching for whatever walked the dunes now, human or otherwise, carrying humming death.

Joe sat in his sleeping bag, stripped down to his boxer shorts, and clicked on another girlie picture. Yolanda. He found the earthquake, a 4.5 in Kobe, Japan, and sighed as the squiggles of the earthquake rose and died on his computer screen. There had to be something he was missing. Something that they all had missed.

"Would you put that thing away?" Rosen said. He was a few feet away, his big feet in Joe's old sleeping bag crowding Joe's feet. Daniel Grantham muttered support under his breath, rolled up in a bag that had to be Sam Williams's own.

They were jammed in the living room like boys at a slumber party. Joe could tell the other men didn't like it any more than he did. They were all strangers to one another. There was something else, too: the flavor of impending battle. It made them nervous with one another.

"I usually don't sleep much at night," Joe said. "I'm a computer geek, remember?"

"We all need to sleep tonight," Rosen said. "That Paris guy is going to be here at six o'clock."

"For breakfast," Daniel said. "If Beth weren't fixing him breakfast, he wouldn't be here before noon."

"Great," Joe said, his eyes on his screen, finding earthquake "Doreen" in Costa Rica. "We're depending on some weirdo millionaire to get us into the dunes before Mitchell turns Kansas City into soup."

"He's reliable, I'll say that much," Daniel said. He rose up on an elbow and looked over at Joe. "What do you mean, soup?"

"Kansas City is built on what used to be mud flats from the Mississippi," Joe said, watching Doreen's earthquake again. "When an earthquake of magnitude six hits—and remember, the New Madrid is supposed to be an eight—the vibration turns the ground into a thick soup. Essentially, it liquefies. Down go houses, people, cars, skyscrapers. Then when the shaking stops, the ground hardens. A really awful way to die, I think. Like being buried in Portland cement. That's just Kansas City."

"Oh," Daniel said. Joe glanced over at him and he was blinking, eyes gazing into the distance, his mouth working soundlessly. He didn't look like a happy man. That was okay with Joe. He wasn't all that happy, either.

"So I'm learning all about earthquakes," Joe continued. "You know about how all the continents are really just big plates floating on the liquid core of the earth. I kind of knew that before, but I really understand it now. There are lots of fractures in these plates and when they shift against each other, we humans get all shook up. Hey, do you know why Mount Everest is so tall?"

"Why?" Rosen asked, in a voice that meant he knew Joe would tell them anyway.

"Because India is an island that crashed into Asia. India is still crashing, by the way, shoving its nose under the big Asia plate and lifting up parts of Asia. That's the Himalayas. So Mount Everest is the result of a big continental car crash that's still happening—we just can't see it. Pretty cool, huh?"

"This is not something I think humans should mess with," Daniel said, his brow furrowed even more. "Who knows what they could set off by accident or ignorance? Did they cause the one we just had?"

"Yeah, they sure did," Joe said. "And that was just a 3.5, a baby one. I can't imagine what an eight pointer would feel like."

"Maybe the Tesla machine can't produce an eight pointer," Daniel suggested.

"I think it can," Joe said. "I've been reading about Nikola Tesla. Alan thought that maybe the government had the plans to the real Tesla earthquake machine. Turns out when Tesla died, his hotel room in New York was sealed by the FBI. Everything within it was confiscated by the government."

"No one protested?" Daniel asked.

"Tesla never married. He didn't have any family to protest for him. He had a family of doves, one white dove in particular that he loved dearly and kept in his room when he was older. But no family. There's something else about him, too," Joe said. He shut down his program and closed his laptop. He looked over at Rosen, who was propped up in his sleeping bag watching him. Daniel, too, was looking at him.

"He was asked to join the Manhattan Project. He refused. Every other prominent scientist said yes, but Tesla said no. He didn't think wholesale slaughter was a good weapon design. He designed something he called a death ray, that would shoot down missiles. It, too, disappeared into the FBI's hands."

"He wouldn't approve of what they're doing," Rosen said unexpectedly.

"That's right," Joe said. "Exactly right. He didn't approve of murder, and that's what they're doing if they set off earthquakes without warning people. Secrecy is necessary for some things, but not for that. And killing Krista and Jim Leetsdale only proves that they don't care who they hurt."

"We have to stop them," Daniel said.

"We'll stop them," Rosen said. "So shut the hell up, Joe. I need sleep."

"Aye aye, Captain Bligh," Joe said sarcastically. But he set his laptop aside. Whatever mystery remained would be solved on the dunes, not in his computer. He patted his Frankenputer affectionately. It wasn't her fault. He lay down in his sleeping bag. He tried very hard not to think of Eileen, somewhere out there in the sand and the snow and the darkness. She was with Alan Baxter, who Joe was sure would die to defend her. He was not a murderer, could not be. Joe was sure of it. He had to be sure of it, or he would not sleep an instant tonight. Holding that thought tightly, Joe closed his eyes and was asleep.

Great Sand Dunes, San Luis Valley, Colorado

"Good morning," Eileen said. Alan opened his eyes with a start. He saw that Eileen had unfastened the flap. She was staring out the small hole she had made, her face lit by strong morning sunshine. The fiercest light, the most unkind light. Her skin was fresh and clear and beautiful, as pretty as a child's. Her eyes were sparkling and she was smiling. "You should look outside. We're completely hidden. Nobody could see us from a foot away, I swear. They'd have to step on us. Take a look."

Alan rolled over cautiously, trying not to appear too stiff and elderly. He edged on his elbows to the entrance and looked out. The dunes were brilliantly tan in the dawn light. Their tracks were gone. The sand lay around them perfect and smooth. Alan remembered how their efforts to bury the tent had stirred the sand up and down the slope. He couldn't see far to either side, but what he could see was reassuring. Their idea for a hiding place was a good one. The cold morning air tasted wonderful, even with the smell of the dunes in his nose.

"We need to get to our spot as soon as possible today," Eileen said. She had already turned away from the entrance and was getting into her clothes. Her movements were as small and tidy as a cat's, with the same economical grace. She was already dressed before Alan started. As he dressed, she braided her shoulder-length hair, taking pieces from the top of her head and braiding down the back in a complicated sort of weave. She finished it off with a small elastic band and snapped it on with a mouth of distaste.

"I hate dirty hair," she said. "If I braid it, I can keep from getting too grossed out."

"I hate dirty teeth," Alan said. "You will let me brush before we leave, won't you?" He grinned at her, and she smiled back. For a second her smile was natural, then it turned inward and became something forced. She turned away and rummaged in her bag.

"Let's eat on the dunes," she said. "I want to stretch my legs."

When Alan scrambled from the tent entrance, he immediately turned and looked at the slope. He couldn't have hoped for better camouflage. The tent was completely invisible. The sand had smoothed over the marks they had made digging into the slope, and now the only thing visible was the slit of the tent opening. Eileen followed him and looked carefully in all directions before she, too, examined their hiding place.

"Very nice," she said. Her breath misted in the cold morning air. It was already degrees warmer than yesterday morning. By noon, the dunes were going to be as hot and dry as though the snow had never happened. Alan stretched and rotated his head on his neck, then leaned forward and did a few runners' stretches to limber up his muscles.

"I have a surprise for you," Eileen said. Alan turned to her and saw a Thermos in her hand. She'd taken it from her pack. It wasn't the same Thermos as the one they'd shared the night before.

"Is that?" Alan asked.

"Coffee," Eileen said with a grin. "Beth packed us two bottles."

"Oh, my," Alan sighed happily. He smoothed a place for his rump in front of their tent entrance. "Let's pack up the tent later."

Their coffee and breakfast done, Alan scrambled over the nearest dune and Eileen headed in the other direction. He dug a deep hole and did everything he needed in the hole, tooth-brush foam and all, then covered it well and headed back with a light step. Eileen was already at the tent, carefully pulling sand away from the sides. He shook the tent out and stored it in the little tent bag, and they were done. He looked around and nodded. There were few tracks. Eileen brushed the last of the sand from her arms and took a little bottle from her pocket.

"Sunscreen?" she offered. "It's going to be a hot day." She'd changed into shorts while she was over her dune, Alan noticed. The clothes must have been loaned from Susan Williams. He took the little bottle and spread some goo on his nose and cheekbones and arms, more to make her happy than anything else. The sun, lighting the sky for some time now, suddenly crested a dune. The light was blinding. They both turned their backs and stood together as they consulted their GPS receivers.

"This way," Alan said, and Eileen nodded. They walked together. Eileen did not speak, but Alan felt her silence was different from the night before. He might have a chance with her, after all.

The Williams's Ranch, San Luis Valley, Colorado

Paris Linsley was everything Joe had been led to expect. Maybe even a bit more. He was tall and young and had a full head of curly, dark blond hair. He had a big smile full of white teeth. He wore an elegant white shirt and pleated khaki pants as though he were going to ride a camel into the dunes and open a mummy's tomb. Joe could understand immediately why Susan Williams disliked him, why Daniel Grantham rolled his eyes at the thought of spending time with him. He was just altogether too much.

His Humvee, named Babe, was painted an incredibly vivid shade of purple. Joe had never been close to a Humvee and was faintly astonished at the size and height of the thing.

Not to mention the paint job. There were faint gold flakes in the purple paint, which were going to make it sparkle in the sun when the sun climbed over the mountains to the east.

Paris, having jumped from Babe and posed nonchalantly against the wheel to give everyone a chance to admire his car and his attire, stood to a kind of attention as Beth came out of the house, wiping her hands on her apron. Everyone else in the strange group had left the breakfast table when Paris rang the bell at the gate. Joe thought of them as earthquake hunters and had heard Rosen mutter something about a motley crew as he shaved in the small guest bathroom. Joe and Daniel and Rosen had shuffled in and out of the bathroom and tried to keep their elbows out of each other's ribs, with limited success.

"Mrs. Williams!" Paris exclaimed. "Tell me you have sweet rolls!"

"I have sweet rolls," she smiled. "Come on in, Paris."

Joe expected Paris to have perfect highbrow pronunciation, given the color of the car and the elegant clothing. Paris, instead, had a voice that belonged with a mud-spattered pickup and a varmint rifle, a voice that was as deep and country as a twanging guitar.

"He's a nut," Daniel said softly to Joe, startling him badly, as they followed Beth back into the kitchen. "Out there. He does his own thing. I think his IQ is off the chart."

"You read minds, or what?" Joe said, and noticed Marcia's grin as she held the door for them.

"Not usually," Daniel replied. "I could just tell what you were thinking. Once you get past Paris being Paris you'll find he's a good guy. He's a lot deeper than he looks."

Paris, his mouth stuffed full of sweet roll and a cup of coffee in his free hand, looked undignified and unbrilliant.

"Okay, fill me in," he said between swallows, waving at everyone and no one.

"We'll get to the details on the way," Rosen said. The star that Gonzalez had given him the night before was pinned undramatically to his shirt front. "In brief, we have two people in the dunes and, potentially, a serial murderer out there as well."

"At dawn tomorrow, where X marks the spot," Marcia murmured, in a voice that Joe thought was too low for anyone but him to hear. Paris, however, gave Marcia a still look over a mouth ringed with icing flakes. His eyes brightened.

"Sounds like a job for Paris," he said, wiping his mouth and flashing his teeth in a movie-star grin. Rosen looked at him steadily and said nothing. Paris grinned even wider and pointed at Rosen's star. "But of course you're in charge, am I correct?"

"Only if I need to be," Rosen said. As Paris looked at Rosen, Joe saw something interesting. Paris had dark hazel eyes, and for a moment they went queerly light, as though blinds were being pulled up. For a moment, something wise and powerful looked out through Paris's eyes, something that was very much "out there" and "off the chart." Then the blinds lowered and the eyes darkened and Paris took a big swig of Beth's good coffee and grinned.

"You're the boss, Boss," he said. "Babe and I are at your service." Daniel blinked and Beth looked visibly startled.

"Can anybody else drive your hummer but you?" Joe asked.

"Sure, she's easy to drive," Paris said. "I'd better handle it when we get to the dunes, though. Why?"

"Because I want to show you my computer simulation," Joe said. "While we tell you all the rest of this story."

Joe was half-afraid Paris would use his X-ray vision, or whatever it was, when Paris turned his gaze to him. But his eyes remained muddy and friendly. Joe wanted to show Paris the New Madrid. Maybe Paris would pull up the blinds and figure out why Jacob Mitchell and his friendly gang were going to kill millions of people. Or whatever it was they were going to do.

"I'll drive Babe," Daniel offered.

"Okay," Paris said mildly.

"Let's go, then, people," Rosen said. "We have less than twenty-four hours."

"Twenty-four hours?" Paris asked.

"Twenty-four hours before the New Madrid goes off, set off from here, and we'll explain it all to you on the way," Marcia said briskly. "Anyone have to pee? No? I'll ride with Paris and Joe in the back, if you and Rosen want to ride in the front, Daniel."

As Babe rumbled off down the ranch road, Joe forgot to look back. He was too busy showing Paris his Frankenputer, showing off, really, too busy trying to fill Paris in on the details of their wild story and make it believable. When he thought to look back, to wave at Beth Williams who had taken him in and fed him and given him shelter and blessed his journey, she was out of sight. He felt a chill, looking out the back window, as Paris delightedly punched buttons on his simulation and watched the earthquakes wiggle. He hadn't waved goodbye. Somehow it seemed vitally important that he had forgotten that, as though he hadn't waved goodbye at the last bit of light and love and warmth he was going to have for a long time.

The dunes lay ahead of them, a different kind of lightness. Hard light, like going into a different sun. As Babe rolled down the highway, he started to smell the burnt spice of the dunes in his nose.

23

Great Sand Dunes, Latitude 37.47.50, Longitude 105.33.20, San Luis Valley, Colorado

Eileen, participant in many stakeouts, was patient. Alan Baxter, catcher of fish with fake flies, was also patient. What they were not was patient with each other. Eileen could not bear to touch him with her shoulder or leg, but the constriction of the tent opening meant that they had to brush up against each other. They were both sweaty and sandy from their efforts to bury the tent and erase their tracks. Since they didn't know how long it took to set up the Tesla machine and make it go, they were both in a hurry to get well hidden as soon as possible.

Now the sun stood high and moveless, and the heat shimmered on the sand. In the tent it was stuffy but cool. The latitude 37.47.50 and longitude 105.33.20 was at the bottom of a long spill of sand below them and to their left. A rise of dune in front of them nearly cut off their view of the spot but would keep their tent opening from being seen. Eileen had checked this out herself by standing in the exact crosshairs of their destination and looking at the spot where they'd finished burying the tent. She could see the opening but it looked like a dune shadow. At least that's what she hoped.

Standing with her GPS receiver displaying the exact center of the dunes gave her a funny feeling. Here was where the Colorado earthquake had originated, or so she believed. Here was where the Burbank earthquake in California had begun, the earthquake that had toppled a cement wall on Lori Leetsdale and started a chain of events that led inexorably to this moment in time, this crossing of paths. Tomorrow morning, at dawn, there would be a kind of showdown, a battle between the people who believed they should interfere and people like herself, who believed they should not interfere. That was the best way she could figure it. While they walked last night in the ghostly white darkness of the sand, she thought about what she was doing here, what she meant to do.

Ultimately, she thought that Jacob Mitchell and his people had crossed a line when they started setting off earthquakes. Once the line was crossed, Krista Lewis's death was only an addition, not the start, of their evil. Jacob Mitchell—not her father, not Alan Baxter, her heart whispered—believed that he was somehow above other people, better than they were. He believed he could alter people's lives without their permission because he was something more than they were. Murderers like Teddy Shaw were the same way.

Then wasn't she, too, an alterer of destinies? She had certainly altered Teddy Shaw's destiny, permanently. But she was an officer of the law, a person sworn to keep the peace. When she shot Teddy Shaw, she was defending her life, not executing him. If he'd thrown his gun down, she would have taken him alive. She didn't believe in her own superiority. She believed, simply and ultimately, that people knew what was best for themselves. Even if Mitchell was setting off small quakes in order to stop a big one, creating bleeder earthquakes was only justified in the light, with everyone knowing about it and making their own decisions about what they were going to do. Creating chaos without warning was evil. The end did not justify the means.

Suddenly Eileen realized that Alan was waving at her, gesturing for her to come to the tent. She was standing stock-still in the heat of the late afternoon with her feet on the invisible X, and at any moment a helicopter or a vehicle could come over the horizon. She scrambled up the dune toward the tent opening, brushing out her tracks clumsily as she went, and arrived at the buried tent sweating and panting, her heart pounding.

Now, an hour later, her sweat had dried sticky and sandy and she was bored and uncomfortable. No helicopters had come swooping over the dunes. Nothing moved in the late day's glare, not even insects. She sat far too close to this man, her father, and didn't know what to say to him.

"Water?" he said.

"No thanks, I have my own," she replied stiffly.

They waited.

Great Sand Dunes, San Luis Valley, Colorado

Babe took the first hill of dunes without enthusiasm. She waddled, she sputtered sand, she complained.

"What a pig," Joe said.

"You couldn't get up the first ridge in anything else," Daniel said loudly. Babe's engine was amazingly quiet for a girl her size but Paris had her in a low roar as he side-walked up the second slope. Paris said nothing, eyes intent on the sand, his hands dancing over the wheel and gearshift.

"An ATV could make it," Joe said. He'd folded up his modified laptop a long time ago and stored it in a laundry bag he'd brought along for it. An ordinary laptop case wouldn't hold the whole contraption, and he didn't want sand to get inside Frankenputer's guts. Now he was well braced in the rocking vehicle and ready to bitch at somebody, anybody.

The whole approach to the dunes had taken far too long. The bright glare of the sand seemed to be just over the next hill, but every time Babe crested a rolling hill there was another beyond it, and the dunes no closer. Then when they'd finally gotten onto the sand, they'd roared across the low sandy creek at less than a walking pace, Paris intent and silent behind the wheel that he'd taken from Daniel before they'd started into the sand.

The day was blazing toward noon and they hadn't even

gotten out of sight of the creek and the edge of the dunes. Rosen wore Old Spice deodorant and his sweaty body slammed into Joe's shoulder every time Babe rocked on the sand, which was every few seconds. Joe had never liked Old Spice, and now he hated it with a passion. It caught in his nose and throat, and the queer smell of the dunes seemed to sneak in around it and choke him further.

More, there was no sign of Eileen and Alan Baxter. No sign of earthquake people. Joe had never met Jacob Mitchell, so his mental image of the earthquake people was based on his imagination. He thought of them as trolls in lab coats, men with twisted bodies and hairy eyebrows and long hands like tentacles. He knew they wouldn't look like that on the outside, but then again murderers never did. He'd worked with a murderer for months, a murderer who killed his best friend, and he'd never known. The murderer, a fellow war gamer, looked nice to the last, when he'd tried to kill Joe with a sharpened screwdriver. He hadn't looked like a hairy troll on the outside, either.

"An ATV could make the first stretch," Daniel corrected him. Marcia, sitting on the other side, looked with bright curiosity out the window. She didn't seem bothered by anything, and she didn't appear to need to sweat. Joe hated her, too. "The dunes are compressed up against the mountains. They're higher than any dunes you've ever seen. They didn't exist here ten thousand years ago, did you know that? No one knows why they appeared. Ute Indians describe in their verbal history about arriving one season in the valley and there the beast was, lying against the slope of mountains like something that had moved in and found that it liked it."

"I read sand is pushed across the valley floor by winds from the west, piling up against the Sangre de Cristos in the east," Marcia shouted. "Is that why they're so high?"

"I guess so," Daniel said. "Anyway, nobody's ever taken a vehicle in here except Paris, and that was to rescue two hikers four years ago."

"Did he find them?" Marcia asked.

"Yes," Paris said abruptly, his profile as intent as something carved from stone. "Dead. Not murdered. They died of hypothermia and dehydration."

"How could you die in such a small space?" Joe asked. "I can see the mountains from here. Just walk towards the mountains for a day or two and you're out. The Sangres?"

"Look at them now," Daniel said. "We'll lose them as soon as we go deeper into the dunes. You can only see the mountains at the highest peaks, and by the time you get to another peak, you've been wandering in circles. The dunes have a huge amount of iron in the sand, so your compass is going to go nuts."

"The GPS is working fine," Marcia said, examining the object in her hands.

"Let's hope it keeps working fine," Daniel said. "We lost some hikers who had a GPS receiver. Who knows what happened? Sand in the works, something else?" He glanced over at Marcia, who gave a small nod. That was right, Joe thought. These two were UFO nuts. They probably thought the hikers had been abducted and murdered by their little gray men. He wanted to snarl in exasperation. Rosen slammed into his shoulder again, Old Spice reeking from his armpits, his face quiet and calm.

"When are we going to reach the center?" Rosen asked, just as Paris reached the top of the dune crest.

"Sometime tonight, after dark," Paris said. "If we don't hit a ridge too high to go over. We don't have much of a moon so we can't travel in the dark. I could flip Babe and we'd be in real trouble."

"Why, because we'd have to walk out?" Joe asked pleasantly. Rosen glanced at him, and Joe realized his voice perhaps wasn't that pleasant after all.

"Because we might not get out," Paris said, idling Babe and contemplating the dunes in front of him. To Joe they looked like ocean waves frozen as though in a picture, ocean waves in a storm. For a moment he could imagine them moving toward him, and he had to blink hard. It made him dizzy and slightly sick. "We'd be buried under Babe, and she'd sink in this stuff like a stone in mud. Rolling over wouldn't do any of us any good." Paris shut up again and rolled Babe down the dune with care, his fingers like a surgeon's on the wheel and gearshift. Joe saw Rosen nod, and he remembered how Sam Williams had shrugged and agreed with Gonzalez that the only person to call was Paris Linsley. Now he knew why. But it didn't help his mood or his shoulder when Rosen came slamming against him for the thousandth time. And there were no tracks of Eileen and Alan Baxter, no tracks at all. They hadn't even found the Bronco, though they'd taken the same route Sam Williams mapped out for Alan and Eileen.

Joe blinked again, trying to keep the waves of sand still like he knew they had to be, looking for a long track in the sand that would mean Alan Baxter was in the dunes with his daughter, the woman Joe Tanner loved and wanted to make his wife. Alan couldn't be a murderer. He wouldn't be. Joe squeezed his eyes shut on the image of Alan Baxter driving down some New Mexico highway, humming a tune, his hands freshly washed of blood, laughing at the idiots who were searching the dunes for him.

He didn't realize he'd made some sound until Rosen nudged him. He opened his eyes and Rosen was offering him a water bottle. Joe blinked at Rosen and saw somewhere in those black eyes the same fear, the same maddened impatience.

"Keep hydrated," Rosen said. "We need to be ready."

"Thanks," Joe said. Rosen's words were steadying. They were also battle words, and that was good too. Joe was ready. He was ready.

He braced himself against the door frame, watching Paris nurse the wheel and coax Babe up another dune, and he drank deeply.

Great Sand Dunes, Latitude 37.47.50, Longitude 105.33.20, San Luis Valley, Colorado

"I figured out why they're going to set it off tomorrow," Eileen said. She felt better as the day started to wind down towards night. The long horrid afternoon was behind them. She'd washed with a dampened washcloth, swabbing at her grimy face and hands and using just a little bit of water on the cloth because they had to conserve what they had left. They had to walk out, too, after this was all over, and they'd need water for that.

"Why?" Alan asked. He, too, had washed his face and hands as they prepared to eat their meager supper. He looked more cheerful as well. Waiting was hard, even if you were good at it.

"Because it's Saturday morning," Eileen said. "Saturday morning when everyone is at home in their beds. Saturday at five o'clock here is six o'clock, seven o'clock in the Midwest. The big office buildings will be empty, the highway bridges will be deserted, and the bars will be closed. Saturday morning is the best time for an earthquake. I'll bet the least loss of life in earthquakes is on Saturday mornings."

"That's why the Colorado earthquake was so early," Alan said.

"At least we know they don't want to kill as many people as they can. But they can't set every one off on Saturday and Sunday, that would be too suspicious," Eileen said. She bit into a crumbly energy bar and grimaced at the dry taste.

"So maybe they don't know they're setting off one so big," Alan said. "Maybe they think this one is a bleeder too. Maybe they think it won't kill anyone, the way the Colorado earthquake didn't kill anyone."

"That's why we have to talk them into stopping it before they start it. We can't just barge in and start shooting like some action movie. Who knows how many people it takes to do this? They might be good people who really think they're saving lives."

"They killed Jim Leetsdale," Alan said stubbornly. "And Krista Lewis."

"We don't know who killed them," Eileen said patiently. "Whoever killed Krista was a rapist, not an executioner. She might not even be related to this." Eileen watched Alan Baxter carefully and swallowed the chunk of dry energy bar in her mouth. It felt like a rock going down her throat. Alan frowned and looked out the tent flap, and if he were a rapist and a murderer Eileen couldn't tell. Her gut twisted like a hanged thing, and she folded the wrapper around the rest of the energy bar. Her supper was done.

Great Sand Dunes, San Luis Valley, Colorado

"Thank you, Paris," Marcia said as Paris handed her a plate. Paris Linsley was a sweetheart through and through, despite the accident of birth that had left him with such a handsome face and build.

Paris had kept his balance, it appeared. He'd put on armor like a medieval knight, like Lancelot, who was so handsome he never smiled. Right now Paris, smiling, was handing out cold chicken and potato salad and rolls from Beth Williams's inexhaustible kitchen, a surprise cooler that he and Beth had hidden in the back of Babe while everyone else was scrambling for their gear.

Marcia bit into her chicken, her plate balanced on her knees, watching Paris. He moved like a dancer, perfectly in tune with his body. Joe Tanner took a plate and forced a thanks. Joe had been wired tight all day. He was desperately concerned about Eileen. There was something additional going on with him and Rosen, some secret they held between them that interested her. Something in their glances when they spoke of Alan and Eileen. Marcia wondered what it was.

She and Daniel had their own secret, their own fears. Here in the dunes things could happen. Things happened in the San Luis Valley, things she'd only read about until now. There might be a human killer out here, but that was not the only thing that walked the dunes at night.

She shivered suddenly, uncontrollably. The sun was gone over the dune heights and the sky was darkening.

"Better bundle up, the temperature's going to drop like a stone," Paris said, sitting by her side with his plate piled high with chicken and coleslaw and fruit salad.

"Let me guess," Marcia said with a smile. "You can eat anything and not gain an ounce, right?"

"Of course," Paris said with a smile that held bitterness

like a dash of salt, bitterness that perhaps only Marcia Fowler could taste.

"Babe is a wonderful beast," she said, aiming with her chicken to where the Humvee sat, ticking slightly, in the fold of sand where they were going to spend the night. As far as they could tell, they were less than a quarter mile from the center of the dunes. At three o'clock, they had agreed, they would walk in. This agreement was not come to easily. Joe nearly set off on his own before Rosen talked him out of it. Finally he'd subsided, muttering darkly, looking terribly worried. Now he sat with his chicken, untouched, in his lap. Rosen said a few words to him, and he nodded and picked up a piece of food. He ate like he was feeding a machine.

"She'll get us out, which is important," Paris said. "What brings you on this posse?"

"I found Krista," Marcia said simply.

"Oh," Paris said. He ate a piece of chicken with surgical neatness. "And you're MUFON, right?"

"That's right," Marcia said, and didn't bother asking Paris how he knew.

"So the Taos Hum is caused by this Tesla machine?"

"We think so."

"So we have to stop it before they set off the New Madrid," Paris mused. "I get it, I guess. But why kill Krista? I can't figure that out."

"I can't either," Joe said, squatting at Marcia's side with his empty plate in one hand. Daniel and Rosen were still eating their supper, sitting in different slopes of sand. Everyone wanted to be far apart from one another when Babe finally stopped.

"Maybe Krista was killed by a boyfriend. Maybe her murder set off this whole chain of events by accident."

"That's one theory," Joe said unhappily, and Marcia read his untold secret in his face in one flashing computation.

"You suspect Alan Baxter, don't you?" she said, and she realized her voice was far too loud even as she spoke.

"I don't know," Joe said. He wouldn't meet her eyes. "I can't believe it, but—"

"But we don't have the luxury to take chances with

Eileen's life," Rosen said. He walked to join them, moving in a quiet way that Marcia admired. He was so light on his feet he hardly left tracks in the sand.

"That's ridiculous," Marcia said. "He'd die to protect Eileen. He wouldn't harm a fly."

"How long have you known Alan Baxter, ma'am?" Rosen asked levelly.

"Less than a week," Marcia said, her chin up. "And I don't care. He's not a murderer."

"I don't think he is, either," Rosen said. "But yes, we need to make sure he isn't."

"But that means anyone could be a murderer. Daniel lives here. He could be one."

Daniel looked at her with sad eyes. "Already occurred to me," he said. "Try being an adult male in a community when a woman is raped and murdered, Marcia. Right, Paris?"

"Not me," Paris said. "I'm suspected of being everything from a closet gay to an alien, but not a rapist."

"Why?" Joe asked.

"Because I'm too good looking," Paris said loftily.

"So was Ted Bundy," Rosen said. Paris frowned and opened his mouth, then shut it and looked down at his plate.

"Women can be murderers, too," Marcia said, and almost felt insulted when the men grinned at her as one. "Well, I *could*."

"You could," Joe assured her. "Don't worry, Marcia, we'll suspect you if that makes you feel better."

"What a mess," Paris said, his good humor restored. "And all is going to be revealed—what, at dawn tomorrow?"

"Yes," Joe said.

"Yes," Daniel said, looking afraid.

"Yes," Rosen said, looking as though he were ready to paint on war stripes.

"Well, then," Paris said, with a movie-star grin. "Let's get to bed, shall we? I'll set my alarm for what, three a.m.? We'll get out of here by four and sunrise will be at six or so. Plenty of time to get there."

"No lights tonight," Marcia suggested. "Let's stay as quiet as we can."

"No sense in drawing the wrong kind of attention, eh?" Paris said with a mocking grin.

"No sense in drawing any kind of attention," Daniel said. "Of any kind."

Great Sand Dunes, Latitude 37.47.50, Longitude 105.33.20, San Luis Valley, Colorado

The wind had not yet begun to blow the cool night wind that smoothed the dunes. Eileen woke, totally alert in an instant. There was a sound, an enormous sound, approaching.

"What is that?" Alan whispered in the darkness beside her.

"I don't know," she whispered back. For a moment she felt dizzy, unreal. Had Alan whispered to her, and had she whispered back? Or had they simply communicated mind to mind, like some science-fiction tale? His hand was real, though, fumbling for hers in the darkness and taking it into his own. His hand was larger than hers. Both their hands were cold. Eileen realized she was terrified. The sound grew louder.

"Is it—" Alan started, then stopped with the caution of a deer coming to a halt in the brush, head held high and nostrils smelling the wind. Eileen pressed his hand, not daring to answer. She didn't move. She wondered if their heat signature was sufficiently buried underneath the sand, or if their body outlines would show up in infrared detectors.

The sound grew impossibly loud. It wasn't the heartbeat of helicopter blades or the roar of tanks or the purr of trucks. It wasn't the sound of a jet engine. Eileen thought dizzily that it sounded something like a boat engine in water, only that was impossible. The bubbling sound started to fade just as Eileen thought she had pinpointed the location. It was just over the ridge to their left, whatever it was, and it sounded huge.

As quickly as it came, it was gone. The silence grew and stretched out. Eileen heard a tiny tapping at the tent door, and her heart leaped in fright before she realized it was sand. The early morning winds were starting to blow.

"Was that the Tesla people?" Alan whispered.

"I don't think so," Eileen said doubtfully, trying to get her breathing under control. "They'll have to have equipment, and that means the Tesla machine. Maybe that was just a reconnaissance of the area to make sure no one is here."

"That sounds reasonable," Alan whispered. His hand squeezed hers and let it go, a squeeze that felt like a kind of wink. We were both scared, said the squeeze, weren't we?

Eileen thought she would wait until dawn, sure that she couldn't sleep any more that night. She heard Alan's breath even out and take on the slow, measured breaths of sleep, and without thinking she lengthened her breaths to match his and felt herself drift back into sleep.

24

The sun approached over the earth. The dunes were dark but
the sky was clear and light. The morning winds had blown
themselves out and the sand was still and silken and unmarked.

Eileen, under the sand, awoke at a sound. It was the beating-
heart sound of a helicopter. A Blackhawk by the tempo of the
rotors and engine, and she was right. She could have guessed
that they would come in a Blackhawk, the military transport
helicopter. It rose over the skyline, a black humped shape like
a surfacing whale, and she reached out to wake Alan. He
clasped her hand in his own. His hand was cold and damp.
Her heart was kicking in her chest and she struggled to
breathe normally and deeply. Whatever had patrolled the sand
last night had not seen them. Their prey was coming into the
trap.

Someone on that helicopter should have a bruise over his
heart. Someone on that helicopter should have DNA that
matched the curly pubic hair found on the dead body of Krista

Lewis. Someone on that helicopter had posed Jim Leetsdale's dead body by a cannon.

Someone on that helicopter was a murderer, not the person holding her hand.

The Blackhawk was lit by the rising sun as it came into sight, but it dropped into the shadows as it came down into the dunes. It swirled into a landing at exactly the spot she'd stood the day before. The blades kicked up a hurricane of sand then slowed to idle speed. The Blackhawk was painted in desert colors, tan with splotches of white and light gray. She could see the pilot behind the glass, and for a terrified moment she thought he was looking straight at her.

Then the man looked down and raised a container to his lips. He was opening a Thermos in his lap and staring out the window as he did, that was all.

Someone stepped out of the helicopter. Eileen saw with a fierce pulse of satisfaction that the man was Jacob Mitchell. He was dressed in khakis that looked faintly military. He wore a broad-brimmed Stetson. Another two men dropped lightly to the ground behind him, both also in civilian clothing. Three uniformed soldiers jumped from the helicopter and lowered a box shrouded in canvas to the sand. The box was big enough to give the three men trouble as they hauled it out of the helicopter.

"The Tesla machine," Alan whispered. "That must be it."

Eileen nodded and squeezed his hand to make him let her go. Her fingers were going numb. It was five o'clock.

The soldiers dropped several packages out of the helicopter, things that looked like ordinary supplies, perhaps tents and food and water. Then they hopped back on board with nods and waves. They showed all the excitement of parcel deliverymen. One of the other civilians jumped lightly into the helicopter as the rotors started to speed up. Jacob Mitchell and the other man put their faces into their elbows as the sand whipped up around them.

Then the helicopter was gone over the ridge, leaving only a dwindling sound like a fading heartbeat.

"Only two of them," Eileen whispered. "I think we can walk up on them without a problem."

"What time is it?" Alan whispered back. "How much time do we have?"

"It's five-fifteen. We have less than forty-five minutes."

"If I can get out of the tent when they're turned the other way, they won't know where I came from," Alan said. Eileen raised her eyebrows.

"I?" she hissed. "What do you mean, I?"

"I think you should stay here," Alan whispered. "What if they shoot on sight? Somebody needs to watch and see what happens."

"That somebody should be you," Eileen said. "I'm a police officer. This is what I do for a living, Mr. Baxter." She peered at him in the gloom of the tent, and she could see a stubborn set expression to his mouth. *Prom*, she thought despairingly.

"I'll tell you what," Alan whispered angrily. "We can start to argue and then we'll fight and the tent will collapse and we'll roll down right to their feet. Then we'll see what happens."

Eileen put both hands over her mouth to hold in a great honk of laughter. She put her face to her sleeping bag and her stomach muscles heaved for a few moments. Finally she lifted her face and looked over at Alan.

"Don't do that again," she said, grinning like a fool, like someone who wasn't within fifty yards of a pack of serial killers. "We'll go together, if you won't stay here."

"I don't want you to go," Alan whispered. His eyebrows were drawn together and his face was flushed in the dim light from the tent opening.

"We go together," Eileen said. "Let's get this over with, Mr. Baxter."

Great Sand Dunes, San Luis Valley, Colorado

It was Humvee versus Blackhawk, a showdown at the Techno Corral, and Joe was sure that the Blackhawk was going to win. It could fly, after all, out of this crappy dragging sand. The Blackhawk stood at the top of a dune crest, blades slowly revolving at idle speed. Three uniformed soldiers stood halfway down the dune, hands at their side arms and looking at the posse with faces like planks.

Paris stood against the purple door of Babe, his hands in his pockets, his shirt as immaculately crisp as the day before. How the hell he managed that, Joe had no idea. What he did know was that these three goons were going to keep them from Eileen and the killer Tesla machine.

He looked at Rosen, as blank-faced as the soldiers, and at Daniel and Marcia. Marcia had the same despairing look on her face that Joe knew he had on his own. Daniel looked furious, an expression Joe hadn't seen before. Daniel Grantham seemed like a low-key guy, a scholar with the light bones and flat muscles of a bicycle rider. He seemed more bird than man. Yet here he was with his jaw muscles clenched, hands in fists, his hair askew on his head, his eyes red and savage.

"These are not *your* dunes," Daniel said in a low voice.

"I'm a deputy with the Alamosa sheriff's department," Rosen interrupted. "We're on a search and rescue mission and we have authority here, as you well know."

"You're not allowed in this part of the dunes," the lead soldier said. Joe recognized the insignia of a captain but couldn't read the nametag from the distance separating them. The captain had the robot-soldier look, all blond hair and freezing blue eyes and muscles on his muscles. If there was a person in there, Joe couldn't see it. Inside the helicopter the pilot looked out, bored, picking his teeth with a toothpick.

"This is not military property," Rosen said.

"This is *my* property, as a citizen," Daniel said. "And technically, you work for *me*."

The helicopter had swept over a dune and caught them as their GPS receivers led them back to Babe the hummer for the second time. Joe was ready to scream with frustration. They'd gotten up at three in the morning, the five of them alert without coffee, wide-eyed as owls in the low flicker of Paris's penlight flashlight. They'd shouldered their packs and headed out by three thirty. The fifth dune they'd climbed showed Babe the hummer at the bottom, their own tracks leading up the opposite slope. Paris consulted his GPS and Marcia consulted hers. She and Daniel exchanged worried looks. They both re-calibrated their machines.

At five fifteen, Babe appeared in front of them once again. The sky was lightening. Three sets of tracks led out of the little hollow; two sets leading out and one set leading in. It was impossible, but there the hummer was. They had gone in an enormous circle *again*. They no longer had time to walk to the center of the dunes before six o'clock. Joe was beginning to believe the dunes weren't going to let them get there at all.

"We need to drive in," Joe said.

"So much for the element of surprise," Paris said, and shrugged.

"If we can get there at all," Marcia said. Her face was a pale circle in the false dawn, her eyes black holes. She sounded worried and afraid. Joe wasn't afraid. Then the helicopter sound thudded in their ears and the Blackhawk swept over the dune.

Joe was afraid now. He wasn't afraid of the three soldiers in front of him. He dealt with soldiers every working day, armed ones and flag officers and men who'd seen the elephant, as Kipling said, men who'd killed other men. Joe knew these men wouldn't kill their little posse. They weren't part of the earthquake people, they were being used by them. But they were soldiers, and they had their orders. Joe was afraid of the Tesla machine, he was afraid of the New Madrid earthquake. And he was afraid for Eileen, all alone without him.

"Enough of this," Marcia said suddenly, in her teacher voice. She stepped forward and put her fists on her hips. "Look. We know about your project. We're here to stop it, if we can. The machine that you carried out here in that Blackhawk is a Tesla machine and it's going to kill about a million people today if we don't stop it. It's going off at 6:45 this morning. You're due back here before noon, aren't you?"

The soldiers never moved. The rising sun, relentless, started creeping down the dune face toward them.

"It's an earthquake machine," Joe said. "I have the simulation here. I can show you. You can't let this happen."

"You're not allowed in this part of the dunes," the captain repeated. His pale eyes didn't change, and Joe thought despairingly of UFO nuts trying to sneak into Area 51. They, too, had desperation and courage. They were nuts, and Joe knew that his group sounded just like them. Nuts. They weren't going to reach the human inside the soldier. To him, they were the ones who weren't really human.

"Think," Marcia said suddenly. "Damn you, *think*. Why are there only a few of these people out there today? There's only, what, four or five people doing their little experiments. Why? Shouldn't there be fifty people wandering around taking notes and getting in the way? That's the way government experiments run. Three people for every one that actually works. Quality assurance to make sure everything is filled out in triplicate. Radios and camcorders and tracking equipment. There's none of that today, is there? Why not? I'll tell you. Because they're doing something *bad*. Something secret because it hurts people. We can show you . . ." She trailed off, breathing hard, her hands clenched. The captain frowned slightly and shifted a little in the sand.

"It doesn't matter what we're here for, Captain," Rosen said. "What matters is the law, and I represent the law. You may not stop us because we are not on a federal base. If you continue to stand in our way, I will arrest you."

One of the soldiers snorted, and the blue-eyed captain made a short, sharp movement with his hand that chopped off the other soldier as though gagged. The captain was still for a few moments, looking at Rosen as though he were a new and interesting species of ant.

"You're not allowed in this part of the dunes," he said finally. Marcia and Daniel groaned in unison, Paris shifted against the hummer and Joe clenched his teeth shut on a very bad word. Rosen stood like a man at a chessboard contemplating his next move as the seconds ticked by.

Joe looked at his watch. Six-twenty.

Great Sand Dunes, Latitude 37.47.50, Longitude 105.33.20, San Luis Valley, Colorado

"Hello, Mr. Mitchell," Eileen said pleasantly.

Jacob Mitchell spun around and the look on his face was a pleasure to see. His mouth dropped open, his eyes bulged, his face turned gray in the dawn light. His companion dropped the balled-up tarpaulin in his hands and started to reach toward his armpit.

"No no," Eileen said, raising her gun and aiming very carefully. "Let's put our hands right on top of our head, shall we?"

"Do it, Scott," Mitchell said. He put his hands on his head as though it were the latest fashion at dinner parties. His eyes had lost their surprised look and he smiled at Eileen and Alan, who stood behind her.

"You're Alan Baxter, yes? What are you doing here—oh." Mitchell stopped, looking back and forth between Alan and Eileen. "I wasn't aware that you're father and daughter. How interesting."

Behind Mitchell the Tesla device sat on the sand, revealed at last. It was beautiful. Two wooden platforms held a series of what looked like metal spools, each one sprouting wires from the top like multicolored hair. The wires twisted together into a thick braid that led into the bottom of a glass globe of the earth.

Eileen focused on Mitchell and tried to ignore the globe. It caught the eye, round and glowing and colored green and blue and brown. In the midst of the wire and the metal spools it looked totally out of place, like a work of priceless art caught inside a piece of industrial machinery.

On the sand next to the machine sat a black car battery on a wooden crate, a car battery with wires that led into the metal structure that held the cool glowing crystal of the globe.

"You run the Tesla machine with a *car* battery?" Alan asked. Mitchell narrowed his eyes but his voice remained light and friendly.

"Jim Leetsdale, right? He left you something on his computer, or in his files? I was surprised when you took his computer so quickly. I didn't expect you'd be able to break his encryption or his system. Ah, well, water under the bridge." Mitchell started to lower his hands and raised them again as Eileen made a slight movement with her gun.

"We'd like to stop your experiment for today, Mr. Mitchell," Eileen said, her voice as calm and friendly as she could make it. "We're going to escort you back to Alamosa, and we'll find out if your DNA, or your friend Scott's here, matches the DNA from material left on Krista Lewis's body. If not, you're free to go."

"Why didn't you just arrest me in Colorado Springs?" Mitchell asked, a smile playing on his lips. He seemed totally unafraid. Eileen felt a freezing doubt sweep her and suppressed it.

"I think you know," she said. "I know about the New Madrid. I don't know why, though I'd like to find out. But officially, Mr. Mitchell, I'm just here to talk to you in the Great Sand Dunes because that's where Krista Lewis was raped and killed. By placing yourself in the vicinity of the crime, you allow me to bring you in for questioning. We're also going to get a court order for DNA testing."

"Are you arresting me, Detective Reed?" Mitchell asked.

"Only if you don't wish to voluntarily come in for questioning, Mr. Mitchell."

"Of course, I'd be happy to. But have you tested Alan Baxter, Miss Reed? Your father?"

"Excuse me?" Eileen said coldly.

"He was in the dunes that night too, you know. Scott and—and I have each other for alibis. We were here conducting earth resonance experiments. What was your father doing that night?"

"I was driving down from my home in Wyoming," Alan said stiffly. "I don't know what you're trying to pull. I never met Krista Lewis."

"Or so he says," Mitchell said. "Let's both go in and get tested, shall we?"

Eileen made the mistake of looking at her father. As her eyes left Mitchell another man rose up from the sand. He was the other person in civilian clothes from the helicopter and he was holding a gun aimed directly at her.

"Don't move, ma'am," he said politely. He was gray-haired, black-eyed, as competent looking as a rattlesnake. He got to his feet slowly, giving her no chance to correct her aim.

Eileen didn't move. Her pistol had wavered from Mitchell and she couldn't aim it at the new man in time. She was caught by the simplest of traps, and she tried hard to keep her face from showing her dismay. She should have thought of the third man, jumping back into the helicopter. It was like that elementary school test, Which-object-does-not-belong? The third man, not in uniform, belonged to Mitchell and not in the helicopter. He'd been dropped over the dunes to make a sweep of the area. She'd flunked a test and she and Alan were going to die because of it.

"I'm not moving," she said, keeping absolutely still. Her voice did not waver and for that she was very glad. "But I'm still a police officer, and you are under arrest."

"Drop your gun, ma'am," the gray-haired man said.

Eileen let her gun's trigger guard drop through her index finger. Her gun fell against her wrist and was completely useless to her as a weapon. It was, however, safely out of the sand.

"One of you clowns should have a very sore chest," she said. "Which one is it?"

"That would be me," Scott said, with an expression of hungry satisfaction. "Broken ribs." He stepped forward and, keeping clear of his companion's line-of-sight, took the gun from Eileen's hand. He looked at Eileen, close, and smiled into her face. Alan made a stirring movement, the first he'd made.

"Now, now," the gray-haired one said. "Let's not get everyone all riled up. We're professionals here."

"No you're not," Alan said. "You're about to become the biggest mass murderers in American history. There's nothing professional about that."

Scott stepped away from Eileen and handed Mitchell her gun, her beloved Sig Sauer with the clean trigger pull and the sleek, elegant shape. It was the prettiest gun she owned, but it wasn't the only one. Her Ladysmith was in her ankle holster, oiled and loaded. If she could distract the gray-haired one, if she could alter the situation slightly, she could turn everything around. She was perfectly willing to risk rape to do that. Being raped was much better than dying.

Mitchell took Eileen's Sig Sauer from Scott and clicked the safety on. He stuck it casually in his pocket and Eileen realized that he was making no attempt to keep his fingerprints from marking it. He wasn't planning on giving it back. She felt a chill at the small of her back.

"We're not mass murderers, Alan," Mitchell said with a pained expression. "I would never do something like that. The New Madrid is going to go sometime this century. Better now than later."

"That's crap," Alan said. "You're playing God with people's lives, you're—"

"Why are you doing this, Mr. Mitchell?" Eileen interrupted. "I can't figure it out. This isn't a bleeder earthquake, like the rest of them. This is a big one. Why?"

The sun caught Eileen in the eyes and then moved on. They were in full early morning daylight now and the sun felt good after the chill of dawn. Eileen wondered briefly if the dunes were the last thing she was ever going to smell, and she suppressed it hard.

Mitchell glanced at his watch. Eileen could see him in the Oval Office, behind the big desk, looking at his watch with the same expression of genial calculation. Sure, there's enough time, he'd say. We'll talk to the Boy Scouts from Rapid City, South Dakota, today. We'll meet with the Akron, Ohio, Ladies Club today.

"Sure, there's enough time," he said. "The New Madrid is going to cause a lot of disruption, Eileen, Alan. Just as it would if it went off on nature's timetable instead of my own. As FEMA director I've been preparing for this earthquake for the better part of two years. We have food, clothing, water, and tents, all ready to go. We have National Guard units in Colorado, Wyoming, the Dakotas, Idaho, Montana, and New Mexico fueled and ready to mobilize. Instead of panic and chaos, I'll be directing relief efforts that will minimize loss of life and property. I'm actually saving lives by doing this."

"The nation will be grateful to you, too, won't it?" Eileen said. "You'll have more airtime than the President. You'll be the country's biggest hero."

"I'm no hero," Mitchell said modestly. "I'm just a civil servant doing his job, that's all."

"But you want to be President, don't you?" Eileen said.

"Yes, I do," Mitchell said, his voice still civilized and calm. But underneath Eileen could hear the starving hunger, the lust. The overwhelming desire to be The Man, the President.

"You worthless shit," Alan said. "You're going to kill hundreds of thousands of people so you can get on television giving the survivors leftover *clothing?* You're going to kill women and children so you can run for *President?* What kind of—"

"Alan," Eileen said without turning her head. "Shut up."

"Oh, there's no need, really," Mitchell said. "You're almost out of time anyway."

"This is crap," Alan said. "This is too huge to risk just to get good PR. You ran for President before, remember? You couldn't win. You couldn't even hold on to your job as a congressman—"

"Shut your trap," Bennett said viciously, taking a step towards Alan.

"Now, Bennett," Mitchell said soothingly. He smiled at Eileen, ignoring Alan. "Who said anything about *running* for President?"

"Oh," Eileen said.

"Oh my God," Alan whispered.

"Exactly," Mitchell said. "Scott, if you would take over for Bennett. Bennett, the program is ready to go."

Scott drew a gun from a side holster and held it on Alan and Eileen with casual competence. Bennett let his own arms down with a sigh and rolled his shoulders. He holstered his gun and took a tiny white stick from his pocket. He put it in his mouth like a toothpick and chewed it as he walked to the Tesla machine.

"So who killed Krista?" Eileen said. "I'm curious."

"I don't know," Mitchell said absently, joining Bennett at the Tesla machine. He was intent on the console, watching Bennett press buttons. Bennett wrote down numbers from the console and compared them to papers on a clipboard. The clipboard was attached to the battery crate. Bennett chomped on his stick until it broke with a wet little snap. He spit it into the sand and immediately produced another from his pocket. Eileen watched this with interest. There was something about the stir sticks that tugged at her mind.

"We have to stop this," Alan whispered desperately to Eileen.

"We don't have to do anything yet, Alan," Eileen said. "Just stay still." The freezing at her spine had invaded her stomach and her legs. She was afraid if she looked down her legs would be trembling. She'd never been so afraid in her life and she had to keep calm. If she lost it, her father would die trying to protect her. She knew this in every fiber of her being, without thought. He would not let her be hurt if he were still alive. She had to keep him alive, then, by staying in control. And she had to stay alive herself.

"Almost ready," Bennett said. Mitchell glanced at his watch and gave a merry smile to Eileen.

"Six-forty," he said.

Great Sand Dunes, San Luis Valley, Colorado

Stalemate. Unless someone had something extra, Kansas City was going to disappear like a T. Rex into a tar pit. Joe could hardly keep still.

"Well," Rosen said, shrugging his shoulders, "I can't think of anything else to say. Anyone?"

The soldiers stood in the same places they had before. Everything Rosen had said had fallen on professionally deaf ears. For fifteen minutes they had tried, while the sun rose in the sky and heated the sand.

"What do we do now?" Marcia said.

"We drive on," Rosen said calmly. The robot captain reacted to this. He blinked.

"What?" Daniel said.

"We drive on," Rosen repeated, looking at the captain. "We're driving in, captain. If you shoot an Alamosa deputy on public land you are going to be prosecuted to the fullest extent of the law. You think your commander is going to stand up for you if you do?"

"And four civilians, too," Joe said. He gave a little hop in the sand and turned to Babe. "Let's get going, guys."

"You can't do this," the captain said. His calm was broken but his face hadn't changed. "I have authority to use deadly force."

"Your authority will melt like yesterday's snow if you kill a cop," Daniel said. "He's a *cop*. He's not some sheepherder's boy like El Paso or some religious nuts like Waco. You better think about it."

Marcia said nothing but scrambled into the back of the Humvee. Her face was pale and frightened. Daniel joined her. Paris shrugged elaborately and climbed into the driver's seat.

"What *do* I get into," he murmured to himself, and started the engine. Rosen stepped up into the vehicle and closed the door.

"You think they'll shoot us?" Paris said casually, as though he were asking about the weather.

"Don't know," Rosen said.

"Okay," Paris said, and gunned his engine. "Let's give it a try."

The soldiers stood where they had before, all but the captain showing faces of anger and dismay. His face was still and silent, looking remarkably like Rosen's. He raised his hand in the air and Joe swallowed and clenched his hands into fists.

Another hummer roared over the dune, nearly taking to the air. It skidded down the slope. It was covered in sand and painted Army green and a slender hand waved a badge out the window as it came to a sandy stop between Babe and the Blackhawk helicopter. The face behind the wheel was Sheriff Gonzalez. A huge grin split his face.

"Hold it, everybody," a voice yelled. The voice belonged to an Asian-American man who jumped from the hummer. He waved his badge, trying to get it in everyone's vision at once. Joe didn't need the badge to know who this was and felt his heart leap in joy.

"Lucy came through!" he shouted, and opened the door.

Fred Nguyen, FBI agent, saw Joe and gave a great sunny laugh.

"Hey, Joe!" he said. "I came as fast as I could. We have a warrant to arrest anybody we want to out here, military or not. Plus I get to confiscate materials stolen from the Defense Archives, if I find them. How's them apples?"

"Like the freakin' cavalry over the hill," Daniel said reverently from behind Joe's shoulder.

"You drove in here?" Paris asked the sheriff, who had rolled his window down. Gonzalez rested a meaty arm on the door and gave Paris a lazy grin.

"I was driving in here in Volkswagen dune buggies before you were born, son," he said. "I just don't have the time anymore."

"We've got less than ten minutes," Rosen said. "And we may have a hostage situation. Can you follow us in?"

Gonzalez nodded and looked at Fred Nguyen. Fred stood for a moment, eyes flashing, smile still on his face. Joe had met Nguyen several times, through Lucy Giometti. He was no slouch.

"We'll follow, of course," Fred said. "We're going to need you there too, gentlemen." This was said to the Army captain, who nodded politely.

"I'll need to see the warrant, then I'm at your disposal," he said. The other two soldiers heaved unprofessional sighs of relief.

"Go on," Gonzalez said to Rosen and Joe. "We'll catch up." Nguyen leaned into the hummer to rummage for the warrant that Lucy, the angel, had gotten them. Joe didn't see if Nguyen found the warrant because he was pressed back into his seat. Paris had hit the gas. Babe swarmed up the dune, spitting sand as she went.

"How much longer?" Paris asked.

"Three minutes," Rosen said.

"We've got three minutes to come up with a battle plan, then," Paris said. "One plan is that I just try and run the Tesla machine over. Any other ideas?"

There were several, and everyone shouted over the scream

of Babe's engine and the relentless ticking of the clock. Six-forty-two.

Great Sand Dunes, Latitude 37.47.50, Longitude 105.33.20, San Luis Valley, Colorado

"So who killed Jim Leetsdale? Did you, Mr. Mitchell?"

"Still trying to solve your murder cases? A little irrelevant now, isn't it?" Mitchell asked in amusement. He stepped away from the Tesla machine and unrolled a sandwich bag he took from his pants pocket. He started rolling ear protectors in his fingers, the little yellow tubes that expanded to fit inside the ear and protected shooters from hearing loss.

"I killed Leetsdale," Mitchell said. "At least, it was my orders. Bennett and Scott carried out the actual execution. Poorly, I might add. He was supposed to be identified as a suicide. You figured out he was a homicide immediately, didn't you?"

"Yeah, it was a lousy faked suicide," Eileen said, still searching her mind for a way to get to her gun. "Did you see Krista? Was she ever here?"

"She was here," Mitchell said. He put the tubes in his ears. They were almost out of time.

"Ready, sir," Bennett said. Scott had his gun steady on Eileen and hadn't wavered.

"Let's go, then," Mitchell said. He looked at Eileen with sparkling eyes. "Then we'll celebrate."

Eileen knew what he meant. Alan's lack of reaction meant that he didn't. She breathed a prayer that if it came to rape, she'd have the courage to keep her wits about her. She'd met rape victims who did, and they usually survived their attack. Not without being raped, of course, she remembered with a freezing and distant coldness. Not without being raped. Well, if it came to that, it would come to that. She would feel about it later.

Mitchell pressed a button on the console of the Tesla device with a flourish and stepped away.

For a few moments there was nothing. Then the machine

gave a kind of shiver, almost too slight to be seen. Eileen stared at it, fascinated and horrified. The lovely crystal globe within the machine began to spin slowly, then sped up. The etched colors blurred into a blue-green blur. A low sound started in her teeth and head and toes and then invaded every part of her. It was a sound but it was a vibration too, a vibration so quick and high that it felt like ants crawling over her body. Beside her, Alan made a sound of disgust and fear.

"It won't hurt you," Bennett said, stepping behind Scott and putting earmuffs on the other man's ears. He never passed between Scott's gun and Eileen. He moved away and put earmuffs on his own ears as the sound started to increase. "It gives you a hell of a headache without ear protection, though," he shouted.

Eileen felt the insect sensation increase, invading the inside of her body as well as her skin. Then the hum began, the atonal pulsing hum that filled the sky and the sand and her bones. It was loathsome.

Mitchell raised his face to the sky and pumped his fists in the air, grinning and shouting something.

"I'm going to try," Alan said calmly and softly. "We have to stop this."

"No," Eileen hissed. "You'll get us both killed." It was hard to speak over the waves of sound. Her head ached fiercely and she knew that she had lost. Alan was going to take out Scott and he might just give her a chance to get to her gun. At the cost of his life. The life of her father. She couldn't do this, she couldn't let him die in front of her. Not when she had just found him. But if Alan gave her a chance to stop these men they could save millions of lives. Maybe even America itself. She felt like something had seized her by the throat as she understood, finally, that she didn't have to be raised by him to love him. She loved him. And she wasn't going to have a chance to tell him, because she was going to let him sacrifice himself. For her. She took a deep breath.

Alan started to move, and Scott shook his head tiredly and raised the gun. He was going to fire.

Mitchell turned, Bennett turned, and Scott turned as a growling snarl burst over the dunes to their right. An enormous Humvee soared over the dune crest and skidded down the sand and that was all Eileen saw before she crouched, drew, and fired at Scott.

His gun whirled like a Frisbee, switching ends back and forth, and he flew backwards into the sand. She hadn't drawn a breath. She was vaguely aware of figures tumbling out of the Humvee. Bennett, next. His eyes were still widening and his arm was still moving toward his armpit when her second shot took him full in the chest. She drew her first breath. Easy shots, both of them, and as he thumped backward, she ran at him.

She landed with both knees on his chest and felt the reassuring solidity of the body armor. She drew her second breath. He was gasping underneath her, face pasty gray but alive. She reached under his jacket and removed his gun. She twisted on her knees and faced Mitchell, who had her gun in his khaki pocket. She drew her third breath.

The bodies piling out of the still-moving Humvee seemed endless, like clowns erupting from a circus car. Two of them were racing toward the Tesla machine and one of them looked like Joe Tanner. Someone else was running toward Jacob Mitchell and she saw with a surging sense of relief that it was Dave Rosen.

"Gun!" she shouted as loud as she could, over the groaning waves of the Tesla machine. It felt like her head was going to burst open. Rosen blurred into a speed he'd only hinted at before and took Jacob Mitchell to the sand with bone-crunching force. Someone dropped to her side and knelt on Bennett's right arm. Eileen caught a glimpse of gray hair and an elderly, kindly, frightened female face. She looked at Scott, who was lying in the sand with Alan Baxter and someone else on him, a tall man with dark blond hair.

"Come on!" screamed the dark blond guy, and Eileen realized he was screaming at Joe Tanner and the other man. They were standing in front of the Tesla machine and looking at the console, clearly trying to figure it out.

Alan Baxter got up from Scott's chest and ran at the Tesla machine like he was sixteen and on the football team. He dropped his shoulder and hit the battery crate with enough force to snap the cables and send the little crate tumbling over. Alan tumbled over in the sand and lay still.

The hum stopped. The air shimmered like a pan of boiling water. The crystal globe slowed in its cage of wire and metal. Silence came back.

"I never thought of that," Joe said into the silence.

"Did we get it in time?" The gray-haired woman next to Eileen was sobbing. "Did we?"

"We won't know until we can get to a television," Joe said. "I don't know."

"It didn't go very long," Alan said, sitting up in the sand. His hair stood up wildly and he was very pale.

"It doesn't matter," Jacob Mitchell snarled. His face was caked with sand and he spit a few times to clear his mouth. Rosen held an arm twisted up behind him and he grimaced in pain. "You'll all go to jail for interfering with a top-secret project. You have no authority to do this!"

"Authority," Rosen said with satisfaction, "is on the way."

"And you won't be using this machine any time soon," Joe said. "Paris?"

The dark blond-haired man tossed Joe a tire jack from the Humvee. Joe caught it with both hands and used the momentum to swing the jack into the lovely crystal globe caught inside the wires of the Tesla machine. Every line of his body went into the effort and for a moment he was something more than human. He looked like an angel, the kind who spears devils and throws them down into hell.

"No!" Mitchell shouted as the jack made a very satisfying noise. The globe shattered with a musical, echoing sound, and glass flew into the air. Joe struck again and wires and metal spools cracked like china plates. Joe took two more hits and the wooden platform itself splintered and threw wood fragments across the sand.

"My turn," said the tall man who'd gone to the Tesla machine with Joe. Joe handed him the jack and the man made two direct hits, his face wrinkled with effort. The interior of the bigger spools held two fragile onion-shaped metal devices mounted on a labyrinth of bracing. They collapsed into shards of metal. Something black and greasy ran into the sand. A thin sheaf of papers fluttered out from the main console and several landed in the grease.

Joe took the jack back but he had little to do. He took a couple of good whacks at the twisted metal pieces. The machine was destroyed. Crystal fragments and shards of metal sparkled in the morning sun. He set the jack handle on the sand and leaned against it nonchalantly, like an Englishman with a cane.

"Hi, baby," he said to Eileen, winking.

"Hey there," she said, laughing. "You must be the cavalry."

"No that would be Lucy," Joe said. "Let me introduce my friends. This is Paris Linsley, Marcia Fowler, Daniel Grantham, and of course you know old-what's-his-name."

"Alamosa Deputy Rosen," Rosen said with a hint of satisfaction. "You are under arrest, Mr. Mitchell. Anything you say can and will be used against you in a court of law."

"Don't give me that bullshit," Mitchell shouted angrily. "You had no right to destroy my machine. You can't arrest me."

"Oh yes, we can," Eileen said. Bennett coughed weakly underneath her. She belatedly remembered Scott. "Is he okay?"

"He's breathing," Paris said. "His eyes are rolled up in his head, but there's no blood on his mouth. He hasn't punctured a lung or anything. How did you know he had body armor on?"

"He had it on the last time he tried to shoot me," Eileen said absently. She looked at the woman Joe had named Marcia Fowler, kneeling on Bennett's arm. "Can you hold his arm down for a minute?"

"As long as he stays passed out, I can," Marcia said nervously.

Eileen got to her feet and stretched her arms to the sky. She wanted to run in circles, shout with crazed laughter, throw up on the sand. She was alive.

"Are you okay? They didn't hurt you?" Rosen asked.

"We're both fine," Eileen said. "I know who killed Leetsdale."

"And Krista?" Rosen asked levelly. Alan, sitting in the sand near Joe and the other man, Daniel Grantham, looked at Eileen.

For a moment there was only Alan Baxter for Eileen, only his tired face in her vision. He looked at her with sadness and love and acceptance. If she arrested him for the murder of Krista Lewis he wouldn't fight, he wouldn't argue. He'd go into Gonzalez's prison cell and wait quietly and when his DNA came back negative for the hair found on Krista's body, he would disappear from Eileen's life forever. He'd never stop loving her, she knew. But that would be a betrayal that could never be healed.

Thank goodness he hadn't done it, then. Eileen felt herself grinning like a fool.

"Yes," she said. "I do know."

25

Great Sand Dunes, Latitude 37.47.50, Longitude 105.33.20, San Luis Valley, Colorado

"Hey, cool!" Joe shouted. He still hadn't gotten over the Tesla machine's enormous sound. "Just like Agatha Christie!" He took on a phony English accent. "You may be wondering why I've gathered you here today." His voice dropped back to normal tones. "Someone here did it, right?"

"That's right," Eileen said, her beautiful face glowing. When Paris gunned Babe over the dune crest, Joe had eyes for no one but Eileen. There she'd stood, pale as death, hands in the air. Joe nearly broke the plan by heading for the creep that was holding a gun on her. He saw the Tesla machine as Paris skidded Babe to a stop, and he remembered what he was supposed to be doing. Sure enough, Rosen was right. Eileen could take care of herself.

Daniel Grantham stirred nervously. Joe looked at him, then saw Marcia and Alan Baxter and even Paris Linsley looking apprehensive. He remembered, suddenly, that each one of them was in the San Luis Valley the night Krista Lewis was murdered. Any one of them could have done it.

"So?" Rosen asked, as though he were sitting comfortably at a desk instead of kneeling in the Great Sand Dunes holding Jacob Mitchell's arms behind his back. Rosen's short black hair was as unruffled as always, but great dark patches stained the back of his shirt and armpits. Joe knew he, too, had sweated through his deodorant and his shirt. The sun was already turning the sand into an early morning oven.

"Krista found this spot while Mitchell and his goons were setting up for the Colorado earthquake. She found this place because she was researching ground water contamination in Medano Creek. Right, Mr. Mitchell?"

"That's right," he said, his face calm again. "We escorted her out of the area. And that's all we did——"

"That night, someone followed her tracks and raped her and killed her. Then the murderer cut two slices of skin from her shoulder and arm, two flaps of skin. Why?"

"To make her look like a UFO abduction," Marcia said.

"That was the red herring, wasn't it?" Eileen said with a twinkle. Joe pressed his lips together to keep from laughing out loud. She was enjoying this as much as he was.

"What do you mean?" Paris asked.

"I didn't know until I saw Bennett in action. He got his little chew sticks out, right before they set off the earthquake machine. I watched you bite them. You're a biter, Bennett. You like to *bite* things."

There was a vast and echoing silence in the cup of sand. Joe's internal laughter died.

"He bit her," Alan Baxter said in a choking whisper.

"He bit her," Eileen said. "Then he cut the bitten skin from her body to keep anyone from matching the bite marks to his teeth."

"What a story," Mitchell said, his brow furrowed. "Ridiculous."

"That son of a bitch," Alan said.

"We have a pubic hair from her body," Eileen said. Joe was watching her face and not Mitchell's. She wasn't angry or sad. She was implacable, as stony as a blind marble statue holding the scales of justice. "Bennett used a condom when he raped her and he cut her skin off where he bit her. He stripped her naked and brushed her off. But he left one little hair. Just one little hair. And that's all we need. Bennett is under arrest for the rape and murder of Krista Lewis."

For a moment there was no sound at all, just the blue sky above them and the sand below them and the pieces of the Tesla machine twinkling in the sun. Joe could smell greasy oil and sweat and underneath it all the smell of the dunes, uncaring about what these little creatures were doing on its great tan hide. Marcia still knelt on Bennett's arm and Paris was kneeling astride the prone body of Scott. Daniel stood at Joe's side and Alan Baxter sat on the sand next to them. Eileen and Rosen and Mitchell stood a few feet away and Babe stood beyond them, her big front wheels nearly buried in the sand.

"No," Mitchell said, twisting forward in Rosen's grasp. His eyes were narrowed to tiny slits like slices of hell. "It can't be. He couldn't. He *wouldn't!*"

Joe saw Alan suddenly rise to his feet and bolt forward. Joe couldn't move fast enough as Marcia went flying off the body of Bennett, the man who appeared to be completely unconscious but who was shamming, he was faking it. Joe should never have left Marcia alone with him.

Bennett had another gun. He had been carrying two just like Eileen always did. It was in his grasp and he was aiming at Eileen. Joe saw Rosen shove Mitchell into the sand with a shout and start to reach for his own gun but it was going to be far too late.

Alan Baxter slammed into Bennett's side, his arms low and reaching for the little pistol. A single shot snapped in the air, an unimportant sounding crack. Bennett went down and didn't get off another shot. Eileen had his gun arm and she jerked and twisted, and Joe clearly heard the sound of bones popping. Bennett shrieked, a thin high whistle of a sound.

Marcia was screaming, her arms around Bennett's kicking legs. Paris was shouting something, still holding Scott's arms. He wisely wasn't going to leave Scott. Joe fell across Bennett's back, jostling Eileen, before Marcia lost her grip on Bennett's flailing feet. Rosen was cuffing Mitchell with lightning speed, ignoring Mitchell's muffled screams as he pressed the man's face into the sand.

Someone else was screaming. It was Eileen, her voice high and thin and breathless. She clicked the safety on Bennett's gun and threw it toward Rosen and fell to her knees beside Alan Baxter.

There was a great spreading pool of red beneath him. The hungry sand soaked it up as fast as it spilled from his body.

"Daddy," Eileen said in a broken voice.

"Can't breathe," Alan whispered, his eyes looking into the empty blue sky.

Joe put his arms around Bennett and bodily picked him up. The man's broken arm flopped in a horrible way as Joe staggered away from Eileen and Alan. He fell down with Bennett underneath him and heard the breath leave the other man in a pained whistle. He didn't care if he killed him. Joe's vision was blurred with rage.

Paris Linsley sprinted past. Joe turned his head to see Daniel Grantham on top of Scott. Paris threw open Babe's door and lunged inside. He fell out of the Humvee with the cooler. His face was sweaty and his hair flopped over his forehead. He threw open the lid and threw things out of the cooler. Chicken and potato salad flew into the air. He ran back past Joe with two plastic bags, which once held chicken, in his hands.

He fell to his knees beside Alan Baxter. Joe twisted on top of Bennett so he could see. Paris elbowed Eileen roughly aside. She let him shove her out of the way. She knelt, her face puffy and flooded with tears, and twisted her hands together. Alan turned his head slowly to look at Paris. Alan's lips were stained with frothy red blood, and he was deadly pale. The right side of Alan's chest was covered with bright red bubbles. Paris put one plastic bag against Alan's chest and rolled him on his side to put the other on his back. Alan groaned.

"It went right through you," Paris said loudly. "It's a Kevlar-piercing round and it didn't mushroom, all right? You're shot through the lung but you're going to live through this, all right? You're losing blood but I'm going to take care of that. Don't die on me, mister, you're not going to die if you don't want to."

"Don't want to," Alan mouthed, and Paris gave him a sunny smile.

"That's right, pal," he said. "Lady, hold these bags against his shoulder here while I get the first-aid kit. His back, that's the exit wound and that's the biggest one. The shot didn't hit any arteries but we've got to keep his lung from collapsing. This is what we call a sucking chest wound, and we can deal with it. Put a lot of pressure on it."

Someone dropped to the sand near Joe, and he turned his eyes to see Rosen holding a roll of duct tape from the Humm V. Bennett, still squirming weakly, shrieked again as they bound his arms to his sides with duct tape. The injured arm was roughly splinted and Bennett couldn't move. Joe appreciated Rosen's detachment in caring for Bennett's injury. Joe didn't care if Bennett's arm came completely off. Rosen was trotting toward Scott when Sheriff Gonzalez's Humm-V hauled itself over the horizon and, blessedly, the helicopter followed.

"We need to get this man to a hospital," Paris shouted as Fred and Gonzalez got out. Fred looked with dismay at Alan Baxter and the duct-tape bound Bennett, still groaning.

"This guy needs to go, too. He's unconscious and his breathing's bad," Daniel Grantham said reluctantly.

"They all have to go. I need to go in the helicopter with the prisoners, Paris," Rosen said crisply. "And Eileen will be going with Alan. Can you—"

"Of course," Paris said. "The sheriff and I are the only ones who can drive out of here. Eileen, keep the pressure on the bandage and keep him flat for the shock. Get some warm blankets around him. That's all you can do until you get him to the hospital." He stood up as the helicopter crew came down the slope of sand. The captain had been reprogrammed to be on their side now, evidently. His crew carried stretcher boards for Bennett and Alan. Joe breathed a sigh of relief as they competently loaded the injured men on the stretchers. It was nice to be on the side of the good guys again.

Eileen held the pressure bandage on Alan as they carried him to the helicopter. She didn't look at Joe as they loaded Alan in. In seconds the blades were throwing up sand as the helicopter rose into the air. The big machine turned directly above them, and for a moment Joe caught a glimpse of Eileen's face, white and strained, at the side window. She was looking right at him. Then the helicopter accelerated into the sky and was gone.

The silence seemed huge. Marcia made a harsh little sound. She was weeping.

"He's going to survive," Paris said to her. "And it's not your fault."

Marcia held her hands over her face, still on her knees in the sand. Joe dropped into the sand next to her and put his arms around her. Paris packed his first-aid supplies back in his big green box. Daniel came over to help.

"Are you all right, ma'am?" Fred Nguyen asked.

"I'm fine," Marcia said underneath her hands. "I'm a little upset, that's all."

"Where will they take them?" Joe asked Gonzalez.

"To Pueblo, that's the nearest trauma center," Gonzalez said. "We'll go right there."

"What happened to the Tesla machine?" Fred asked.

"Somebody bumped into it and it got broken," Joe said. Fred regarded him in silence.

"I see," he said finally. "We have to pack up what's here, then we'll head out." He regarded the shards of the Tesla machine and shook his head slowly back and forth.

"I'd like to get to Pueblo," Marcia said, putting her hands down. Her face was tear-stained but calm.

"Me, too," Joe said.

"Yes," Daniel said. They all looked at Paris.

"Of course," Paris said. He stood up with the first-aid box in his hands. Joe helped Marcia to her feet. Daniel dusted his hands off. They looked at Fred Nguyen and Sheriff Gonzalez, who looked back at them. Both men looked furious.

"You should have waited for us," Gonzalez said.

"There'd be about a million people dead if we had," Joe said. "I hope there aren't a million people dead right now."

"Babe has AM *and* FM radio," Paris said. "And we're not getting closer to Pueblo just standing here."

Marcia stood for a moment more, looking at the bright red

sand where Alan Baxter had bled. She stepped forward and
kicked sand over the stain with savage little movements. Tears
ran down her face.

"Let's go," she said.

North of the Great Sand Dunes, Colorado

Alan was unconscious, his face sweaty and gray. The big
gauze pads that she was holding over the plastic bags were
slowly soaking through with blood. If they didn't get to a hospital soon, she believed he was going to die. She looked at the
front of the helicopter but there was no point in asking for
more speed. She could hear the engines herself and they were
shrieking at full power.

The helicopter was crowded. Rosen sat next to Mitchell
and Scott, who had also been bound with duct tape. Mitchell
was still trying to shout orders and arguments but Eileen
couldn't understand what he was saying. Rosen had pressed a
length of duct tape over his mouth shortly after takeoff.

Eileen turned back to Alan. Her arms were beginning to
tire of the strain of holding the pads, but she welcomed the
pain. It should have been her. She was younger. She could
take the trauma better than a sixty-year-old man. She was so
delighted at finding the murderer that she forgot he might
want to fight back. She was stupid, stupid. She shouldn't be a
detective. All she ever did to solve cases was wander around
and kick at rocks until something crawled out. She wasn't
brilliant. She wasn't even bright. She was stupid.

"I was trying to get Mitchell," Bennett's voice said at her
right elbow. She looked in surprise to see him looking up
at her, his arms bound at his side, his face sweaty and ill looking.

"Really?" she said, uninterested.

"Really. I'd never kill a cop. That's Scott, he doesn't care.
He killed Leetsdale and he shot at you at your apartment. I
wanted Mitchell, that son-of-a-bitch."

"Why?" Rosen asked.

"Because I joined his team to get to the White House,"

Bennett said. Echoing in his voice was the same lust for power Eileen heard in Mitchell's voice. She wished she wasn't sitting so close to him. "He screwed it up. He screwed me up. He had to start killing people, and look where it got us."

"Krista Lewis?" Rosen asked.

"She was just a chick. It was an accident," Bennett said with an attempt at a shrug that caused his face to grow sweaty. "I didn't kill anybody but her, and she was an accident. Wouldn't stop fighting, was what. I can do ten years for that, but I don't want to go to prison for trying to kill a cop. I'll get life. I don't want that."

Disgusted, Eileen turned back to Alan, who seemed no worse than before. She wished the helicopter didn't smell so badly of fuel and oil. She wished the stretcher weren't so hard. She wished they were there already, damn it, how long?

"You should have waited for me," Rosen said abruptly to her.

"I did what I had to," Eileen said. She didn't want to turn her head but she did. "I had to go."

"If you don't trust me, maybe we shouldn't work together," Rosen said. His jaw was tight. He was furious with her.

"You'll have to decide that," Eileen said hoarsely. "I had to go after him, Rosen." Her throat closed up to a pinhole, and she felt the pressure of tears in her nose and eyes. Was she going to lose Rosen too? She deserved no less. She was so stupid. She bent her head and blinked two fat tears out of her eyes. She watched them fall to the dirty floor of the helicopter with a sense of distant surprise. When was the last time she had cried?

She felt the first warm touch of the blood soaking all the way through Alan's pressure bandage and turned back to him. He was so pale. She closed her eyes. Nothing was important now but getting him to the hospital. She didn't matter anymore. Alan Baxter mattered. Somewhere inside her, in the roaring dark, she held her father's love. Her father was no murderer. Her father loved her. The helicopter pounded and shuddered around her and she held the wet bandage tighter and she prayed desperately that they would get there soon.

Great Sand Dunes, San Luis Valley, Colorado

Paris lifted his hand in a wave to Gonzalez as Babe chugged over the top of the dune. Joe fiddled with the radio as they wallowed down the next slope. The radio on all bands played nothing but music and commercials.

"That's a good sign," Daniel said.

Joe said nothing. His heart thudded heavily in his chest. Eileen had looked out the window, looking for him, as the helicopter took her away. That had to mean something. It had to.

"Is Alan going to make it?" Marcia asked. Her voice was husky with emotion but her eyes were calm.

"If they get him to the hospital within the next half hour or so, and they have a trauma doctor who's not completely useless, I should think so," Paris said.

"How'd you know how to do that?" Daniel asked Paris.

"EMT training, and about six months up in Denver working for an ambulance company," Paris said. "We did runs into Denver General and University Hospital. I hadn't invented anything in a year and was feeling useless. So since being a doctor seemed extreme, I thought I'd be a paramedic. Just for kicks, you know."

"Were there kicks?" Joe asked, turning down the radio volume. Paris shrugged, his arms corded with muscle as he held Babe's steering wheel and aimed her into the slope of a dune.

"Yeah, there were. Not like today. I know I saved Mr. Baxter back there, but didn't we just save the world, too?"

"I think so," Joe said, and laughed.

"America, anyway," Daniel allowed.

"America is the world," Paris said with a sideways smile at Daniel.

"Let's say the world," Marcia said, and blew her nose with an enormous, unladylike honk. She put her tissue back into her pocket and shrugged. "Set off powerful earthquakes wherever you want. Who's going to stop you from taking over the world?"

"We are," Daniel said.

"Just don't make me wear any stupid superhero outfit with tights," Paris muttered.

Joe laughed with the rest, but his thoughts were with Eileen, and Alan. He sent thoughts, prayers, whatever he could, toward Pueblo and the hospital and the trauma doctor who should not, could not be useless. Hold on, he thought, and held on to the dashboard. Hold on.

"We interrupt this program to bring you a special news report," said the tinny voice of the radio announcer.

There was abrupt silence in the Humm-V.

"Oh, God, no," Marcia whispered.

"Turn it up," Daniel hissed. Joe fumbled with the knob and turned it too far. The announcer's voice boomed into the truck.

"We have reports of an earthquake in the Midwest. Is that right, Ben? Check the AP wire for me. Are you sure it isn't California?"

Paris came to a stop at the top of a dune and let Babe idle. He rested his forehead on his arms. Joe slumped back in his seat.

"We were too late," Joe said in a dull little voice. "After all that, we were too late."

"Shh," Marcia said.

"No, that's right, the Mississippi Valley," the announcer said. "Maybe our earthquake here in Colorado was a precursor, or pre-trembler, or whatever it's called. Okay, here's the report from the AP wire. 'An unexpected earthquake shook the Midwest at 8:23 this morning. The earthquake made buildings sway from Kansas City, Missouri to Chicago, Illinois and was felt as far away as Denver, Colorado. The earthquake, measured at 3.7 on the Richter scale, damaged some older buildings in Memphis, Tennessee. No fatalities were reported. The earthquake was along a little known fault line named the New Madrid.' That's all we've got so far. Looks like some flatlanders got their shorts scared off of them today, just like we did last week. Stay tuned for updates, and in the meantime, here's an oldies tune to match the day, 'Shake, Rattle, and Roll.' "

"He did say 3.7?" Joe asked.

"He said 3.7," Paris said. He gunned Babe and she spit sand and headed down the slope of the dune. "That would be less than four. Less than four!"

"We did it," Daniel shouted. "We really did it!"

"We did," Joe said. "Alan *has* to live now. He has to."

"He will," Marcia said. "How fast can this thing go on the highway, Paris?"

"We're going to find out," Paris said. "Just as soon as I can wrestle her back on to solid ground, that is."

Joe leaned back in his seat and closed his eyes. He kept seeing Eileen's face in the gritty window of the helicopter. Her face was strained and dirty and exhausted, but there was something different about her. There was something different in her eyes. Did she even know they'd won? At this point, he didn't think she cared. She would, later on, when Alan Baxter was out of danger. Then she would care that their little band of earthquake hunters had won.

"What a strange team we were," Marcia said, echoing his thoughts.

"I was thinking that, too," Daniel said. "Two police detectives, two ufologists, an inventor, a computer programmer, and a retired English professor. What a crew."

"Two computer programmers," Joe said.

"Two?"

"Two," he said quietly. "Me, and Jim Leetsdale. He gave his life to give me the codes I needed. He's the real hero."

"You're right," Daniel said in a low voice. "I wish he knew."

"Oh, I think he does, somehow," Marcia said.

"We'll turn a glass for him," Paris said. "We'll toast his memory at the biggest stinkin' party the valley has ever seen, when Alan gets out of the hospital."

"Damn right," Joe said.

"Is that Medano Creek?" Marcia said.

"Yeah, we're almost out," Paris said. Babe slid down the last slope, taking an avalanche of sand with her, and roared toward the creek. Joe could see the glitter of sunlight on the water and the glorious fall colors of the cottonwood trees that lined the edge of the dunes.

"We're out," Daniel said, as Babe crossed the creek.

Joe reached for the water container and took a long drink. The water felt delicious going down his throat, washing the last taste and touch of the dunes away.

"Here," he said, handing the water to Paris. Each of them drank. Daniel, the last, poured a measure of water from the window as Babe hauled herself back on to the roadway.

"Water for our lives," he said, with a sideways look at Marcia and Joe. "Thanks to Gaia, for sparing us."

"Gaia?" Joe asked.

"The earth goddess," Marcia said crisply. "Let's ask her for Alan's life, while we're at it."

"I already am," Joe said. "Every second."

Paris put Babe's wheels on the highway and leaned over the steering wheel. The engine revved up to a near scream and Babe took off like a rocket.

"Give her all she's got, Scotty," Joe shouted, laughing. Behind him the dunes receded, flat and tan and uncaring.

In the center of the dunes, tiny left-behind shards of the Tesla machine were lying on the sand. Tonight the wind would come, Joe thought, and the grains of sand would cover the remains, and tomorrow the sand would be silken and unmarked. Pure, and silent, and clean.

26

The Rio Grande River, San Luis Valley, Colorado

Eileen squinted and set her jaw and cast the fly rod like she
was trying to beat a carp to death. Joe laughed so hard he staggered in the water and nearly fell down. She looked at him
with flashing eyes and a tight mouth. Then her mouth relaxed
and she grinned.

"I'm trying," she said.

"I know, I know," he laughed. "I can't help it, though. You
look so cute!"

Eileen sloshed over to him and he put an arm around her.
She was dressed in a fleecy jacket against the cold November
day. She was wearing winter Neoprene waders that came up
past her waist. She made waders look good. The winter sunshine had heated her hair. He smelled flowers as he buried his
face in the gloss of her hair.

"Say it," he said roughly.

"I love you," she said instantly. "Want me to say it again?"

"Yes."

"I love you, I love you, I love you," she said, hugging him

with her free arm. "Don't try to make love to me here, Alan is coming back down the river to check on me."

"Okay," Joe sighed. "He's still pretty slow, though. We might be able to get in a quickie before he gets back."

Eileen pulled back and glared at him, which gave him a perfect opportunity to kiss her thoroughly.

Alan came around the river bend as Eileen was getting her fly rod sorted out for another try at casting. Joe was a good six feet down the river, innocently untangling a knot in his leader.

Alan was a little slower, Joe thought. He moved slowly and carefully but he managed the fly line. Good thing he'd been shot in his non-casting side. Best of all was the way he looked when he saw Eileen and waved.

She waved back, unsmiling, her face as radiant as morning.

"How's it going?" he asked as he joined them.

"Not so well," Eileen said. "I'm not so good at casting."

"Let's try together," Alan said. He stepped behind his daughter and put his arm on her casting arm. He held the back of her hand, and as she held the line in her other hand he moved her arm back, then forward. The fly line floated over the water and sailed back again, making a perfect loop.

"Like this," Alan said, "Now let go." The fly line settled on the water and the whitish fluff of the fly landed on the water. "This is a good cast. I know there's fish in this bend, that's why I put you here."

The water sparkled in the winter sun, cold and clear as melted ice. The fly floated downstream. Joe watched Alan and Eileen. Their eyes never left the tiny fluff. Beyond the river, the winter grasses were golden yellow, speckled with snow. Joe shifted in the river, his toes protesting the lack of movement. The icy water was making his feet go numb. Alan was still, Eileen was still, and the fly suddenly disappeared underneath the water.

"Now!"

Alan pulled up Eileen's hand and the line and the tip of the fly rod abruptly bent down. The line tightened and went straight into the water. Eileen laughed as the line suddenly moved underneath the water. It darted to the left, then to the right. Under the water, there was a fish with Eileen's fly caught in its hard little mouth.

"Got one!" Joe crowed.

"Oh, wow, what do I do, oh wow," Eileen panted, her cheeks flushed pink with excitement.

"Keep your rod tip up," Alan said, his eyes never leaving the fly line. He was grinning. "Let the line out until you've got the fish on your reel. There we go. Now reel in slowly. Don't pull too hard."

It seemed like forever but it was only a few moments before Alan scooped up the fish in his net. It was silvery purple and spotted and not as big as Joe expected. Maybe a foot long.

"So small," Eileen gasped. "I thought it would be bigger."

"This is a wild rainbow trout," Alan said reverently. He took a pair of forceps from his vest and expertly slipped the hook from the jaws of the fish. "This isn't a hatchery fish. See the fins, how they're perfectly shaped? Hatchery fish have worn fins from swimming along the concrete bottoms of hatchery ponds. Wild trout have perfect fins and they fight like demons. Aren't they fun to catch?"

"Oh, my," Eileen said. "That was incredible." Alan let the net release the fish without touching it. It flipped a few drops of water at them as it swam off, as if outraged at losing the game. They all slogged to the bank and sat down together. The day was cold but there was no snow. With the sunshine, it was a gorgeous day to be outside in the wild. Joe tilted his head back and sighed.

"We ought to get back pretty soon," Eileen said. "Supper."

"We don't want to miss Beth's cooking," Joe agreed. "And Marcia said she was bringing Daniel and Lady Jane and Sara down tonight." They all grinned at each other. Watching Beth and Lady Jane learn to be friends was like watching two elephants get to know each other. There was a lot of stomping and ear flapping and trunk blowing.

"Marcia is really moving down here?" Eileen asked.

"That's what she says," Alan said. He eased his shoulder in the sling. "Some people just get taken with this place, she says. Looks like she's one of them. Anyway, she can visit her friends up in Fort Collins whenever she gets the urge. That's what she says."

"That's what she says," Joe repeated mildly. Alan gave him a sharp glance but Joe said nothing more. Joe grinned to himself and wondered when Alan was going to be leaving the San Luis Valley. By the looks of it, not any time soon.

"So you'll be going back to the Springs tomorrow night?" Alan asked.

"Yeah, got to get back to work," Joe said.

"You can't take a few more days?"

"Rosen is still mad at me for taking off after you," Eileen said. Her face brightened. "He didn't ask for reassignment, though. So I'm trying to keep on his good side. But we'll be back for Thanksgiving, for Susan's wedding to Frank. We wouldn't miss that."

"It's going to be huge," Alan said with a smile. Joe grinned too. Susan Williams had allowed her mother to plan her wedding. She didn't care, she told Joe, and her mother did. Whatever her mother wanted was fine with her. As rumor had it, the wedding train was long enough to reach from the front of the church to the back. Frank's family was coming out from New Jersey. Joe wondered what the easterners would think of the San Luis Valley.

"You'll have to come up for a while after that," Eileen said suddenly. "The trial."

Mitchell's trial was going to be in early December and Alan had been called by the prosecution as a witness. Bennett's trial was scheduled for May.

"Okay," Alan said. "I'll come up early. The kokanee salmon are going to be running in eleven-mile reservoir any time now. That's the big reservoir west of Colorado Springs. Kokanee are really fun to catch."

"It's about time to go," Joe said, glancing at his watch.

"I want to fish one more bend," Alan said, climbing gingerly to his feet. "I'll meet you back at the truck in about fifteen minutes."

"Okay," Eileen said. She looked doubtfully at her fishing gear and Joe knew she'd had enough. Why spoil the experience of catching the pretty little rainbow?

"Let's just sit here a while," Joe said as Alan disappeared upriver. He'd reach the truck before they did, which was fine with Joe. He had something to talk to Eileen about.

Alan stepped out into the river to cast at the far bank. The water was freezing cold and they'd been fishing all day. His shoulder was starting to ache fiercely. It was time to go, but the fishing had been terrific today. As his fly floated down-river his eye was caught by the figures of Joe and Eileen. They'd been hidden around the curve of the bank.

He watched them, puzzled, ignoring his fly. They were on their feet and almost looked like they were arguing. He felt the slightest of tugs on the fly and knew he'd missed a strike from a fish. They didn't see him. He couldn't hear them over the sound of the river and he couldn't catch their expressions. The sun touched at the horizon and painted the winter grasses with gold.

Suddenly Joe knelt down as though he were going to pick something up or retie his wading shoe. It took Alan a moment longer to realize what Joe was doing, and he turned his back to them immediately. There was a tightness in his throat, a sense of happiness and loss so mixed he could hardly breathe. Was this what fathers felt like when their daughters married? The river doubled, then tripled in his vision. He felt absurd and yet the feeling was pure and good and sweet.

This was what it felt like to be a father. He laughed at the river, at the fish underneath it, at the dark blue winter sky and the beginnings of the stars coming out directly overhead. He was a father. He waded to shore, reeling up his fishing line and trying not to stumble. He'd meet them at the truck. What was that line that Joe always muttered?

"All will be well, and all will be well," he said to himself, grinning like a foolish old dog. "And all manner of things will be well."

Colorado Springs, Colorado

"Well, here we are," Gerri Matthews said, leaning back in her chair. Eileen wrapped her fingers around her own mug and grinned at Gerri like they were little girls at a tea party. The Victorian house hummed with psychologists and social workers working on marriage problems and abuses and relationships. The place no longer bothered Eileen. In fact, she believed she was going to miss it.

"Last session, right?" Eileen hadn't killed either Bennett or Scott, as it turned out. She'd re-broken two of Scott's ribs when she shot him the second time.

"Last session," Gerri said. "You've come a long way. And you're taking your father up to Wyoming to meet your parents?"

"Right after New Year's," Eileen said. "I think they'll love him as much as I do."

"And you love Joe Tanner," Gerri remarked.

"Love, love, love," Eileen said comfortably. "Yes, I can say love. I even think I can *do* love, now."

"Too bright for the ordinary traps, as always," Gerri laughed. "I just have one question, Eileen. For me, not for my notes."

"Okay," Eileen said.

"What happened that night you killed Teddy Shaw? Why did you lie to me about it?"

Eileen was still for too long. Gerri looked at her solemnly. Caught by Gerri after all, and at a time she was least expecting. She looked down at her hands. Thoughts of Teddy Shaw had faded so much from her mind that she'd forgotten what she'd done, how she'd lied.

"I'll tell you," she said slowly. "But you won't think very well of me."

"I think well of you, Eileen," Gerri said calmly. "That's not going to change."

Eileen grimaced and twisted her tea mug around in her palms. It was empty and dry but still smelled faintly of sweet herbs.

"I have to start way back, if you want to understand why I did what I did," she said. "All the way back."

"At the traffic accident where your parents found you."

"Yeah. I didn't tell the whole story there, either, Gerri. My Dad—that's my adoptive dad, not Alan—had climbed in next to me and steadied my head. He'd put his own shirt on the cut on my arm. But I was starting to pull all the fuses. Too much had happened, I think. I was just—shutting down. He saw that, and he tried to get me to talk to him, to tell him my name and where I was from. But I was just fading. I remember what it was like, just easier not to pay attention to what was going on out there in the world around me.

"Dad, he knew he was losing me. Maybe I was going catatonic or maybe I was going into shock and I was going to die. I don't think he knew. We never talked about what he did. But he did it. He reached around to my mother and pulled her head over so I could see her. She was dead and her eyes were open." Eileen swallowed hard.

"'She's dead,' my dad shouted into my face. 'She's dead and you're alive and you're going to stay alive.'"

"That brought you back?" Gerri said.

"Like being slapped across the face," Eileen said. "I don't think I've ever thought about it clearly until now. He showed me the worst demon of my life and she was dead. I couldn't shut down. I couldn't die. I know she was ill, she wasn't really a monster, but then and there she was to me. Even with all the love mixed in, I was more afraid of her than anything else. If I died, I might end up right back with her."

"You did the same to Jeannie Bernowski?"

"Oh, worse," Eileen said with a wry smile. "She'd pulled almost all the fuses. She was almost entirely gone, which is what I would be in the same situation. I knew it, too. But there was something there, something behind her eyes that was still alive. So I pulled her up and showed her Teddy Shaw lying in the grass in front of her. I used the same line on her that my dad used on me." Eileen looked out of her tea mug and into Gerri's face. "And I know I'm not a professional therapist. That's why it isn't in my report. I broke the rules."

"I see," Gerri said. She took an absent mouthful of cold tea and made an awful face. She put the mug down and picked up her pen. "And?"

"And I put my pistol in Jeannie's hands," Eileen said. "I aimed it at Teddy Shaw's body and I told her that if she needed to, just go ahead and pull the trigger. Shoot him again and again until she knew that he was gone and was never going to hurt her again."

Gerri closed her eyes and leaned back in her chair.

"I sure hope you don't plan on writing this down," Eileen said.

"Only if you promise never to do such a boneheaded thing again," Gerri said.

"But it did work," Eileen said. "She came back. She put the fuses back in and turned on the lights in her head, just like I did. She never pulled the trigger. Just knowing she could gave her back enough to want to stay alive."

"Let's just leave the shock therapy to the professionals from now on, okay?"

"Well, it worked," Eileen said again. She tried a smile on Gerri. Gerri glared at her for a moment, then sighed and relaxed into a smile.

"Okay," she said. "I won't put it in my report."

"Thank you."

"There's a trade-off, though," Gerri said, fixing Eileen with a stern glance.

"What?"

"Once a month, my tea, your time. Finding your birth father and getting married is a pretty tough transition. You're going to need my help. I'll give you a good deal on cost and you never, ever lie to me again. Deal?"

Eileen thought it over for a few moments. She liked Gerri. Most of all, she liked the Eileen that Gerri seemed to see. Flawed and not entirely grown up, but decent just the same. A good person.

"Deal," Eileen said. "I'll even keep drinking your crappy tea."

Epilogue

Lucy hung up the phone and jumped up from her office chair. Hank, examining a toy in his playpen with the intensity of a research scientist, looked up. Fancy woke out of her daytime doze in her padded bed and perked up her ears.

Lucy danced around the office, arms above her head, making cheerleader sounds. She scooped Hank up into her arms, Tonka truck and all, and whirled around and around.

"I get to be a maid of honor," she said to Hank. "I've never been one, did you know that? Lots of times a bridesmaid, but never the maid of honor. Oh, wait, I'm the matron of honor. This is going to be such fun. And she's getting married next summer, so Daddy and you and I can take a whole week's vacation."

She turned to her computer and hit the key to save her report. She'd upset her boss, Steven Mills, once again. Involving herself, even unofficially, in what was definitely an FBI case was strictly against policy. Fred Nguyen had written a glowing report that gave her credit for her involvement and got her into furious hot water. For a while she wondered if she were going to keep her job.

Then her two new friends came through. Tate and Randy had more clout than she realized. They seemed like college students down in their archive dungeon, but they weren't. They'd gone through Pentagon channels to give her credit for the recovery of the Tesla file. Exposing Jacob Mitchell's "earth resonance" project had shaken the Pentagon's black program management to the core and might lead to a congressional review.

Lucy didn't care much about that, but she did care that Mills was off her back again. She might even get a raise. A raise would be very nice.

Tate and Randy had been to the house to celebrate the return of the Tesla file and Lucy and Ted had fixed them an Italian dinner to remember. After a couple of bottles of good red wine, they'd all agreed, Ted included, that it was for the best that Tesla's earthquake designs were damaged. The documents were stored within the machine itself and machine oil had obliterated some of the crucial ink drawings when Joe Tanner had destroyed the machine. Tate and Randy carefully stored the damaged documents anyway back in their original folder with Tesla's handwriting on the cover.

"So how did Mitchell find the Tesla machine in the first place?" Ted asked, one arm holding a sleepy Hank and the other a wineglass.

"The FBI transferred a section of files from their own archives to ours. The section included the whole Tesla grouping," Tate said. His face darkened. He was still angry about the theft. "Mitchell must have heard about the Tesla file from someone in the FBI. So he got to them before they came to us."

Then Tate had coughed delicately into his fist and set down his wineglass and, after a look at Randy, had offered her a job. They often encountered puzzles and mysteries, and they needed an analyst who had some time to investigate them. An analyst might have prevented Jacob Mitchell from carrying off the Tesla file, for example. They had approval for a generous salary and they'd make great bosses, they earnestly declared. They *liked* her.

Lucy, flattered and astonished, had told them she'd think it over. She still hadn't decided, even though the long string of Christmas beads haunted her mind. What were the stories locked in those boxes?

Hank shifted in her arms, and she looked down into his glorious dark eyes.

"Woolgathering again, Hank," she said. "I don't know about this job. But I do know I have to lose weight. You're weaned and I have no more excuses. I want to look good for Eileen's wedding. We'll have such fun!" She danced around with Hank, and Fancy leaped to her feet and joined them, panting.

Lucy was sure they looked like idiots, the three of them. She didn't care. Hank laughed in her arms and Fancy barked and turned in circles and grinned her doggy grin, wagging her tail as though it would never stop.